THE HORUS HERESY

Graham McNeill

THE OUTCAST DEAD

The truth lies within

BLACK LIBRARY

For Amber, our little girl.

A BLACK LIBRARY PUBLICATION

First published in Great Britain in 2011 by
The Black Library,
Games Workshop Ltd.,
Willow Road, Nottingham,
NG7 2WS, UK.

10 9 8 7 6 5 4 3 2

Cover and page 1 illustration by Neil Roberts.

See the Black Library on the internet at

www.blacklibrary.com

Find out more about Games Workshop
and the world of Warhammer 40,000 at

www.games-workshop.com

Printed and bound by CPI Group (UK) Ltd, Croydon, CR0 4YY

THE HORUS HERESY

It is a time of legend.

MIGHTY HEROES BATTLE for the right to rule the galaxy. The vast armies of the Emperor of Earth have conquered the galaxy in a Great Crusade – the myriad alien races have been smashed by the Emperor's elite warriors and wiped from the face of history.

The dawn of a new age of supremacy for humanity beckons.

Gleaming citadels of marble and gold celebrate the many victories of the Emperor. Triumphs are raised on a million worlds to record the epic deeds of his most powerful and deadly warriors.

First and foremost amongst these are the primarchs, superheroic beings who have led the Emperor's armies of Space Marines in victory after victory. They are unstoppable and magnificent, the pinnacle of the Emperor's genetic experimentation. The Space Marines are the mightiest human warriors the galaxy has ever known, each capable of besting a hundred normal men or more in combat.

Organised into vast armies of tens of thousands called Legions, the Space Marines and their primarch leaders conquer the galaxy in the name of the Emperor.

Chief amongst the primarchs is Horus, called the Glorious, the Brightest Star, favourite of the Emperor, and like a son unto him. He is the Warmaster, the commander-in-chief of the Emperor's military might, subjugator of a thousand thousand worlds and conqueror of the galaxy. He is a warrior without peer, a diplomat supreme.

As the flames of war spread through the Imperium, mankind's champions will all be put to the ultimate test.

~ DRAMATIS PERSONAE ~

The City of Sight

NEMO ZHI-MENG — Choirmaster of the Adeptus Astra Telepathica

ANIQ SARASHINA — Mistress of the Scholastica Psykana

EVANDER GREGORAS — Master of the Cryptaesthesians

KAI ZULANE — Astropath seconded to Navigator House Castana

ATHENA DIYOS — Astropath of the City of Sight

ABIR IBN KHALDUN — Astropath of the City of Sight

The Outcast Dead

ATHARVA — Adept Exemptus of the Thousand Sons

TAGORE — Sergeant, 15th Company, World Eaters

SUBHA — Warrior of the 15th Company, World Eaters

ASUBHA — Warrior of the 15th Company, World Eaters

SEVERIAN — Warrior of the 25th Company, Luna Wolves The 'Wolf'

ARGENTUS KIRON — Warrior of the 28th Company, Emperor's Children

The Hunters

YASU NAGASENA	Seer Hunter of the Black Ships
KARTONO	Bondsman to Yasu Nagasena
MAJOR GENERAL MAXIM GOLOVKA	Commander of the Black Sentinels
SATURNALIA	Warrior of the Legio Custodes

The Lords of Terra

| ROGAL DORN | Primarch of the Imperial Fists |

The Petitioner's City

PALLADIS NOVANDIO	Priest of the Temple of Woe
ROXANNE CASTANA	Supplicant of the Temple of Woe
BABU DHAKAL	Clan lord of the Dhakal
GHOTA	Dhakal enforcer

Wonders are many on Earth, and the greatest of these is Man, who rides the Great Ocean and makes his way through the deeps, through wind-swept valleys of perilous seas that surge and sway.

– Attributed to the Tragedean
Sophocles, pre-M1

Dreams are mirrors in which are reflected the true character of the dreamer. What should happen when the individual face of the dreamer sees himself reflected in the collective dream mirror of all humanity?

– Aniq Sarashina,
Oneirocritica Sarashina, Vol XXXV

Your vision will become clear only when you look into your heart. Who looks outside, dreams. Who looks inside, awakens.

– Nemo Zhi-Meng, Choirmaster of
the Adeptus Astra Telepathica.

From: **Chirurgeon Bellan Tortega (BT)**,
certified neuro-psychic attendant
To: **Patriarch Verduchina XXVII,**
House Castana, Navis Nobilite
Observed period: Cycles 15-18
Subject: **Zulane, Kai (KZ)**
Evaluation summary: NON-FUNCTIONAL/
POTENTIALLY SALVAGEABLE

Excerpted from 4423-4553: Full Case
Notes to follow.

TRANSCRIPT EXCERPT BEGINS.

  BT: Can you tell me what happened on
the *Argo*?
  KZ: No.
  BT: No?
  KZ: No.
  BT: Why not?
  KZ: I don't want to.

BT: With respect, you are in no position to withhold anything you know. The incident involving the *Argo* represents a significant financial deficit for House Castana, not to mention the considerable loss of prestige with respect to the XIII Legion.

KZ: Take it up with Nemo. I was only loaned to Castana, I don't care about their losses.

BT: You should. You should also know that my evaluation will play a significant part in deciding whether you can continue with House Castana. Or continue at all for that matter.

KZ: Like I said, I don't care.

BT: Do you WANT to be sent to the hollow mountain?

KZ: Of course not. No sane person would.

BT: Then I would co-operate if I were you.

KZ: You don't understand, it's not about co-operation.

BT: Then enlighten me, Kai. What IS it about?

KZ: It's about hearing ten thousand men and women die. It's about hearing every single last thought as their bodies were torn apart by *things*. It's about hearing the terror of people about to die every time I close my eyes. It's about not putting myself through that nightmare again. [Subject breaks down. Three minutes of sobbing.]

BT: Are you finished?

KZ: For now.

BT: Then do you feel like talking about what happened?

KZ: Terra, no! Maybe someday, but even when I do, it won't be with you.

BT: Why not?

KZ: Because you're not here to help me.

BT: That's EXACTLY why I'm here, Kai.

KZ: No it's not, and stop calling me Kai as if we're friends. Your only purpose in being here is to show the XIII Legion that House Castana can keep its house in order. I'm an embarrassment to your precious patriarch.

BT: No, you are part of the family. All Patriarch Verduchina wants is to help.

KZ: Then leave me alone. The *Argo* isn't a memory I want to go back to. Not yet, maybe never.

BT: Confronting the past is the only way you can face the future. Surely you can see it's not healthy to dwell on such macabre memories. Purge them and you can return to your duties.

KZ: You're assuming I WANT to return to my duties.

BT: Don't you?

KZ: [One minute pause] I don't know.

TRANSCRIPT EXCERPT ENDS.

Addendum:

Sire, as this excerpt clearly shows, Kai Zulane displays classic symptoms of denial, paranoia and an inability to face the truth of his ordeal. It is my conclusion that he believes he is responsible for the events that led to the loss of the *Argo*, though the truth of this is for others, more qualified in the fields of multi-dimensional overlaps, to determine. However, I do not believe any individuals could live through so traumatic an experience without some psychic scarring, none of which is evident in Kai Zulane's aetheric aura. I would, therefore, venture the opinion that Kai Zulane is not beyond recovery. Kai Zulane represents a significant investment in time and effort (both by House Castana and the Adeptus Astra Telepathica) and to simply 'cut our losses' and send him to the hollow mountain would, at this point, be premature.

In summary, it is my recommendation that Kai Zulane be returned to the auspices of the Adeptus Astra Telepathica for immediate rehabilitation. This will reaffirm our commitment to the XIII Legion, and effectively allow House Castana to pass the burden of responsibility elsewhere.

I remain your humble servant in all things, and can offer further clarifications, should they be required, on Kai Zulane's psychic pathology at your convenience.

Bellan Tortega
Neuro-psychic attendant 343208543.

Antonius, do what the unctuous little chirurgeon says. Throw Zulane back to the City of Sight. He can be their problem instead of ours.

V.

It is the hour before dawn when the hunters come for them.

Nagasena checks his rifle, already knowing it is fully functional. On a day like today he needs the solace of things done in the right order. Too many of this newly emergent Imperium's people rush around without taking the time to ensure they are properly prepared. Truth and order are Nagasena's watchwords, for they provide a centre from which all other things can flow. He has learned this from the teachings of a wise man born in these parts in an age now long forgotten.

Those teachings survive only in scattered texts comprising gnomic aphorisms and proverbs, each one passed down from mentor to student over thousands of generations in secret script known only to a chosen few. Nagasena has lived his life by these teachings, and he feels they have guided him well. His life has been lived truthfully, and he has few regrets.

This day's hunt will, he thinks, be one of them.

He uncoils from the cross-legged position in which he sits and slings his rifle across his shoulder. Around him, men come to their feet, energised by his sudden movement.

'Is it time?' asks Kartono, handing him a long bladed sword with just the barest hint of a curve. It is a wondrous weapon,

13

sheathed in a scabbard of lacquered wood, jade and mother of pearl. A master of the metal arts crafted this blade to Nagasena's exacting specifications, yet it is no sharper, no lighter or in any other way superior to the millions of sword blades churned out by the armouries of Terra. But it was crafted with love and an attention to detail that no machine can ever replicate.

Nagasena knows the weapon as Shoujiki, which means Honesty.

He nods respectfully to Kartono as Golovko approaches, bullish and bearing the scent of gun oil, sweat and lapping powder. In an elder age Nagasena's ancestors would have considered him a barbarian, but now he is an honoured man. Golovko's armour is bulky, cumbersome and designed to intimidate. His face looks much the same.

He gives no greeting and his lip curls in instinctive distaste as he sees Kartono.

'We should have struck in the middle watches of the night,' he says, as Nagasena slips his sword through the black sash tied at his waist. 'We would have surprised them.'

'It would make no difference what time we came,' says Nagasena, smoothing out his long black hair and settling a long scalp-lock over his shoulder. 'Such men as we hunt will never truly be at rest, and there will never be a best time to fight them. As soon as the first is taken, most likely even before then, the rest will be instantly alert and dangerous beyond imagining.'

'We have three thousand soldiers,' points out Golovko, as though numbers are all that matter at a time like this. 'Black Sentinels, Attaman Janissaries, Lancers. Even the high and mighty Custodians sent a squad.'

'And it may still prove to be insufficient,' says Nagasena.

'Against thirty?' says Golovko, but Nagasena has already dismissed him from his thoughts.

He turns away from the bellicose general and moves through the assembled soldiers silently awaiting his signal. They are nervous, dislocated. Most of all, they are horrified that they are about to take up arms against those who fight in their name on worlds far distant from Terra.

Nagasena looks up at the building that houses the Crusader Host. It is known locally as the Preceptory, and it is a triumphant structure of rearing golden lions, fluted columns and warrior statuary, capped by a lightning-shot dome of black marble. Heroic imagery adorns the fresco of the pediment high above the portico, and the grand approach leading to the entrance is paved with enormous flagstones bearing the names of worlds the Legiones Astartes have brought to compliance.

Every day these flagstones are cut with fresh tallies, and Nagasena wonders how these men of war feel to see the litany of their brothers' victories grow ever larger while they remain on Terra, ever more distant from the bloody edge of the Imperium's frontier.

'What are your orders, lord?' asks Kartono.

His companion is unarmed, but needs no weapons to be lethal. His former masters trained him to such a high degree of lethality that he is a weapon himself. Many people dislike Kartono for reasons they can never quite articulate, but Nagasena has long since grown used to his presence. He looks at the soldiers, confident that they are well hidden in the warren of gilded avenues and columned processionals that garland this region of the Imperial Palace like jewellery around the neck of a favoured concubine.

Three thousand armed men await his signal to advance, and Nagasena knows that by giving that signal, many of those men will die. Maybe all of them. He relishes few of his hunts, but this one in particular sits ill with him. He wishes he were back in his mountain villa, where his only concerns are the mixing of paints and tending to his garden, but his likes and dislikes are immaterial here.

A mission has been set, and he is duty bound to obey. And though he does not like this order, he understands it.

'Walk with me, Kartono,' says Nagasena, stepping out onto the grand walkway of victories. Kartono trots after him, surprised at his master's sudden movement. Nagasena hears Golovko through the vox bead situated in his ear and pulls it free. The man's protests become tinny and distant.

'They will know we are coming for sure now,' says Kartono, and Nagasena nods.

'Your presence alone will have alerted at least one of them,' he says. 'Did you really think so many armed men could approach a place like this without its occupants knowing of it?'

'I suppose not,' agrees Kartono, glancing over his shoulder. 'The Major General will not be pleased. He will make trouble for us.'

'That is a problem for another day,' says Nagasena. 'I will be sufficiently pleased if we live through this morning. It is highly likely we will die here.'

Kartono shakes his head. 'You are fatalistic today.'

'Perhaps,' says Nagasena as they climb the first steps of the Preceptory. 'I dislike rising before the sun. It feels impolite.'

Kartono knows his moods well. Nagasena has grown tired of hunting, but this task has been given to him by a man whose orders come with the highest authority. Refusal was not an option. He feels the chill of the day through his silken robes, but does not allow it to lessen his focus. Knowing that his armour would afford him little protection against the weapons of his prey, he did not have Kartono encase him within its lacquered plates of bonded ceramite and adamantine weave.

A figure steps into view on the portico above, and Nagasena feels his heart beat just a little quicker. He is tall and broad shouldered, as one would expect for a warrior genhanced to be the pinnacle of physicality, but there is a gracile quality to him that is unexpected. His hair is longer than is usual, tied in a short ponytail, and his face is broad, with the congenital flatness of features so common amongst his kind. Nagasena is reassured to see that he wears no armour, perhaps indicating that he has not come to fight. His robes are crimson, edged in ivory, and a jade scarab set in amber rests upon his chest.

The man watches as he and Kartono climb to the top of the steps, his face unreadable and without expression. No, that is not quite correct. There is a sadness to him, visible only in the tiniest descending curve at the corner of his lips and a tightness around his eyes. At last Nagasena reaches the top of the steps and stands before the man, who towers over him like the oni of legend. The oni were also said to dwell in the mountains, but the old myths told of ugly creatures possessing horned skulls and wide mouths filled with terrible fangs.

There is nothing ugly about this warrior; he is a perfect specimen.

'Oni-ni-kanabo,' whispers Kartono.

Nagasena nods at the aptness of the expression, but does not reply.

The warrior nods and says, 'Oni with an iron club?'

'It means to be invincible or unbeatable in battle,' says Nagasena, trying to hide his surprise that the warrior knows this ancient tongue of Old Earth.

'I am aware of that,' says the warrior. 'Another meaning is "strength upon strength" whereupon one's innate power is bolstered by the manipulation of some kind of tool or external force. Very apt indeed.'

'You are Atharva?' asks Nagasena, now understanding how he can know their secret language.

'I am Adeptus Exemptus Atharva of the XV Legion,' confirms the warrior.

'You know why we are here?'

'Of course,' says Atharva. 'I expected you sooner.'

'I would have been surprised if you had not.'

'How many soldiers did you bring?'

'Just over three thousand.'

Atharva mulls over the number. 'My brothers will be insulted you came with so few. You should have brought more to be certain.'

'Others thought such numbers sufficient.'

'We shall see,' observes Atharva, as though it is no more than an intellectual exercise they are considering and not a terrible, unthinkable waste of Imperial lives.

'Will you fight us, Atharva?' asks Nagasena. 'I hope you will not.'

'You brought your clade pet hoping it would dissuade me,' replies Atharva, with a curt gesture towards Kartono, 'but do you really think he can stop me from killing you?'

'No, but I hoped his presence might give you pause.'

'I will not fight you, Yasu Nagasena,' says Atharva, and the sadness in his eyes is achingly visible. 'But Tagore and his brothers will walk the Crimson Path before they allow themselves to be taken.'

Nagasena nods and says, 'So be it.'

PROLOGUE

ABIR IBN KHALDUN exhaled cold air and saw myriad patterns in the swirling vapour of his breath, too many to examine fully, but diverting nonetheless. An inverted curve that augured danger, a genetically dense double helix that indicated the warriors of the Legiones Astartes, and a black planet whose civilisation had been ground to black sand by a cataclysmic war and the passage of uncounted aeons.

The mindhall was quiet, the metallic-tasting air still and cool, yet there was tension.

Understandable, but it made an already difficult communion that much harder.

The presence of the thousand-strong choir of astropaths surrounding Ibn Khaldun was like the sound of a distant ocean, or so he imagined. Ibn Khaldun had never heard any Terran bodies of water larger than the vast, basin cisterns carved within the lightless depths of the Urals and Alpine scarps, but he was an astropath and his life was swathed in metaphors.

Their psychic presence was dormant for now, a deep reservoir of energy he would use to distil the incoming vision from its raw state of chaotic imagery to a coherent message that could be easily understood.

'Do you have communion yet?' asked the Choirmaster, his voice sounding as though it came from impossibly far away, though he stood right next to Ibn Khaldun.

'Give him time, Nemo,' said Mistress Sarashina, her voice maternal and soothing. 'We will know when the link is made. The astropaths of the Iron Hands are not subtle.'

'I am aware of that, Aniq,' replied the Choirmaster. 'I trained most of them.'

'Then you should know better than to rush this.'

'*I* know that well enough, but Lord Dorn is impatient for news of Ferrus Manus's fleet. And he has a gun.'

'No gun ever helped speed things up in a good way,' said Sarashina.

Ibn Khaldun smiled inwardly at her gentle admonition, though the mention of the lord of the Imperial Fists reminded him how important this communion was to the Imperium.

Horus Lupercal's treachery had overturned the natural order of the universe, and emissaries from the palace were shrill in their demands for verifiable information. Expeditionary fleets of Legiones Astartes, billions-strong armies of mortal soldiers and warfleets capable of planetary destruction were loose in the galaxy, and no one could be sure of their exact locations or to whom they owed their allegiance. News of world after world declaring for the Warmaster had reached Terra, but whether such stories were true or rebel lies was a mystery.

The old adage that in any war, the first casualty was truth was never more apt than during a civil war.

'Is it dangerous to link over so great a distance?' asked Maxim Golovko, and Ibn Khaldun sensed the man's natural hostility in the flaring crimson of his aura. 'Should we have Sentinels within the mindhall?'

Golovko was a killer of psykers, a gaoler and executioner all in one. His presence within the Whispering

Tower was decreed by the new strictures laid down after the great conclave on Nikaea, and Ibn Khaldun suppressed a spike of resentment at its hypocrisy. Bitterness would only cloud his perceptions, and this was a time for clarity like no other.

'No, Maxim,' said Sarashina. 'I am sure your presence alone will be sufficient.'

Golovko grunted in acknowledgement, oblivious to the veiled barb, and Ibn Khaldun shut out the man's disruptive psyche.

Ibn Khaldun felt a growing disconnection to the individuals around him, as though he were floating in amniotic gel like the princeps of a Mechanicum war-engine. He understood the urgency of this communion, but took care to precisely enunciate his incubating mantras. Rushing to link with an astropath he didn't know would be foolhardy beyond words, especially when they were halfway across the galaxy and hurtling through the warp.

En route to an unthinkable battle between warriors who had once stood shoulder to shoulder as brothers.

Not even the most prescient of the *Vatic* had seen *that* coming.

Ibn Khaldun's heart rate increased as he sensed another mind enter the sealed chamber, a blaze of light too bright to look upon directly. The others sensed it at the same instant and every head turned to face the new arrival. This was an individual whose inner fire was like the blinding glare of a supernova captured at the first instant of detonation. Mercury-bright traceries filled his every limb, blood as light, flesh woven from incomprehensible energies and sheathed in layers of meat and muscle, skin and plate. Ibn Khaldun could see nothing of this individual's face, for every molecule that made up his form was like a miniature galaxy swarming with incandescent stars.

Only one manner of being was fashioned with such exquisite beauty...

'Lord Dorn?' said the Choirmaster, surprise giving his voice a raised tone that turned his words into a question. 'How did you…?'

'None of the gates of Terra are barred to me, Choirmaster,' said Dorn, and his words were like bright streamers ejected from the corona of a volatile star. They lingered long after he spoke, and Ibn Khaldun felt their power ripple outwards through the awe-struck choir.

'This is a sealed ritual,' protested the Choirmaster. 'You should not be here.'

Dorn marched towards the centre of the mindhall, and Ibn Khaldun felt his skin prickle at the nearness of such a forceful, implacable psyche. The majority of mortal minds simmered with mundane clutter close to the surface, but Rogal Dorn's mind was an impregnable fortress, hard-edged and unyielding of its secrets. No one learned anything from Dorn he did not want them to know.

'My brothers are approaching Isstvan V,' said Dorn. 'I *need* to be here.'

'Communion has yet to be established, Lord Dorn,' said Sarashina, clearly understanding the futility of attempting to eject a primarch from the mindhall. 'But if you are to stay, then you may only observe. Do not speak once the link is achieved.'

'I do not need a lecture,' said Dorn. 'I know how astropathic communion works.'

'If that were truly the case, then you would have respected the warding seal upon this chamber,' said Sarashina, and Ibn Khaldun felt the momentary flare of anger from behind the monolithic walls of Rogal Dorn's mind fortress. Almost immediately it was followed by a mellow glow of begrudged respect, though Ibn Khaldun sensed this only because Dorn *allowed* it to be sensed.

'Point taken, Mistress Sarashina,' said Dorn. 'I will be silent. You have my word.'

Ibn Khaldun dragged his senses away from the primarch; a difficult feat in itself, for his presence had a gravity that drew in nearby minds. Instead, he splayed his mind outwards into the echoing space of the vast chamber in which he lay.

Fashioned in the form of a great amphitheatre the heart of the Whispering Tower, this chamber had been shaped by the ancient *cognoscynths* who first raised the City of Sight, many thousands of years ago. Their unrivalled knowledge of psychically-attuned architecture had been hard-won in a long-forgotten age of devastating psi-wars, but their arts were long dead, and the skill of crafting such resonant structures had died with them.

Amid the blackened mindhalls of the City of Sight, the Whispering Tower reached the farthest into the gulfs of space between the stars, no matter what lofty claims the Emperor's grand architects might make of the ornamented spires they had built around it.

A thousand high-ranking astropaths surrounded Ibn Khaldun, seated in ever-ascending tiers like the audience at some grotesque spectacle of dissection. Each telepath reclined in a contoured harness-throne, appearing as shimmering smears of light in Ibn Khaldun's consciousness, and he sharpened his focus as a subtle change in the choir's resonance tugged at the edge of his perceptions.

A message was being drawn towards the tower.

Whisper stones set within the ironclad walls shone with invisible light as they eased the passage of the incoming message, directing it towards the centre of the mindhall.

'He's here,' said Ibn Khaldun, as the presence of the sending astropath swelled to fill the chamber like a surge tide. The sending was raw and unfocussed, a distant shout straining for someone to listen, and Ibn Khaldun folded his mind around it.

Like strangers fumbling to shake hands in a darkened room, their thoughts slowly meshed, and Ibn Khaldun gasped as he felt the hard texture of another's mind rasping against the boundaries of his own. Rough and sharp, blunt and pugnacious, this sending was typical of astro-paths who spent prolonged periods assigned to the Iron Hands. Cipher codes flashed before him in a complex series of colours and numbers, a necessary synesthesia that confirmed the identity of both astropaths before communion could begin.

'You have it?' asked the Choirmaster.

Khaldun didn't answer. To grasp the thoughts of another mind from so far away demanded all his con-centration. Fluctuations in the warp, random currents of aetheric energy, and the burbling chatter of a million overlapping echoes sought to break the link, but he held it firm.

As lovers gained a slow understanding of their part-ner's rhythms and nuances, so too did the union of minds become easier. Though to call anything of this nature *easy* was to grossly understate its complexity. Ibn Khaldun felt the cold wastes of the immaterium all around him, roiling like a storm-tossed ocean. And like the oceans of Old Earth, it was home to creatures of all shapes and sizes. Ibn Khaldun sensed them swarming around the bright light of this communion like cautious predators circling potential prey.

'I have communion,' he said, 'but I won't be able to hold it for long.'

The spectral outline of somewhere far distant began to merge with Ibn Khaldun's sensory interpretation of the mindhall, like a faulty picter broadcasting two sepa-rate images on the same screen. Ibn Khaldun recognised the hazy image of an astropath's chamber aboard a star-ship, one that bore all the stripped-down aesthetic of the X Legion. Figures appeared around him, like faceless ghosts come to observe. They were mist-limned giants of burnished metal with flinty auras, angular lines and the cold taste of machines.

Yes, this was *definitely* a ship of the Iron Hands.

Ibn Khaldun ignored the additional presences and let the body of the message flow into him. It came in a rush of imagery, nonsensical and unintelligible, but that was only to be expected. The psychic song of the choir grew in concert with his efforts to process the message, and he drew upon the wellspring of energy they provided him. Will and mental fortitude could cohere simple messages sent from planetary distances, but one sent from so far away would need more power than any one individual could provide.

Khaldun was special, an astropath whose skills in metapsychic cognition could transform confused jumbles of obscure symbolism into a message that even a novitiate could decipher. As the raw, urgent thoughts of the expeditionary astropath spilled into his mindscape, his borrowed power smoothed their rough edges and let the substance of the message take shape.

Ibn Khaldun interpreted and extrapolated the images and sounds together, alloying astropathic shorthand with common allegorical references to extract the truth of the message. There was art in this, a beautiful mental ballet that was part intuition, part natural talent and part training. And just as no remembrancer of a creative mien could ever truly explain how they achieved mastery of their art, nor could Ibn Khaldun articulate how he brought sense from senselessness, meaning from chaos.

Words sprang from him, reformed from the encrypted symbolism in which they had been sent. 'The world of black sand. Isstvan,' he said. 'The fifth planet. The Legion makes good speed. Lord Dorn's retribution flies true, yet the sons of Medusa will strike before even the Ravens or the Lords of Nocturne. Lord Manus demands first blood and the head of the Phoenix.'

More of the message poured through, and Ibn Khaldun felt some of the astropaths in the tiers above him perish as their reserves of energy were expended. Such was the import of this message that losses amongst the choir had been deemed acceptable.

'The Gorgon of Medusa will be the first warrior of the Emperor upon Isstvan. He will be the speartip that cleaves the heart of Horus Lupercal. He will be the avenger.'

Ibn Khaldun slumped back in his harness as the message abruptly ended, and allowed his breathing to return to normal. His mind began the tortuous process of re-ordering itself in the void left by communion's end, but it would take many days rest to recover from this ordeal.

As always, he wanted to sit up and open his eyes, but the restraints of his harness and the sutured veil of skin over his empty eye sockets prevented him from doing either.

'It is done,' he whispered, his words echoing around the chamber as though he had shouted at the top of his voice. 'There is no more.'

Mistress Sarashina took his hand and stroked his glistening brow, though his consciousness was already fading after such strenuous mental exertion. Lord Dorn loomed over him, a glittering nimbus of light playing around the golden curves of his battle plate, and the proximity of such naked power was like a defibrillating jolt that kept Ibn Khaldun from slipping into a recuperative trance.

'Damn your impatience, Ferrus, you will be the death of me,' hissed Dorn, his voice betraying a measure of the terrible burden he bore. 'The plan requires you to follow my orders to the letter!'

The primarch of the Imperial Fists turned to the Choirmaster. 'There is no more? You are sure this is the entirety of the message?'

'If Abir Ibn Khaldun says there is no more, then there is no more,' stated the Choirmaster. 'The cryptaesthesians will filter the Bleed for any residual meaning or hidden subtexts, but Ibn Khaldun is one of our best.'

Rogal Dorn rounded upon the man. '*One* of your best? Why would you not employ your best telepath for so crucial a message?'

The Choirmaster exchanged a look with Sarashina, and Ibn Khaldun felt their unease as they formed the image of an astropath who had long since left the Whispering Tower for the lofty heights of secondment to a patrician house of the Navis Nobilite.

'Our best is not yet among us,' said the Choirmaster.

'I ordered you to utilise every and all means to bring me reliable information from the frontier,' said Dorn his hand closing over the onyx and gold pommel of his heavy-bladed sword. 'Do any of you people understand what is at stake? I am forced to wage a war I cannot see, to fight a foe I cannot gauge, and the only way I can do that is if I know *exactly* what is happening en route to Isstvan. To save the Imperium, I need you to use only your best operatives. The truth is all that matters, do you understand?'

'We understand all too well, Lord Dorn,' said the Choirmaster after a moment's hesitation.

'Our best operative is returning to us as we speak,' added Sarashina, 'but he will not be in any state to help us. Not yet.'

'Why not?' demanded Rogal Dorn.

Sarashina sighed. 'Because his mind must be remade.'

PART 1
DREAMS OF THE RED CHAMBER

ONE

Roof of the World
Little Girl
Homecoming

THROUGH THE PETRIFIED forests of Uttarakhand and the barren rad-wastes of Uttar Pradesh the travellers climbed. Then through the Brahmaputra valley, drawing closer to the roof of the world with every passing day. Onto the Terai-Duar flatlands, now colonised by the shipwrights of the Mechanicum for their dry-dock repair yards. Through those acetylene-lit cathedrals of iron, they rose still higher, into the thin air of the Bhabhar, where the land was cut with collimated streambeds that had once carried meltwater from the highest peaks to the plains below.

Vast swathes of subtropical forest had once flourished here, before ancient wars had destroyed almost everything living on the surface of the world. Oceans had boiled, continents burned and so much of what made this land special had been lost in those wars, but the world had endured. This particular forest had been dominated by the *sarja*, a tree favoured by an ancient god of a long dead empire that had once dominated the lands hereabouts.

One of the few surviving myths of that empire was

that its greatest queen had given birth to a mortal god while gripping the branches of a *sarja* tree in a village of the Sákyans. This god had spawned a new religion, but nothing now remained of his teachings and no tales told whether he had been a wrathful or benevolent god.

The travellers knew nothing of the region's history, for the Bhabhar was now a desolate hinterland of sprawling worker camps that filled the landscape as far as the eye could see. Millions of craftsmen, labourers and hulking *migou* gathered together in industrious cities of canvas and prefabricated plasteel, the raw meat and muscle driving the engine of construction that now enveloped the farthest reaches of the mountains.

Higher still, into the Shiwalik belt of upland rock, where the travellers rested overnight in the statue-lined Chitwan Processional before making the push through the Mohan Pass into the Mahabharat Lekh, where the first of the great gates reared from the titanic peaks like a sepulchral portal into the lair of a sleeping giant.

This was the Primus Gate, and in more peaceful times, the sunlight had made the damascened silver and lapis lazuli coffers shine like dew on the morning of the very first day in creation. Those coffers were now obscured by adamantium panels, the exquisite lapidary that had been a traveller's first sight of the Emperor's palace now locked away in secure vaults. Towering cranes and bulk lifters sprouted from its battlements, and cascades of sparks fell from phosphor-tipped welding torches.

Thousands of petitioners and supplicants gathered before the gate, patiently waiting their turn to pass through its towering magnificence. Not all would reach the lofty heart of the palace. The climb would prove to be too arduous for many, the journey too long or the wonders too great to bear. A phalanx of soldiers in gleaming breastplates of ivory and jade kept watch on the petitioners, and the air was charged with frightening strangeness. A lone figure armoured in all-encasing gold plate moved through the crowds, and the crimson of his helm's horsehair plume stood out like a bloodstain on snow.

Never before had the Primus Gate been shut, and the stark fact of its closure struck a clear note that the axis of the galaxy had tilted. Humanity had a new enemy, one that wore a familiar face, and whose agents might even now be among them.

No longer could Terra's citizens walk freely within the domain of their master.

Until now, the travellers' journey into the peaks had been largely unhindered by the rigorous new security that surrounded the continental palace of the Emperor, but they had drawn too near the bright flame at the heart of the Imperium to pass unnoticed. Millions of migrant workers had come to the palace, and so many faces needed watching.

As it transpired, the Primus Gate was traversed without much in the way of inconvenience, for they had come with documents affixed with the seal of one of the great Navigator houses, and its amethyst hue was given due deference by the gate's castellans as the way was opened. Passing beneath its shadow took many hours of travel, and once beyond the gate the magnificence of the palace proper began.

It had been described as a crown of light atop the world, a continental landmass of unrivalled architectural brilliance, and the greatest work of man, but such descriptions failed to capture its epic immensity, the sheer weight of awe it engendered and the colossal impossibility of its very existence. Many supplicants who had spent their life's worth to see the palace passed its first gate and climbed no further, humbled to the point of insensibility by even its least noteworthy avenues, processionals and towers. It was a monumental endeavour built not to the scale of men, but the scale of gods.

Beyond the docking rings and landing fields of the Brahmaputra Plateau rose the tallest peaks: the Naked Mountain, the Great Black, the Turquoise Goddess, and once mightiest of them all, the Holy Mother. None of them had escaped the attentions of the Mechanicum or the Emperor's warmasons, their summits planed flat, and their bedrock burrowed deep to anchor the footings of the mighty palace.

'Impressive,' said Bellan Tortega from the back of the luxurious, up-armoured skimmer.

Kai Zulane fixed the chirurgeon with a hostile stare. 'I hate you,' he said.

THE INTERIOR OF the skimmer was panelled with off-world wood from the broadleaf forests of Yolaeu, its metallic surfaces edged with chased platinum and inset with smooth pict slates that displayed a rolling series of serene alien landscapes. The seats were plush amethyst velveteen, with the crest of House Castana embroidered in gold. Subtle lighting kept the hard edges of the interior soft, and a well-stocked chill-bar meant even a long journey could pass in comfort. All that spoiled the elegant luxury of the interior was the presence of four House Castana armsmen.

Clad in loops of gleaming black carapace and bonded leather armour, they filled the interior of the skimmer with their augmented physiques. Castana was pre-eminent among the families of the Navis Nobilite and could easily afford the ruinous cost of Mechanicum enhancements for their security personnel. Their faces were invisible behind glossy black helm visors, and each was wired with crystalline psi-dampers – as was the skimmer itself – to shield them from psychic intrusion.

Ostensibly, these men were here as a protective escort, but the combat shotguns gripped tightly in heavy leather gauntlets left no doubt in Kai's mind that he was little better than a prisoner. He eased his back into the wide seat, finding himself unable to enjoy comfort he had once taken for granted. He cradled a glass of mahogany-coloured amasec, swirling the drink in a cut crystal glass that would cost more than most citizens would earn in a year. Idly he thought of throwing the glass out the window, but decided that such petty rebellion would only irritate him afterwards.

Besides, the liquor dulled the ache of psi-sickness that had plagued him since his return to Terra.

Across from Kai, Bellan Tortega stared out of the window with open-mouthed delight. It was the chirurgeon's first time visiting the palace, and it showed. He had been naming landmarks and marvelling at the sheer number of people within the palace precincts ever since they had passed beneath the Primus Gate, nearly twenty hours ago. Their route took them over the Brahmaputra Plateau, and Kai kept an artfully bored expression glued to his face. He knew it was an honour to see the cradle of humanity up close, but was too wrapped in his own misery to take much notice of his surroundings.

'I believe that covered amphitheatre, the one encased in scaffolding, is the Investiary,' said Tortega. 'The statues of the Primarchs within are hooded with mourning shrouds.'

'Why?' asked Kai.

'What do you mean?'

'I mean why hood a statue? It's not like it can see.'

'It's symbolic, Kai,' said Tortega. 'It represents the desire of the Emperor to shield his sons from the treachery of their brothers.'

'Represents a waste of time if you ask me. I would have thought the Emperor had more to worry about than pointless symbolism.'

Tortega sighed. 'You know your biggest problem, Kai?'

'I am well aware of my problems, good chirurgeon,' snapped Kai. 'You never tire of reminding me of them every day.'

'You take no appreciation of how lucky you are,' said Tortega, as if Kai hadn't spoken.

Kai bit back a caustic response and took another drink.

'Patriarch Verduchina would have been well within his rights to have you cast out of the Telepathica, and then what would you have done? You'd have been picked up by the psi-hounds within a day.'

Kai used to try and defuse these lectures while in the medicae facilities of House Castana on the island crag of Kyprios, but time and apathy had made him realise that once Tortega had begun, there was no stopping him.

'You think you could have afforded those ocular augmetics without the Castanas?' continued Tortega. 'Disgrace the House and they'll take them back, mark my words. You have a lot to be thankful for, young man, and it's time you realised that before it's too late.'

'It's already too late,' said Kai. 'Look where we are, where I'm going.'

'We're in the bosom of our species, Kai. And when the Imperium is reunited after this silly war, people will flock to this place,' said Tortega, leaning forward and placing a hand on Kai's knee.

The sensation was painful, and Kai flinched at the chirurgeon's unwarranted over-familiarity.

'Don't touch me,' said Kai. 'Don't you know anything about telepaths? Do you really want me to know all your dirty little secrets?'

Tortega snatched his hand back, and Kai shook his head. 'Idiot. I've no talent for psychometry, but you were worried, weren't you? What are you keeping from old Verduchina? Drug abuse? Illicit liaisons with your patients? Aberrant sexual deviancy?'

The chirurgeon reddened, and Kai laughed. 'You're a pathetic little man, Tortega. You think Verduchina values you? Likes you? You're nothing to him, just another disposable functionary. That is if he even knows your name.'

Tortega's back stiffened, but he refrained from rising to Kai's bait. Instead, he returned his gaze to the wonders passing their skimmer.

'There,' said Tortega archly, 'that's the Hamazan Ossuary. I've seen picts, but they don't capture the grandeur of its scale. You really have to see it to appreciate the harmony of its proportions. And there, I believe that colonnaded

archway with the golden finials and weeping domes
leads to the Astartes Tower. They say it's the last place the
Emperor and the primarchs spoke before the expedition
fleets set off to the far corners of the Imperium. The
glorious arias of Kynska's *The Score of Heroes* tells of each
day the Emperor spent with his sons.'

'I'll bet he wishes he'd spent longer,' said Kai idly, finishing his drink and placing the glass on the polished
mahogany rest beside him. He wanted another, to drain
the entire bottle. Anything to dull the ache.

'What do you mean?' said Tortega.

'Maybe if the Emperor had spent longer than a day
with Horus Lupercal, we wouldn't be in this mess.'

'Hush,' said Tortega. 'You cannot say such things, not
here, not in this place.'

'Who is to stop me?'

Tortega shook his head. 'What pleasure do you get
from being so provocative?'

Kai shrugged. 'I was just pointing out that had the
Emperor spent more time with his primarchs, then perhaps they might not have turned on him. It's hardly a
treasonous thought.'

'Who is to say what is treason these days?' sighed
Tortega.

'Just ask the Crusader Host,' said Kai. 'I'm pretty sure
they could tell you.'

IT TOOK ANOTHER day to reach their destination, and Tortega spent his time cataloguing wonders of the palace
he would probably never see again: The Gallery of Winter, Upanizad's Tomb, the Petitioner's Hall, the Crystal
Observatory, the fire-blackened Preceptory, the Long
Room and the Forge of Flesh and Steel, where the historic pact between the Martian priesthood and Terra had
finally been sealed. Its double-headed eagle capstone
was fashioned from ouslite and porphyry. In the dying
sunset it looked bloody.

Kai sensed the presence of the City of Sight long before

he saw it over the horizon, a grimly empty space amid this teeming anthill of mental activity. The psi-dampers fitted to the skimmer had blocked virtually every stray thought from the billions of workers, labourers, scribes, technicians, artisans and soldiers within the palace walls, but Kai had still sensed the background thrum of so vast a populace.

Approaching the headquarters of the Adeptus Astra Telepathica, there was nothing, no trace that anyone lived in this forsaken part of the palace. Kai knew better, having spent nearly a decade within its bleak towers, learning how to harness his abilities for the betterment of the Imperium. Thinking back to those days, he felt a fleeting touch of nostalgia, but quelled it bitterly, for this was no joyous homecoming.

Where other regions of the palace were celebrations of Unity, the builders of the City of Sight seemed to have gone out of their way to craft something calculated to weigh on the soul. Beyond the domain of the astro-telepaths, the architecture of the palace was raised up in glorification of mankind's achievements, its statuary fashioned to remind a grateful populace of all that had been rebuilt in the wake of the terrible, world-spanning wars that had almost dragged the species down into extinction.

None of that was to be found in the City of Sight, and Kai felt only aching despair as the skimmer passed beneath the Obsidian Arch in its outer walls. Tortega twisted his head as he stared at the forest of iron towers, lightless garrets and silent thoroughfares within. The streets of the palace beyond the glossy black archway were alive with the heaving, vibrant mass of humanity, but only solitary ghosts in hooded green robes populated these streets.

'A lot of memories here for you, I expect,' said Tortega.

Kai nodded and said, 'I *really* hate you.'

* * *

IT WAS FOOLISH to be out on the streets this late, but Roxanne had little choice but to risk the darkness. Though it was night, the Petitioner's City was never truly dark. Drumfires cast flickering illumination on the walls of the buildings around her, and hooded lanterns hung from hooks on makeshift lamplighter posts.

Fumes from chemical burners clung to leaning structures built from prefabricated panels stolen from the spoil heaps of the Mechanicum or the construction fields before the palace walls. Whip antennae reached up into the smoky haze hanging over the ad hoc city from some of the larger dwellings, and cloth bunting was strung from corner to corner in a failed effort to leaven the appearance of squalor. The wall next to her was plastered with Lectitio Divinitatus flyers, crudely printed on old propaganda sheets.

Roxanne's every instinct had counselled against her leaving the temple, but the sight of Maya's crying children had persuaded her that there was no other option. The infections ravaging their tiny frames were well advanced and, without medicine, they would be dead by morning. Two of Maya's offspring were already laid at the feet of the Vacant Angel while their mother wept and wailed to its featureless face.

Palladis had given her directions to the Serpent House, and Roxanne took care to follow them exactly. She had never travelled so far from the temple, and the experience was fearful and exciting in the same breath. To a girl raised a virtual prisoner by her own family, the sense of danger was liberating and intoxicating.

And just as the city was never truly dark, nor was it ever truly silent.

Metal hammered on metal, children cried, mothers shouted, lunatic preachers read their holy writ of the Emperor, and drunks yelled obscenities at the air. Roxanne had read volumes of history in the family library that spoke of Old Earth's cities, how they had been teeming slums where millions of people lived cheek by jowl with one another in appalling poverty.

That, her carefully-vetted tutors told her, had been an ancient age, an age before the coming of the Emperor. To Roxanne's freshly-opened eyes, it didn't look like much had changed. It seemed absurd that poverty like this could exist in the shadow of the palace, the living symbol of this new age of progress and enlightenment. The gilded halo around the palace bathed the tallest buildings of heroic architects with lambent illumination, but little hint of the light and wonder the Emperor's armies were bringing to the galaxy fell upon the Petitioner's City.

Roxanne wondered if her family had sent anyone to find her, if there were, even now, agents of her father scouring the streets of the city looking for his wayward daughter. Perhaps, but most likely not. The dust had yet to settle from the scandal surrounding her last voyage, and she imagined there would be those amongst the family hierarchy who would be more than happy to see her lost amongst the faceless masses.

She put such thoughts from her mind and concentrated on the route ahead.

Dangerous enough to roam the streets of the City this late without letting her mind dwell on the injustices of the world or the life on which she had turned her back. *This* was her life now, and it was about as far from the one she had known as it was possible to get.

Swathed in a hooded robe of rough muddy brown fabric that Roxanne wouldn't have dreamed of wearing a few months ago, she was an innocuous enough presence on the streets. The few people she passed carefully avoided her glances and made their own furtive ways through the streets. She kept her hood pulled tight around her head, keeping her features in the shadows and walking with the hunched gait common amongst the city's inhabitants.

The less notice she attracted the better.

The Serpent House was deep in Dhakal territory, and

she most assuredly did not want to run into any of the Babu's men before she got there. At best they would kill her quickly and rob her. At worst they'd take their time in violating her before dumping the mutilated corpse in the gutter.

Roxanne had seen the body of a girl who'd run into Ghota, the Babu's most feared enforcer, and she found it impossible to comprehend that a human being could do such terrible things. The girl's father had brought her to the temple and handed over everything he owned. Palladis had tried to stop the man leaving, knowing full well where he would go, but the father's grief was unassailable. His dismembered body had been found hanging from iron meat hooks on the edge of the Dhakal territories the following night.

Yes, it was dangerous to be out in the Petitioner's City after sundown, but Maya's little ones needed counterbiotics and Antioch was the only chirurgeon who had medicine that hadn't been cut with too many impurities to do any good. The old man's prices were ruinous, but that didn't matter to Palladis when it came to children.

In any case, what price could you put on a life when the temple was never short of money?

The bereaved were generous with their coin, as though fearing any hint of pecuniary reticence would somehow prevent their dead from finding peace. Imperial truth owned to no life beyond the corporeal, that death was the end of a person's journey, but Roxanne knew better. She had stared into the tenebrous realm that lay beyond the hideously permeable borders of reality, and seen things that made her question everything she had been told.

She shook off such dangerous thoughts, feeling her breath quicken and her heartbeat race. Suppressed memories threatened to surface, horrors of skinless bodies on fire from the marrow, wet organs hanging from ruptured torsos and skulls licked clean from the inside, but she fought to quell them by fixing on something inconsequential.

The wall next to her was daubed with graffiti, and she focussed the entirety of her attention upon it as her memory recalled the smell of blood and the ozone stink of failing shields. It was a mural depicting hulking warriors of the Legiones Astartes atop newly conquered worlds, gaudy in colour and robust in vigour if not aesthetic merit. The artist was clearly ignorant of their true scale, as the armoured figures were not much bigger than the mortal soldiers accompanying them.

Roxanne had seen the terrible might of the Legiones Astartes, and knew just how unnaturally swollen they were, their bulk freakishly ogre-like, yet surprisingly supple and graceful.

The mural had been vandalised, and several of the figures were partially obscured with hurled whitewash and slogans that reassuringly told her that the Emperor protected. The purple of the Emperor's Children and the blue of the World Eaters was almost completely gone, while the white and ochre green of the Death Guard poked out from a numerous angry brush strokes. A Luna Wolf howled from behind a wide splash of paint, while an Iron Warrior's face had been unfairly hacked from the wall and lay in pieces on the hard-packed earth.

Roxanne's breathing slowed and she reached out to touch the mural, letting the reassuring solidity of the wall bring her back to a place of equilibrium. She closed her eyes and rested her forehead against the rough brickwork, taking in slow breaths and imagining the expanse of an empty desert wasteland. The metallic reek of innards faded, and the pungent odour of roasting meat and stale sweat returned with its all-too-human aroma. The toxic smell of bac-sticks waxed strong in the mix.

'In the desert there is no life,' she said, repeating the mantra her tutors had taught her so long ago. 'In the desert I am alone and nothing can touch me. I am inviolate.'

'Too bad you're far from a desert, little girl,' grunted a voice behind her.

Roxanne turned in fright, all thoughts of equilibrium and deserts falling from her mind like leaves in autumn. Three men in heavy furs and rough canvas work over-alls lounged on the wall opposite the mural. All three smoked, and clouds of blue hung like a fog over their heads. Swarthy and rough-skinned, they were brutish and clumsy looking, but Roxanne knew better than to dismiss them as common drunks or thugs.

'I am not looking for trouble,' said Roxanne, lifting her hands, palm up, towards the men.

They laughed, and a man with thin eyes and a long drooping moustache stepped forward.

He flicked his bac-stick away. 'That's too bad, little girl, because trouble's found you.'

'Please,' said Roxanne. 'If you are Babu Dhakal's men, you should walk away. It would be better for everyone if you just left me alone. Trust me.'

'If you know we work for the Babu, then you know we're not going to let you go,' said the man, beckoning his companions to his side. Roxanne saw heavy pistols stuffed into the waistbands of their overalls, and crude, hand-made shanks strapped to their thighs. The mous-tachioed leader pulled a gleaming weapon from his belt, a long knife with the blade angled forward. He lifted it to his lips and ran a yellowed tongue over the cutting edge of the knife. Blood dripped down his chin and he smiled, exposing reddened teeth.

'You're from the death church, aren't you?' said the man.

'I am from the Temple of Woe, yes,' confirmed Rox-anne, keeping her voice as neutral as possible. 'That is why you should leave me alone.'

'Too late for that, little girl. I'm guessing you're head-ing for Antioch's, and that means you must have plenty of coin to afford his prices. Hand it over now and we'll go easy on you, maybe only cut you a little.'

'I cannot do that,' said Roxanne.

'Of course you can. Just reach inside that robe and

hand it over. Trust me, it'll be easier for you if you do. Anil and Murat aren't kind like I am, and they already want to kill you.'

'If you take my money, you will be killing two children,' explained Roxanne.

The man shrugged. 'They won't be the first. I doubt they'll be the last.'

With a gesture, the two men either side of the lead thug rushed towards her. She turned and ran for the end of the road, screaming for help though she knew no one would answer. A hand grabbed her robe. She squirmed free. A fist punched her on the shoulder and she stumbled, reaching out to the wall to steady herself.

A portion of the adobe wall came loose and she cried out as she fell to her knees. She found herself face to face with a piece of brickwork bearing the helm of a warrior in armour of red and white. A foot planted itself between her shoulder blades and shoved hard. Roxanne's face slammed into the earthen street and blood filled her mouth as she bit the inside of her cheek. Rough hands rolled her onto her back.

Roxanne's hood fell back, along with a knotted bandana, and her assailant leered a gap-toothed grin.

'Pretty, pretty!' he spat. His shank caught the light of a nearby torch.

A second pair of hands tore open her robe and Roxanne thrashed in their grip.

'Get off me!' she screamed, but Babu Dhakal's men weren't listening.

'I warned you,' said the leader of the thugs, almost amiably.

'No,' said Roxanne. 'I warned *you*!'

The thug pawing at her belt suddenly spasmed as though a high voltage electric current was passing through him. Blood-flecked froth burst from behind his teeth and his eyes boiled to glutinous steam within their sockets. He screamed and rolled off Roxanne, clawing at his smoking skull and thrashing as though assaulted by a host of invisible attackers.

'What did you do?' snarled the second man, scrambling away in terror.

Roxanne sat up and spat a broken tooth, her anger and hurt too powerful for any thoughts of mercy to intrude. She fixed the frightened man with her gaze and, once again, did the very thing her tutors had always warned her never to do.

The man screamed and bright red blood squirted from his nose and ears. The life went out of him in an instant, and he slumped against the wall like a drunk. Roxanne climbed unsteadily to her feet as the third man backed away from her in horror.

'You are *boksi*!' cried the man. 'A daemon witch!'

'I told you to leave me alone,' said Roxanne. 'But you wouldn't listen.'

'I'll kill you!' screamed the man, reaching for his pistol.

Before the weapon cleared his overalls, he fell back with sizzling brain matter leaking from every orifice in his skull. Without a sound, he toppled sideways and his head caved in like an emptied air bladder as it hit the ground.

Roxanne steadied herself against the wall behind her, breathless and appalled at the violence she had unleashed. Swiftly she retrieved her bandana, and pulled up the hood of her robe, lest anyone see her face and recognise her for what she was.

Once again, blood and death had followed her. She was what ancient mariners had once called a Jonah, and it seemed that no matter where she hid, ill-fortune and death would surround her. She hadn't meant to kill these men, but raw survival instinct had kicked in and there was little she could have done to prevent their deaths.

She saw the clan markings tattooed on the arm of the man she had killed first, and the cold realisation of what she had done flooded her.

These were Babu Dhakal's men!

He would demand blood in return for their deaths,

and the Babu was not a man given to restraint in his vengeance. When retaliation came it would be exponentially worse.

'Throne, what have I done?' she whispered.

Roxanne fled into the night.

THE SKIMMER EASED through the City of Sight, its blue and amethyst colours bright in the overlong shadows that filled its gloomy precincts. Few statues were raised here, and though many of the pale, columned buildings were grandly shaped and heroically proportioned, they were brooding, monolithic structures that pressed down on the skin of the mountains like architectural black holes, sucking in the available light and warmth of the failing day.

Kai knew he was being melodramatic, a trait he despised in others, but couldn't help himself from such indulgence. He had long thought himself done with this bleak place, but here he was again, cast back like a failed aspirant.

The image was an apt one, he realised, for wasn't that exactly what he was?

The hollow mountain loomed above the city, casting its shadow over Kai. Though he affected an air of disinterest, the idea of being taken there sent breathless jolts of fear through his body. He pushed thoughts of that dreadful place from his mind and concentrated on the road ahead. Tortega had turned away from the window, proving that even a fool could sense the weight of solemnity that pervaded the City of Sight. Kai reached out with the tiniest measure of his psychic senses to determine exactly where he was. Thanks to his augmetic eyes, precision-fashioned ocular implants ground and crafted by Mechanicum adepts bonded to House Castana, he had little reason to employ his blindsight, and it took a moment for him to adjust his perceptions from visual to psychic.

He closed his eyes, feeling the weight of the nearby

buildings and the aetheric bulk of the many high towers of psykers. It took a moment to orient himself, but
in seconds he had shaped the surrounding architecture
into ribbons of light and gleaming threads of colour.
The skimmer was passing the Gallery of Mirrors, a vast,
cathedral-like building through which successful initiates passed on their way to the awe-inspiring caverns
beneath the city. Far beneath the palace, they would
kneel before the Emperor and have the impossibly complex neural pathways of their mind agonisingly reshaped
to better resist the dangers of the warp.

Kai remembered being shepherded through the gallery by a company of Black Sentinels, nervous, excited
and unsure of what was to come. He supposed the mirrors were there to give the aspirants a last look at their
faces before their eyes were seared from their sockets by
a force so potent it was beyond imagining. In the years
since Kai had taken that walk, he had never been able to
decide if that was merciful or cruel.

He shook off the memory, unwilling to relive such a
singular moment in the presence of those who would
misread his pained expression as fear of where they were
going. Instead, he cast his mind-sense forward, along
the flat plane of the road towards the tallest tower of the
city. Alone of all the structures around it, the Whispering
Tower shone with a lattice of silver light, though it was a
light that existed beyond the sight of most mortals.

Yet for all its brightness, its glow was eclipsed utterly
by the burning lance of light that speared from the hollow mountain. That brilliance was of another order of
magnitude entirely, and Kai was able to tune it out of his
perceptions only with difficulty.

'Why are there no telepaths on the streets?' asked Tortega. 'I'm only seeing servitors, sherpa-couriers and a few
Mechanicum thralls.'

Kai opened his eyes, and the cityscape of light and
colour vanished from his mind, replaced with the prosaic geometry of its mundane stones and stolid angles.

Though he had jumped at the chance to have his sight restored, it was at moments like this he almost wished he had not.

'The students and adepts of the Telepathica mostly travel by means of a network of tunnels and crossways cut into the rock beneath the city. Very few come above ground if they can help it.'

'Why is that?'

Kai shrugged. 'Feeling sunlight on your skin is just another reminder of what you've lost.'

'Of course, I see,' nodded Tortega, as though grasping some complex insight into the human psyche instead of something that should have been obvious.

'The city walls and the rock below us are threaded with psi-disruptive crystals, which makes it quieter too,' said Kai. 'Travelling above ground is noisy for an astropath. You keep hearing undisciplined thoughts, random chatter and wild emotions. You're taught to tune it out, of course, but it's always there in the background. It's just easier to travel where you don't hear it.'

'Are you hearing anything now?'

'Just your incessant prattle,' said Kai.

Tortega sighed. 'Your hostility is just a defence mechanism, Kai. Let it go.'

'Spare me,' said Kai, resting his head on the soft fabric of the headrest and closing his eyes. His blindsight picked out the shimmering glow of the Whispering Tower and the minds that waited at its entrance.

One was welcoming, while the other bristled with hostility not even a shielded helmet could contain.

The skimmer glided to a halt and the batwing doors hissed as they swooped up with a hiss of high-end pneumatics. Three of the armsmen climbed from the skimmer, while the fourth gestured to Kai and Tortega to disembark with a curt swipe of his shotgun barrel. Tortega hurriedly got out, but Kai poured himself another measure of amasec, taking his time and delaying his inevitable fate as long as possible.

'Get out,' said the armsman.

'One last drink,' said Kai. 'Trust me, they don't have anything like this good in there.'

He drained the glass in one swallow, and coughed as the liquor set his throat on fire.

'You done?' asked the blank visor across from him.

'So it would appear,' said Kai, lifting the bottle from the chill-bar and tucking it under his arm as he climbed from the comfortable warmth of the skimmer.

The freezing air of the mountains hit him like a blow, and he took a frigid breath that burned his throat more thoroughly than the amasec. He'd forgotten just how bone-achingly cold it was here. Kai had forgotten a lot of things about the City of Sight, but he had never forgotten the kindness of the woman who stepped from the arched entrance to the tower.

'Hello, Kai,' said Aniq Sarashina. 'It is good to see you again.'

'Mistress Sarashina,' he said with a short bow. 'I hope you will not take this the wrong way, but I cannot say the same.'

'No, I expect not,' she said with a sad, but wry smile. 'You never could conceal how much you wanted to be away from this place.'

'Yet here I am,' said Kai.

The man beside Sarashina took a step forward, his bullish manner more than matched by the rippling haze of belligerence surrounding him. Encased in beetle-black armour and with the craggy, unforgiving lines of his face concealed by a reflective helm, he wore his power like a mailed fist.

He received a rolled parchment from the lead armsman and broke the waxen seal. Satisfied with its contents, he nodded and said, 'Transfer is acknowledged, Kai Zulane is now in the custody of the Black Sentinels.'

'Custody, Captain Golovko?' said Kai, as a group of soldiers in contoured breastplates of burnished obsidian and tapered helms, not unlike an early make of

Legiones Astartes armour, emerged from the tower. Each was armed with a long, black-bladed lance, their hafts topped with sparkling crystalline spearheads.

'Yes, Zulane. And it's Major General Golovko now,' said the man.

'You've gone up in the world,' said Kai. 'Were all the senior members of your organisation killed in some terrible accident?'

'Kai, one does not begin the healing process with insults,' said Tortega.

'Oh, shut up, you bloody imbecile!' said Kai. 'Just go away, please. Take your precious patriarch's skimmer and get out of here. I can't stand to look at you anymore.'

'I'm just trying to help,' said Tortega with a hurt pout.

'Then leave,' said Kai. 'That's how you can help me best.'

Kai felt a soft hand take his arm, and calming energy filled him, easing his barbed thoughts and imparting a measure of serenity he hadn't felt in months.

'It's alright, Chirurgeon Tortega,' said Aniq Sarashina. 'Kai is home and he is one of us. You have done all that you can, but it is time to let us take care of him.'

Tortega nodded curtly and turned on his heel. He paused, as though about to say something, then thought the better of it and climbed back into the skimmer. The Castana armsmen followed him, and the doors slammed down with a solid clunk.

The skimmer spun on its axis and sped away as though eager to be gone.

'What an odious little shit,' said Kai, as the skimmer vanished from sight.

TWO

The Cryptaesthesian
Temple of Woe
Homecoming

IN THE DEPTHS of the Whispering Tower, a lone figure hooded in a robe of embroidered jade stood in the centre of a domed chamber that echoed with the myriad voices of a departed choir. Garbled and indistinct sounds swirled around him like a corrupted vox-signal or a transmission hurled across galactic space in ages past.

At the dome's apex was a crystalline lattice pulsing with internal illumination that cascaded from its multi-angled facets in a waterfall of shimmering light. Evander Gregoras stood in the centre of the swirling mist, his arms sweeping out like the conductor of an invisible orchestra. Hazy shapes formed around him, innumerable faces, objects and places. They surfaced in the light like phantoms then faded into the mist, each one summoned and dismissed with a precise gesture.

The voices rose and diminished, snatches of wasted words and redundant phrases that would be meaningless to anyone not trained in the art of the cryptaesthesian. Gregoras sifted the Bleed with the efficiency of a surgeon, discarding that which was of no importance and

51

memorising those items that piqued his interest.

Gregoras was not a man whose company others craved. Though entirely average in appearance, he had seen the secret, ugly face of humanity and such sights made a man melancholy of aspect. Where others might talk of love, truth and a new golden age, Gregoras saw lust, deceit and the same tired melodramas played out in the psychic waste of every communiqué that passed through the City of Sight.

Never more so than now.

With the treachery of the Warmaster and the departure of Rogal Dorn's annihilation fleet, the astro-telepathic choirs were operating beyond capacity to satisfy the demands of waging a distant war against this rebellion. Horus Lupercal had cast his treacherous spark into an unstable galaxy, and entire systems were declaring for his forces in wave after wave of defection.

It seemed the Emperor's dream of galactic Unity was slipping away day by day.

Aetheric space was awash with telepathic communication, and messages were being hurled into the void that screamed for help or simply blared hatred. The trap chambers beneath the iron towers of the city were filled with psychic residue from the thousands of messages, and Gregoras's cryptaesthesians could barely keep up with the brutal pace. In the face of treason, every message sent to Terra had to be carefully scrutinised, no matter how mundane it might appear. The Bleed was scoured for signs of encryption that might be a communication intended for embedded agents of the Warmaster.

Insane amounts of communication traffic was coming from the palace every day, and the City of Sight's astropaths were burning out with greater rapidity than ever before. The captains of the Black Ships attempted to spread their nets ever wider for emergent psykers to replace these burn-outs, but the war had cut off many of the more promising systems.

New astropaths arrived every week, but the Imperium's

need was continually outstripping demand.

Yet amongst this fresh influx there was one addition to the tower's roster of astro-telepaths that Gregoras believed to be a liability.

He had railed against allowing Kai Zulane to return to the tower, arguing that the man should be dismissed to the hollow mountain, but the Choirmaster had ignored his objections. Sensing Sarashina's hand in Zulane's repatriation, Gregoras had confronted her at the Obsidian Arch as she returned from another conference with the Sigillite's emissaries. Her steps were weary, but Gregoras had cared nothing for her lethargy.

'Your student returns to us then?' he had said, not bothering to disguise his venom.

She turned to him, and he felt her brief surge of irritation, quickly suppressed.

'Not now, Evander,' she had said. 'Can I at least enter the tower before you berate me?'

'This won't wait.'

She sighed. 'Kai Zulane. Yes, he will be here within the week.'

'I assume you know Castana are just dumping him here to save face with the XIII Legion. If you cannot fix him, the blame falls on us, not them.'

'I will not need to "fix him", because he is not broken,' Sarashina had said, walking briskly towards the tower. 'Everyone experiences loss and trauma at some point in their service.'

Gregoras shook his head. 'Not like Zulane did. He and the girl should have had a bullet in the back of their heads as soon as the Space Marines found them. Verduchina knows it, so does the choirmaster, but not you. Why is that?'

'Kai is stronger than any telepath I have ever trained,' said Sarashina. 'He is more resilient than he knows.'

'But what they saw and heard…'

'Was more terrible than you or I can imagine, but they survived, and I will not condemn them for that. I believe they survived for a reason, and I would know what that reason is.'

'The *Vatic* have seen nothing to validate that belief,' said Gregoras. 'I would know of it.'

'Not even you can uncover every potential, Evander.'

'True, but I see more than you. Enough to know that Kai Zulane should not be here.'

'What do you know?' asked Sarashina. 'What have your grubby little scavengers found that I should hear?'

'Nothing concrete,' admitted Gregoras, 'but there are dark currents in the echoes of every vision we parse from the Bleed, hidden things without form or presence. I do not understand them, for the do not appear in any of my *Oneirocritica*.'

'You have consulted the *Alchera Mundi*?'

'Of course, but even in Yun's collection I can find no correlation of imagery beyond the vulgar texts of pre-Unity dreamers: daemons, gods and the like.'

'You should know better than to give credence to the dreams of those who professed belief in the divine and the sorceries of magicians. I am surprised at you, Evander.'

No more had been said, and despite his continued objections, the Choirmaster had allowed Kai Zulane to return to the City of Sight. For once, Gregoras had found himself in accord with Maxim Golovko, a situation that was almost too ridiculous for words.

He pushed thoughts of Kai Zulane aside as yet more psychic emanations spilled into the chamber, the aftermath of the messages sent in the wake of Abir Ibn Khaldun's communion with the X Legion. The knowledge that Ferrus Manus was racing ahead of his main fleet for personal revenge had prompted a barrage of messages from Rogal Dorn, urging caution and rigid adherence to his order of battle, but whether any would be heeded was another matter entirely. With wide sweeps of his hands and deft strokes of his fingertips, Gregoras began the process of psychic examination, hoping he might see yet another fragmentary hint of the pattern that had been his passion for over a century.

Gregoras sat at the crossroads of the Imperium, where lines of communication crossed and re-crossed. From here, expedition fleets were despatched, recalled or regrouped. The fate of tens of thousands of worlds was decided within the walls of the palace, and it all passed through the City of Sight. To sift through the vast quantity of psychic debris that was left in its wake was the task of the cryptaesthesians, a task few relished but which Evander Gregoras had made his life's work.

Telepaths on every world of the Imperium had been sending their thoughts to Terra for nearly two centuries, and each one had eventually come to him in this chamber. They spoke of wars, of lost branches of the species, of heroes and dastards, of loyalty and betrayal and all the millions of trivial matters in-between.

He had sifted the psychic waste of millions of astro-telepaths for over a hundred years, and uncovered all manner of hidden vice, greed and sedition in the detritus of transmitted messages. He had seen the very worst of people, the dark, petty, ridiculous, malicious subtexts hidden in a thousand different places in everything they said without ever realising.

And amid the countless dream-borne messages that came to the City of Sight, Evander Gregoras had begun to see a pattern emerge. For decades he had studied any Bleed that carried a tantalising hint of this emergent cohesion, learning more of its brilliant complexity with every scrap he uncovered. Perhaps only one in every hundred messages would contain a veiled reference to it, then one in a thousand, ten thousand. Each time, the truth of the message would be veiled in secrecy or lunacy, buried in subtextual codes so subtle that few would ever recognise it as a cipher – even the senders of such messages.

Through the decades, it became clear that there was a secret to the Imperium that was known only to a fragmented diaspora of madmen who were wholly ignorant of each other's existence, yet who hurled their desperate messages into the void in the impossible hope that their warning would be heeded.

Only here in the Whispering Tower did their disparate scraps converge, like a single song straining to be heard amid a cacophony of voices.

Gregoras had not fully deciphered the truth of this song, but had come to one inescapable conclusion.

It was getting louder every day.

DAWN BROUGHT LIGHT, but no respite from the cold. The mountains above were achingly white with snow, but little of that lay upon the roofs of the Petitioner's City. Thousands of people clustered together in such confined spaces raised the ambient temperature enough to prevent the snow from lying, but kept it cold enough to bite. Roxanne pulled her robes tighter about her body and shivered as she pushed open the sheet steel door of the temple. It squealed noisily, setting her teeth on edge, and slammed heavily behind her as she entered the echoing space given over to grief.

Like most buildings in the Petitioner's City, the temple had been constructed from random materials appropriated from the endless cycles of construction, repair and rebuilding that now engulfed the palace. Its walls were raised with marble offcuts stacked and mortared by itinerant *migou* expelled from the Masonic Guilds for habitual usage of narcotics.

That stonework had been shaped and carved into a menagerie of forms: distraught angels with upraised arms, weeping cherubs with silver trumpets and great birds with golden wings dipped in sorrow. Mosaics of mourners fashioned in Gyptian pebble looked down from brick corbels and death masks of stillborn children stared out from painted frescoes assembled from crushed glass.

A mish-mash of pew-like benches filled the temple,

many occupied by wailing families gathered round the body of a loved one. Sometimes these bodies were old, mostly they were not. Roxanne kept her head bowed as people looked up at the sound of the door slamming. She was known here, but not known enough for people to want to speak to her, which was just how she liked it. Someone like her would attract attention, and that was the last thing she wanted.

At the far end of the temple was its crowning glory, a tall statue of dark-hue that had come to be known as the Vacant Angel. Thanks to some imperfection in the Syryan nephrite, the warmasons had rejected the base material and cast it on the spoil heaps. Like most things discarded by the palace, it had found its way to the Petitioner's City.

Carved in the form of a kneeling man, its muscular body was classically proportioned and in need of finishing. The face was blank, no doubt intended to be completed in the likeness of some Imperial hero by a Masonic sculptor. It had stood in the temple for over a year, but Palladis had – for reasons he kept to himself – chosen not to give it a face, though Roxanne could never shake the feeling it was looking at her with eyes just waiting to be carved.

Compared to the chambers in which Roxanne had spent her youth, the temple's ornamentation was crude and unsophisticated, yet the grieving statues possessed a grace that far surpassed anything she had grown up around. What made it all the more incredible was that it was all the work of one man.

Palladis Novandio stood beside Maya, who knelt weeping at the feet of the Vacant Angel. She cradled an unmoving infant close to her breast, as though expecting to suckle it once again. Maya's tears fell on the child's eyes and rolled down its cold cheeks. Palladis looked up and gave Roxanne a nod of welcome as she took a seat to one side of the nave. She sat within sight of the Imperium's secular heart, and yet here she was in a temple. The thought made her smile, as precious little else had done since she had returned to Terra in disgrace.

A stoop-shouldered man touched her arm, and Roxanne jumped. She hadn't heard him approach. He stood next to her, his face draped with the emptiness of loss.

'Who have you lost?' he asked.

'No one,' she replied. 'At least no one recently. You?'

'My youngest sons,' said the man. 'That's my wife at the statue.'

'You are Estaben?'

The man nodded.

'I'm so sorry for your loss,' she said.

The man shrugged, as though the matter were of no consequence. 'Maybe better this way.'

Before Roxanne could ask him what he meant, Estaben handed her a folded sheaf of papers and made his way down the nave. He limped over to Maya and lightly took her by the shoulder. She shook her head, but her husband bent to whisper in her ear and her wails took on a new pitch of misery as she put down her dead son.

Estaben led her away from the statue, and Roxanne bowed her head as they passed, ostensibly leaving them to their sorrow, but secretly fearing their grief and ill-fortune might be contagious. She looked up in time to see Palladis taking a seat in the pew in front of her. She gave him a weak smile.

'Did you get the medicine?' he asked without preamble.

She nodded. 'Yes, though it took a while to rouse Antioch from a qash stupor.'

'The man likes to sample his own wares,' said Palladis shaking his head. 'Foolish.'

'Here,' said Roxanne, handing over a cloth bag the size of her fist. 'It should be enough for both children.'

Palladis took the medicine and nodded. His hands were rough and callused, the nails permanently edged in black from long years working stone with rasp and chisel. He was a man of middling years, with greying hair and a face weathered like the side of a cliff from a life-time spent in the open air, carving statues, columns and detailed adornments for pediments and vaulted arches.

'Maya will be grateful to you,' said Palladis. 'Once she has finished her mourning.'

'You paid for it, I just went to get it.'

'At no small risk to your person,' pointed out Palladis. 'You encountered no problems?'

She lowered her head, knowing she had to tell him what had happened, but fearing his disappointment more than any censure.

'Roxanne?' he said when she didn't answer.

'I ran into some of Babu Dhakal's men,' she said at last.

'I see,' said Palladis. 'What happened?'

'They attacked me. I killed them.'

He sighed. 'How?'

'How do you think?'

Palladis raised a placatory hand. 'Did anyone see you?'

'I don't know, probably,' said Roxanne. 'I didn't mean to kill them, not at first, but they'd have cut my throat as soon as they were done with me.'

'I know, but you must be more careful,' said Palladis. 'The Babu is a man of great rages, and he will find out what happened to his men. He will come here, that much is certain.'

'I'm so sorry,' she said. 'I didn't mean to bring you trouble. That's all I ever seem to do.'

Palladis laced his big, callused hands in her fingers and gave a slow smile.

'One problem at a time, Roxanne,' he said. 'Let tomorrow look after itself. Today we are alive and have medicine to give two children a chance to see another dawn. If you learn anything in your time here, let it be that death surrounds us in all its myriad forms, just waiting to catch you unawares. Bend all your efforts to keeping it at bay. Honour death in all its forms. Appease it and you will be spared its cruel attentions for a time.'

He spoke with the passion of a zealot, yet there was

kindness in his eyes. Roxanne knew little of his past, save that he had once been a master craftsman under the suzerainty of Warmason Vadok Singh. That he had suffered loss was obvious, but he had never spoken of what had driven him to raise a temple from the ashes and debris of the Petitioner's City.

Roxanne bowed her head. She knew all too well how easily death could reach out and completely change the course of a life, even one spared its attention.

'What did Estaben give you?' asked Palladis.

She looked at the papers as though seeing them for the first time. The paper was thin and looked like whatever was printed on it now wasn't the first ink it had known.

'The usual,' she said, flicking through the palimpsest and picking out phrases at random. She read them aloud.

'The Emperor of Mankind is the Light and the Way, and all his actions are for the benefit of mankind, which is his people. The Emperor is God and God is the Emperor, so it is taught in the Lectitio Divinitatus, and above all things, the Emperor will protect...'

'Let me see that,' said Palladis, with a sharpness she had not heard in his voice before.

She held out the pamphlet, and he snatched it from her hand.

'Not this Lectitio Divinitatus nonsense again,' he said with a sneer of contempt before ripping the pamphlet in two. 'A bunch of desperate people beguiled by a glittering light and who have yet to discover that all that glitters is not gold.'

'They're harmless enough,' said Roxanne with a shrug. 'It's comforting even.'

'Nonsense!' snapped Palladis. 'It's dangerous self-delusion, and I hear they've even spread these fantasies off-world. This is the very worst kind of lie, for it comforts people with a hope of protection that does not exist.'

'Sorry,' said Roxanne. 'He just gave me it. I didn't ask him to.'

Palladis was immediately contrite. 'Yes, of course, I'm sorry. I know that, but I don't want you reading anything like this. There is only one truth, and that is the finality of death. This is the worst kind of lie, because let me tell you, the Emperor most assuredly does *not* protect.'

KAI HAD HEARD a wise man say that you can never go home, and until now he had never understood the sense of that. Born to a wealthy family of the Merican hinterlands, Kai had travelled extensively with his father, a cartel agent who brokered trade contracts between Terran conglomerates and the surviving mercantile interests of newly-compliant worlds.

As a youngster, Kai had scaled the heights of the mid-Atalantic ridges, explored the majestic ruins of Kalagann's cities of Ursh, bathed in the glow of the pan-pacific magma-vents, and descended into the Mariana Canyon to gaze in awe at the great cliff sculptures carved by geological artists of a forgotten age. He had spent much of each year travelling the globe, following his father from negotiation to negotiation.

Life had been one adventure after another, but no matter how exhilarating each trip was, Kai would always relish the sight of the family home, perched high on the cliffs of what had once been a carven monument to long-dead kings of antiquity. His mother would be there with a welcoming smile that was just a little bit sad because she knew it wouldn't be long until her husband and son would be travelling again.

Home was more than just a physical place, it was a state of mind, and even after he had come of age, and the men of the Black Ships had come for him, he always longed to return home to see that sad, welcoming smile.

The City of Sight had become his home, but it was one to which Kai had never wanted to return. The interior of the tower was lightless, cold and high-ceilinged, but Kai's augmetic implants compensated for the low light and his surroundings swam into focus with a lambent green glow.

It wasn't that the builders had set out to make the tower inhospitable, it was more the purpose it had been put to and the mien of its inhabitants that coloured it so. Kai imagined that with the gilt-edged hangings and dazzling lights that illuminated every other structure in the palace, the Whispering Tower could be just as impressive.

The stonework of its walls tapered inwards, planed smooth and cut with mason's marks that helped the newly blind discern their location. Here and there, an inset whisper stone glinted in the dim light, and Kai wondered what secrets they passed between each other in such troubled times. Kai followed Sarashina along the narrowing chamber towards a curved wall, machined smooth and silver, incongruously modern amidst the ancient stone. Two Black Sentinels stood guard before a psi-sealed doorway in the silver wall, and they stood aside as Golovko waved a data wand before them. Kai watched the glowing hash of code cyphers reflected in the visors of the soldiers, automatically storing the binaric information before it faded.

The door slid open, and a cold gust of air sighed from within. Kai shivered as the psychically charged air caressed the skin of his face. Inside the silver chamber was a grav-lift shaped in the form of a double helix that ran the full length of the tower. A nimbus of light surrounded the gravity field, and Kai's augmetics picked out the differing waveforms that rippled up and down the shimmering cascade.

Around the outer walls of this silver chamber, sealed doors led into iron-clad mindhalls, where choirs of astropaths distilled messages sent from all across the galaxy, while others led to vaulted libraries, filled with arcana gathered from the distant corners of Terra.

'We are going to the novitiates level,' said Sarashina, stepping into the leftmost curve of the double helix. The grav-lift enfolded her in its gentle embrace and carried her with smooth grace down into the tower. Kai hesitated at the edge of the light, knowing that once he took this step, there would be no going back.

'Hurry up, Zulane,' said Golovko. 'I have better things to do than baby-sit you.'

'I seriously doubt that,' said Kai, stepping into the light.

Any step was a good one if it carried him away from Golovko.

The light surrounded Kai, and carried him into the tower. He travelled down the spiral, turned around as he descended into the bowels of his former abode. He passed numerous jutting steps where he could have stepped from the grav lift, but Sarashina had said they were going to the novitiates level, and that was right at the bottom of the Whispering Tower.

At last Kai felt the reassuring feel of solid ground beneath him, and stepped out of the light. His eyes adjusted immediately to the brightly lit surroundings. Not everyone who navigated these passages was blind, and bare lumen globes hung from the brickwork ceiling on linked loops of brass cabling. This chamber had been hacked from the bedrock of the mountains and faced with ceramic tiles of bottle green. It had the feel of a medicae chamber, and a number of locked doors led deeper into the guts of the tower. Some led to the novice libraries, where new additions to the tower learned astropathic shorthand, common symbols and the basic mantras of the *nuncio*. Others led to the novices' cells, yet more to communal facilities for eating and ablutions, while yet others ended in hermetically-sealed isolation chambers.

In the moments before Golovko and his Sentinels arrived, Kai took a moment to study his former mentor.

Aniq Sarashina had aged since Kai had seen her last, and the naked light from the lumens was unflattering. Her hair had lost the last of its blonde lustre and was now completely silver. Puckered lines radiating from the plastic hemispheres inserted into her eye sockets had grown deeper and more pronounced. She had been old when Kai had last been here, but now looked positively ancient.

'Do I look so different?' asked Sarashina, and Kai blushed at being caught in his frank appraisal of her appearance.

'You look older,' he said at last.

'I *am* older, Kai,' said Sarashina. 'I have travelled the warp for too many years, and it has left its mark upon me.'

She reached up and ran her fingers over the rumpled skin of his face, her touch feather-light and tender. 'As it has on you too.'

The curse of the Astropath was premature ageing, and Kai didn't need Sarashina to tell him that he had lost the clean lines of his high cheekbones and his growth of fine, salt and pepper hair. Though he was in his late thirties, he had the appearance of a man in his fifties, at least. The face that looked back at him in the mirror – on those days he could face his reflection – was gaunt and hollow, with pinched cheeks and sunken eyes. Only the most expensive juvenat treatments could conceal the damage constant warp travel wreaked on a human being, and no astropath, even one of House Castana, was worth that indulgence of vanity.

Kai backed away from her touch. 'I never thought I would return here,' he said, anxious to change the subject.

'Few of us ever do,' agreed Sarashina.

'Should I be honoured at being one of those few?'

'That depends on how you view your return.'

'As a punishment,' said Kai. 'What other way is there to interpret it?'

'I will leave you to ponder that question for now,' said Sarashina as Golovko stepped from the grav-lift.

His Black Sentinels swiftly followed, and when they were all assembled, Sarashina unlocked the door to her immediate left. Kai frowned at this new direction.

'I am not a novice,' he said. 'This route leads to the training halls set aside for initiates of the *nuncio*.'

'It does indeed, Kai,' agreed Sarashina. 'Where else would your training begin?'

'Begin? I've served the Telepathica for over a decade, and I know the rites of incubation. I don't need to be treated like a child.'

'We'll treat you how we damn well please,' snapped Golovko, pushing him towards the open door. 'You don't have any say in the matter, and if it was up to me, I'd never have allowed you back. You're dangerous, I can feel it.'

'You should watch those "feelings", Golovko,' said Kai, shrugging off the man's grip. 'Things like that will get the psi-hounds sniffing around you. And I don't think you've got what it takes to cut it here.'

'Enough, both of you,' said Sarashina. 'Your petty posturing is ridiculous, and will only cause tremors in the aether.'

Kai said nothing, knowing she was right and remembering the low-grade irritation he'd felt whenever outsiders had let their emotions get the better of them in close proximity to a whisper stone. Without further protest, Kai followed Sarashina along the passageway, the brickwork faced with tiles of ochre ceramic and the glow of the entrance hall fading behind them. Reinforced doors punctuated its length, each one marked with a number and name. Within each marked cell, an initiate of the Scholastica Psykana slumbered, perhaps dreaming, perhaps not. With the psi-shielded doors, it was impossible to know for sure. The darkness soon became absolute, yet Kai could still see perfectly well.

'You are not using your blindsight,' said Sarashina, with a slight incline of her head. Kai thought he detected a hint of disappointment in her tone.

'No, my augmetics allow me to see perfectly well in the darkness.'

'I know that, but what need of them did you have?'

'I didn't like being blind. Properly blind, I mean. I missed reading.'

'There are books for those without eyes.'

'I know, but I prefer to let the words come to me,' said Kai. 'There is more to the written word than lifting the words from the page with my fingertips. Language has visual beauty that touch-script can never match.'

'I would debate that with you, but that is a discussion for late at night with a good book between us and a pot of hot caffeine. Could it be that you wished eyes again to hold onto some aspect of your life before entering the Telepathica?'

'I don't know,' said Kai. 'Maybe. I don't see how it's important.'

'It may be crucial to understanding why you can no longer master the *nuncio* and open yourself to the dreams of your brothers.'

'I know the *nuncio*,' said Kai defensively. 'I mastered it within a year.'

'Then why are you here? Why does House Castana send its pre-eminent astropath back to the City of Sight?'

Kai did not answer her, and she stopped beside the open door of a cell.

'I am here to help you, Kai,' said Sarashina. 'You were my greatest student, and if you have failed, then I have failed.'

'No,' said Kai. 'It's not that, it's just... what happened on the *Argo*...'

Sarashina raised a hand to stop him.

'Do not speak of it here while others are abed,' she said, gesturing to the rows of cells that lined the corridor. 'Sleep. Meditate for a while if it helps you. Refresh yourself, and I will speak to you in the morning.'

Kai nodded. Though his thoughts ran amok, his body craved sleep, and no matter that the bed of a novice was far from comfortable, it would be welcome. He stepped into the cell, catching a ghostly susurration of a distant voice in the darkness as he crossed the threshold. A whisper stone glinted on each side of the doorway, and he wondered into whose dream or memory he had briefly intruded.

Memories were all too common in the walls of the City of Sight, and most of them were ones you wouldn't want. No one dwelled too long on memories if they valued their sanity.

Kai knew that better than anyone.

THE DOOR TO Kai's cell closed with a heavy thud of wood on stone. There was no click of a lock, as was common for novice cells, but he could sense the presence of two Black Sentinels outside. Sarashina might talk to him like a prodigal son, but Golovko was another matter entirely. Kai could only imagine the nightmares Golovko's bilious presence was provoking among the true novices.

His travel trunk hadn't yet made it to his cell, and he supposed the Black Sentinels were examining his personal effects for any hint of something dangerous. They wouldn't find anything. Kai had wanted nothing from the *Argo*, and his possessions amounted to little more than a few undershirts, his hygiene kit, a finely-tailored suit from the seamstress-houses of the Nihon peninsula, and, of course, his many leather-bound *oneirocritica*.

The books would mean nothing to the Black Sentinels, but the cryptaesthesians would examine them thoroughly to ensure there was no latent symbolism that was cause for alarm.

They wouldn't find anything, but he understood they had to check.

The interior of the cell was bare and devoid of anything that might have indicated who had lived here before him. That was sensible, for any lingering sense of a previous occupant would influence Kai's dreaming. A cot bed lay along one wall, with a simple footlocker at its base. A small writing desk and chair sat opposite the bed, and a black notebook lay on a blotting pad, next to an inkhorn and pen.

Empty shelves lined the wall above the desk, ready to be filled with an astropath's steadily growing *oneirocritica* collection. The shelves were short, for a novice would take time to build a comprehensive library of imagery, symbolism and dream recordings.

Kai placed the bottle of amasec he'd taken from the Castana skimmer on the table and lifted the notebook from the desk. He idly fanned its thick pages, smelling the crisp newness of the paper. Each page was blank, ready to be filled with dream perceptions, and he carefully placed the book down. It was empty, but the potential of what *might* fill its pages was like a loaded gun.

Given his level of expertise, Kai wanted to feel offended at being put in a novice's cell, but the anger wouldn't come. It made sense, and he realised the lack of responsibility it implied was refreshing. He lay back on the bed and closed his eyes, letting his breathing slow as the ache of psi-sickness gnawed at his bones.

Though his thoughts were troubled, sleep was a state few astropaths had trouble attaining. With the right mantras and incubation techniques, any state of mind was possible.

Sleep came easily to Kai, but his dreams were not restful.

THREE

The Best Move
Rub' al Khali
Arzashkun

'YOUR EMPRESS IS exposed,' said the Choirmaster of Astropaths with a grin.

'I am aware of that,' replied Sarashina, moving the carved piece of coral from the ocean world of Laeran across the board. 'Do you think this is the first time I have played regicide?'

Nemo Zhi-Meng smiled and shook his head. 'Of course not, but I do not want to win through your inattention.'

'You are assuming you are going to win.'

'I normally do.'

'You won't today,' said Sarashina, as Zhi-Meng took a Castellan with his Chevalier and laid it on the carpeted floor. The board and its pieces had been a gift of the Phoenician himself, and the ornamentation on each figurine was wondrous. Each figure was worked to an obsessive degree, with a character all of their own, as one would expect from the hand of a primarch who was the embodiment of such attention to detail. The feel of them was exquisite, and to touch such pieces was as pleasurable as the game itself.

'I think you are wrong,' said Zhi-Meng as Sarashina pushed her Divinitarch across the board.

'You should think again,' said Sarashina, reclining on the wealth of sumptuous cushions spread over the floor of the Choirmaster's chambers. 'You see?'

Zhi-Meng leaned over the board and laughed as he perceived the arrangement of pieces on the grid.

'Inconceivable!' he said, clapping his thin, sculptor's hands. On the heart finger of his left hand was an onyx ring carved with intertwined symbols that might have been language, but was more likely ornamentation. Zhi-Meng had told her the ring was purchased from a man who claimed to have journeyed from the Fourth Dominion, but Sarashina suspected this was another one of the Choirmaster's mischievous boasts. If he had retained his eyes, they would have twinkled as he told the story. Instead, his almond shaped eyes were sewn shut, telling anyone who knew of such things that he had been blinded over a century ago when such techniques were common.

The Choirmaster shook his head and he scanned the board again, as though checking he was truly beaten. 'I am defeated by the assassin's blade hidden in the velvet sleeve. And here I thought I had planned enough moves ahead to win with ease.'

'A good regicide player thinks five moves ahead,' said Sarashina, 'but a *great* regicide player–'

'Only thinks one move ahead, but it is always the best move,' finished Zhi-Meng stroking the long forks of his white beard. 'If you're going to quote Guilliman to me, at least have the decency to let me win first.'

'Maybe next time,' answered Sarashina as a blinded servitor entered the Choirmaster's chambers. Robed in white and with no thoughts of its own, it was a ghostly apparition, its presence visible as a blur of murky light in her mind. Elements of the servitor's brain had been removed with gemynd-shears, and only the most rudimentary cognitive functions remained.

'Do you know why I insist we play regicide?' asked Zhi-Meng.

'To show off?'

'Partly,' admitted Zhi-Meng, 'but there's more to it than that. Regicide helps us develop patience and discipline in choosing between alternatives when an impulsive decision seems very attractive.'

'Always teaching, is that it?'

'Learning is always easier if the subject doesn't know it's being taught.'

'Are you teaching me?'

'Both of us, I think,' said Zhi-Meng as the servitor deposited a steel-jacketed pot of tisane, and the smell of warm, sweetened honey came to Sarashina.

'You and your sweet tooth,' she said.

'It is a weakness, I confess,' said Zhi-Meng, dismissing the servitor with a gesture and reaching over to pour two small cups of the warm liquid. He handed her a cup and she sipped it gingerly, savouring the sweet taste.

'It gives me solace,' said Zhi-Meng, with a smile. 'And in such times, solace must be taken wherever it can be found, don't you agree?'

'I thought that was what the qash in the hookah pipe was for.'

'Solace comes in many forms,' replied Zhi-Meng, removing his belt and letting his robe fall to the floor. His body was thin and wiry, but Sarashina knew that there was strength in those limbs that belied their frail appearance. His skin was parchment taut and pale, every centimetre covered in tattoos inked by his own hand with a needle said to have been snapped from the spine of a fossilised beast found in the bedrock of the Merican rad-wastes. A cornucopia of warding imagery was wrought on the canvas of his flesh: hawk-headed birds, snakes devouring their tails, apotropaic crosses, eyes of aversion and gorgoneion.

That such symbols flew in the face of the Imperial Truth mattered little to the Choirmaster, for he was the oldest living astropath in the City of Sight, and his knowledge of what protective wards would guard against the dangers of the immaterium was second to none.

He lay down next to Sarashina, and he stroked her arm with great tenderness. She smiled and rolled onto her front, letting Zhi-Meng massage her back and ease the tensions of yet another arduous day of passing increasingly desperate messages from the mindalls to the Conduit and onwards to their intended recipients. Zhi-Meng had studied with the ancient wise men who had dwelled in these mountains before the coming of the Emperor and his grand vision of a palace crowning the world, and his touch spread healing warmth through her aged bones.

'I could let you do that all night,' she purred.

'I would let you,' he replied. 'But such is not our lot, my dear.'

'Shame.'

'Tell me of the day's messages,' he asked.

'Why? You already know what's passed through the tower today.'

'True, but I like to hear what you think of it,' he said, working a stubborn knot of tension in her lower back.

'We have been getting a lot of traffic from worlds demanding Army fleets to keep them safe from any rebel forces.'

'Why not ask for Legion forces?'

'I think people are afraid that if four Legions can turn traitor then maybe others will too.'

'Interesting,' said the Choirmaster. His hand kneaded the bunched muscles around her shoulders and neck as he spoke. 'Go on. Tell me of the Legions. What news comes to Terra of our greatest warriors?'

'Only fragments,' admitted Sarashina. 'Some Legions send daily for tasking orders, a few are beyond our reach and others appear to be acting autonomously.'

'Tell me why Space Marines deciding their own orders sets a dangerous precedent,' asked Zhi-Meng.

'Why do you ask questions that you already know the answer to?'

'To see if *you* know the answer, of course.'

'Very well, I'll indulge you, since you're making me feel human again,' said Sarashina. 'Once loosed, such power as the Legions possess will be difficult to shackle to Terra once more.'

'Why?'

'To think that the Space Marines are simply gene-bred killers is to grossly underestimate them. Their commanders are men of great skill and ambition. Free to act on their own authority, they will not take kindly to being brought to heel once again, no matter who demands it.'

'Very good,' nodded the Choirmaster.

'But it will not come to that,' said Sarashina. 'Horus Lupercal will be crushed at Isstvan. Not even he can stand against the force of seven Legions.'

'I believe you are right, Aniq,' said Zhi-Meng. 'Seven Legions is a force with a power beyond imagining. How long will it be until Lord Dorn's fleet reaches Isstvan V?'

'Soon,' said Sarashina, knowing the vagaries of warp travel made precise predictions impossible.

'Something bothers you regarding the coming battle? Aside from the obvious, I mean.'

'The primarch of the VIII Legion,' said Sarashina.

'I hear from the Raven Guard that he is reunited with his warriors.'

'Exactly, but Lord Dorn was adamant that we not send the fleet assembly orders for the Isstvan expedition to Konrad Curze, only to the Night Lords Chapters stationed within the Sol system.'

'And this has caused alarm within the palace?' said Zhi-Meng, more to himself than Sarashina. 'That a primarch rejoins his Legion?'

'To say the least,' said Sarashina. 'No one seems to know where Curze has been since the Cheraut compliance.'

'Lord Dorn knows, though he will not say,' replied

Zhi-Meng, 'He bade me send a message to Lords Vulkan and Corax.'

'What kind of message?'

'I do not know,' said Zhi-Meng. 'It was composed in a manner unknown to me, some form of battle-cant known only to the Emperor's sons. I can only hope it reaches them in time. But enough of matters upon which we can have no further effect. Tell me of Prospero. Why do you think we have had no contact for months?'

'Perhaps Magnus is still smarting after his treatment at Nikaea,' said Sarashina.

'That is certainly possible,' agreed Zhi-Meng. 'I saw him after the Emperor pronounced his judgement, and it is a sight I will never forget. His anger was terrible indeed, but even worse was the hurt betrayal I felt in his heart.'

'I can assign more choirs to reaching Prospero,' offered Sarashina.

Zhi-Meng shook his head. 'No. Magnus will re-establish contact before long, I am sure. As hurt as he was by the judgement, he loves his father too dearly to remain estranged for long. There, you are done.'

Sarashina turned onto her front, rolling her shoulders and rotating her neck. She smiled, feeling her joints and muscles flex and rotate freely.

'Whatever the holy men of the mountain taught you, it has potency,' she said.

Zhi-Meng laced his fingers together and flexed them outwards with a smile. 'I taught you what they taught me, remember?'

'I remember. Lie down,' she said, sitting up as he lay face down in the space she had just vacated.

She straddled him, and worked her fingers along the length of his tattooed back. Hawk-headed men and grinning snakes stretched and swelled beneath her fingertips.

'Tell me of Kai Zulane,' he said. 'I felt the power of his nightmares through the whisper stones.'

'There were few in the tower who did not,' noted Sarashina.

'His mind is damaged, Aniq, badly damaged. Are you sure it is worth the effort to save him from the hollow mountain? The great beacon will always need fresh minds. Now more than ever.'

Sarashina paused in her massage. 'I believe so. He was my best student.'

'Once, maybe,' said Zhi-Meng. 'Now he is just an astropath who can send no messages. One who *chooses* not to send or receive.'

'I know that. I've assigned my best seeker to bring him back. I think you'll approve.'

'Who?'

'Athena Diyos,' said Sarashina. 'She has a rare skill in rebuilding damaged minds.'

'Athena Diyos,' mused Zhi-Meng with a contented purr as Sarashina walked the heels of her palms over his shoulder blades. 'Throne help him.'

'MISTRESS SARASHINA TELLS me you can no longer master the *nuncio*,' said Athena, her voice dripping with venomous scorn. 'The most basic of the telepathic disciplines, without which no astropath can function. Not much of an astropath are you?'

'I suppose not,' said Kai, trying not to stare.

'Is there something wrong?'

'Ah, well, it's just that you're not quite what I expected.'

'What did you expect?'

'Not… this,' replied Kai, knowing how ridiculous that sounded.

To say that Athena Diyos was not what Kai had expected was an understatement of magnificent proportions. After a night of restless dreams, Kai had been summoned to one of the anonymous training cells on the novitiates' level. Bereft of furniture beyond a single chair, the cell was as bare of signifiers as it was possible to be.

Athena Diyos had been waiting for him, and Kai immediately sensed the sharpness of her personality.

Her body reclined in a floating chair, contoured to the twisted shape of her spine and what little remained of her limbs. Athena's legs had been amputated at mid-thigh, and her left arm was a puckered mass of scar tissue. In place of her right arm, a thin manipulator augmetic tapped an impatient tattoo on the brushed steel of the chair. Her skull was hairless and the skin there was like the weathered surface of an ancient ruin. The sockets of her eyes were concave hollows of vat-grown skin, the only part of her face that had escaped the trauma of whatever fate had seen her consigned to this chair.

'Use those fancy ocular augmetics to blink-click a pic-ture,' snapped Athena. 'You can study it at your leisure once we're done. But for now we have work to do, under-stood?'

'Of course. Yes, I mean, sorry.'

'Don't be sorry,' she said. 'I don't want your pity.'

Her chair spun around and drifted to the other side of the chamber, and Kai took the opportunity to apply a medical filter over his augmetics to examine her one remaining arm. Dermal degradation and scar density told him she had suffered these wounds no more than a few years ago. Evidence of tissue crystallisation indicated her wounds were at least partially caused by vacuum damage.

Athena had been crippled on a starship.

If nothing else, they had that in common.

'Sit,' said Athena, turning to face the room's only chair.

Kai took a seat, and the padded chair encased his body. Pressure sensors shifted internal pads to match his bone structure. It was the most comfortable seat Kai had ever known.

'Do you know who I am?' asked Athena.

'No.'

'I am Athena Diyos, and I am a seeker. That means I am going to find the pieces of your ability that still work and put them back together. If I succeed you will be of use again.'

'And if you fail?'

'Then you will be sent to the hollow mountain.'

'Oh.'

'Is that what you want?' asked Athena, her augmetic arm ceasing its relentless tattoo on the arm of her chair.

'At this point I'm past caring,' said Kai, crossing his legs and rubbing a hand across his stubbled cheeks. The light in the room was offensively bright and shadowless, making it feel horribly clinical. Athena's chair hovered close to him, and he smelled the counterseptics and pain balms slathered on her ruined arm. He noticed a gold ring on her middle finger, and zoomed in on the tiny engraving at its centre: a feathered bird arising from a cracked egg in the midst of a raging fire.

She saw his glance, but didn't acknowledge it.

'Do you know what happens in the hollow mountain?' she asked.

'Of course not,' said Kai. 'No one speaks of it.'

'Why do you think that is?'

'How should I know? A rigorous code of silence?'

'It's because no one who goes into the hollow mountain ever comes out,' said Athena. She leaned forward, and Kai fought the urge to press himself further back in his own chair. 'I've seen what happens to the poor unfortunates who go in there. I feel sorry for them. They're gifted with power, just not enough to be useful in any other way. It's a noble sacrifice, but sacrifice is just a pretty way of saying that you're going to die.'

'So what happens to them?'

'First your skin cracks, like paper in a fire, falling from your bones like dust. Then your muscles waste away, and though you can feel the life being drawn out of you, it's impossible to stop. Piece by piece, your mind dies: memory, joy, happiness, pain and fear. It all gets used. The beacon wastes nothing of you. Everything you were is sucked from your frame, leaving nothing but a withered husk, a hollow shell of ashen, dry skin and powdered bones. And it's painful, agonisingly painful. You should know that before you so lightly dismiss this last chance of life I'm offering you.'

Kai felt the heat of her breath on his skin, hot and scented with a sickly sweet aroma of medicines.

'I don't want that,' he said.

'Didn't think so,' said Athena, the manipulator augmetic pushing her away from Kai.

'So how are you going to help me?'

'How long since you entered a receptive trance?' asked Athena.

The question took Kai aback. 'I'm not sure.'

'If I am going to keep you from the hollow mountain, then you need to give me something to work with, Kai Zulane. If you ever lie to me, ever hold anything back or make me think that in any way you are impeding my work or putting a single living soul within this city in danger, then I won't hesitate to write you off. Am I making myself clear?'

'Amply,' replied Kai, now understanding that his life was in this disfigured woman's lap. 'It has been several months since I've entered a receptive trance.'

'Why? That must be painful to you,' said Athena. 'Are you psi-sick?'

'A little,' admitted Kai. 'It hurts in my joints and I have a low grade headache all the time.'

'Then why avoid a trance?'

'Because I'd rather be sick than feel what I felt on the *Argo*.'

'So it's nothing to do with any lack of ability. That's a relief. At least I'll have something to work with.'

Athena's chair slid towards him again, and she held out her hand. The skin was puckered and tight, ribbed with buckled ridges of hardened, discoloured flesh. It was glossy and wet looking, and he hesitated for the briefest second before taking her hand in his own.

'I'm going to enter a *nuncio* trance,' said Athena. 'You'll follow my words, but I want you to form the dreamscape. Whatever you normally use to blank the canvas prior to a message, do nothing different. I will be with you, but all we're doing is forming the dreamscape. We're not going to send or receive a message. Understand that before we go in.'

'I understand,' said Kai. 'I don't like it, but I understand.'

'You don't have to like it. Just do it.'

Kai nodded and closed his eyes, slowing his breathing and running through the preparatory mantras that would expand his consciousness into the dreamscape. This part was easy. Anyone could do it, even a non-psyker, though all they would get out of it was a sense of relaxation. It was the next part that would be troublesome, and he tried to force down his apprehension.

'Rise into the dreamscape,' said Athena, her voice losing its harsh edge and becoming almost pleasant.

A mild sensation of vertigo tugged at Kai's mind as he let the mantras lift consciousness from his body. He heard the suggestion of singing, like a choir in a far distant theatre. The tower's astropaths were busy, but that was only to be expected in such turbulent times. A million sibilant voices filled the tower, but the whisper stones kept them separate. Kai dismissed any thoughts of the rebellion on the edge of Imperial space, picturing a soothing light enveloping his body in a protective sheath.

Now he was ready.

He could feel Athena's presence as her consciousness flowed alongside his own. In such a mental state, there was no such thing as up or down, but human perceptions couldn't help but shape so formless a space. Each astropath entered a receptive state in their own way, some surrounding themselves with imagery relating to the telepath whose projections they were attempting to receive, others by focussing on the key symbolic elements common to most senders.

Kai employed neither method, preferring to create his own mental canvas upon which to imprint the sending telepath's imagery. All too often, a message could be distorted by the mental architecture of the receiving mind, and such misinterpretations were the bane of every astropath. In all his years of service, Kai had never yet wrongly interpreted an incoming vision, but had heard – as had all students of the City of Sight – horror stories of telepaths who had misread desperate pleas for aid or despatched expeditionary fleets to destroy worlds whose inhabitants were loyal servants of the Throne.

He felt heat and his skin prickled with sweat.

False heat, but real enough in this place of dreams and miracles.

Kai opened his eyes and the desert stretched out for kilometres all around him.

WHITE SAND SHIMMERED in the heat haze, a vast empty landscape of nothingness that was completely free of anything troubling. Nothing disturbed the achingly empty vista – it was as though all life and character had been utterly erased from the world.

Kai's dreamscape had been this way ever since his return to Terra.

Hypnopompic drugs had kept him awake aboard the salvage cutter, but the human mind could not long escape the need to dream. Denied such sleep-depriving narcotics in the Castana medicae facility on Kyprios, his first night back on Terra had almost shattered his fragile psyche, before his training had kicked in and he had taken control of his dreaming. Aside from last night, he had come to this place in his dreams and wandered its wondrous emptiness until he woke.

Such sleep refreshed the body, but left the mind without any form of release.

'This is your canvas?' asked a voice behind him, and Kai turned to see Athena Diyos walking towards him. Her long robes flowed around her shapely body, and long hair, auburn with a hint of gold red flowed to her shoulders.

'You look surprised,' she said.

'I suppose I am,' replied Kai, as taken aback as when he had first seen her.

'You shouldn't be. This is the realm of dreams after all. You can shape your form to how you wish yourself to be.'

'But not you,' said Kai, catching the well-honed deflection. 'This is the real you.'

Athena swept past Kai, and instead of the medically-prescribed chemical reek of her skin, she smelled of cinnamon and almonds.

'You are beautiful,' said Kai.

She looked over her shoulder with a smile, and her face came alive. 'You are kind. Most people say you *were* beautiful.'

'You'll come to understand that I'm not "most people".'

'I'm sure,' said Athena. 'So this is your dreamscape?'

'Yes, this is the Rub' al Khali,' said Kai.

'I don't know what that means.'

'It means the Empty Quarter,' said Kai. 'It was a desert of Old Earth that grew and grew until it merged with another great sandscape that eventually filled the midterrene oceans to create the dust bowl.'

'It is the mental mindscape of a dreamer who does not want to dream,' said Athena. 'It is not healthy to inhabit a level of cognition that denies the subconscious mind any release. No symbolism, nothing to remind a dreamer of the waking world and nothing to reveal so much as a single aspect of the dreamer.'

'So what do we do now?' asked Kai.

'We explore,' said Athena. 'I need to get a feel for your mind before I can see the cracks.'

'There isn't much to explore in the Rub' al Khali.'

'We'll see. Tell me why you are here.'

'In this trance?'

'No, in the City of Sight. I read your file. You were attached to the Ultramarines Legion aboard the *Argo*, a helot-crewed frigate en route to the Jovian shipyards for a structural refit prior to making the translation to

Calth. Tell me about why you are here and not en route to Ultramar.'

'I don't think we should talk about that,' said Kai. The landscape on the far horizon rippled as though something vast moved just below the surface of the sand. He tried to ignore it, but the featureless wasteland of his dream shifted to accommodate this new intrusion.

Athena followed his gaze, seeing the cascade of white sand from the ridge above them.

'What is that?' she asked.

'You read my file,' said Kai, straining to keep the fear from his voice. 'You should know what it is.'

'I want you to tell me.'

'No,' said Kai.

Something broke the surface of the sand, something glistening and metallic, cobalt blue and gold, like the scaled hide of a serpent breaking the surface of the ocean. It moved with a hunter's grace and a killer's patience before vanishing beneath the surface.

'We're very exposed out here,' said Athena, matter-of-factly.

'I know that,' snapped Kai.

'Don't you think we ought to find somewhere safe?'

'Where would you suggest?' snapped Kai. 'We're in the desert.'

His heart was hammering against his ribs, and his palms dripped sweat. His mouth felt dry and his bladder wanted to empty itself. He shielded his eyes from the blazing sun and scanned the horizons for any sign of the subterranean predator.

'No, we are not,' said Athena. 'We are in your mind, sharing your fear. Whatever is out there is part of you, and the only one who will let it hurt us is you. Come on, Kai, have you forgotten the first principles of psychic defence?'

'I can't stop it from coming.'

'Of course you can,' said Athena, taking his hand. 'Craft whatever it is that kept you safe before.'

Kai saw the glint of metal breaking the sand over
Athena's shoulders, and all thoughts of even the most
basic training tenets fled from his mind. The fear was
all-encompassing, and he heard the sound of screaming,
a host of terrified voices that seemed to ooze from the
sand like the cries of an entire army buried alive.

'You can do this, Kai,' said Athena, glancing down at
the sand. 'Hold on to my voice.'

Athena began reciting the basic exercises of the *nuncio*,
and the soothing cadence of her voice was like a calming
soporific. 'This is the dream I craft for myself. It a place
of tranquillity. I am the master of this domain. Say it
with me, Kai.'

'I am the master of this domain,' said Kai, trying to
force himself into believing it. The shadow of the thing
beneath the sand spread on the surface, a gathering darkness that wouldn't fade. It was circling beneath them,
rising to the surface with lazy sweeps of its metallic body.
It knew its prey was vulnerable, and was in no hurry to
rush the kill.

'Say it like you mean it!' hissed Athena. 'I don't want to
see that thing any more than you do.'

'I am the master of this domain!' yelled Kai.

'Now craft us somewhere safe,' said Athena.

Kai tried to clear his thoughts as the sand shifted
beneath them. The screaming voices were closer to the
surface now. A leviathan moved beneath him, and its
bulk was impossibly vast, stretching out kilometres to
surround Kai and Athena.

He knew what it was, but that knowledge only made
him more determined to avoid it.

'I know somewhere safe,' he said.

'Show me,' said Athena.

Slowly, stone by stone, Kai pictured the construction of
a fortress of light in the raw fecundity of his mindscape.
Fictive turrets, domed towers, pleasure gardens and tree-
lined processionals erupted from the sand around them,
rising higher and higher with every passing moment.

Gilded arches, ornamented balconies and minarets of jade, mother of pearl and electrum formed from the building blocks of imagination and recall.

This was a fortress of ancient times, a wonder of the world that no longer existed.

Athena's eyes widened at the sight of the magnificent fortress, its walls glittering with hoar frost and polished smooth as though formed from vitrified sand. The ground rose beneath them and they were carried into the air on a high wall, hundreds of metres from the undulant sand.

'What is this place?' asked Athena as their dizzying ascent halted.

A fierce wind whipped around them and Kai held her tight as it sought to hurl them from the walls.

'It is the Urartu fortress of Arzashkun,' said Kai. 'It once stood at the headwaters of a great river that was said to have its source in the garden that birthed humanity.'

'Does it still stand?' asked Athena as more towers, higher walls and yet more barred gateways formed from the shimmering sand of the dreamscape.

'No, it was destroyed,' said Kai. 'A great king razed it to the ground many thousands of years ago.'

'But you know its likeness?'

Kai heard the rumble of something vast approaching the surface of the sand, but kept his attention firmly focussed on Athena's question. If he allowed his thoughts to stray beyond the walls of the fortress they would come crashing down. Instead, he cast his mind back to the glass walls of an incredible library that nestled amongst towering highland forests.

'Not long after I took up my position with the XIII Legion, I was lucky enough to be allowed access to the Crystal Library on Prandium,' said Kai, focusing on the past to avoid the present. 'You should see it, Athena, tens of millions of books and paintings and symphonies contained within resonant crystals set all along the length of the canyon walls. The warden showed me one of Primarch Guilliman's works, just set in the cliff like it was nothing out of the ordinary. But it was incredible, and it wasn't what I'd expected either. There wasn't any illuminated scriptwork or exquisite calligraphy, just a painstaking attention to detail that no mortal writer could ever match.'

'And this fortress was in the book?' said Athena.

'Yes. On a page that told of Lord Guilliman's time on Terra before his Crusade fleets set out into the galaxy. I saw a sketch of this fortress, so real that I could feel the hardness of its stone and the strength of its walls. It was a footnote really, a veiled reference to when the primarch's father had travelled there and studied its architecture. I have been to those lands, and nothing remains of Arzashkun now, not even memory, but Lord Guilliman's skill had rendered it as clearly as if Rogal Dorn himself had handed him the plans.'

'If only that were true,' said Athena, and Kai followed her gaze beyond the walls.

His breathing quickened and he struggled to keep his equilibrium as a bloom of red appeared on the sand, like a splash of blood in milk. His racing heart rate increased still further, and he swallowed as he felt the furious tugging of memory. A child's pleading voice intruded on his thoughts and the red stain expanded at a geometric rate.

The shadowy hunter beneath the ground surged towards the spreading crimson mass, hot and urgent in its desire. It broke the surface beyond the walls, all angles, blades and red noise. A ghost ship brought to the surface of the deepest ocean, it breached like an ambush hunter and crashed back down with a thunderous boom. Its flanks were iron and blue, gold and bronze. It was a world killer, a monster capable of unimaginable destruction, and his fortress of light was no match for its terrible power.

It came on a tide of screams, ten thousand voices shrieking in terror and pain. It knew his name and it wanted him to join the dead whose bones and blood filled its wailing corridors and chambers.

Kai was catapulted from his dreamspace with a terrified shout as the fortress was overwhelmed in a terrifying crescendo of leering faces, black blades and tearing fangs.

His eyes flicked open and he jack-knifed upright in his chair. The whisper stones glowed angry red as they dissipated the psychic residue of their connection into the trap chambers beneath the tower. Kai pressed the heels of his palms into his face, feeling the chill ceramic and steel of his artificial eyes against his skin. Revulsion, guilt, sorrow and terror vied for space in his frontal lobes and a strangled sob burst from a throat that was raw from screaming.

No tears fell, but the anguish he felt was no less potent.

The desert was gone and the blunt, geometric forms of Athena's chamber rushed to fill his senses with bland, clinical reality.

'That was the *Argo*?' said Athena.

Kai nodded. He realised he was still holding her hand, his knuckles white with tension. Tiny crescents of blood welled from where his nails had cut the thin layer of her regrown skin. Instantly contrite, he pulled his hand away.

'I'm so sorry,' he said. 'I didn't mean…'

Athena closed her fingers into a pained fist.

'I felt it,' she said, taking his hand again. 'Everything you felt as they died. I felt it all.'

Kai wept tearlessly for the lost souls of the *Argo*.

But most of all he wept for himself.

FOUR

Ghota
Old Gods
Faces of Death

WORKING WITH THE dead was thirsty work, and Palladis Novandio took a sip of brackish water from the wooden barrel set up at the door of the crematorium. The men who worked to load the bodies into the incinerator were hard men, inured to the cold, stiff reminders of their own mortality. They worked without words, hauling the pallets of the dead towards the giant furnace built into the rock, stripping them of their clothes and dignity before taking them by ankles and wrists and swinging them into the fire.

The Petitioner's City had no shortage of dead, one of the few commodities it had in abundance.

The piles of clothes were sorted and cleaned by the women of the temple before being distributed to those in need. On some days it seemed as though the population of the city never changed, and you might stop someone, thinking they were miraculously returned to life, but who was simply wearing the coat of a dead man. Palladis took a measure of comfort in knowing the dead could yet give something to those they left behind.

Most of them, anyway.

He wiped the ashen residue of the incinerator from his face with a mixture of the water and his own sweat. The taste of cinders and fat was always at the back of his throat, but it never occurred to him to do anything else. Without any meaningful civic authority, bodies were a common sight on the streets of the Petitioner's City, those who had given up or simply been in the wrong place at the wrong time. Death could take you in any number of ways, too many to count.

The millions of people coming to Terra filtered through the mountains en route to the Palace, but only a fraction of those numbers made it this far. That still left thousands who clamoured at the gates, beseeching the faceless warriors who marched along the battlements to grant them passage. The streets of the Petitioner's City were filled with those who sought meaning in their life, answers to their questions or those who simply came to view the magnificence of the Emperor's demesne.

Palladis remembered a time when the Petitioner's City had retained a semblance of an ordered community, when it had been small enough to maintain a form of order and stability. But as more and more people found their way to the walls of the palace, its ordered structure had begun to break down. The buildings that appeared overnight and pushed the city limits further down the mountains became steadily more temporary, more numerous and altogether more squalid.

Then the gangs had moved in, sensing opportunity amongst the desperate petitioners like vultures circling a wounded man in the desert. Gangs from the mountains, gangs from the plains and gangs from the battlefields of Unity were drawn to the ever-expanding city, sensing vulnerable people ready to be exploited. The killings had begun, bloody and designed to spread fear like a contagion.

Babu Dhakal's gang had been the worst. His men were stronger, faster and more ruthless than any others, and there was no level of mutilation and degradation

to which they would not stoop. Palladis had seen one
of his men stabbed though his eyes and left to bleed to
death on the steps of a medicae facility. That man's killers had their limbs hacked off and their broken bodies
left impaled on tall spears for the carrion birds to devour.
Revenge killings, honour killings, random killings. None
of it made any sense, and by the time the worst of it was
over, only Babu Dhakal was left standing.

No one knew where the feared gang warlord had come
from, but there were many rumours. Some claimed he
was a member of the Legio Custodes who had never
come back from a Blood Game. Others said he was one
of the Emperor's thunder warriors who had somehow
survived the end of the wars of Unity. Yet more claimed
he was a Space Marine whose body had rejected the last
stage of his elevation to post-human and had fled before
he could be put down. Most likely he was simply a ruthless bastard who had proved to be more of a ruthless
bastard than anyone else.

But his evil reputation didn't put off those who desperately sought entry to the Palace, and day by day, year
by year, the Petitioner's City grew ever larger. Armed
forces from the palace periodically swept the streets of
the city, gathering up the dregs and lowlifes too slow or
too stupid to hide, but it achieved little more than salv-
ing the consciences of the noble born lords of Terra. For
all intents and purposes, the Petitioner's City was a law
unto itself.

Imperial heralds escorted by hundreds of armed men
occasionally ventured as far as the Proclamation Arch to
read the names of those whose luck had finally turned
and would be allowed to enter the Palace. Few of those
called ever made their way through the archway to the
Petitioner's Gate. Most were either lying dead in a nameless alley or, having given up all hope of ever attaining
entry, had simply returned to whatever corner of the
globe they had once called home.

Palladis had been one of the lucky ones, called to the

palace with his family while the Petitioner's City was still a place of quiet order. He had come from the southern lands of the Romanii, where he had plied his trade as a crafter of stone and worker of marble in the palaces of the burgeoning technocratic cartel houses that rose from the drift sand at the edge of the dust bowl. But as the megastructures rose higher and higher and steel and glass replaced the ancient weight of stone, Palladis found himself forced to seek work elsewhere.

With his wife and newborn sons, Palladis had crossed a landscape still bearing the scars of global war that had raged for as long as anyone could remember. Only now was it beginning to reveal the potential glory spoken of by the Emperor's heralds. In search of that glory, he had crossed the peaks of Serbis and followed the Carpathian Arch before entering the homeland of the Rus and following the trade caravans along the ancient Silk Road across the plains of Nakhdjevan. There they turned east through Aryana and the newly-fertile lands of the Indoi, before the ground began to rise and the mountains that marked the edge of the world came into view.

It had been an awe-inspiring sight, one that would be forever etched on his memory, but one that had become bittersweet in the years that followed.

Palladis turned from the memories of murder and pushed through the plastic slats that kept the worst of the ash from leaving the crematorium. The air was thick with it. The incinerator would need to be emptied soon, as the remains of the dead were backing up in the fire-box. He hung up his rubberised apron and removed his heavy canvas gauntlets. The wetted cloth around his mouth and nose came off next, followed by his ash-smeared goggles.

Taking a moment to run his hands through his unkempt hair, Palladis stepped through the doorway into the main area of the temple. As always, it was crowded with mourners, and the soft sound of weeping women and men drifted to the stoic angels worked into the eaves. Palladis felt his eyes drawn to the smooth curves of the Vacant Angel, and placed his hand on its cool marble surface.

The dark nephrite was from Syrya, hand finished and polished to a degree of smoothness that only an artisan's love could fashion. And yet Vadok Singh had rejected it and cast it aside. He felt his hands bunch into fists at the thought of the Emperor's warmason. So obsessed with his art was Singh that he cast aside anything that did not match his exacting demands: materials, tools, plans or people.

Especially people.

His gaze was drawn to the featureless face, again wondering whose likeness had been planned for its unfinished surface. It didn't matter now. It would never be completed, so the question was immaterial. He dragged his eyes from its blank countenance as he heard someone call his name, and looked across the chamber.

Roxanne sat with Maya and her two surviving children, both of whom had responded well to the counterseptics she had obtained from Antioch. The woman's husband, Estaben, sat to one side, and Palladis felt a stab of annoyance. He had forbidden the man to distribute more of his Lectito Divinitatus leaflets, knowing it was unwise to attract additional attention to a place people insisted on calling a temple.

Roxanne raised her hand, and he returned the gesture, knowing it was only a matter of time until she brought trouble down upon them. Someone like her could not remain hidden forever, even in a place like the Petitioner's City. No one here knew it, but she was an exceptionally rare woman, and her family would eventually demand that she return to them. By force if need be.

He walked over to her, giving smiles of sympathy to those who mourned and nods of understanding to those who stood with them. Roxanne looked up as he approached and put her hand on the head of the child nestled in Maya's arms.

'Looks like the medicine is working,' she said. 'I think they'll both be fine.'

'I'm glad to hear it,' said Palladis, tousling the hair of the boy beside Maya.

'His name's Arik,' said Maya, reaching out to stroke the child's cheek.

'A good strong name,' said Palladis, addressing the boy. 'Do you know what it means?'

The boy shook his head, and Palladis made a fist. 'Arik was one of the Emperor's lightning-bearers in the first epoch of Unity,' he said. 'They say he was taller than the hollow mountain and that he carved the pass at Mohan with his fists. Give it time and I think you might grow as big.'

The boy smiled and made a fist too. Maya reached out and placed a palm on her son's shoulder.

'Emperor love you,' she said. 'Are you blessed with children?'

Palladis sighed wearily, but nodded. 'Two boys.'

'Are they here?' asked Maya. 'I would love to meet them and tell them what a kind father they have.'

'They were here,' said Palladis. 'They died.'

'Oh, I am so sorry,' said Maya. 'I didn't know.'

'What happened to them?' asked Arik.

'Hush now, Arik!' cried Maya.

'No, it's alright,' said Palladis. 'He should know and understand such things.'

Palladis took the boy by the shoulders and looked him straight in the eye, wanting him to understand the gravity of what he was about to hear.

'I once worked for a powerful man who desired I work for no other,' said Palladis. 'I did not like such restrictions, and secretly accepted a commission from another, though I knew the price of discovery would be high. The powerful man learned of my other work and sent men to my house to express his displeasure. I was working in a limestone quarry west of the palace, but my wife and two boys were home. The men cut my wife's throat and shot my boys in the heart. I returned from the quarries to find all three lying where they had fallen.'

The boy's eyes widened, and Palladis knew he had frightened him. That was good. Fear would keep him alive to the many ways in which death was stalking him.

'You poor man...' said Maya, while pulling her son away from Palladis.

He deflected her fearful sympathy and his own rising grief by looking over at her husband, who sat to one side. His face was expressionless, crushed and empty, as though all the life had had been drained from him.

Palladis knew that expression well. Sometimes he felt it was the only one he wore.

'Estaben?' said Palladis, but the man didn't look up.

He repeated the man's name, and at last his head came up.

'What?'

'Your sons are recovering, Estaben,' he said. 'You must be relieved.'

'Relieved?' said Estaben with a shrug. 'Vali and Chio are with the Emperor now. If anything, they're the lucky ones. The rest of us have to live in this world, with its suffering and pain. Tell me, priest, why should I be relieved?'

Anger touched Palladis. 'I am sorry for your loss, but you have two sons who need you. And I am not a priest.'

'You are,' said Estaben. 'You don't see it, but you are a priest. This is a temple, and you are its priest.'

Palladis shook his head, but before he could rebut Estaben's words, the crack of splintering timber filled the building, followed by the heavy thud of a door falling from its frame. Cries of alarm sounded, and people began moving from the entrance.

Seven men stepped over the ruin of the door. Big men. Hard men. Dangerous men.

They were swathed in furs, leather straps and plates of steel beaten into the semblance of armour. Two wore spiked helmets, one carried a vicious, flanged mace of pig iron, while another carried a bulky gun with a flared barrel and lengths of copper piping running along the barrel to a sparking cylinder filled with tiny arcs of lightning. Swirling tattoos writhed on the muscles of their beefy arms, and each man bore a jagged brand of a lightning bolt above his right eye.

'Babu Dhakal's men,' hissed Roxanne, but Palladis waved her to silence.

He stepped into the central aisle, his hands held up before him.

'Please,' he began. 'This is a place of peace and solemnity.'

'Not any more,' said a broad-shouldered figure, entering the building behind his vanguard. He towered over the seven dangerous men, making them look small in comparison. Crossed bandoliers of knives made an X on his chest, and a trio of jangling meat hooks hung from his belt next to a holster containing a wide pistol that was surely too heavy for any normal man to fire without losing his arm to recoil. Barbed iron torqs encircled his biceps, making the pulsing veins throb like writhing snakes beneath the skin.

The man's flesh was emblazoned with the tattooist's art, myriad representations of lightning bolts, hammers and winged raptors. What little of his natural skin tone remained was the unhealthy pallor of a corpse, and a thin line of blood oozed from the corner of his mouth.

But it was the man's eyes that told Palladis who had come for retribution. Pupils so fine they were little more than black dots in a sea of petechial haemorrhages, the man's eyes were literally red with blood.

'Ghota,' said Palladis.

ATHENA ROSE THROUGH the central spine of the Whispering Tower, carried aloft on the double helix of gravity-defiant particles. It made her skin itch abominably, and the scar tissue that capped her amputated thighs throbbed painfully in the flux. Why the Whispering Tower's builders had thought a pneumatic lift was unnecessary was a constant mystery, and she never failed to curse them whenever she was forced to move vertically through its structure.

She badly needed to see Mistress Sarashina, and rose through the levels of the tower towards the upper wing of the *Oneirocritica Alchera Mundi*, the great dream library of the City of Sight. A stack of papers and dream logs rested in her lap, a volatile record of her latest flight into the Immaterium that required a second interpretation. No one had a better understanding of *Vatic* prognostication than Aniq Sarashina, and if anyone could provide clarification of her latest vision, it would be her.

At last the stream of particles came to a diffuse end, and she used her manipulator arm to work the controls of her chair. It lurched as one repulsor field was exchanged for another, and Athena winced as the drum-taut tissue of her ravaged limbs pulled tight.

Passing through the arched entrance of the library, Athena nodded to the detachment of Black Sentinels stationed by the heavily armoured doors. She felt the humming machine spirits set into the arch cast their unfeeling eyes over her, ensuring she brought nothing forbidden into the library.

Towering shelves, rearing hundreds of metres into the air filled this section of the *Oneirocritica Alchera Mundi*, groaning stacks radiating from the central hub filled with interpretive texts, dream diaries, vision logs and the many books of common astropathic imagery. Every vision received and sent from the City of Sight was here, a complete record of communication that passed between Terra and the wider galaxy.

Scores of hunched astropaths drifted through the stacks like green ghosts, seeking clarification of a vision, while elder telepaths added freshly approved symbols to the ever-growing library. Every addition to the library was ratified by Artemeidons Yun, the Custodian of this invaluable repository, and Athena saw the corpulent old telepath shuffling through the stacks with a gaggle of

bobbing lumen globes and harried aides following in
his wake.

Athena circled the hub until she sensed Sarashina's
presence in the section devoted to elemental symbolism
in visions. She floated towards Sarashina, and her former
tutor looked up as Athena approached. Though astropaths lacked traditional visual acuity, their blindsight
allowed them to perceive the world around them just as
well as sighted individuals.

'Athena,' said Sarashina with a smile of genuine
warmth. 'How are you?'

'Pained and tired,' said Athena. 'Is there any other way
for an astropath to feel?'

Sarashina nodded in understanding. Athena caught
the brief flare of sympathetic regret, and swallowed her
anger at Sarashina's pity.

'Have you come to talk to me about Kai Zulane?' asked
Sarashina, ignoring Athena's brusque tone.

'No, though Throne knows he is damaged.'

'Beyond repair?'

'Hard to say for sure,' said Athena. 'There's a lot of aversion in him, and he's psi-sick because of it, but I think I
can bring him back.'

'So if you are not here to talk about Kai, what else is
troubling you?'

'I had a precept concerning the X Legion,' said Athena.
'Right after I saw Zulane.'

Sarashina gestured to the end of the stack furthest
away from the hub, where numerous reading tables and
data-engines were spread along the curved inner face of
the tower. Sensing Athena's unease, Sarashina picked
an empty table far from astropaths studying the touch-
script books and manuscripts.

Athena floated behind Sarashina and deposited her
dream logs on the table.

'This precept,' asked Sarashina. 'Have you logged it
with the Conduit?'

'Not yet, I wanted to speak to you first.'

'Very well, but log it immediately after we speak. You know the purpose of the X Legion's expedition?'

'Of course,' said Athena. 'And that's what scares the crap out of me, because I don't think it's a true precept.'

'What do you mean?'

'I mean I don't think it's a vision of the future. I think it's happening *right now*.'

'Tell me what you saw,' said Sarashina. 'Leave nothing out.'

'I was on a sun-parched desert when I saw an obsidian statue rise from the sands, a muscular figure clad in a breastplate of burnished iron and chained to a rock. The statue's fists were encased in silver, and sitting on one of them was an amber-eyed falcon with ocean-green plumage and a hooked beak.'

'The statue is obvious enough,' said Sarashina. 'Prometheus.'

Athena nodded. A vision of the Titan of ancient myth who signified belief in humanity even over divine decree was a common visual metaphor used by astropaths to represent the primarchs. The silver of the statue's gauntlets was the final confirmation of this one's identity.

'Yes, Ferrus Manus,' said Athena. 'Primarch of the Iron Hands.'

'So what happened in this vision?'

'A shadow fell across the sun, and I looked up to see darkness eclipsing the face of its brightness until it resembled a world of black, granular sand. It's a new symbol, but it's one I've seen a lot of recently.'

'Isstvan V,' said Sarashina.

Athena nodded. 'No sooner had the sun gone black than the statue of Prometheus pulled against the chains holding it fast to the rock. The falcon took to the air as the metal links shattered, and a spear of fire appeared in the giant's fist. The statue surged forward and cast the spear into the heart of the black sun, and the tip punched into its heart in a shower of blazing sparks.'

'That bodes well for Lord Dorn's fleet,' noted Sarashina.

'I'm not finished yet,' said Athena.

She took a deep breath before continuing. 'Even as the statue slew the sun with its spear cast, I saw it had left much of its inner substance behind. Chunks of obsidian remained stuck to the rock, and I knew the giant had struck prematurely, without his full weight behind the blow. Then the statue sank beneath the sand, and the falcon flew back to the rock. It swallowed the chunks of obsidian and then took to the air with a caw of triumph.'

'That is everything?' asked Sarashina.

'That's everything,' agreed Athena, tapping her dream records. 'I checked my *Oneirocritica* and it makes for uncomfortable reading.'

Sarashina extended her hands, nodding in agreement as her fingers danced over the raised words and letters.

'Ferrus Manus always was impetuous,' she said. 'He races ahead of his brothers to Isstvan V to deliver the death blow to the rebels, while leaving much of his force behind.'

'Yes, but it's the hawk with the amber eyes that concerns me,' said Athena.

'The importance of the falcon is paramount,' agreed Sarashina. 'Its obvious implication is troubling. What elements Ferrus Manus leaves behind will be devoured. What other interpretation do you give the falcon?'

'It's a symbol of war and victory in most cultures.'

'Which, in itself, is not troublesome, so what gives you cause for concern?'

'This,' said Athena, opening her oldest *Oneirocritica* with her manipulator arm and turning it around. As Sarashina's fingers slipped easily over the pages, her serene expression turned to a frown as the words imprinted on the pages went on.

'This is ancient belief,' said Sarashina.

'I know. Many of the gods worshipped by these extinct cultures displayed hawks as symbols of their battle prowess, which just confirms the more obvious symbolism. But I remembered the text of a rubbing taken from a

marble sculpture uncovered by the Conservatory only
a year ago in the rubble of that hive that collapsed in
Nordafrik.'

'Kairos,' said Sarashina with a shudder. 'I felt its fall. Six
million souls buried under the sands. Terrible.'

Athena had been aboard Lemurya, one of the great
orbital plates circling Terra, when Kairos hive sank into
the desert, but she had felt the aetheric aftershock of its
doom like a tidal wave of fear and pain. An empathic
shudder of grief pulsed from Sarashina's aura.

'The hive's fall exposed a series of tomb-complexes further west, and among the mortuary carvings were hawks.
It's said that the Gyptians considered the hawk to be
a perfect symbol of victory, though they viewed it as a
struggle between opposing elemental forces, especially
the spiritual over the corrupt, as opposed to physical victory.'

'And how does that fit within your precept?' asked Sarashina.

'I'm getting to that,' said Athena, pushing a sheet of
paper towards her. 'This is the text of a scroll I copied
a few years ago from a deteriorating data-coil recovered
from the ruins of Neoalexandria. It's just a list, a pan-
theon of old gods, but one name in particular stuck out.
Taken together with the amber eyes and the colouring of
the hawk's plumage...'

'Horus,' said Sarashina as her finger stopped halfway
down the list.

'Could the hawk with the amber eyes represent the
Warmaster and his rebels?'

'Pass this to the Conduit,' said Sarashina. 'Now!'

'PLEASE,' SAID PALLADIS. 'Don't hurt these people, they
have already been through enough.'

Ghota took a step into the temple, his heavy, hob-
nailed boots sounding like gunshots as he crushed glass
and rock beneath them. He swept his gaze around the
terrified throng, finally settling on Roxanne. He smiled,

and Palladis saw his teeth were steel fangs, triangular like a shark's.

Ghota pointed at Roxanne. 'Don't care about others,' he said. 'Just want her.'

The man's voice was impossibly deep, as though dragged unwillingly from some gravelled canyon in his gut. It sounded like grinding rocks, flat and curiously not echoing from the stone walls of the temple.

'Look, I know there was some blood spilled, but your men attacked Roxanne,' said Palladis. 'She had every right to defend herself.'

Ghota's head cocked to one side, as though this argument had never been put to him before. It amused him, and he laughed, or at least Palladis guessed that the sound of a mountain avalanche coming from his mouth was laughter.

'She was trespassing,' growled Ghota. 'She needed to pay a toll, but she decided it didn't apply to her. My men were enforcing the Babu's law. She broke the law, now she has to pay. It's simple. Either she comes with me or I kill everyone in here.'

Palladis fought down his rising tension. All it would take would be one person to panic, and this temple would become a charnel house. Maya sheltered her two boys, while Estaben had his eyes closed and muttered something inaudible with his hands clasped before him. Roxanne sat with her head bowed, and Palladis felt her fear hit him like a blow.

So easy to forget how different she is…

He took a step towards Ghota, but the man raised his hand and shook his head.

'You're fine where you are,' said Ghota, 'but I can see you're hesitating, trying to think if there's some way you can talk your way out of this. You can't. You're also thinking if there's any way the *boksi* girl can do what she did to the men she killed. She might be able to kill a couple of them, but it won't work on me. And if she tries it I'll make sure she doesn't die for weeks. I know *exactly* how fragile the human body is, and I promise you that she'll suffer. Agonisingly. You know me, and you know I mean what I say.'

'Yes, Ghota,' said Palladis. 'I know you, and trust me, I believe every word you say.'

'Then hand her over, and we'll be gone.'

Palladis sighed. 'I can't do that.'

'You know what she is?'

'I do.'

'Stupid,' said Ghota, drawing his heavy pistol with such swiftness that Palladis wasn't sure what he'd seen until the deafening bang filled the chamber with noise. Everyone screamed, and went on screaming as they saw what the gunshot had done to Estaben.

It had destroyed him. *Literally* destroyed him.

The impact pulped his upper body, hurling it across the chamber and breaking it apart over the chest of the Vacant Angel. Ribbons of shredded meat drooled from the statue's praying hands and sticky brain matter and fragments of skull decorated its featureless face.

Maya screamed and Roxanne threw herself to the floor. Weeping mourners huddled together in the pews, convinced they were soon to join their loved ones. Children screamed in fear and mothers let them cry. Roxanne looked up at Palladis and reached for the hem of her hood, but he shook his head.

Ghota flexed his wrist, and Palladis found himself looking down the enormous barrel of a weapon that could obliterate him. Coils of muzzle smoke drifted from the gun, and Palladis could smell the chemical reek of high-grade propellant. The dim light of the temple reflected from an eagle stamped on the pistol's barrel.

'You are next,' said Ghota. 'You'll die and we'll take the girl anyway.'

Palladis felt his body temperature drop suddenly, as though a nearby meat locker had just opened and gusted a breath of arctic air into the chamber. The hairs on his arms stood erect, and he shivered as though someone had just walked over his grave. Sweat beaded on his brow and though every one of his senses was telling him the chamber was warm, his body was shivering like it had on the nights he'd spent on the open plains of Nakhdjevan.

The sounds of frightened people faded into the background, and Palladis heard the snorting, wheezing emphysemic breath of something wet and rotten. Colour drained from the world and even Ghota's colourful tattoos seemed dull and prosaic. The cold air bloated the chamber, a sudden swelling of icy breath that seemed to swirl around every living thing and caress it with a repulsively paternal touch.

Palladis watched as one of Ghota's thugs stiffened, clutching his chest as though a giant fist had reached inside his ribcage and squeezed his heart. The man turned the colour of week-old snow and he collapsed into a pew, gasping for breath as his face twisted in a rictus mask of pain and terror.

Another man fell as though poleaxed and without the drama of his comrade. His face was pulled tight in a grimace of horror, but his body remained unmarked. Ghota snarled and aimed his pistol at Roxanne, but before he could pull the trigger, another of his men shrieked in abject terror. So stark and primal was his scream that even an inhuman monster like Ghota was caught unawares.

Colour flooded back into the world, and Palladis threw himself to the side as Ghota's pistol boomed with deafening thunder. Palladis didn't see what he'd shot at, but heard a buzzing crackle as it hit something. More screaming sounded from the far end of the chamber, frantic, urgent and terrified. Palladis squirmed along the floor between the pews, knowing something terrible was happening, but with no idea what it was.

His breath misted before him, and he saw webs of frost forming on the back of the timber bench at his side. He flinched as Ghota fired again, roaring with an anger that was terrifying in its power. The sound of his rage went right through Palladis, penetrating to the marrow and leaving him sick and paralysed with terror.

No mortal warrior could vent such battle rage.

Pinned to the floor with terror, Palladis wrapped his hands over his head and tried to shut out the sounds of terrified screams. He kept his face pressed to the cold flagstones of the temple floor, taking icy air into his lungs with every terrified breath. The screaming seemed to go on without pause. Shrieks of terror and pain, overlaid with angry roars of thunderous defiance in a strange battle-cant that sounded like the fury of an ancient war god.

Palladis remained motionless until he felt a drop of cold water on the back of his neck. He looked up to see the frost on the back of the bench was melting. The freezing temperature had vanished as swiftly as it had arrived. He felt a hand touch his shoulder, and cried out, flailing his arms at his attacker.

'Palladis, it's me,' said Roxanne. 'It's over, he's gone.'

Palladis struggled to assimilate that information, but found it too unbelievable to process.

'Gone?' he said at last. 'How? I mean, why?'

'I don't know,' said Roxanne, peeking over the top of the bench.

'Did you do it?' asked Palladis, as a measure of his composure began to return. He pulled himself upright and risked a quick look over the top of the bench.

'No,' said Roxanne. 'I swear I didn't. Take a look. This isn't anything I could have done.'

Roxanne wasn't lying. Ghota was gone, leaving a greasy fear-stink in the air and a fug of acrid gunsmoke.

Seven bodies lay sprawled by the entrance to the temple: seven hard, dangerous men. Each one lay unmoving with their limbs twisted at unnatural angles, as though they had been picked up by a simpleminded giant and bent out of shape until they broke. Palladis had seen his share of abused corpses, and knew that every bone in their bodies was crushed.

'What in Terra's name just happened?' said Palladis, moving to stand in the centre of the temple. 'What killed these men?'

'Damned if I know,' said Roxanne, 'but I'm not going to say I'm not grateful for whatever did it.'

'I suppose,' agreed Palladis, as heads began appearing over the tops of benches. Their fear turned to amazement as they saw Palladis standing amid the ruin of seven men. Palladis saw the awe in their faces and shook his head, holding his hands up to deny any part in their deaths.

'This wasn't me,' he said. 'I don't know what happ...'

The words died in his throat as he looked back down the central passageway of the temple towards the Vacant Angel. The viscera that had been blown out of Estaben's guts hung from the statue like grotesque festival decorations, and Maya wailed like a banshee at this latest agonising loss.

For a fleeing second, it was as though a pale nimbus of light played around the outline of the statue. Palladis felt the lingering presence of death, and was not surprised to see a leering, crimson-eyed skull swimming in the dark-veined marble of the statue's face. It vanished so suddenly that Palladis couldn't be sure he'd seen anything at all.

'So you have come for me at last,' he whispered under his breath.

Roxanne was at his side a moment later.

'What did you say?'

'Nothing,' said Palladis, turning away from the statue.

'I wanted to thank you,' said Roxanne.

'For what?'

'For not letting them take me.'

'You're one of us,' he said. 'I'd no more let them take you than anyone else.'

He saw the disappointment in her eyes, and immediately regretted his thoughtless words, but it was too late to take them back now.

'So what happened here?' said Roxanne.

'Death happened here,' said Palladis, fighting the urge to look over his shoulder at the Vacant Angel. He lifted his voice so that the rest of his congregation could hear him. 'Evil men came to us and paid the price for their wickedness. Death looks for any chance to take you to into his dark embrace, and to walk the path of evil is to bring you to his notice. Look now, and see the price of that path.'

The people of the temple cheered, holding one another tight as his words reached them. They had stepped from the shadow of death and the light beyond had never seemed brighter. The colours of the world were unbearably vivid, and the comfort of the loved one nearby had never been more achingly desirable. They looked at him as the source of their newfound joy, and he wanted to tell them that he had not caused these men to die, that he was as shocked as they were to still be alive.

But one look at their enraptured faces told him that no words he could summon would change their unshakable belief in him.

Roxanne gestured to the dead bodies. 'So what do we do with them?'

'Same as all the rest,' he said. 'We burn them.'

'Ghota won't take this lightly,' said Roxanne. 'We should get out of here. He'll raze this place to the ground.'

'No,' said Palladis, picking up the strange rifle one of Ghota's men had carried. 'This is a temple of death, and when that bastard comes back, he's going to find out exactly what that means.'

FIVE

Old Wounds
The Unthinkable
The Troubled Painter

KAI AND ATHENA descended the tower, making their way down the grav-lifts towards the mess facilities near the base of the tower. They hadn't spoken since breaking their most recent connection to the *nuncio*, and both were drained with the effort of maintaining a shared dreamspace. An appraisal of his improvement could wait until they had the distraction of a drink and the barrier of a table between them.

The mess halls of the tower were iron-walled, stark and low-lit, reminding Kai of the serving facilities aboard a starship. He wondered if that was deliberate, given where most astropaths were destined to spend much of their lives. Solitary figures were scattered around the echoing chamber, lost in thought, trailing their fingers over an open book or adding fresh interpretive symbols to their *Oneirocritica*. They found a table and sat in silence for a moment.

'So, am I getting better?' asked Kai.

'You already know the answer to that,' replied Athena. 'You managed to send a message to an astropath in the Tower of Voices, and it almost drained you.'

'Still, it's an improvement, yes?'

'Fishing for praise won't do you any good,' said Athena. 'I won't give it out for anything less than the full return of your abilities.'

'You're a hard woman.'

'I'm a realistic one,' said Athena. 'I know I can save you from the hollow mountain, but I need you to know it too. You have to be able to send messages off-world, to starships a sector over, and you need to send them accurately. You'll have a choir for the last part, but you know as well as I do that the best of us work alone. Are you ready for that? I don't think so.'

Kai shifted uncomfortably in his seat, fully aware that Athena was right.

'I don't feel safe hurling my mind out too far,' he said.

'I know, but you're no use to the Telepathica unless you will.'

'I… I want to, but… you don't know…'

Athena leaned forward in her chair, the electro-magnetics of its repulsor plates setting Kai's teeth on edge.

'I don't know what? That we take risks and brave horrors that even the most heroic Army soldier or Legionary wouldn't be able to comprehend? That every day we could be corrupted by the very powers that make us useful? That we are in the employ of an empire that would collapse without, yet fears us almost as much as the enemies at our frontiers? Oh, I am *very* much aware of that, Kai Zulane.'

'I didn't mean–'

'I don't care what you meant,' snapped Athena. 'Look at me: I'm a freakish cripple that any medicae worthy of the name would have let die the moment he laid eyes on me. But because I'm useful I was kept alive.'

Athena tapped her scarred palm on the metal of her chair. 'Not that this is any kind of life, but we all have our burdens to bear. I have mine, and you have yours. I deal with mine, and it's time you dealt with yours.'

'I'm trying,' said Kai.

'No, you're not. You're hiding behind what happened to you. I've read the report of what happened on the *Argo*. I know it was terrible, but what good do you do by letting yourself get drained in the hollow mountain? You're better than that, Kai, and it's time you proved it.'

Kai sat back and ran a hand over his scalp. He smiled and spread his hands out on the table. 'You know that was almost like a compliment.'

'It wasn't meant as one,' replied Athena, but she returned his smile. The tight skin at her jawline stopped the right corner of her lip from moving, and the gesture was more like a grimace. A robed servitor brought them two mugs of vitamin-laced caffeine. He took a sip and sucked his cheeks in as the bitter flavour filled his mouth.

'Throne, I'd forgotten how bad the caffeine here is. Not as strong as they make it on Army ships, but pretty damn close.'

Athena nodded in agreement and pushed away the mug in front of her. 'I don't drink it anymore,' she said.

'Why not? Aside from the fact it tastes like bilge water and you could repair blast damage on a starship's hull with it.'

'I acquired a taste for fine caffeine aboard the *Phoenician*. Her quartermasters and galleymen were the very best, and when you've tasted the best, it's hard to go back.'

'The *Phoenician*? That sounds like an Emperor's Children warship.'

'It was.'

'Was?'

'It was destroyed fighting the Diasporex,' said Athena. 'It took a lance hit amidships and broke in two.'

'Throne! And you were aboard at the time?'

Athena nodded. 'The engine section was dragged into the heart of the Carollis Star almost immediately. The forecastle took a little longer. A secondary blast took out the choir, and venting plasma coils flooded the ventral compartments in seconds. My guardians got me out of the choir chamber, but not before... Not many of us escaped.'

'I'm so sorry,' said Kai, with a measure of understanding. 'I'm glad you got off though.'

'I wasn't,' said Athena. 'Not for a while, at least. I was living with a lifetime's worth of pain every day until Mistress Sarashina and Master Zhi-Meng taught me tantric rituals to make it bearable.'

'Tantric?'

'You know how Zhi-Meng works,' said Athena neutrally.

Kai considered that and said, 'Maybe they could teach me?'

'I doubt it. You're not as broken as me.'

'No?' said Kai bitterly. 'If feels like I am.'

'Your body is still in one piece,' pointed out Athena.

'Your mind is still in one piece,' countered Kai.

Athena gave a gargled chuckle. 'Then between us we have a functioning astropath.'

Kai nodded, and the silence between them was not uncomfortable, as though in sharing their hurts they had established a connection that had, until now, been missing.

'Looks like we are both survivors,' said Kai.

'This is surviving?' said Athena. 'Throne help us then.'

AT THE HEART of the web of towers within the City of Sight lay the Conduit, the nexus of all intergalactic communication. Carved by an army of blind servitors from the limestone of the mountains, these high-roofed chambers were filled by black-clad infocytes plugged into brass keyboards and arranged in hundreds of serried ranks. Once each telepathic message had been received and interpreted – and sifted by the cryptaesthesians – it was processed and passed on by the Conduit to the intended recipient by more conventional means. Looping pneumo-tubes descended from the shadowed ceilings like plastic vines, wheezing and rattling as they sped information cylinders to and from the clattering, clicking keystrikes of the infocytes.

Overseers in grey robes and featureless silver masks drifted through the ranks of nameless scribes on floating grav-plates that disturbed the scattered sheets of discarded meme-papers covering the floor. The smell of printers' ink, surgical disinfectant and monotony filled the air alongside a burnt, electrical smell.

Those of the Administratum who had seen the Conduit found the sight utterly soulless and monstrously depressing. Working as an administrator was bad enough, where faceless men and women were lone voices among millions, but at least there was a slim possibility that talent might lift a gifted individual from the stamping, filing, and sorting masses. This repetitive drudgery allowed for no such escape, and few administrators ever returned to the Conduit, preferring to turn a blind eye to its harsh necessity.

Vesca Ordin drifted through the Conduit on his repulsor plate, information scrolling down the inside of his silver mask as his eyes darted from infocyte to infocyte. As his eye glided over each station, a noospheric halo appeared over its operator with a host of symbols indicating the nature of the message being relayed. Some were interplanetary communications, others were ship logs or regularly scheduled checks, but most were concerned with the rebellion of Horus Lupercal.

In all his thirty years of service in the Conduit, Vesca had always prided himself on making no judgement on the messages he passed. He was simply one insignificant pathway among thousands through which the Emperor ruled the emerging Imperium. It did not become a messenger to get involved. He was too small in the grand scheme of things, just an infinitesimally tiny cog in an inconceivably vast machine. He had always been content in the certainty that the Emperor and his chosen lieutenants had a plan for the galaxy that was unfolding with geometric precision.

The Warmaster's treachery had seen that certainty rocked to its foundations.

Vesca saw the glaring red symbol that indicated a more urgent communication, and he flicked his haptically-enabled gauntlets to bring a copy of the message up onto his visor. Another missive from Mars, where loyalist forces were struggling to gain a foothold in the Tharsis quadrangle after insurrection had all but destroyed the red planet's infrastructure.

The Martian campaign was not going well. The clade masters had taken it upon themselves to insert numerous operatives in an attempt to decapitate the rebel leadership, but the killers were finding it next to impossible to penetrate the rigorous bio filters and veracifiers protecting the inner circles of the rebel Mechanicum Magi. This was yet another death notice bound for one of the clade temples. Callidus this time.

Vesca sighed, flicking the message back to the station. It seemed distasteful that the Imperium should rely on such shadow operatives. Was the threat of the Warmaster so great that it required such agents and dishonourable tactics? The fleets of the seven Legions despatched to bring Horus Lupercal to heel were likely even now waging war on Isstvan V, though confirmation of victory had yet to filter through from the various astropathic relays between Terra and the Warmaster's bolthole.

The daily vox-announcements spoke of a crushing hammerblow that would smash the rebels asunder, of the Warmaster's treachery inevitably destroyed.

Then why the use of assassins?

Why the sudden rush of messages sent from the Whispering Tower to the fleets forming the second wave behind the Iron Hands, Salamanders and Raven Guard? These were concerns that normally did not trouble Vesca, but the assurances being passed throughout the Imperium seemed just a little too strident and just a little too desperate to sound sincere.

More and more messages wreathed in high-level

encryption were being sent from Terra to the expeditionary fleets in order to determine their exact whereabouts
and tasking orders. A veteran of the Conduit, Vesca had
begun to realise that the Imperium's masters were desperately trying to ascertain the location of all their forces
and to whom they owed their loyalty. Had the Warmaster's treachery spread further than anyone suspected?

Vesca floated over to a terminal as a request for confirmation icon shimmered to life over the terminal of
an infocyte. Despite each operative being hard-wired
to a terminal, the staff of the Conduit were not lobe-
cauterised servitors. They were capable of independent
thought, though such things were frowned upon.

A noospheric tag appeared over the head of the infocyte.

'Operative 38932, what is the nature of your query?'

'I... uh, well, it's just...'

'Spit it out, Operative 38932,' demanded Vesca. 'If this
is important, then clarity and speed must be your watchwords.'

'Yes, sir, it's just that... it's so unbelievable.'

'Clarity and speed, Operative 38932,' Vesca reminded
him.

The infocyte looked up at him, and Vesca saw the man
was struggling to find the words to convey the nature of
his request to him. Language was failing him, and whatever it was he had to ask was finding it impossible to
force its way out of his mouth.

Vesca sighed, making a mental note to assign Operative 38932 a month's retraining. His repulsor disc floated
gently downwards, but before he could reprimand
Operative 38932 for his lax communication discipline,
another request for confirmation icon appeared over a
terminal on the same row. Two more winked to life on
another row, followed by three more, then a dozen.

In the space of a few seconds, a hundred or more had
flickered into existence.

'What in the world?' said Vesca, rising up to look over

the thousands of infocytes under his authority. Like the visual representation of a viral spread, white lights proliferated through the chamber with fearsome rapidity. The infocytes looked to their overseers, but Vesca had no idea what was going on. He floated down to Operative 38932's terminal and ripped the sheet of meme-paper from his trembling fingers.

He scanned the words printed there, each letter grainy and black from the smudged ink of the terminal. They didn't make sense, the words and letters somehow jumbled in the wrong order in a way that was surely a misinterpretation.

'No, no, no,' said Vesca, shaking his head and relieved to have found the solution. 'It's a misinterpreted vision, that's all it is. The choirs have got this one wrong. Yes, it's the only possible explanation.'

His own hands were shaking and no matter how hard he tried to convince himself that this was simply a misinterpreted vision, he knew it was not. An incorrect vision might have triggered two or three requests for confirmation, but not thousands. With a sinking feeling in his gut that was like having the air sucked from his lungs, Vesca Ordin realised his infocytes were not requesting confirmation on the veracity of the message.

They were hoping he would tell them it wasn't true.

The meme-paper slipped from his fingers, but the memory of what was printed there was forever etched on the neurons of his memory, each line a fresh horror building on the last.

Imperial counter-strike massacred on Isstvan V.

Vulkan and Corax missing. Ferrus Manus dead.

Night Lords, Iron Warriors, Alpha Legion and Word Bearers are with Horus Lupercal.

HIGH ON THE western flank of the mountain known as Cho Oyu, a graceful villa of harmonious proportions sits upon a grassy plateau. Sunlight reflects from its white walls and shimmers upon the red-clay tiles of the roof. A thin line of smoke curls from a single chimney, and a number of custom-bred doves sit along the ridgeline of the roof. A thin, square tower rises from the north-eastern corner of the villa like a lonely watch tower on a great wall or a lighthouse set to guide seafarers to safety.

Within this tower, Yasu Nagasena stands before a wooden stretching frame, upon which is a rectangle of white silk held in place with silver pins. Cho Oyu is the old name for this mountain, words in a language that has long since been assimilated into a tongue that in turn has been outgrown and forgotten. The *migou* say it means the Turquoise Goddess, and though the poetry of that name appeals to Nagasena, he prefers the sound of the dead words.

The tower overlooks the Imperial Palace and affords a spectacular view of the hollow mountain to the east. Nagasena does not look at the hollow mountain. It is an ugly thing, a necessary thing, but he never paints it, even when he paints the landscapes of the east.

Nagasena dips his brush into a pot of blue dye and applies it lightly within the boundary lines he has previously applied to prevent the colour bleeding into the material. Painting in the freehand *mo-shui* style, he lays depths of sky to the fabric and nods to himself as he watches the colour flow.

He is tired. He has been painting since dawn, but he wants to finish this picture today. He feels he might never finish it if he does not do so today. His bones ache from standing so long. Nagasena knows he has seen too many winters to indulge in such foolishness, but he still climbs the seventy-two steps to the tower's uppermost chamber every day.

'Well, are you coming in or not?' asks Nagasena without turning. 'You are distracting me just standing there.'

'Apologies, master,' says Kartono, moving from the doorway to stand at his master's right shoulder. 'And to think some of the servants believe your hearing is going.'

Nagasena snorts in amusement. 'It keeps them on their toes, and you would be amazed what insights you pick up when people think you cannot hear them.'

They stand in silence for some moments, Kartono intuitively recognising it will be for Nagasena to decide when to speak. Kartono keeps his eyes averted from the painting, knowing that Nagasena detests people looking at incomplete works. One should only look upon art when it is complete is one of his favourite sayings.

Instead, Kartono stares over Nagasena's shoulder through the wide openings in the walls. Nagasena designed the chamber at the top of the tower specifically for painting, and the width of the world is laid before him.

Shutters on each wall keep the wind out, and even when Nagasena does not paint, he often climbs the many steps to enjoy the views over the landscape when he needs a place of serenity. At present, the northern and easternmost shutters are thrown open and the Imperial palace is spread out in all its glory.

Gilded roofs, jagged spires and mighty towers jostle for space, and the vast city-palace heaves with motion like a living thing. Suppliants, servants, soldiers and scribes fill its vast districts with life and noise. Smoke rises from the cook fires of the Petitioner's City, but the air is clearer than Nagasena remembers it. He tastes the fragrances brought to the palace on the wind like travellers from far off lands.

'What do you see?' asks Nagasena, pointing to the window.

'I see the palace,' replies Kartono. 'And it is a fine sight. Robust and healthy, full of life.'

'And beyond the city?'

'More mountains and a world rebuilt. The sky is clear, like a spring stream, and there are clouds like the breath of giants around the peaks of Dhaulagiri.'

'Describe the mountain,' commands Nagasena.

'Why?'

'Just do it, please.'

Kartono shrugs and turns his gaze upon the mountain, its tall, rugged flanks shining like silver in the sunlight. 'It gleams like a polished shield rising from the landscape, and I think I can see the high peaks of the Gangkhar Puensum behind it.'

'You can see Gangkhar Puensum?'

'Yes, I think so. Why?'

'It is a bad omen, my friend. The *migou* legends say that when Pangu, the ancestor of their race died, his head turned into Gangkhar Puensum and that it is the emperor of all mountains. The ancient *migou* kings would climb its slopes to petition the gods and seek the blessings of heaven. So far none have ever reached its summit, and the *migou* say this is why they remain bonded as virtual slaves.'

'*Migou* kings? The *migou* have no kings or ancestors,' points out Kartono. 'They are a gene-forged race of labourer creatures. They have no past to have had any kings.'

'That is as maybe,' answers Nagasena. 'You know that and I know that, but do the *migou*, I wonder? Have they invented a fictitious history and mythical past to justify their place in the world? Does it make it easier to bear a life of servitude if you believe it is the will of the gods?'

'Is seeing the mountain a bad omen?' asks Kartono.

'So the *migou* say.'

'And since when do you consult omens?' asks Kartono. 'Such things are for the simple minded and the *migou*.'

'Perhaps,' says Nagasena, 'but I have painted the landscape to seek guidance.'

'Painted the landscape? Is that some new form of prognostication introduced by the remembrancers?' laughs Kartono. 'I confess I have not heard of it.'

'Do not be flippant, Kartono,' snaps Nagasena. 'I will not stand for it.'

'Apologies, master,' says Kartono, instantly contrite. 'But I find the idea of divining omens through painting... unusual in these times.'

'That is because you do not paint, Kartono,' points out Nagasena. 'The ancient artists believed a spark of the divine moved in every artist. They believed it was sometimes possible to discern a portion of heaven's scheme for mankind if one had eyes to see it. Jin Nong, the great artist of Zhou, was said to have painted the greatest picture in the world, and when he looked upon what he had wrought, he saw the will of heaven and went mad, for such things are not for mortals to know. He burned the painting, foreswore his previous life and became a hermit in the mountains, where he dwelled alone with his secrets. Those who desired a quick and easy route to wisdom would seek him out and beg him to teach them what he knew, but Jin Nong would always send such fools away. Eventually, a band of unscrupulous men captured Jin Nong and tortured him in an attempt to prise the secrets of the divine from him, but Jin Nong told them nothing and eventually his captors threw him from a cliff.'

'Not a happy story,' says Kartono. 'I hope you do not plan on following Jin Nong's footsteps?'

'I am talented, Kartono, but I am not *that* talented,' says Nagasena. 'Anyway, the story does not end there.'

'No? So what happened next?'

'When Jin Nong's soul departed his body, the gods interceded and allowed the artist his choice of existence for his next life on earth.'

'He was reincarnated?'

'So the legends say,' replies Nagasena.

'What did he choose to return as?'

'Some say he reincarnated as pomegranate tree in the Lu Shong gardens, while others claim he came back as a cloud. Either way, he achieved the favour of Heaven, which is something to be proud of.'

'I suppose it would be,' says Kartono. 'So... do you see anything in your painting?'

'You tell me,' answers Nagasena, stepping away from the stretcher frame.

Kartono turns to look at the painting and Nagasena watches his eyes roam the colours and lines rendered there. Nagasena knows he has talent as an artist, and the landscape beyond the shutters is rendered on the silk with uncommon skill.

He is not seeking approbation, but confirmation of something that has been troubling him all day.

'Speak,' commands Nagasena, when Kartono does not say anything. 'And be honest.'

Kartono nods and says, 'The tops of the palace buildings gather like conspirators, and the mountains tower over everything. They cast a cold shadow over the land. I thought the peaks shone like silver, but you have painted them in the white of mourning. The clouds hang low and brood like dissatisfied children amid the heavy sky. I do not like this picture.'

'Why not?' asks Nagasena.

'I sense threat from it, as if something malevolent lurks in the warp and weft of the silk.'

Kartono looks up from the picture, frowning as he sees nothing of its content in the world beyond the windows of the tower. The sun shines golden on the mountains, and lazy clouds drift like wandering minstrels across an invitingly open blue sky.

'You painted this today?' asks Kartono.

'I did,' confirms Nagasena.

'I do not see what you see, master.'

'Nor would I expect you to. We all see with different eyes, and how we perceive the world around us is coloured by the landscape within our heart. You look on the world and see the optimism of a life spent away from hunting and killing, but I see…'

'What? What do you see?'

'Ah… I am an old man, Kartono, and my eyes grow dim,' says Nagasena, suddenly reticent. 'What do I know?'

'Tell me what you see,' pleads Kartono.

Nagasena sighs and looks into the depths of the painting. 'I see a time of darkness ahead for us. The world knows it and it is afraid of the bloodshed to come. I fear we are about to walk into the lair of a sleeping dragon and awaken the most terrible danger imaginable.'

Kartono shakes his head. 'You are speaking of Horus Lupercal. What have we to do with the rebel Warmaster? His army will be ashes by now. Ferrus Manus and the rest of Lord Dorn's strike force will be celebrating victory even as we speak.'

'I fear you are wrong, Kartono,' says Nagasena. 'I believe the Warmaster is a more terrible threat than anyone can imagine. And I believe that Lord Dorn has gravely under-estimated how far his reach has spread.'

Nagasena puts down his brush and makes his way from the tower. He descends its seventy-two steps and enters his rose garden, wishing he could spend more time here, but knowing that such a desire is impossible. Kartono follows him, and they move through the delicately proportioned and harmoniously appointed chambers of the villa like ghosts.

'What are you planning?' asks Kartono, as Nagasena enters his private chambers. Three walls are painted white, adorned with long silk hangings and ancient maps of long vanished lands, while the other is covered with shelves laden with rolled up scrolls and heavy textbooks. A narrow desk of dark walnut sits low in the centre of the room, and writing implements are arranged neatly on its polished surface.

'I am preparing,' answers Nagasena cryptically, running his hands over the one bare wall in the chamber in a series of complicated patterns.

'Preparing for what?'

The wall in front of Nagasena slides back to reveal a deep compartment filled with racked weapons and armour. Conversion generators, web-guns, long rifles, energy blades, digital lasers, plasma pistols, cestus gauntlets, shot-casters, fire-lances, photon-nets and stasis grenades. Implements of pursuit and capture.

'For the hunt,' says Nagasena.

'Who are we hunting?' asks Kartono, exasperation beginning to enter his voice.

Nagasena smiles, but there is no warmth in it, for he knows the answer will only confound his friend further.

'I do not know yet,' says Nagasena.

SIX

Woe-weavers and Doomsayers
Acceptance
The Red Eye

NEWS OF THE massacre on Isstvan V spread, as all bad news does, with gleeful rapidity, as if those who bore it took unseemly relish in passing it on. The effect on the populace of the palace was immediate and contradictory. In the worker habs of the Brahmaputra Plateau, riots broke out between those who railed against the notion of the Warmaster's treachery and those who decried him as a faithless oath-breaker. In the precincts of Ter-Guar, ten thousand wailing women knelt before the towering fortress of the Eternity Gate and begged the Emperor to give the lie to the news.

Woe-weavers and doomsayers roamed the streets, screeching of brother turned on brother as they wailed and gnashed their teeth with zealous frenzy. Panic swept through the palace like the dreaded Life-eater virus, leaving ashen hopes and broken dreams in its wake. Men wept openly before their wives and children, their faith in the infallibility of the Emperor shaken to the core. That Horus Lupercal could have betrayed his father was terrible beyond imagining, but to learn that so many of the Emperor's sons had followed him into rebellion was more than many could bear.

The people of Terra were waking up to a very different reality, one with which many of the globe's inhabitants found themselves unable to cope. To have a dream so precious that its demise made life unbearable was the cold reality of the day following the news of the bloodshed on Isstvan V.

Hundreds of inconsolable citizens of Terra threw themselves from the cliffs of the palace or quietly took blades to their necks and wrists in the cold confines of their homes. On the Merican plains of Jonasburg, the seven thousand men and women of a bio-weapons storage facility exposed themselves to a pernicious strain of the newly-developed gangshi virus and perished in the flames of automated decontamination procedures rather than live in a world where the Emperor could be betrayed.

When word reached the Diemensland prison island, the inmates declared themselves loyal servants of the Warmaster and slaughtered their overseers. Regiments drawn from the Magyar Ossurites mustered in the Meganesian heartlands, but the battle to retake the island would take many bloody weeks.

All over the globe, the solid certainty of the Imperium's invincibility was crumbling, but worse was to come. As the sun reached its zenith above the hollow mountain and the shadows hid, word came that one of the Emperor's sons had fallen on the sands of Isstvan V. Ferrus Manus, beloved gene-sire of the Iron Hands was dead, slain, it was said, by the hand of his most beloved brother.

It was impossible to believe, ridiculous. That a demigod could be slain was preposterous, the lunatic notion of a delusional fool. Yet as the hours passed and fragments of information eked from the City of Sight, it became harder to deny the truth of Ferrus Manus's death. People tore out their hair and mortified their flesh in bloody honour of the Emperor's fallen son. Vulkan too was rumoured to be dead, though no one could yet say for sure whether this was true or fevered speculation. Yet even as cold facts spread into the global consciousness, they came on a tide of wild rumour and manic embellishment that grew with every retelling.

Some tales spoke of the Warmaster's fleet breaching the outer perimeter of the solar system, while others had his warships on the verge of entering Terra's orbit. False prophets arose on every continent, spreading a credo of falsehoods and misinformation until Imperial Arbitrators or gold-armoured warriors of the Legio Custodes silenced them. As more and more lies spread across the world, suspicions began to form in the minds of Terra's leaders that not all were the result of panic and the mutational power of rumour and distance, but of deliberate misinformation by agents of the Warmaster.

The cryptaesthesians passed word to the Legio Custodes of numerous messages sent to Terra with concealed subtexts, hidden encryptions and suspicious routings. Acting on such information, the Custodians made numerous arrests, all of which only fanned the flames of unrest. The notion of the enemy within turned brother upon brother, neighbours into potential spies, and any word of dissent marked a man out as a traitor.

In such a climate of fear, the people of Terra turned to whatever gave them comfort. To some it was the solace of loved ones, to others it was the oblivion promised by alcohol or narcotics. Some swaddled themselves in hope that the Imperium was strong enough to weather this terrible storm, placing their faith in the Emperor's wisdom and the power of his remaining armies.

Others' faith in the Emperor was of a radically different stripe, and the clandestine churches of the Lectitio Divinitatus grew from small gatherings of like-minded individuals to massed congregations that met in secret basements, echoing warehouses and other such unremembered spaces.

In time of turmoil, the human mind seeks solace

wherever it can, and never more so than in times of war. For it was clear to everyone on Terra that the Warmaster's treachery was no longer simply an isolated rebellion.

It was nothing less than galactic civil war.

THE TEMPLE HAD never been busier, which was ironic given that it was likely to be razed to the ground sometime soon. Ghota had not returned, but Roxanne knew it was only a matter of time. She wondered if she could have done anything different, if there was something she could have done that might have avoided this inevitable doom. No, she had been defending herself, and were it not for her unique abilities then she would have suffered a lingering, degrading and painful death.

Roxanne had come to the temple believing that she deserved such a fate, but time and distance had given her a perspective on what had happened aboard the *Argo*. It hadn't been her fault, despite what her father and brothers kept telling her. The vessel had been commissioned at the outset of the Great Crusade and the demands of war had kept it from its regularly scheduled maintenance refits. With such inherently unstable technology as Geller Fields, it had only been a matter of time until disaster struck.

She swallowed hard as a mouthful of bile rose in her throat at the memories of being trapped in her crystal dome, protected and left to wonder what had become of the crew, but knowing full well what their fate had been.

Roxanne rubbed the heels of her palms against her eyes and took a deep breath.

'Calm is the way that the eye sees,' she said. 'The storm parts before me and the swells of the ocean rise to meet me in glorious concord.'

'Talking to yourself is a sign of madness,' said a voice at her shoulders. 'That's what my dad always said.'

Roxanne looked down and saw the tiny and lost features of Maya's eldest surviving son.

'Arik,' she said. 'Your father was a clever man. I think he was onto something.'

'Are you mad?' asked the boy.

Roxanne considered the question seriously. She wasn't sure she knew the answer.

'I think we all go a little mad sometimes,' replied Roxanne, sitting next to Arik on a wooden bench. 'But it's nothing to worry about.'

'I though I was going mad when my brothers died,' said Arik, staring at the Vacant Angel at the end of the building. 'I kept seeing faces on that statue, but mum kept telling me I was making it up and that I was being stupid.'

Roxanne risked a glance at the faceless statue, unwilling to spare it more than a glance. Palladis had told her what he thought he'd seen there after Ghota's men had been killed, and now she wondered what manner of presence might have fleetingly turned its gaze upon them. Roxanne knew from long experience that there were innumerable *things* that could be drawn to strong emotions, but she had never heard of them existing in this world.

'I don't think you should be looking at it like that,' she said, turning his small face away with gentle pressure of her fingertips. He was resistant at first, but at last his head turned away.

'They say that we're all going to be dead soon,' said Arik.

'Who says?'

The boy shrugged.

'Who says that?' pressed Roxanne. 'Who's been telling you that?'

'I listen and I hear things,' said Arik. 'Too many people crowded in here not to hear what they're saying.'

'And what are they saying?'

'That Horus is coming to kill us all. His fleets are on their way to Terra right now and he's going to slaughter us all. Just like they say he did with the Iron Hands.

He's burning up all the worlds out in space, and folk are scared he's going to do the same to us.'

The boy began to cry softly, and Roxanne put her arm around him. She pulled him close and looked for Maya, but Arik's mother was nowhere to be seen. She had spent a day and a night shrieking at the feet of the Vacant Angel, but Palladis had eventually led her away as the crowds of people flocking to the temple grew ever larger.

Word of what had happened spread through the Petitioner's City faster than news of a name being called to the inner precincts of the palace, and the curious, the desperate and the needy had flocked to the temple. Palladis had turned them away at first, but it quickly became a futile effort. Over three hundred people filled the temple, many with truthful grief to vent, others here simply to feel part of something bigger than themselves.

Roxanne let the boy cry and tried to think of something hopeful to tell him.

'The Warmaster is a long way away,' she said. 'It will take him a long time to get to Terra from Isstvan V, but the Emperor's fleets will stop him long before he gets here.'

Arik looked up, his face red and puffy with snot and tears.

'You promise?'

'I promise,' said Roxanne. 'Trust me, I know these things. I used to work on a starship, so I know how long it takes to get from one side of the galaxy to the other.'

Arik smiled, and she tried to keep the truth of the matter from him. True, Isstvan was incredibly distant from Terra, but with fair tides and a steady course, the Warmaster's forces could reach the heart of the Imperium within months.

Not for the first time, Roxanne wondered what she was doing here, surrounded by people she didn't know. For all its faults, her family had always drawn tight around its members, even the ones who – rightly or wrongly – were believed to have brought shame upon the good name of Castana. Even she had been brought into the bosom of the family in the wake of the loss of the *Argo*, albeit with the crushing power of imposed guilt.

With Babu Dhakal's inevitable retribution looming like an oncoming storm, she knew it would be far safer for her to leave this place. She wore a silver ring that could send a locator pulse to the Castana estates and have a skiff en route to her within minutes. Inside an hour she could be back in the gilded halls of her family's sprawling Galician manor house, with its great libraries, portrait-hung galleries and luxurious appointments. Without even realising it, she was twirling the ring around her right index finger, her thumb hovering over the activation stud and the first code phrases forming in her mind.

Roxanne took her thumb away from the ring, knowing that however much she might desire to flee, she would never abandon these people. No matter that Babu Dhakal's thugs had given her no choice, it was her fault they would come and destroy this place and everyone in it. She could no more abandon these people to their fate than she could trick her heart into stopping beating.

Arik reached up and wiped his nose and eyes with his sleeve. His eyes were swollen with tears, but he had found a place of calm within himself.

'What did you used to do on a starship?' he asked.

Roxanne hesitated, not yet ready share her identity with the people around her. Like the blind astro-telepaths of the City of Sight, her people were vital to the continued existence of the Imperium, but were feared as much as they were needed. Like most misunderstood things, fear of their abilities had made them outcasts.

'I helped to make sure it reached where it was supposed to go,' said Roxanne.

'That's why you wear that bandanna under your hood,' said Arik.

'In a manner of speaking,' said Roxanne, suddenly wary.

'You're one of them Navigators, ain't you?'

Roxanne's head jerked up and she looked around to see who had heard the boy's question. If anyone was listening, they gave no sign of it. She lowered her head towards Arik and whispered to him.

'Yes,' she said. 'I am, but you can't tell anyone. People don't really understand what we are and how we do what we do. That makes them afraid, and frightened people can do terrible things to the things that frighten them.'

Arik smiled through his tears. 'You don't have to worry about that.'

'What do you mean?'

'Everyone knows what you are,' he said. 'They've known ever since you came here. My dad told me what you were a while ago. Even before you went to get the medicine for me.'

Roxanne was astonished. 'People know what I am?'

'Yeah, I heard people talking about it weeks ago.'

She sat back on the bench and let the weight of secrecy fall away from her. All her life she had been taught that the common man feared her and would seek to persecute her if given the chance. The words of one small boy and the actions of the people around her had given the lie to that notion in one fell swoop, and the sudden lightness of being that filled her was like an elixir of purest light poured into her veins.

She looked at the plain, unassuming, ordinary faces that surrounded her, seeing them now for the wonderful, powerful and determined individuals they were. She was accepted amongst them simply because she was here, not through any familial connection, trade agreement or covenant of service.

'Is it true you've got another eye under that bandanna?'

Roxanne nodded. 'Yes.'

'Can I see it?'

'No, I'm afraid you can't, Arik.'

'Why not?'

'It can be dangerous,' explained Roxanne.

'I hear you can kill people with it.'

Roxanne ruffled the boy's hair. 'You shouldn't believe all you hear about Navigators, Arik. Yes, people can get hurt by looking at it, but that's why I keep it covered up. I don't want to hurt anyone.'

'Oh,' said Arik, but shrugged off his disappointment to ask, 'But you can see the future, right? With your hidden eye, I mean?'

'I'm afraid not,' replied Roxanne. 'We just guide starships, that's all.'

Arik nodded, as though he fully understood the complexities and nuances to being one of a caste that was both shunned and required for the Imperium to function. A group that was both powerful and wealthy, yet could never take a rightful place amongst the people they served.

A sudden thought occurred to Roxanne, and she said, 'Does Palladis realise that everyone knows?'

'Nah, he thinks he's the only one,' said Arik. 'I think losing his boys must've rattled some of the marbles loose in his head. He don't trust anyone.'

'I think you might be right,' whispered Roxanne. 'You're a clever boy, Arik, do you know that?'

'That's what my mum always tells me,' he said with a proud smile.

She pulled Arik close and gave him a kiss on the forehead.

'You have no idea how precious a gift you have just given me,' she said.

He looked confused, but nodded with a child's seriousness.

'Here, let me give you something in return,' said Roxanne, tugging at her finger and placing something in the centre of his palm. She closed his fingers over it before anyone could see what she'd given him.

'What is it?' asked Arik.

Roxanne smiled. 'It's a magic ring,' she said.

* * *

THE WHITE SANDS of the Rub' al Khali rose and fell in end-less dunes beyond the walls of the fortress of Arzashkun. Kai wandered the empty ramparts and deserted tow-ers with a pleasant aimlessness to his steps. The sands beyond the walls were silent and dusted by a warm sirocco that carried a pleasing scent of roasted meat, mulled wine and exotic perfumes.

He trailed his fingers over the silver-gold battlements, letting the peace and emptiness of his surroundings calm him. Nothing moved in the sands, no shadowy hunters or buried memories threatening to burst to the surface, for Kai was merely dreaming. His metacognitive pow-ers were developed enough that he could understand he was dreaming and shape his surroundings to a degree beyond most sleepers.

Though Arzashkun was his refuge from the dangerous presences of the immaterium, it was much more than that. It was a place where he could find peace and a measure of solace and isolation. No one else could come here, save by his express invitation to a shared dream-space, and Kai revelled in the silence that filled every vaulted chamber and domed cupola of the ornately dec-orated structure.

Kai descended the steps to the courtyard, his steps light and the black mood that had been his constant companion since the disaster on the *Argo* lightening by degrees. The fear was still there, lurking at the threshold of his perceptions, but he refused to acknowledge it. To remember was to feel, and to feel was to experience. Ten thousand deaths screaming in his head had unhinged his mind for a time, and he wasn't entirely sure it had returned to him intact.

Yet the few times he was able to escape to Arzashkun were where he could heal in private, where he could experience all the human mind could conjure without fear of dreadful memories and sympathetic terrors. Kai pushed open the doors to the main hall, and breathed in the aroma of scented lanterns and fresh growths. A circular pool glittered in the centre of the hall, its base tiled with a gold and scarlet lozenge pattern, and a silver fountain in the shape of a trident-bearing hero shimmered in the sunlight drifting down from a stained-glass dome.

Palm fronds waved gently in the breeze from the opened door, and the scent of lemongrass and hookah smoke was strong. The air was redolent with the fragrances of distant kingdoms of long ago, and the connection with the past was a potent anchor to Kai in this realm of imagination and dreams. Had he wished, Kai could conjure anything his consciousness desired into being, but this was all he needed. Peace and solitude and an end to the thousands of voices that clamoured for his attention.

Pillars of marble and nephrite supported the roof, and Kai wove a path through them as he made his way to the wide staircase that swept up to the cloisters above. Battle flags of crimson, emerald and gold hung from the graceful arches, honours won in battles no one now remembered. Strange how something so terrible and vital to the lives of thousands of people could so easily be forgotten. The men who had fought in these battles were naught but the sand of the Empty Quarter, but their lives had mattered once. No matter that the tide of history had ground each of them down to insignificant specks of grit, they had once been important, they had once made a difference.

That the difference existed now only in a dream did not lessen their lives. Kai recalled them, even if it was a borrowed memory from a primarch's writings. In time, he too would be forgotten, but instead of frightening Kai, the thought made him smile. To be forgotten in times like these would be a blessing. To be lauded by everyone, to be depended upon by so many would be a burden no one should ever have to bear.

Kai wondered how people like Malcador, Lord Dorn or the Choirmaster stood it.

He paused by at the bottom of the wide staircase, closing his eyes and letting the burbling sound of the fountain wash over him. His blindsight trembled and a breath of wind sighed across the skin of his face, as Kai inhaled the scents of a land long since consigned to history. Smell was one of the strongest senses in the dream landscapes, and the heady aroma of alinazik, habesh and mahlab transported Kai's thoughts to an open-air souk, its thronged pathways filled with jostling, sweating bodies: chattering vendors, haggling customers and slit-mouthed cutpurses.

Kai could taste the smoke of cookfires, the billowing clouds of hashish and the potent reek of papazkarasi as it was poured from clay ewers into pewter mugs nailed to drinking posts. So real was the sensation that Kai had to hold onto the carved balustrade to keep himself from sinking to his haunches at the aching sadness he felt.

Tears pricked at the corners of his eyes, and Kai wondered at how he could know these sounds and smells. This was no fantasy conjured from the depths of his imagination, these were sense-memories that belonged to a mind other than his own. These sensations had been dredged from the depths of a memory so ancient that it staggered Kai that any one mind could contain so much history.

Kai gasped and opened his eyes. The world wavered as his grip on its solidity faltered for an instant. His breath came in sharp hikes, though he knew in this dreamspace he was not truly breathing. Kai's body lay asleep on his cot bed, but certain laws still held true in the world of dreams as they did in the real world – though such a term was almost meaningless to one whose existence was lived in a world beyond the comprehension of most mortals.

A flicker of movement caught his eye, and Kai looked up to the cloister in time to see a figure move out of sight. He stood dumbfounded for a moment, unable to believe what he'd just seen. Someone else in his dreamscape? Kai had heard fanciful tales of powerful psykers who were able to invade the dreams of sleepers and alter their mindscapes, but the last such cognoscynth was said to have died thousands of years ago.

'Wait!' cried Kai, turning and taking the stairs two at a time. He was out of breath by the time he reached the landing, and turned ninety degrees to mount the last flight of stairs. The terrazzo floor was patterned in a square-edged spiral motif, a maze with only one way in and out, and Kai rushed along the cloister towards where he had last seen the mysterious figure.

Silken curtains bellied out from arched openings, carrying the beat of a distant drum that echoed like a heartbeat from another epoch of the world. Kai could see no musicians, and knew the sounds were as impossible as the sight of an intruder in his dreams. He ran along the cloister, leaving the sound of percussion in his wake, and passed through a curtained doorway into a chamber of light and verdant growth. Trees grew through the floor as though nature had reclaimed this fortress after thousands of years of neglect by man. Creeping vines hung like gilded wall hangings from the pilasters, and waving fronds garlanded the window openings.

At the far end of the chamber a tall figure in long robes of white and gold stepped towards a doorway. Too distant to make out his features, his eyes were pools of great sorrow and infinite understanding of the price men pay for their dreams.

'Stop!' cried Kai. 'Who are you, how can you be here?'

The figure did not answer and stepped out of sight. Kai ran through the room, brushing drifting leaves and questing vines from his path as he fought towards the doorway through which the robed figure had passed. The scents of spices, fresh growths and old memory was strongest here, and Kai shouted out in triumph as he finally reached the doorway. The smell of salt water and hot stone came from beyond the door, and – now that he had reached it – Kai found himself strangely reluctant to pass through.

Summoning up what little courage he possessed, Kai stepped over the threshold.

He found himself on a balcony he had never known existed, high on the side of the central tower of the fortress. The sun was a burning eye of searing red, and a lake so vast it better deserved to be called an ocean stretched out before him, wondrously blue and almost painful to look at. Birds flocked over the water, and small fishing boats bobbed close to the shore.

The balcony was deserted, which was impossible, as there was no way the intruder could possibly have escaped. Save the door behind him, a drop of hundreds of metres was the only way off the balcony. Only the creator of the dreamspace had the power to alter the laws that governed the logic of a dream, and even then it was dangerous, so how this mysterious stranger had escaped Kai was beyond him.

Kai walked to the edge of the balcony and rested his hands on the sun-warmed stone. He took a breath of the clean air, sharp and free of the chemical tang that pervaded every breath of the Terran atmosphere.

'Where is this place?' said Kai, knowing somehow that the man he had been chasing would hear him.

A hand clamped his shoulder with a powerful grip. The touch was electric, and Kai had the sense that had he chosen to do so, the owner of this hand could break him into tiny pieces with a simple twist of his wrist.

'It is Old Earth,' said a voice at his ear. Soft, lyrical, but with a core of steel.

'How?' asked Kai, enthralled by the man's voice.

'The human mind is impossibly complex, even to one such as I,' said the man, 'but it is no great feat to share my memories with you.'

'You're really here?' asked Kai. 'I'm not imagining this?'

'You are asking if I am really here? In a dream you created?' said the man with a wry chuckle. 'That's one for the philosophers, eh? What is reality anyway? Is this any less real to you than your life in the Whispering Tower?

Does fire in a dream not warm you just as well as one of timber and kindling?'

'I don't understand,' said Kai. 'Why are you here? With me, right now.'

'I wanted to see you, to know more about you.'

'Why? Who are you?'

'Always the obsession with names,' said the man. 'I have had many names over the long years, and one is as good as another until it is shed for the next.'

'So what do I call you?'

'You don't call me anything,' said the man, and the power of the grip on Kai's shoulder increased exponentially. Kai winced as the complex arrangement of bones in his shoulder ground together. 'You just listen.'

Kai nodded, and the pain in his shoulder eased a fraction. The birds over the lake swooped down over the fishing boats, their caws echoing from the water as though from a great distance. Kai narrowed his eyes. Staring at the vivid blue of the lake was hurting his eyes, and his augmetics had no power to help him in this dream.

'Great and terrible forces are abroad in the galaxy, Kai, and the billions upon billions of threads they weave into the future are beyond the comprehension of even the greatest of the eldar seers, but one particular thread I have seen entwines with my own. Can you guess whose that is?'

'Mine?' ventured Kai.

The man laughed, the sound so infectious it made Kai smile despite the growing ache in his shoulder. Yet it felt somehow insincere, as though this man had not laughed in a very long time and had forgotten how it was supposed to sound.

'You, Kai Zulane? No, you are not destined to be remembered by the saga-tellers of the ages yet to come,' said the man, and Kai felt him look into the glaring red eye of the sun. 'It is of another I speak, one who has the ability to undo all that I have achieved and cut my thread, but whose face is hidden from me.'

'So why are you here talking to me?' asked Kai. 'If you are who I think you are, then there must be a million things more important than me for you to deal with.'

'Very true,' agreed the man. 'But I am here talking to you because you will bear witness to my ending. I sense you are being pulled along by the unseen thread that leads to my death. And if you can see it, then I can know it.'

'And you can stop it?' asked Kai, as the red sun began to descend.

'That remains to be seen.'

THE REGICIDE BOARD lay untouched. This was no time for games, and they all knew it.

Nemo Zhi-Meng paced his chambers with a harried expression creasing his already craggy and lined features. Since the Conduit had passed word of the disaster at Isstvan V, he had not slept, and the strain was beginning to show.

'Sit down, Nemo, you're wearing me out,' said Sarashina.

'And put some damn clothes on,' added Evander Gregoras

'I can't,' he said. 'I do my best thinking on the move. And it helps being naked, the energies flow through me so much better.'

'You know that's nonsense,' said Sarashina.

Zhi-Meng's head snapped up and he waved her objections away. 'You know as well as anyone that whatever works for you only works because you make it so.'

Sarashina lay back on a contoured couch, trying to let its massaging texture ease out the terrible cramps in her shoulder and neck muscles. It was a hopeless task. Days of constant telepathic communion with astropaths all over the Imperium had pushed them all to the end of their endurance. The Choirs were operating far beyond safe limits, and hundreds had burned out like quick-burning star shells fired over a midnight battlefield.

Over a dozen had suffered catastrophic intrusions that had required the intervention of Golovko's Black Sentinels. Thankfully such incidents had been contained and the cells of those poor unfortunates were now sanitised by fire and sealed with psi-locks.

'And the *Vatic* saw no sign of this?' Zhi-Meng asked. 'We're sure of that?'

'Nothing was logged with the Conduit apart from the dream vision of Athena Diyos,' said Gregoras, flicking through reams of sifted data on his dataslate. 'Not even any residuals or imagery they interpreted wrongly.'

'And you're sure about that, Evander?' demanded Zhi-Meng. 'The palace wants heads on spikes for this, and we're next in line at the chopping block.'

'I am sure, Choirmaster,' said Gregoras in a tone that conveyed his irritation at the idea his people might have missed something. 'If there was something to be found, the cryptaesthesians would have seen it.'

Zhi-Meng nodded and resumed his naked pacing.

'Damn it, but why didn't Athena send her vision straight to the Conduit? Why did she waste time going to you, Aniq?'

'I'll let the insult in that question go this time, Nemo, but don't ever speak to me like that again.'

'Sorry, but you know what I meant.'

Sarashina smoothed out her robes and said, 'It would have made no difference, and you know it. By the time Athena interpreted her vision it was already too late. The traitors had already struck. There was no way we could have warned Ferrus Manus or the others.'

'I know that, but it rankles,' said Zhi-Meng, pausing to suck on the coiled pipe of a gently smoking hookah. Aromatic fumes, redolent of desert mountains, filled the air. 'Lord Dorn is ready to break down the Obsidian Arch and drag me out by scruff of the neck for this. He wants to know why we didn't see this coming. What am I supposed to tell him?'

'You tell him that the currents of the immaterium

are always shifting, and that to think that you can use them to predict the future with anything other than best guesses is like shooting an arrow on a windy day and predicting which grain of sand it will hit.'

'I told him that,' said Zhi-Meng. 'He wasn't impressed. He thinks we failed, and I'm inclined to agree with him.'

'Did you tell him that we are not seers?' asked Gregoras. 'That if we *could* predict the future, we'd be locked up in the Vault with the Crusader Host and the rest of the traitors the Custodians have rounded up?'

'Of course, but Lord Dorn is a blunt man, and he demands answers,' said Zhi-Meng. 'We all know that it *is* possible to see potential futures, echoes of events yet to come, but for not one single astropath in this city to get so much of a glimpse of this strikes me as awry. Not one of your *Vatic* caught so much of a whiff of this, Aniq, not one!'

'Apart from Athena Diyos,' said Gregoras.

'Apart from Athena Diyos,' repeated Zhi-Meng. 'How is that possible?'

'I do not know,' said Sarashina.

'Find out,' ordered Zhi-Meng.

'Perhaps this is the pattern,' said Gregoras.

'You and your pattern,' cried Zhi-Meng, throwing his arms into the air and slapping them down on the top of his head. 'There is no pattern. You are inventing things, Evander. I have seen the things you have seen, and I detect no pattern.'

'With all due respect, Choirmaster, you do not live in the detritus of dreams as I do, and you do *not* see what I see. I have studied the pattern for centuries, and it has been building to something terrible for many years. All the voices speak of a great red eye bearing down on Terra, a force of awesome destruction that will forever change the course of history.'

Zhi-Meng stopped his pacing. 'That's what your precious pattern is telling you? I don't need Yun's *Onei-rocritica* to tell me what that means. A novice could tell you the red eye represents Horus Lupercal. If that's all your years of looking for patterns that aren't there has told you then you've been wasting your time, Evander.'

'The eye does not represent Horus,' said Gregoras.

'Then who does it represent?' asked Sarashina.

'I believe it to be Magnus the Red,' said the cryptaesthesian. 'I think the Crimson King is coming to Terra.'

'Don't be ridiculous, Evander,' hissed Zhi-Meng. 'Magnus is still on Prospero, nursing his wounded pride after Nikaea.'

'Are we sure about that?' asked Gregoras.

SEVEN

Cognoscynths
The Cave
The Gate is Broken

EVEN IN A place as lightless and silent as the Whispering Tower, the lair of the cryptaesthesians was gloomy and foreboding. Kai and Athena moved swiftly through the melta-bored tunnels, pausing every now and then to run their fingers along the wall to check for the notched guide marks. Astropaths soon learned to navigate the familiar corridors of their tower, but none visited the deep levels where the cryptaesthesians plied their trade without very good reason.

'This is a bad idea,' said Kai, feeling the psychic pulse of whisper stones bleeding the residue of hundreds of astropathic visions into the trap chambers.

'I know, but it was your idea,' Athena reminded him, the sound of her support chair sounding disproportionately loud in the angular corridor. 'I distinctly recall telling you it was a bad idea several times. You don't go looking for the cryptaesthesians, *they* find you.'

Hundreds of metres below ground, the temperature was low and Kai's breath misted before him. The dimly lit corridor stretched out before him for hundreds of metres, unmarked doors blending with the walls, and only the occasional mark on the walls giving any indication as to how far they had travelled.

'You can always go back,' said Kai.

'And miss seeing you get chewed up by Evander Gregoras? No chance.'

'I thought Sarashina told you to help me.'

'She did,' said Athena. 'And right now I'm helping you by making sure you get out of this level with your brain still in your skull.'

'Now you're being dramatic.'

'Tell me that when Gregoras has you wired up to his machines, then we'll see how dramatic I'm being.'

Kai knew Athena was right. It *was* foolish to seek out the cryptaesthesians, for the towers of the astropaths were awash with dark rumours of their powers. Some said they could pluck secrets from the darkest parts of a person's psyche, others that they could brainwash any individual into any act imaginable. Yet more told that they could read the minds of the dead.

Such talk was just that, talk, but Kai had no clear idea of how these most secret astro-telepaths worked. He suspected they were associated with the security of the City of Sight, assessing the messages that came to the towers for any warp-borne corruption. Where the Black Sentinels protected the physical aspects of the city, Kai believed the cryptaesthesians looked to its psychic defences.

He reached out to run his fingers along the wall, feeling the particular notches that told him he was on the right level and a few metres away from his destination.

'This is it,' he said as they stopped before a plain door of brushed steel.

'You don't have to do this,' she said. 'I told you, it was just a dream. You know anything can happen in a dream. Especially the dreams of a telepath. They don't have to mean anything.'

Kai shook his head. 'Come on, you are *Vatic*, you know better than that.'

'You're right, I *do* know better than that, but I also know that his is a dangerous door to open, and one that will not easily be shut. To invite a cryptaesthesian to examine the interior architecture of your mind is to forever alter it, to bare the darkest, secret parts of the mind to their scrutiny. Once a cryptaesthesian is in your head, nothing is hidden from them.'

'I have nothing to hide,' said Kai.

'We all have something to hide,' said Athena. 'Something we don't want the rest of the world to know. Trust me on this. I've seen the astropaths the cryptaesthesians have questioned, and they *all* ended up being sent to the hollow mountain.'

'Well if that's where I'm heading anyway, then this can't do any harm.'

Athena reached up with her twisted arm and took hold of his elbow.

'Of course it can,' she said. 'Mistress Sarashina told me to bring you back, but I can't do that if the cryptaesthesians have reduced your mind to a fractured mess. Kai, think, *really* think about what you're doing.'

'I have,' said Kai, rapping his knuckles on the brushed steel door.

The sound drifted down the corridor with mocking echoes, and Kai waited for the door to open with held breath. Finally it slid into the wall, and Kai found himself face to face with Evander Gregoras.

Looking at the man's sallow, pinched features he could see why so few sought him out. Though his features were completely unremarkable to the point of being bland and forgettable, there was a calculating sharpness to his gaze that made Kai feel like a specimen on a dissection table.

'The whisper stones are awash with your incessant chatter, and I need to rest,' said Gregoras. 'Why are you disturbing me?'

Kai was momentarily taken aback, and struggled to find his voice. Beyond Gregoras, he saw a room at odds

with the bland-faced man, but Gregoras quickly stepped
between Kai and his view of the interior.

'I am a busy man, Kai Zulane, as are we all in these
times,' said Gregoras. 'Give me one reason not to send
you on your way with a reprimand.'

'I want to know about the cognoscynths,' said Kai, and
the dismissive expression in the cryptaesthesian's eyes
was replaced with one of guarded interest.

'The cognoscynths? Why? They are long gone.'

Kai took a breath and glanced at Athena, aware that he
was crossing a very dangerous threshold. He shucked the
fabric of his robe from his shoulder to reveal a yellow
purple bruise in the shape of a powerful man's hand.

'I think I met one,' he said.

THE INTERIOR OF the cryptaesthesian's chambers were
superficially similar to a novitiate's: walls of cold stone
and iron, an uncomfortable bed, whisper stones set in
copper settings, but there the resemblance ended. This
chamber was much larger, filled with rack upon rack of
shelves, and where a novitiate's shelves would be empty,
awaiting the amassing of a dream library through time
and experience, Gregoras boasted an impressive collection.

Leather bound books, data-spikes and rolled up
parchments vied for space on bookcases overflowing
with scraps of paper, celestial charts and handwritten
lists. Scores of *Oneirocritica* lay strewn across the floor,
and every square inch of wall was covered in a looping
pattern of chalked curves, angles and scrawls that at once
seemed dreadfully familiar and utterly unknown to Kai.

Evander Gregoras was a man Kai had known of before
he'd left the City of Sight, but he was not a man he had
ever required to meet.

Right now, he wished that were still the case.

'Move some of those books if you want somewhere
to sit,' said Gregoras, sorting through a pile of papers
stacked at random on a wide desk of scuffed dark wood.

'Not you, Mistress Diyos, you don't need to bother.'

Kai wondered if Gregoras was being cruel, but decided he was simply being factual. He shifted a heap of parchments on the bed to make room. He craned his neck to look at the writing on the wall, seeing that the handwriting was the same as filled the parchments. At first glance the designs looked like star charts or some form of celestial cartography, or perhaps the most complex genealogical record imaginable, but none of the symbols and intersecting lines made sense of that interpretation.

'Don't bother trying to understand it, Zulane,' said Gregoras lifting a book from the desk and sweeping a layer of dust from its cover. 'I have been trying for nearly two centuries and I understand only a fraction of it.'

'What is it?' asked Athena, gliding next to him as her manipulator arm tapped a nervous tattoo on the silvered armrest.

'Please stop that, Mistress Diyos, it is most irritating,' said Gregoras before continuing without missing a beat. 'I call it the pattern, and as to what it is...'

Gregoras pulled a chair from the desk and sat before Kai with the book in his lap. He gazed up at the symbols and lines on the wall like a man seeing the landscapes of Kozarsky for the first time. 'I believe it is a fragmented vision of a coming apocalypse. A vision of the future experienced by humanity aeons ago and shattered into billions of unrelated shards that have been spinning in the species consciousness for hundreds of thousands of years. I have been trying to piece it together.'

He had the certainty of a zealot in his voice, and Kai wondered just how much of what he had heard of the cryptaesthesians was due to this man.

'So when is this apocalypse?' said Kai. 'Not for a while, I hope.'

'It is happening now,' said Gregoras.

Kai almost laughed, but thought the better of it when he saw the seriousness of Gregoras's expression.

'You're joking, yes?' said Kai.

'I never make jokes,' replied Gregoras, and Kai believed him.

'Is it about Horus?' asked Athena.

'Possibly, or one of his brothers, but there are many potential interpretations, so I cannot know for sure. There are still too many variables, and much of what I can glean is… of questionable veracity at best. Now, tell me again why you are interrupting my rest cycle.'

'The cognoscynths,' said Athena. 'What can you tell us of them?'

Gregoras leaned back in his chair and shook his head with a sigh. 'The last of the cognoscynths was slain thousands of years ago,' he said, 'Why do you wish to know of an extinct discipline?'

Kai hesitated before answering. Though there was nothing overtly threatening to Gregoras, he exuded bureaucratic threat with his clinical detachment. The kind of man who would sign a hundred death warrants in the same breath as asking for a pot of fresh caffeine. He had a bland, authoritarian coldness that warned Kai not to let his guard down and say anything foolish.

'I told you, I met one,' replied Kai.

Gregoras laughed, a dry cough of a laugh, and said, 'Impossible.'

'Does this look like something impossible?' asked Kai, pulling his robe away from his shoulder and once again revealing the bruise in the shape of a man's hand. The cryptaesthesian put down his book and examined the bruising on Kai's flesh. Against the paleness of his skin, it was a stark discolouration.

Gregoras laid his own hand on top of the mark. It fitted easily within the bruise. He reached down and pulled Kai's hand up to his shoulder. It too was smaller then the bruise.

'A big man with a large hand,' said Gregoras. 'Are you sure you did not fall afoul of one of Golovko's Black Sentinels and get frogmarched back to your cell? Be truthful, I will find out if you lie to me.'

'I swear to you that mark was not there when I went to sleep,' said Kai. 'I was getting dressed the next morning when I saw it. I can't explain how it got there.'

'Except by the presence of a psyker breed whose powers have been extinct for thousands of years or more,' said Gregoras. 'That is quite a leap of logic.'

'Well how do you explain it?' asked Athena.

'I don't have to explain anything,' said Gregoras, lacing his delicate fingers together on his lap. 'You are the ones who come to me. I *could* go into your mind and look for any lingering traces of another psi-presence, but it is not a delicate procedure, and it is not painless. Are you sure you are ready for such a painful intrusion to your mind?'

'I need to know for sure if I was just dreaming or if it was real.'

'Of course you were dreaming,' said Gregoras, as though that explained everything. 'You had a dream, Zulane, nothing more. As if wasn't bad enough that you return to us broken, you now tell me that you have lost the ability to tell dream from fantasy.'

'It was more than a dream,' insisted Kai.

'Any novitiate would say the same thing.'

'Kai is not a novitiate,' said Athena.

'Really?' snapped Gregoras, rounding on Athena. 'Yet he is quartered with them, and I am given to believe that he can no longer employ the *nuncio*. Nor is he capable of sending or receiving astro-telepathic communion. He is fit only for the hollow mountain. Am I incorrect in any of these statements?'

'As a matter of fact, you are,' said Athena. 'Kai has a long way to go before he is fully recovered from the incident on the *Argo*, but his abilities return with every passing day. I will have him back in the mindhalls before long, you can be sure of that.'

A surge of gratitude washed through Kai as Athena spoke in his defence. They had known each other for a short time only, and though their initial meeting hadn't exactly been a roaring success, their shared damage had at least established a common ground between them. Gregoras sensed her protectiveness and sat back with a slight smile playing around his thin lips. The cryptaesthesian took a shallow breath and brushed a piece of lint from his robe before opening the book in his lap.

'A cognoscynth is a powerful psyker indeed, one with a very distinct modus operandi,' said Gregoras. 'It would be hard for one to use his abilities on Terra without at least one operative of the City of Sight being aware of it.'

'So you don't believe me?' asked Kai.

'Let us say I maintain a healthy degree of scepticism,' replied Gregoras, 'but I will indulge your delusion for the moment and tell you of the cognoscynths.'

HALFWAY ACROSS THE galaxy, two men met in a glittering cave, far beneath the paradise world they called home. The walls of the cave sang with unheard harmonies, the music of a world alive with the background hum of latent psychic powers bubbling beneath the surface of the planet's consciousness.

One of the men was a giant, a towering figure robed in white and bearing a heavy leather book hung with small thurible and parchment strips. His name was Ahzek Ahriman, and among mortal men he was a demi-god, a figure of such awesome power and intellect that few of Terra's greatest minds could match him in contests of wit and knowledge. His face was downcast as he stared at the second figure sitting cross-legged on the rocky floor at the exact centre of the cave.

Though Ahriman was a giant, the seated figure was even bigger. Likewise robed in white, he was a strange individual, with skin like burnished bronze and a mane of crimson hair like that of a furious lion.

On this world, at this time, there could be only one individual that gathered the light and power of the cave into himself.

Magnus the Red. The Crimson King, Primarch of the Thousand Sons and Master of Prospero.

None who knew the primarch would ever give identical descriptions of his face, attribute the same colour to his eyes, or give the same impression of his humours. Inconstant as the wind or the ocean waves, no two aspects of Magnus could ever be the same, and the light from the glittering crystals carried by the hundreds of thralls around the edges of the cave was both reflected and absorbed by his skin.

A faint shimmer of illumination connected Magnus to a strange device hanging from the cavern's ceiling. Shaped like a giant telescope, its surfaces were carved with sigils unknown beyond this world, and silver vanes projected from a platinum rim around a giant green crystal at its centre.

For two nights Magnus had meditated, and for many more he had sat motionless beneath the bronze device as his acolyte read passages from the book in a never-ending recitation of formulae, incantations and numerical algorithms.

Had any of the polymaths of Terra been present, they would have wept at the beautiful complexity and lyrical simplicity of these equations. Devised by Magnus over decades of research and study, they were unique and known only to the Thousand Sons. A lifetime's worth of irreplaceable knowledge was bound within the pages of the book carried by Ahriman, and its incalculable value was beyond imagining.

The Chief Librarian of the Thousand Sons had not faltered in his reading, every complex syllable voiced with a perfection that would have made the most demanding captain of the Emperor's Children proud. He watched over Magnus with a son's love for his father, and though he believed in his primarch's genius and wisdom, he could not disguise the unease he felt at what they attempted here.

Magnus had not moved in four days, his subtle body crossing the unremembered and unknown reaches of the immaterium en route to a fateful meeting.

In his heart Magnus carried a warning for his father's Imperium, but in his actions he carried the seeds of its doom.

GREGORAS TURNED THE book in his lap around to face them, and Kai saw a colour plate spread over two pages depicting a scene of battle. Yet this was no ordinary contest of arms, it was a conflict between warring soldiers of Old Earth, fought beneath a raging, bilious sky that split apart with shards of lightning and grotesque faces pressing through the clouds. A leering sun bathed the scene with a hellish light, and the faces of the combatants were twisted, not in hate, but in terror and anguish.

'*Sargon of Akkad at the Gates of Uruk,*' said Kai, reading the caption beneath the picture. 'I can't say I've heard of this battle.'

'Unsurprising,' said Gregoras, 'though I presume you will have heard of the psi-wars?'

Kai nodded. Athena nodded.

'Of course you have, you would be ignorant psykers indeed had you not. Truth be told, little is known of those global wars with any certainty, just fragments culled from surviving records that escaped the purges of its aftermath. We believe they began, as all wars do, with ambition and greed, but it soon became clear that the warrior kings at each others throats were being directed by the will of power-mad individuals hidden in the shadows.'

'The cognoscynths?' asked Kai.

Gregoras nodded. 'Psykers are an uncommon mutation. Perhaps one child in a million may be born with some latent power. And of those children, perhaps a tenth will have power worth harnessing. The gene-code for the cognoscynth is two orders of magnitude rarer. Now I want you to understand what that means, for it is not just a hyperbolic phrase. Cognoscynths are considerably rarer than any normal psyker, so to have so many arise on Old Earth at once was an event so singular as to demand its own named epoch. Yet no such epoch exists in the records, for some times are best forgotten.'

Kai had heard a bowdlerised version of the early years of the psi-wars, but his knowledge was sketchy at best. That period of psyker history was not well taught at the City of Sight. No one wanted to remember a time where psychic powers almost destroyed the world, least of all the psykers themselves.

'Eventually it came to light that the great states of the world were simply pawns for powerful individuals who set nation against nation for their own savage amusement. No normal telepath could have done this, only one with the unique power of a cognoscynth.'

'Why would anyone want to do that?'

Gregoras shrugged, but said, 'You know the lure of psychic powers, Zulane. Despite the dangers, every astropath acquires a taste for using their powers. Once your mind touches the immaterium, it craves that wellspring of limitless potential like nothing else. Do you remember the first time you used your powers?'

'Yes,' said Kai, 'it was intoxicating.'

'Mistress Diyos?'

'My mind could reach across the heavens, and I felt as though I was part of the fabric of the universe itself,' said Athena.

'Indeed, but no matter how many times you achieve communion after that first time, it is never quite the same,' said Gregoras. 'Every communion is dangerous, but you still willingly hurl your mind into a realm of terrible danger just to feel that rush of its power again.'

'But you never can,' said Kai.

'No,' agreed Gregoras. 'And if you stop trying...'

'You get psi-sick,' finished Athena. 'Your mind aches for what it once had. I felt it when they brought me back from the *Phoenician* and I couldn't use my powers for weeks. I never want to go through that again.'

'The cognoscynths could maintain that first sensation,' said Gregoras. 'Every time they touched the warp was like the first time. They became addicted to the power, and it is said they were virtually immune to the dangers of the warp. No immaterial creature could touch them, and without limits on their power and ambitions, the cognoscynths became obsessed with dominating lesser men, believing that they alone could control the destiny of the species. And they had the power to do it.'

'I've heard rumours of what they could do, but it all seems too overblown, the kinds of powers ordinary folk *think* we have.'

'Whatever you have heard is likely true,' said Gregoras. 'There was little a cognoscynth could not do. After all, if you can control people's minds, you can do anything at all.'

'They could go into your mind and… change things?' asked Kai.

'They could go into your mind and do *anything at all*,' repeated Gregoras. 'For example, I could no more compel you to throttle Mistress Diyos than I could have you slit your own throat with a sharp blade. Nor, I suspect, could I convince you of the dissonant beauty of Dada's *Antisymphony*, no matter how hard I tried. Most people's own innate sense of self-preservation and understanding of right and wrong are too ingrained to overcome, but a cognoscynth could make you his puppet with no more effort than breathing. He could compel you do perform unimaginable acts of horror and make you laugh as you did them. He could erase your memories, graft new ones in their place and make you see what he wanted you to see, feel what he wanted you to feel. Nothing of the spaces in your mind that make you who you are would beyond his reach.'

Kai felt his skin crawl at such invasive psykery.

'No wonder our kind are feared,' he said.

'Our kind have always been feared, even before the psi-wars,' said Gregoras. 'It is the way of men that they fear what they do not understand and seek to bring it to heel. The aftermath of the psi-wars was a perfect excuse to do so. And here we are, shackled to a bleak iron city in the midst of the greatest fortress this world will ever see.'

'How did the wars end?' asked Athena.

'The legends say a great warrior with golden eyes arose, the only man whose will was strong enough to resist the influence of the cognoscynths. He rallied the armies of those few kingdoms left and trained a cadre of warriors like no other, stronger, faster and tougher than any of the great bands of old. One by one, they stormed the citadels of the cognoscynths on the backs of great silver flying machines. Not ever the most powerful cognoscynth could dominate the golden-eyed warrior, and every time he slew one of these psyker-devils, the enslaved armies were freed from bondage, and willingly joined the forces of the great warrior. It took another thirty years, but eventually his armies brought down the last cognoscynth, and the people of the world were free again.'

'And what became of the warrior?' asked Kai.

'No one knows for sure. Some legends say he was killed in the battle with the last cognoscynth, others that he tried to take power himself and was killed by his men.'

Gregoras paused and a wrinkle at the side of his mouth told Kai he was smiling. The gesture was unsettling, like the death grin of a corpse. 'Some even say the warrior still lives among us, waiting for the day when the power of the cognoscynths returns.'

'But you don't believe that?' asked Athena.

'No, of course not. To imagine that any such being could still exist is the stuff of children's tales and foolish saga poets. No, that warrior, if he even existed as the legends recall, is long since dust and bones.'

'Shame,' said Kai. 'The Imperium could use someone like him right now.'

'Indeed,' said Gregoras. 'Now that you know the true measure of a cognoscynth's power, tell me the substance of your so-called encounter with one.'

And so Kai took Gregoras through every stage of his dream: the Empty Quarter, the deserted fortress and the strange sounds and smells of a distant land that emerged from the air itself. He spoke of the harsh blue of the lake and the glaring red eye of the sun that beat down on the desert sands like a burning hammer. Finally, Kai ended his tale with the ghostly figure that drifted through the empty halls of Arzashkun with easy familiarity.

Gregoras sat opposite him as he spoke of his meeting with the figure, the unseen presence and the powerful grip he had taken on Kai's shoulder. He related all that the figure had said, and ended his tale by showing Gregoras the marks on his shoulder once more.

The cryptaesthesian licked his lips, and Kai struggled to hold back an expression of revulsion. The gesture was like a lizard's anticipation of a fresh meal, yet there was a tightness to Gregoras's posture that had been absent when they had first arrived at his chambers. Though it seemed hard to credit, Kai believed the cryptaesthesian to be worried.

'Tell me again of the sun,' Gregoras demanded. 'Speak, and be clear. How did it look, how did it make you feel? What imagery did you use to describe it? The metaphor and the impression. Tell me of them, and do not add or embellish. Just as you saw it.'

Kai cast his mind back to the moment before the robed figure appeared behind him.

'I remember the simmering heat of the desert, the salt-tang of the air and the rippling horizon. The sun was red, vivid red, and it seemed as though it was looking down on the world, as though it was a huge eye.'

'The red eye,' whispered Gregoras. 'Throne, he's almost here.'

'Who?' asked Athena. 'Who is almost here?'

'The Crimson King,' said Gregoras, looking beyond Kai at the impossibly complex pattern sketched out on the wall behind him. 'Sarashina, no! It's happening now. It's happening *right now*.'

* * *

FAR BENEATH THE birthrock of the race that currently bestrode the galaxy as its would-be masters, a pulsing chamber throbbed with activity. Hundreds of metres high and many hundreds more wide, it hummed with machinery and reeked of blistering ozone. Once it had served as the Imperial Dungeon, but that purpose had long been subverted to another.

Great machines of incredible potency and complexity were spread throughout the chamber, vast stockpiles and uniquely-fabricated items that would defy the understanding of even the most gifted adept of the Mechanicum.

It had the feel of a laboratory belonging to the most brilliant scientist the world had ever seen. It had the look of great things, of potential yet untapped, and dreams on the verge of being dragged into reality. Mighty golden doors, like the entrance to the most magnificent fortress, filled one end of the chamber. Great carvings were worked into the mechanised doors, entwined siblings, dreadful sagittary, a rearing lion, the scales of justice and many more.

Thousands of tech-adepts, servitors and logi moved through the chamber's myriad passageways, like blood cells through a living organism in service to its heart, where a great golden throne reared ten metres above the floor. Bulky and machine-like, a forest of snaking cables bound it to the vast portal sealed shut at the opposite end of the chamber.

Only one being knew what lay beyond those doors, a being of towering intellect whose powers of imagination and invention were second to none. He sat upon the mighty throne, encased in golden armour and bringing all his intellect to bear in overseeing the next stage of his wondrous creation.

He was the Emperor, and though many in this chamber had known him for the spans of many lives, none knew him as anything else. No other title, no possible name, could ever do justice to such a numinous individual.

Surrounded by his most senior praetorians and attended by his most trusted cabal, the Emperor sat and waited.

When the trouble began, it began swiftly.

The golden portal shone with its own inner light, as though some incredible heat from the other side was burning through the metal. Vast gunboxes fixed around the perimeter of the cave swung arround, their barrels spooling up to fire. Lighting flashed from machine to machine as delicate, irreplaceable circuits overloaded and exploded. Adepts ran from the site of the breach, knowing little of what lay beyond, yet knowing enough to flee.

Crackling bolts of energy poured from the molten gates, flensing those too close to the marrow. Intricate symbols carved into the rock of the cavern exploded with shrieking detonations. Every source of illumination in the chamber blew out in a shower of sparks, and centuries of the most incredible work imaginable was undone in an instant.

No sooner had the first alarm sounded than the Legio Custodes were at arms, but nothing in their training could have prepared them for what came next.

A form began pressing its way through the portal: massive, red and aflame with the burning force of its journey. It emerged into the chamber, wreathed in eldritch fire that bled away to reveal a being composed of many-angled light and the substance of stars. Its radiance was blinding and none could look upon its many eyes without feeling the insignificance of their own mortality.

None had ever seen such a dreadful apparition, the true heart of a being so mighty that it could only beat while encased in super-engineered flesh.

The Emperor alone recognised this rapturous angel, and his heart broke to see it.

'Magnus,' he said.

'Father,' replied Magnus.

Their minds met, and in that moment of frozen connection the galaxy changed forever.

EIGHT

Take but Degree Away
The Veil is Broken
Dreams of the Red Chamber

ANIQ SARASHINA'S DAY had begun badly. She woke at dawn with the lingering residue of a dream she couldn't remember filling her gut with a nauseous, roiling ache. It felt like the sickness she suffered aboard a starship just before it translated, but more persistent. The fact that she couldn't remember the dream was also troubling. The Mistress of the *Vatic* should have perfect recall of all her visions, for who knew what clues to the future were held there?

The rest of the morning passed in a dull haze, with her blindsight blunted, as though she had been drinking heavily or imbibing mentally unfettering narcotics with Nemo. It had been days since she had taken anything stronger than caffeine into her system, so it was doubly unfair to feel so wretched. For the first time since she had taken her place in the ranks of the Telepathica, Aniq Sarashina felt truly hampered by her lack of eyes.

An oppressive sense of claustrophobia hung over her as she spent a morning digesting the latest red-flagged communications passing through the City of Sight. In the wake of the Dropsite Massacre, as many were taking to calling it, the Imperium's armed forces were reeling, still on the back foot as Legion expeditions and Army groups attempted to reorganise their battle-lines and sort friend from foe.

Of the forces that had been betrayed on Isstvan V, almost nothing was known.

No word had been received from the Raven Guard, lending weight to careless rumours from *Er* scryers that Primarch Corax and his Legion had been destroyed utterly. A few elements of the Salamanders were believed to have escaped Isstvan V in disarray, but the only reports of this were third hand at best. Primarch Vulkan's fate was unknown, but many feared that he too was lost.

The Iron Hands were all but gone, their devastated chapters scattered to the winds in the aftermath of the primarch's death. Despite the completeness of the betrayal, Sarashina still found it hard to accept the idea that a primarch could die. But as shocking as it had been to learn of Horus Lupercal's betrayal, subsequent events were piling impossibility upon impossibility until now nothing was beyond belief.

Rogal Dorn's emissaries to the Whispering Tower demanded answers, but the Choirmaster had little concrete information to give them. Traitor fleets had cut the escape routes from the fifth planet, and for all intents and purposes the system was as dark as a dead moon. Nothing was getting in or out of the Isstvan system, no information, and certainly no loyalist warriors.

Worse, the defeat on Isstvan had galvanised scores of cowardly planets and systems throughout the Imperium to openly declare for the Warmaster. A sense of hurt betrayal and horrified incomprehension was paralysing the Imperium's response to this gross betrayal when decisive action was needed more than ever.

And then a ray of hope. A message from the very edges of the Isstvan system.

Garbled and fragmentary, but bearing all the synesthesia codes of the XVIII Legion.

The Salamanders.

Sarashina rushed immediately to the largest mindhall in the Whispering Tower.

Abir Ibn Khaldun was already in place, surrounded by the Choir Primus. Only the lambent glow of dimmed lumens cast light around the chamber, its ironclad walls coffered and deaf to the psychic white noise that filled it.

Two thousand astropaths of the Choir Primus reclined in their contoured harnesses, each struggling to distil a message hurled from the outskirts of the Isstvan system. Abir Ibn Khaldun sat in the centre of the chamber, wrestling with the confused allegorical concepts and baffling symbolism they were sending him.

Sarashina had briefly linked her mind to his, but could make no sense of the imagery she saw there. A mountain dragon drinking from a golden lake, an orchid emerging from the crack in an obsidian plain that stretched for thousands of kilometres in all directions, a flaming sword hanging motionless over a world utterly devoid of life or geography. Twins conjoined by a single soul, tugging in different directions.

What did any of it mean?

Choir Primus were the strongest second-tier psykers in the Whispering Tower, and could normally distil the interpretation of a message sent from the other side of the galaxy without difficulty, but what they were sending to Ibn Khaldun made no sense.

A voice sounded in her head, cultured and deeply lyrical.

~ *I confess I am all at sea, Mistress Sarashina.* ~

~ *As am I, Abir,* ~ she replied.

~ *It is as though the astropath is quite mad.* ~

~ *That may well be the case, who knows what they have gone through to get this message to us.*

Another thought occurred to her. ~ *Could the incoming message have been intercepted en route to us?* ~

~ *Perhaps, but such interference is patently obvious in most cases. This message evinces no such distortion. I believe that*

*whatever is warping this message is here on Terra, but I have
no clue what it could be.* ~

~ *Keep trying. Lord Dorn is expecting progress.*

Sarashina broke the link to Ibn Khaldun. He would
need every ounce of his concentration to make sense of
the message. Synesthesia confirmed that the message
had originated with an astropath of the Salamanders
Legion, but beyond its identity, nothing of its contents
made sense.

She sighed, feeling the beginnings of a pounding
headache building in her sinuses. Head pains were nothing out of the ordinary for an astropath, especially in
the presence of a demanding communion, but she could
already feel that this would be a bad one. A low-level
irritation had been griping at the back of her mind all
day, a persistent whining drone, like a desperate insect
trapped in a glass jar.

She wasn't the only one feeling it. The whole tower
was on edge, and not just the overtaxed astropaths. Even
the Black Sentinels were jumpy, as though the latent
pressure from the exhausted psykers was somehow
bypassing the psi-shielding of their helmets and racking
up their aggression. It felt like the drawn out moment
before a battle, where the tension stretched to unbearable levels before a single shot began the killing.

Despite the welcome news of contact with a loyal
Legion, Sarashina couldn't shake the feeling that this was
a harbinger of something so terrible that it was beyond
her ability to understand. She knew she was being melodramatic. After all, any event of such magnitude would
have seen by the *Vatic*. Future-scrying was an imperfect
discipline, but could anything as bad as she feared have
escaped the notice of her viewers?

She didn't know, and that scared her more than anything.

Sarashina felt something wet on her top lip. She
dabbed the skin and her fingertips came away sticky.
Blood was flowing from her nose in a steady stream, and

Sarashina let out a small moan as she tasted it on her lips.

'Oh, no,' she whispered as the steadily building pain in her head flared to a white hot spike of agony rammed through the frontal lobes of her brain.

Sarashina's blindsight distorted like a static-filled picter held too close to a powerful magnet, and she staggered as her balance was thrown off. The world tilted crazily, and she fell to the mosaic-tiled floor as an incomprehensibly vast tide of psychic energy surged into the mindhall.

THE CATACLYSM UNLEASHED by the arrival of the Crimson King and the breaking of the mighty wards around the golden gateway in the dungeons spread through the mountains like the blast wave of an atomic detonation. A tsunami of psychic force thundered upwards from the bowels of the palace in a raging torrent that touched every mind on the surface of the globe.

The gilded towers of the palace shook with the force of it, and priceless, irreplaceable statuary toppled from plinths as the shockwave trembled the very rock of the mountains. The madness, fear and panic that hung over the palace roared back to life like a resurgent wave of pestilence.

Mobs of lunatics bearing cudgels and brickbats laid siege to columned palaces and clashed with other mobs for no reason any one person could adequately explain. Blood flowed on the marble paved thoroughfares and golden processionals, madness stalked the illuminated galleries and insanity held court all across the roof of the world.

Yet as quickly as it began, the insanity of their actions became clear to the mobs, and they guiltily slunk from sight to lick their wounds, nurse newly-acquired griev-ances or shut themselves away from revenge attacks. Within minutes of the psychic shockwave, it had passed from the high summits of the palace and spread across the globe like the fiery advance of a plague.

Those on the dark side of the world suffered nightmares the like of which had not been seen since the bleakest watches of Old Night. Genetic memory of that horrific time of madness surged to the fore of sleepers around the world, bringing dreams of blood drenched metropolises, planetary exterminations and species slavery.

Entire cities of Terra awoke screaming and millions died by their own hand as their minds fragmented in the face of such psychic assault. Others awoke with their minds altered in fundamental ways that rendered them into entirely new individuals. Fathers, wives and children forgot one another as mental pathways were erased or rewritten in vulgar ways that wiped entire families from existence.

In places where the barrier between the material realm and the warp was already thin, manifestations of dreams and nightmares stalked the landscape. Black-furred wolves with burning lights for eyes descended from the mountains to devastate entire communities, and no weapon could slay them. Entire populations vanished as their towns and burgs were swallowed whole by catastrophic overspills of warp energy, leaving nothing but eerily empty buildings in their aftermath.

All over the globe, the people of Terra suffered for Magnus's hubris, but nowhere felt the shockwave of his return more powerfully than the City of Sight.

SARASHINA CLOSED HER mind to her abilities and threw up her psychic defences as colossal amounts of raw, unfettered psychic power bloated the chamber, like an overloading plasma reactor in the instant before its coolant system failed. She felt the tsunami of psychic power roaring over the mountains, a horrendous outpouring of warp energy unleashed from the very heart of the palace.

Even disconnected from her higher powers, Sarashina

felt the searing wave of psychic energy trapped in the mindhall find earthing conduits through the astropaths of Choir Primus. Five hundred died instantly as their minds were reduced to blackened cinders by a flash of supercharged psychic energy.

Choir Primus shrieked in unison, each suffering the agony of a slow, searing psi-death. Fully aware of their brains being seared from their skulls, the astropaths howled like wounded animals as their higher functions were burned away, until their crazed autonomic functions spasmed and broke limbs, spines and fractured skulls as they literally thrashed themselves to death.

Sarashina's mental defences were among the strongest in the City of Sight, but even she strained to hold back this unknown attack, her layered wards like a levee pounded by hurricane-driven waves. A cramping pain seized her gut, and Sarashina howled.

When the permeable wall between realities was torn aside by a starship's warp engines, every psyker within ten light years would feel a measure of discomfort.

This felt like she was chained in the terrible heart of a warp engine.

The pain was intense, translation pain, but there was no reason for it.

It felt like Terra itself was about to plunge into the immaterial chaos of the warp. The thought was ridiculous, but it lodged like a splinter in soft skin. In the instant of the thought forming, Sarashina felt a fiery sickness build in her stomach. She cried out and grasped her stomach as hot bile and the partially digested remains of last night's hastily snatched meal erupted from her mouth in a tide of acidic vomit.

The maelstrom of psychic energy raged around her, ravaging the minds and bodies of Choir Primus with its towering, elemental fury. The life-lights of the astropaths were being snuffed out one by one, as easily as a man might snuff out the candles of a mourning chamber.

But the choir did not die easily or quietly.

Sarashina tried to shut her mind off to the death-screams of the astropaths around her, but such a feat was impossible in the face of so unified a death cry. Memories dying, lives left unfinished and the terror of knowing that everything you were was being slowly, agonisingly, destroyed. The horror of your brain disassembling, and knowing there was nothing you could do to stop it. Every defence you had against it was futile, every mantra you had been taught to ward against such attacks useless.

Sarashina felt it all, every emotion, every horror, every last iota of loss and desperation. It flooded through her, permeating every cell of her body with anguish. Yet even as the astropaths died, they fulfilled their last duty. The surging, killing brightness of the psychic energy fuelled their powers to unimaginable heights for the briefest instant, making them – for a last shining moment – the greatest astropaths in the history of the galaxy.

Like madmen and prophets, the dead and the dying, they tapped deeper into the well of infinite knowledge contained in the warp. To the shape of things that had been, and were yet to come to pass. What a radical adept of Mars had sought to harness through technology, they broke open with the very power that was killing them.

It was intoxicating and numbing, overpowering and deadly.

The message from the Salamanders was obliterated, and their song immolated Abir Ibn Khaldun in a thunderclap of psychic discharge. Vast and incomprehensible power was distilled by the last breath of Choir Primus and shaped into a singularity of psychic energy that blared from Ibn Khaldun's last scream and burned with the light of a thousand suns in the heart of the chamber.

Impossible colours, undreamed of light from the universe's beginning and the knowledge of all things hung in the centre of the chamber like the frozen pulse of a neutron star. Even those without ability would have seen its glittering beauty had they somehow survived the initial blast wave of immaterial energy.

The last surviving members of the choir shrieked as geysers of light erupted from their scalps. Howling monstrosities and nightmare aberrations were carried on the light, searing their way into the material universe through living hosts. The majority of these formless spawn withered in the face of the hostile environment of the material universe, but others devoured the flickering remains of their dying brethren and grew stronger. They flocked in dirty scraps of debased light as Sarashina picked herself up from the floor, wiping drooled bile and vomit from her chin.

Klaxons and warning bells were sounding throughout the City of Sight and she heard gunshots from somewhere nearby. Evidently this mindhall was not the only place within the Whispering Tower to suffer breaches in the fabric of reality.

The warp creatures descended from the upper reaches of the mindhall, surrounding the sphere of impossible light where Abir Ibn Khaldun had once sat like weary travellers gathered around a cookfire. None of them were a threat to her, their substance too insubstantial and weak to trouble her, but their presence would draw the Black Sentinels. Already she could hear the soldiers beating at the locks of the sealed mindhall, but she paid the sound no mind, her attention firmly fixed on the shimmering, glittering light in the centre of the chamber.

It swirled like a ball of liquid gemstones, blue and white, green and red and every other colour imaginable. Inconstant and insubstantial, it appeared as dense as a black hole and as transient as mist in the same instant. Sarashina felt the siren song of its magnificent power and felt herself drawn to it as carrion-eaters are drawn towards rotten meat. The imagery disturbed her, for it was not of her own making, but conjured from the depths of this coalesced energy.

Sarashina had been fortunate never to suffer the pain of psi-sickness, but faced with this potency, her mind ached like a novitiate shorn of his power. Her entire

being craved this, and with every step she took, Sarashina knew she would not be able to resist its incredible
potential.

It swam in the air before her, the warp creatures parting
before her like a curtain at a production of the Theatrica
Imperialis. She felt their unthinking hunger for her, a
mindless desire to drain her of her very essence. With a
thought they retreated from her like whipped hounds. A
crashing detonation sounded behind Sarashina, but she
was oblivious to everything except the wondrous light
before her.

It promised so much, this doorway into a realm of
infinite possibilities.

Truth, knowledge, power.

The *Vatic* aspect of her powers saw the potential to
know the course of the future in perfect clarity. With that
knowledge she could forewarn the Emperor's armies and
be instrumental in stamping out the rebellion of Horus
Lupercal. In the space of a breath, she could know the
future of all things.

One touch was all it would take.

Yet still she hesitated, knowing on a primal and conscious level that nothing of the warp could be trusted.
The psi-sickness in her gut intensified, and the unclean
scraps of warp-life swirled around her in streamers of
ghostly light. No matter what warnings her higher brain
functions were screaming, she *had* to touch this power,
just to feel the heat at the heart of creation for one fleeting instant.

Sarashina reached out with trembling fingers and
touched the raw energy of the warp.

And screamed as she saw the red chamber in all its
infinite horror.

NINE

Sentinels
Where You Will Not Go
Saturnalia

EVANDER GREGORAS DRAGGED Kai through the chaos of the Whispering Tower like a child. Almost paralysed by choking terror, Kai stumbled through a red mist of horror as the sights and sounds and smells of the *Argo* returned to him with evil clarity. They had long since left Athena in their wake, darting along low-roofed corridors and narrow tunnels that seemed designed for emaciated midgets. The cryptaesthesian knew the tower intimately, bypassing the commonly trod halls and screaming mindhalls as the psychic shockwave echoed and roared within the city of the astropaths.

Kai had no idea what had just happened, but every scrap of self-preservation was begging him to find a place of safety. Screams clung to the air, the whisper stones carrying them around the interior of the tower like horrible secrets. Alarum bells rang and barking gunshots swiftly followed angry bellows from the Black Sentinels.

'Throne!' bellowed Gregoras. 'Pick up your feet, Zulane.'

'I can't,' sobbed Kai. 'I can't do this again.'

Gregoras stopped and backhanded Kai across the face.

The slap was shocking and sharp, the sound like split-ting wood. Kai flinched from the blow, blood and snot mingling on his top lip as he dropped to the floor like a beaten slave.

'Get up, damn you,' said Gregoras.

'Why?' hissed Kai. 'We're all going to die here. The dae-mons are coming in and they're going to kill everyone. I won't survive a second time.'

Gregoras hauled him to his feet, his previously bland and unremarkable face now clenched in fury. 'I said, get up! This is the pattern. Get up or so help me I will hand you over to Maxim Golovko myself and laugh as he puts a bullet in your brain.'

Kai wiped his bloody nose with the sleeve of his robe, understanding only a fraction of what Gregoras was say-ing.

'Why do you need me?' he asked.

'I don't know,' admitted Gregoras. 'I wish I did not, but this is what I have been searching for all my life. You have glimpsed a portion of it, and you will help me understand it. Do you understand?'

'No, not even a little bit.'

Gregoras shrugged. 'I don't care,' he said. 'You're com-ing with me anyway.'

He hauled Kai by the scruff of the neck, propel-ling him along an iron-framed corridor that looked as though it ran between one of the mindhalls and a sec-tion of the *Oneirocritica Alchera Mundi*. Whisper stones bled thoughts of rape and murder, torture and degra-dation, and Kai fought to keep them out. It had been thoughts like these that had turned the crew of the *Argo* into debased monsters, cannibals and violators of the dead.

Kai had only lived by isolating himself in his astro-pathic chambers, to which no one but the captain and his equerry had access. They had been the first to die when the protective shields collapsed, and though the fiends had clawed at his chambers, none could reach him.

While the monsters and maddened crew could not drag him from his sanctuary, he could not shut his mind to the horrors that devoured their humanity. He heard every scream from their murderous orgies and tasted the loathsome appetites of the creatures that emerged from their bloody murders.

Aboard the *Argo* he had a place of refuge. Here he was horribly exposed.

How could he possibly survive this?

He followed Gregoras blindly, dragged along in his wake, not knowing where they were going or what had happened to the tower. Were they under attack? Had the forces of Horus Lupercal already reached Terra and begun their invasion by crippling the Telepathica?

'What in the Emperor's name is happening?' he shouted.

Gregoras didn't answer, and Kai saw him crouch to run his fingertips over the notched marks on the wall next to him.

'Do you even know where we are?'

'Of course I know,' snapped Gregoras. 'We are in the bleed channels under the Zothasticron.'

'The what?'

'The bleed channels,' said Gregoras, running his hands along the opposite wall. 'The whisper stones gather the excess energies of communion and carry it down to the trap chambers beneath the towers. How else do you think we dissipate the psychic energy?'

'I didn't know we needed to,' said Kai.

'Then you are a bigger fool than you look.'

Despite his dislike of Gregoras, Kai wasn't about to abandon his only anchor of safety in this maelstrom of unleashed horrors. So far they hadn't seen anything beyond running Sentinels, but the flickering images of bloated bodies, fly-ridden corpses and skinless faces parading through his hindbrain told him that the Whispering Tower was now a place of horrors to match the *Argo*.

Gunfire echoed down the channel, followed by an explosion and the dull cough of grenade launchers. Kai heard screams, the sounds amplified by the acoustics of the narrow tunnel, but he couldn't be sure he was really hearing them or if they were being carried into his mind by the whisper stones.

'What's happening here?' asked Kai.

'Magnus is here,' said Gregoras.

'Magnus the primarch?'

'Of course Magnus the primarch, who else could unleash such powerful psychic force?'

'How can he be on Terra? He's halfway across the galaxy.'

'I don't know how, but Magnus the Red is here and his coming has unleashed power unlike anything you can possibly imagine.'

'So is this an attack?'

Gregoras took a breath as he considered the question. 'Not as such. I do not believe Magnus has betrayed us, at least not intentionally, but he has acted with such hubris that there will be no forgiveness for this act. The Emperor will have no choice but to make an example of him.'

'What does that mean?'

'You *know* what it means.'

'No, I don't,' said Kai. 'Tell me.'

'It will mean the Wolves will be loosed again.'

Kai shivered, unsure of what Gregoras meant, but knowing on a primal level that it would be unwise to ask more.

'Back in your chambers you said Mistress Sarashina's name,' said Kai. 'Is she in danger?'

'The very worst kind,' confirmed Gregoras, finally finding the mark he sought on the walls. 'The warp is giving her exactly what she wants. Damn, but I should have seen this. The Maiden and the Great Eye. Truth and the future, all bound together. The silver vixen, the heralds of the final truth. It all makes sense now.'

Gregoras was rambling now, random phrases from

his insane researches spilling from his lips like a madman's stream of consciousness. None of it made sense, but nothing of this made any sense. Who better to make sense of madness than a madman?

'I don't understand what you're talking about, but if Mistress Sarashina is in danger, then we need to help her.'

Gregoras nodded and said, 'If it is not already too late for her.'

KAI AND GREGORAS emerged from the bleed channels in one of the central hub chambers towards the base of the tower. Yellow light flashed from warning lumens and a number of bodies were stacked like cordwood at the entrance to one of the libraries. Kai gagged at the stench of blood and the actinic tang of lasfire. Streams of hard light blasted into the library from a ranked up squads of Black Sentinels.

Another group worked at the door to the Choir Primus mindhall, rigging melta charges to detonators, while Maxim Golovko paced impatiently behind the demolition crew like a caged predator. Alone of the Black Sentinels, Golovko went without a helmet, an open insult to the psykers of the Whispering Tower.

I do not fear you or need protecting from you the gesture said.

A handful of Black Sentinels spun to face them as they emerged from the channel, rifles brought to bear with exacting precision and speed.

'Hold!' cried Gregoras. 'Protocol cryptaesthesian!'

The guns were lowered, and Golovko strode through their ranks as more gunfire blasted into the library. The major general was livid, yet Kai sensed that he was taking great relish in his task of extermination.

'I might have known I would find you drawn to the heart of this,' he said.

'Sarashina is in there?' said Gregoras, pushing past the commander of the Black Sentinels.

'With the Choir Primus,' replied Golovko. 'Do you know what's happening?'

'I have my suspicions, but we don't have time for discussion. You need to get that door open. Now.'

An explosion blew out a choking cloud of dust, splinters and mulched paper from the library, and a howling scream of something unnatural rang from the walls. Whisper stones shattered with glassy pops, and Kai felt a surge of bloodthirsty rage fill him. His teeth bared and his fists clenched, but it passed as soon as Gregoras touched his shoulder. Kai felt the anger pour out of him, blinking away the red veil that had descended on him.

Gregoras had one hand on his shoulder, another pressed against a whisper stone that had survived the psychic surge.

'Think!' snapped Gregoras. 'Maintain your defences.'

Kai nodded, ashamed he had allowed his mental buttresses to become so weakened in his fear of what was happening.

'Get some null grenades in there,' said Golovko, his tone brusque, but clipped and businesslike. 'Don't let that happen again.'

Kai had never liked Golovko, but the man had just endured a psychic attack without flinching. The only sign of the strain of holding it at bay was a pulsing vein at his temple that throbbed like a hydraulic pipe. Golovko saw his look and shook his head with a sneer.

'It'll take more than that to get by this soldier.'

Kai didn't answer, and concentrated on maintaining his own wards against the power washing from the library. Through the smoke and sliced up bodies at the entrance, Kai saw a swirling morass of light and flesh, a patchwork monstrosity formed from still-living hosts and torn flesh given form and mobility by immaterial energies. He looked away as the entity sensed his scrutiny and wisps of light darted towards the door.

'Don't look at it,' hissed Gregoras. 'You of all people should know better than that.'

Another volley of gunfire stitched across the nascent form of the thing in the library, followed by a dull *crump* of psychically resonant grenades. Immediately the air took on a thick, grainy quality, and the raging static of the warp spawn diminished to bearable levels.

'Yeltsa, get in there and push that thing out of my tower,' ordered Golovko, before turning back to the mindhall of Choir Primus. 'How's that breaching charge coming on?'

'Done, sir,' replied the demo-tech, backing away from the rigged door and handing the detonator box to Golovko.

Kai and Gregoras pressed themselves to the walls as Golovko stood in front of the door, unlimbering a bulky grenade launcher from his back.

'Remember that's Aniq Sarashina in there,' said Gregoras.

'We don't know what's in there,' said Golovko. 'But if it's hostile, it's going to die.'

'If you kill her, you'll answer to the Choirmaster.'

Golovko shrugged and pressed the activation thumb-switch on the detonator box.

Kai had been expecting a thunderous detonation and had his ears covered, but the melta charges simply glowed a fiery blue-white, and the only sound was the hiss of metal flashing to superheated liquid in seconds. Gobbets of molten metal drooled down the carven face of the door as the charges burned through the lock.

Golovko dropped the detonator and racked the loading tube of his grenade launcher.

He kicked the door open, and a host of gibbering voices flew from the unsealed chamber. Shrieks of babes yet to be born and corpses cold in the ground for millennia blasted from the mindhall, a chorus of the dead and still to die coalesced in one almighty bellow of fear and regret. Golovko stood firm in the face of this cyclone of the dead, unmoved and uncaring of their torments or lives unlived.

Kai felt the torrent of unleashed psychic energy and winced as it battered the defences of his mind. He felt the horror of each death within the mindhall, and impossible tears spilled down his cheeks as he felt the last moments of each of the astropaths within. A pale light, like a beacon lit far beneath the surface of a clear ocean spilled from the mindhall, wavering and uncertain. It threw Golovko's shadow out behind him and, for a fraction of a second, Kai could have sworn his face was a mask of blood, as though some nightmare parasite had exploded from within his skull.

'Are you coming in then?' asked Golovko, and the impression of his horrific injury vanished. 'I might need your help.'

Gregoras pushed himself from the wall and Kai saw his indecision.

'I'm coming with you,' he said. 'If Sarashina's in trouble, then I want to help.'

Gregoras nodded and they set off after Golovko. A dozen Black Sentinels came with them, and they plunged into the wavering, uncertain light. The mindhall was cold, like a frozen tundra, and the floor crunched with newly-formed ice beneath their feet. Spiderwebs of frost crazed the wooden panels of the lower tiers, and puffs of ventilated smoke rose form the backpacks of the Black Sentinels.

Kai kept close to Gregoras, knowing on a very basic level that the cryptaesthesian was helping to shore up his mental defences. The power at work within the tower was so great that Kai didn't think he'd have been able to resist it were it not for his help.

It was difficult to see exactly what was happening in the mindhall. The light at its centre was so powerful it outshone everything else. Kai had the powerful impression of a black silhouette, a black slice of limbs touching a sun that burned with a blinding sapphire light.

'Mistress Aniq!' he shouted, and the words left his mouth in a trail of colourful smoke, giggling gleefully as they took form and life before dissolving into the fertile air. Gregoras shot him a *say nothing* look, and Kai's mouth snapped shut before he could do anything else stupid.

The Black Sentinels spread out, rifles raised and grenades primed. Golovko marched at their head, the bulky launcher held out before him. He said nothing, but his manner suggested that he had seen this sort of thing before, though Kai couldn't imagine where. He'd heard of warp-spawned creatures using astropaths as vessels to force their way into the material universe, but an entire mindhall?

Scraps of light swirled at the apex of the chamber like flocking birds, and Kai forced himself to look away from them. As his eyes began to adjust to the power of the light, he lifted a hand to his face and looked up into the tiers surrounding the centre of the chamber.

The astropaths of Choir Primus lay rigid in death, their eyes alight with eldritch fire that streamed from their useless sockets like phosphorent smoke. Their mouths were stretched in skeletal grins, and that same dead light burned between their burned lips as though they were screaming light.

The Black Sentinels surrounded the sphere of light, and Kai saw its surface was alive with writhing patterns, sun-bright streamers and spiralling grooves of emptiness. It shone like a miniature sun, but one that was the antithesis of Terra's star. This was a dead sun, one that sucked life from the bodies around it.

Aniq Sarashina stood before the dead sun, her hand outstretched and bathed in the fires of its unnatural energies. Corposant lines of raw energy coiled up her arms, and her flesh was translucent. Veins, bones and muscle were plain to see, and the same light that streamed from the eyes of Choir Primus burned in hers.

Kai wished he could cry, for the sadness he felt was all too real. Mistress Sarashina was dying, any fool could see that, and there was nothing anyone could do about it. He wanted to save her, as she had once saved him from a life wasted, but he could do nothing but watch as the warp light burned her away from the inside.

Ghosts of energy limned her body with ectoplasmic mist, creatures that pressed almost too lightly on the matter of the universe to be seen. They were little more than shimmers of consciousness, barely able to hold their presence in this world, yet they swirled protectively around Sarashina as though she was a prize they were unwilling to relinquish.

'Gregoras?' said Golovko. 'How dangerous are these things?'

'They are nothing,' said Gregoras. 'Base desires given form. They cannot hurt us.'

'Really? This seems like quite an intrusion for something so powerless. Doesn't seem like nothing to me.'

'They are opportunistic parasite creatures. They crossed over when the walls collapsed.'

'And what about that ball of light? Should I be worried about that?'

'When you are dealing with the warp you should always be worried.'

'So how do you destroy it?'

'You don't,' said Gregoras. 'I do.'

Gregoras stepped towards the sphere of light, his hands outstretched, and Kai felt the build up of potent psychic energy. Gregoras was already a powerful psyker, with abilities Kai would never be able to understand or wield, but in the aftermath of the Crimson King's arrival on Terra, his strength was so much greater.

'My mind is untouchable. It is as a locked room,' he said. 'None can enter without my authority. You have no power over me.'

The creatures of light withdrew from him, recognising a more powerful entity than they could hope to overcome. The burning sun seethed in mute rage, its brightness diminished, but still awesomely powerful.

'These are not the fields you know,' continued Gregoras, infusing every syllable with power and will. 'This world is not yours and you do not belong here. Leave and befoul this place no more.'

The creatures hissed soundlessly, but retreated still further. They were not completely cowed, for they had a wellspring of energy to draw upon. The sphere of energy spun with ever greater urgency, as though its purpose here was not yet done, and a keening screech filled the mindhall. Kai's hands flew to his ears, and even Golovko winced at the piercing volume.

The black armoured Sentinel commander took aim over the oversized barrel of his grenade launcher.

'No!' yelled Kai. 'Please.'

At the sound of his voice, Sarashina turned towards him, and Kai felt her pain descend upon him. She knew she was dying, but she had held on for just this moment. Kai sank to his knees as he saw the weight of guilt and sorrow within her. He saw the anguish that she had been forced into this path, but beyond that was the determination that she would not fail, as though the fate of the galaxy itself hung upon what she must now do.

'Don't you move,' warned Golovko, taking a step forward.

Sarashina didn't even acknowledge him and took another step towards Kai.

Despite the cold, Kai was sweating, imagining what kind of dark power burned inside Sarashina. Gregoras shouted at him to move back, but Kai was pinned in place by Sarashina's fiery eyes. They were locked to his, and Kai's body was no longer his to command.

Gregoras began chanting the words of banishment, words taught only to the highest ranking members of the Telepathica, for to use them was to know the powers of the creatures of the warp, and such knowledge was not taught lightly.

Kai felt Sarashina's grip on life slipping, as Gregoras poured his will into stopping her in her tracks. Golovko grabbed Kai's shoulder to haul him away, but a sharp bang of energy threw him back. Smoke rose from where Golovko had touched him, but Kai was unhurt by the fire. Dimly he recalled that was where the robed stranger in his dream, the cognoscynth, had laid his hand.

'Get away from him!' screamed Gregoras, pouring all his power into his words of banishment.

'I am not here to hurt him, Evander,' said Sarashina, the words sounding as though the woman who spoke them was falling farther and farther away with every passing second.

'Then why are you here?'

'To give him a warning.'

'Warn him of what?'

'A warning he must pass on to another.'

Gregoras approached Sarashina warily, as though unsure whether to continue his words of banishment or abandon them in the hope of learning something of value from Sarashina.

'Is it the pattern? Tell me, Aniq, is it the pattern?'

'Yes, Evander, it is,' replied Sarashina, 'but it is so much bigger than you ever knew. Or ever will. Not even the Emperor knows it all.'

'Please, you can tell me,' pleaded Gregoras. 'What is it? What have you seen?'

'Nothing you would ever want to know,' said Sarashina, turning her gaze upon Kai once more. 'Nothing *anyone* should know, and for that I am truly sorry.'

'Sorry?' said Kai. 'Sorry for what?'

Sarashina darted forward, fast as quicksilver, and took hold of Kai's head with both hands. The light that burned in her eyes flared, and Kai screamed as a host of burning, screaming, violent, bloody and sharp-edged images poured through him, filling his brain to capacity and beyond. Kai screamed as his mind sought to process this immense flood of information. A billion times a billion pictures, events, memories and perceptions flashed through his consciousness, the sensory input of a life lived over thousands of years. No mortal brain could contain such a vast repository of knowledge. Such a wealth of experience could only be contained by a mind that existed outside the physical world, a mind that was not constrained by physical limitations of flesh and blood.

Amid the chaos of his overfull mind, Sarashina's voice cut through the crescendo of new thoughts like a diamond blade.

This warning is for one person, and one person alone. You will know who when you see him. Others will seek to know what I have given you, but you must never tell them what you have learned. They will break you open to learn what I have told you, but they will not find it. I will hide it in the one place you will not go.

Kai's augmetic eyes rolled back in their sockets, and tears of blood spilled from his eyes. The world receded to a white point of light.

He heard the booming report of a heavy gun, a splash of warm wetness on his face.

A light was snatched from the world, and the torrent of life flowing into Kai was abruptly cut off, like a data cable wrenched from a Mechanicum logic engine. From a deluge of a thousand images every instant, one single image expanded to crystal clarity.

A face, ancient and wise, ruthless and single-minded.

A man who was so much more than a man: a warrior, a poet, a diplomat, an assassin, a counsellor, a killer, a mystic, a peacemaker, a father and a war-bringer.

All these and thousands more.

Yet it was his eyes that captured Kai's attention.

They were the most beguiling colour of warm honey.

Like coins of the purest gold.

KAI OPENED HIS eyes and found himself looking at the bare iron dome of the mindhall. The watery light from the dead star was gone, and the harsh illumination of arc lights filled the space with an unforgiving clarity. He wanted to sit up, but his limbs were locked to his side. His head ached abominably. Shooting pains stabbed his brain repeatedly, and he groaned as what felt like the mother of all migraines surged to the fore of his skull.

Colours flashed before him, sickening and dizzying. His gut lurched, and he fought to keep his bile from exploding from his gullet. This wasn't psi-sickness, this was overload. Just as too little use of an astropath's powers was painful, too much could be just as debilitating.

'What...?' was all he could manage before a face appeared above him, upside down.

'You're awake,' said Gregoras.

'I think so,' he said. 'What happened?'

'What do you remember?' said Gregoras, moving around so that he was the right way up.

'Not much,' said Kai. 'I feel terrible. Why can't I move?'

Gregoras nodded and looked down at Kai's body. Kai followed his gaze and saw that he was bound at the wrists and ankles by shackles of gleaming silver. Intricate carvings were acid-etched into the metal, and Kai zoomed in on them.

'Warding sigils?' he said. 'Why am I in chains covered in warding sigils?'

Gregoras sighed. 'You really don't remember what happened when Sarashina touched you?'

Kai shook his head and Gregoras looked up at something out of his eye line.

'First of all Golovko shot Sarashina in the head,' said Gregoras. 'Now I never liked her much, but she didn't deserve that. Gunned down like a common criminal.'

'She's dead?'

'Didn't you hear what I said? She was shot in the head by a Black Sentinel. Nobody survives that, Zulane.'

'You still haven't answered my question,' said Kai, the sickening pain in his head shortening his already finite patience. 'Why am I chained?'

'For safety. Yours and mine.'

'I don't understand.'

'No, you don't,' said Gregoras. 'I suspect you never will.'

'What's that supposed to mean?' demanded Kai.

'It means I was right to think you were going to be

trouble.'

Heavy hands came from behind and hauled Kai to his feet. His limbs felt like rubber, as though the strength had been drained from him, and he stumbled as his legs tried to bear his weight. The hand that held him upright kept him from falling without effort. His flesh ached and his skin felt as though a low-grade electric charge ran over its surface.

Kai's own shadow was thrown out before him, an elongated slice of blackness. Two shadows went with it, but these were broader and longer by far, the shadows of giants. Kai turned to see what manner of ogre stood behind him, and the breath caught in his throat as he saw the two figures that had lifted him from the floor as though he weighed nothing at all.

Their armour was unblemished gold, heavy plate and tightly-hammered mail weave, with kilts of segmented leather and brushed steel. Cloaks of the deepest crimson were fixed to their shoulders by carven pins in the shape of lightning bolts. Both wore tapered helmets, one with a dangling horsehair plume of blood red, the other with silver wings affixed to the cheek plates.

They carried tall spears with ivory coloured hafts, each one terminating in a blade as long as Kai's arm and bearing a monstrously large projectile weapon slung beneath the cutting edge. The plates of their armour were not smooth, they bore intricately carved renditions of words that curled around greaves, along the edges of breastplates, beneath pauldrons and around gorgets.

'Legio Custodes...' breathed Kai.

Kai had heard that Custodians earned their names through the course of their enhanced lives, and if that were true, then these warriors were clearly long-lived specimens of the order. They stood immobile as the golden statues said to guard the great subterranean pyramids of the sub-stratum deserts of the Sudafrik, but Kai guessed they could spring into action faster than he could think.

'Kai Zulane,' said one of the golden giants, the one

with the silver wings on his helm.

'Yes,' replied Kai, surprisingly calm at facing such a deadly warrior.

'I am Saturnalia Princeps Carthagina Invictus Cronus Ishayu Kholam, and you are bound by Imperial law to my custody. If you attempt to escape or employ any facet of your astropathic abilities, you will be terminated instantly and without recourse to any higher authority. Is anything I have said unclear?'

'I'm sorry, what?'

The giant leaned forward, and it seemed to Kai that the red eye lenses of his helmet narrowed. Saturnalia's head inclined to the side and Kai tried to imagine what thoughts must be going through the Custodian's mind. Saturnalia looked over at Gregoras.

'Has be been made imbecilic?' asked the Custodian.

'No,' answered Gregoras. 'I believe he is simply confused.'

The Custodian found this puzzling. 'I was quite clear.'

'Nevertheless,' said Gregoras. 'If you will allow me…?'

Saturnalia nodded and stood upright.

'I don't understand what's happening,' said Kai. 'Where are they taking me? I haven't done anything.'

'Sarashina touched you, a powerful telepath who was, if not possessed, then at least acting as a conduit for high level warp intelligences using her *Vatic* abilities. Whatever passed through her is now inside you, and we are going to find out what it is.'

'We? Who is we?'

Saturnalia answered that question. 'The neurolocutors of the Legio Custodes,' said the Custodian. 'You are being taken to the dungeons of the Imperial Palace, and whatever is in your head will be stripped out by men skilled in the obtaining of information at any cost.'

'Wait!' said Kai, turning to Gregoras. 'You can't let them take me! I didn't do anything.'

His cries fell on deaf ears, and the cryptaesthesian simply watched as the Custodians fastened a brass circlet around Kai's temples.

'No! What's that?' cried Kai.

His question was answered a second later as he heard a soft buzzing sound and his nervous system shut down, leaving him limp in the grip of the Custodians

'No!' wept Kai. 'Please, I'm begging you. I don't know anything. She didn't pass anything to me, I swear. You're wasting your time, please! You're making a mistake!'

'The Legio Custodes does not make mistakes,' said Saturnalia.

'Gregoras!' yelled Kai. 'Please help me! I'm begging you!'

The cryptaesthesian did not answer, and Kai screamed as he was dragged from the mindhall towards a steel gurney and interrogators equipped with scalpels, trepanning drills and invasive neuro-psychic probes.

PART TWO

THE VEILED CITY

Can you imagine what it means to be blind?

Truly blind, not the simple removal of the visual sense or the temporary darkness of night, but utterly bereft of sensation. That is what they think they have done to me by severing my connection to the Great Ocean, but such a concept displays a literalness of thought that betrays ignorance of the warp's true nature.

It is all around me, no matter what my gaolers believe, but it pleases me to let them think they have wounded me with their damping collars and walls impregnated with psi-resistant crystals. I felt the cataclysmic arrival of my gene-father in the depths of the palace, and I still feel the havoc that resonates around the globe in its aftermath. I touched the mind of the Crimson King and I saw a measure of what drove him to such desperate action.

Though I am Athanaean, the foresight of the Corvidae and the vanity of the Pavoni are not unknown to me. Nor are the visceral arts of the Raptora or the Pyrae beyond my reach, though it irritates me to wield such vulgar powers. An Adept Exemptus of the Thousand Sons is master of many things and is a more terrible foe than anyone here understands.

But it is well to keep your foes ignorant of your true strength.

All war is deception, and wars are won by those who can best conceal their blows.

I can hear the thoughts of my caged brothers, the controlled anger of Ashuba and the febrile rages of his twin. The dour gloom of Gythua is amusing in small doses, as are the petulant diatribes Argentus Kiron composes. No one who matters will hear them, but his desire to perfect his outrage knows no bounds.

All of them rage at the injustice done to us, not one of them understanding that it could be no other way. Tagore still broods on the insultingly small force sent to apprehend us, but his rage is spread thin: at our captors for coming for us in the first place, at the men who killed his fellow warriors, at his Legion for abandoning him.

But most of all, it is directed at me for not warning them.

How can I begin to explain my reasoning to him when I do not understand it myself?

It was not the words of the psi-hunter that persuaded me to stand aside. His words were as meaningless as the random mind-noise of warp-scraps. Rather, it was the dream that stayed my hand, the dream of the icy, blue-lit tomb that gave me pause.

In my dream I walk its frozen catacombs and I see that the ground is littered with shards of glassy bone. Millions carpet the flagstones, pouring from the broken sepulchres in an endless tide. I see each individual fragment, each one reflective and carrying a memory etched on its vitrified surface.

A great red eye reflected in broken shards of bone.

I know this eye. I know it well, and it is speaking to me of a terrible crime, though I do not yet understand what it is saying.

It is a bleak place, this tomb where I wander in the bleak light of torches frozen in time, their flames unmoving and lifeless. The dead are all around me, I can feel them looking at me. The weight of their accusations is like a curse, to use a pejorative of the ancients.

Though this is a city of death, it is frighteningly beautiful.

Rearing statues of hooded reapers and spiteful angels adorn the grand avenues of the dead, their expressions frozen at their most tempestuous.

Something flits past at the edge of my vision, something vividly coloured in this landscape of the morbid. It darts between the towering, monolithic statuary, a scavenger creature that could not possibly be here. I recognise its tapered snout and rust-coloured fur, the black edging to its ears and feet.

Canis Lupus, a species extinct for thousands of years, yet here it is.

I am no Biologis, but somehow I know this creature will not die here. The wolf shadows my path through the blizzard of bone, drawing closer with every passing moment, though I wave my arms and shout bloody threats at it. Seeing that the wolf will not be dissuaded from its approach, I ignore its presence and concentrate on where my steps carry me.

Towards a monstrous statue, one that was not there a moment ago, but which rears from the landscape like a vast missile emerging from a silo. It is the winged statue of a faceless angel, fashioned from a strange, twilight black stone. Bone dust falls from its wide shoulders, and avalanches big enough to bury one of the Terran hives thunder past. Like any initiate of the word of Magnus, I understand the symbolism of powerful elemental forces, and know full well the times of upheaval they herald.

I sense something within this statue, something malevolent watching through its smooth featureless face.

As I am aware of its presence, it too is aware of me.

The sky above this newly emerged statue gleams with dull metal and golden spires. A starship hangs motionless above this mausoleum city. Its pristine blue paint been burned away, and only the pearlescent stubs of its master's insignia remain to indicate that it was once a vessel of the XIII Legion. The ship's name is etched into its hull in letters hundreds of metres high, the curling script hammered onto its adamantium hull in the shipyards of Calth.

The Argo.

I know this vessel. It is a ghost ship, gutted from within by *nightmarish creatures of sublime horror. Red-scaled skin, oily black tongues and eyes that reflect every vile thought you ever had. Everyone on that vessel is dead, and their deaths weigh heavily on the conscience of one who draws ever nearer.*

He believes it is his fault. I know this with a certainty that is as unshakable as it is ludicrous. What could he possibly have done to condemn that incredible vessel to such a violent death?

Yet certainty is foolish in a place like this, a place where truth and lies can cross the vast gulfs of space in an instant. I deal in the intangible, the allegorical and the phantasmal, yet I assert certitude. The irony is not lost on me.

Only then do I realise I am not alone, there are others with me.

I recognise them and I see that they are all dead. Ghosts yet to be. They lament their passing and try to tell me of the manner of their deaths, but their words are nonsensical and I cannot understand them. By their own choosing, each one of them is outcast and dead. Each one has been slain for reasons only he can know, be it honour, pride, vanity or a hunger for knowledge.

Noble reasons all.

I listen to their doomed mantras and I sing them lustily to the shining beacon of light that reaches out to the farthest extent of the galaxy.

The one the Eye has spoken of is here.

TEN

Praetorians
Psychic Excavations
Blood Protects its Own

BENEATH THE PEAK known as Rakaposhi, the Legio Custodes kept their gaol – where those individuals deemed hostile to the Emperor were isolated from the world above. Dug into the rock of the mountain, its limestone walls were clad in adamantium plate, resistant to virtually all forms of weaponry and deaf to the pleas of innocence that echoed from its cells.

In an ancient, long-dead tongue, it had been known as Khangba Marwu, an all too literal name that gave some clue to its age. Only the most senior Custodians bothered to use its original name, and to those condemned to its cells, never again see the light of day, it had an altogether more prosaic name.

They knew it simply as the Vault.

Khangba Marwu had always been part of the mountain, or at least so it seemed to those who even knew of it. It had always been a site of incarceration, a hidden place to cage the most violent, the most dangerous, and the most reprehensible evils the world had known. No one knew who had first hacked its cells and passageways from the bedrock of the mountain, but its origins went far beyond the limits of memory and surviving documentation.

Stories of the heinous criminals incarcerated in its lightless depths stretched back thousands of years, their names now meaningless and their crimes long forgotten. Yet there were villains aplenty plucked from living memory who had darkened its sterile corridors and died insane within its unfeeling walls.

The lieutenants of the Pan-Pacific tyrant had been brought here, as had the Ethnarch of the Caucasus Wastes, the so-called 'First Emperor' and a being known only as the Reaper – a monster that legend said was an angel sent to cleanse mankind from the world. Uilleam the Red, the tyrannical blood-drinking prince of Albyon had been brought here for execution after his defeat at the Battle of the Blue Dawn. Uilleam's debased followers conquered a quarter of the globe, but were finally halted by an army of powerful warriors raised by a Nordafrik warlord known as Kibuka, who was said to have called lightning from the clouds and granted his warriors superhuman strength. In time, Kibuka himself was hauled in chains to Khangba Marwu, but no history remained to tell of who had overturned his rule.

A persistent rumour told that the Emperor himself had designed a cell especially for Narthan Dume, but which had gone unused following the tyrant's death during the final battle to bring down his inhuman regime. Scurrilous whispers maintained it had been the urging of Constantin Valdor that saw Durme executed in the ruins of his empire, a half-mad, half-genius psychopath deemed too dangerous to live.

Cardinal Tang had been bound for this specialised gaol, but like Durme he never saw the inside of his cell. Inmates who had suffered the worst tortures imaginable in his bloody pogroms broke open his isolation tank and tore his body apart with their bare hands before his transit from Nusa Kambagan could be arranged.

In all its long history, only one individual had ever

escaped Khangba Marwu, a congenital dwarf named Zamora who was said to have once attained the rank of major in the proto-Legio Custodes, a fact that made the stories of his escape all the more ridiculous.

Since the beginning of the Great Crusade, Khangba Marwu had seen no shortage of inmates, deluded fools and doomsayers who raved and ranted of the Emperor's folly or greedy opportunists who sought to exploit this new golden age for their own benefit. None of those incarcerated could boast a pedigree as infamous as Tang or Durme or Uilleam, but that would all change once this rebellion was put down.

Khangba Marwu's most impregnable cellblock was even now being made ready to contain the most dangerous individual in the galaxy.

But could any facility on Terra hope to hold Horus Lupercal prisoner?

PRIMUS BLOCK ALPHA-ONE-ZERO was never dark. The diurnal phases of the planet above were inconsequential to the workings of the Vault or the needs of its inmates. Darkness was an aid to escape, and was thus banished. Uttam Luna Hesh Udar halted before the last security checkpoint before the cells, allowing the bio-metric surveyors in the walls, floor and ceiling to verify his identity.

Air-samplers tasted his breath, body-mass sensors registered his weight and radiation detectors measured the decay rate of isotopes in his blood and bones. Over a hundred such measurements and genetic markers were compared against real-time data logs to ensure no intruders were able to penetrate Khangba Marwu's security net without detection.

Uttam wore the gold armour of a Custodian, the cheek plates of his full-face helm folded back into its layered structure. His features were unmoving and expressionless, the result of a greenskin bacteriological pathogen that had left the upper right quadrant of his face unresponsive to muscle stimulus. His enhanced metabolism had easily purged the toxin, but the after-effects of the injury had reduced his reflexive response times to a level below the minimum required for front line service.

A proud man, Uttam had taken his removal from the fighting ranks of the Legio Custodes hard, but he had adapted and taken to his new role as gaoler of the Vaults with the same determination and attention to detail that had seen him closest to full infiltration in a Blood Game until Amon Tauromachian Leng's most recent attempt.

Uttam had studied the young Custodian's route to the palace, finding no fault with any of his decisions until the final moment when he had chose to throw caution to the wind and leap to the attack like a common assassin. Uttam would have drawn his victim in like a struggling insect in an arachnid's web.

Far better to let the prey do the work and subtly calve it from its protectors.

Uttam stared into the blank slate above the armoured doorway, letting the retinal signifiers examine his eyes. This part always took longer than usual, his damaged eye making the machines work hard to establish his identity. This deep in the Vault, such measures were virtually unnecessary, but protocol was protocol, and Uttam never willingly ignored protocol.

The thought made Uttam turn to glance at the procession of veteran soldiers following him. Chosen from the most professional regiments based on Terra, they were armed with a collection of strange weapons, ranging from web-guns, plasma nets, iso-capacitors and mass-crushers to more commonplace melta-guns and hellguns.

A full head and shoulders over even the tallest soldier, Uttam could barely contain his disdain as they filed past the signifiers. It sat ill with him that these men were not Custodians, for the threat rating of the prisoners kept in Primus Block Alpha-One-Zero was far too lethal for these men to face, regardless of what weaponry they

carried. Significant levels of the Legio's operational
strength had been despatched on a mission to Prospero
alongside the Space Wolves. The purpose of the mission
had not been stated, but there could be only one reason
to send so many of the Emperor's praetorians from his
side at such a time.

Two soldiers in crimson battle plate and gold-mirrored
visors guided a metallic box shaped like an oversized
coffin floating on repulsor fields. A standard nutrition
dispenser, it had been modified by the Vault's Mechanicum staff to provide the specialised foodstuffs of these
prisoners. Uttam found it incomprehensible that these
men had been allowed to live. They were the most dangerous men on Terra, and no good could come of their
continued existence.

The signifiers confirmed the identity of last of the soldiers, and the armoured door slid upwards with a hiss
of pneumatics and a gust of cool air that spoke of a vast
open space ahead. Beyond the door, the iron-sheathed
walls of the prison complex gave way to the rough-cut
stone of the mountain's footings. The smell of cold earth
and stone that had once rested beneath the deepest
ocean blew from within. Glaringly bright lumen globes
provided stark illumination and banished shadows.

Thirty metres in, a pair of servitor-crewed turrets
spooled up and snapped towards them, clicking and
whirring as target locks were established. Heavy calibre
autocannons whined with the rotational speed of their
barrels as Uttam stepped into the killing box.

'Uttam Luna Hesh Udar,' he said, enunciating each syllable with precise modulation.

The augmetic eyes of the servitors changed from red
to green, and Uttam ushered the soldiers through as his
rearguard warrior approached.

Sumant Giri Phalguni Tirtha was a veteran Custodian,
whose name was said to bear at least seventy-six awarded
titles. His armour was polished and carved with words of
approbation in addition to his earned honours. Uttam

did not know how Tirtha had come to Khangba Marwu. He bore no obvious injury and was in prime physical condition, but rumour said he had once questioned an order from Constantin Valdor.

The master of the Legio Custodes was a stern, uncompromising man, and though Uttam had never had the honour of meeting him, he doubted Valdor was so petty as to banish another from his side for so slight an offence. The Legio valued thinking warriors, doggedly determined men who would question and question again until an answer was forthcoming.

'Is there a problem, Uttam?' asked Tirtha. 'Why do you pause?'

'No reason,' said Uttam, ashamed at his lapse into speculation.

'Then let us be on our way,' said Tirtha. 'I dislike being here, the air stinks of them.'

Uttam nodded. The air *did* taste different. The unique physiology of the prisoners made them different from mortals, even Custodians, in many obvious ways, but also in many less evident ones. Whatever crimes a man might have committed, he was still recognisably human, still clearly part of the human race. These prisoners smelled subtly different… almost *alien*, and that rankled almost as much than their betrayal.

Almost.

'Biometrics confirmed,' said Uttam, and the security door slid closed behind Tirtha. As the metres-thick locking bars slid home, he said, 'Primus Block Alpha-One-Zero is now sealed and secure.'

'So confirmed,' said Tirtha, striding to the front of the column. Uttam now took up the rearmost position, and took short steps as Tirtha led them down the wide corridor. Though they were selected from the bravest and most professional regiments still based on Terra, there was no disguising the soldiers' nervousness as they passed between the turrets. Though rigorous safeties had been engaged by Uttam's command, they guns could open fire in a heartbeat, and the green eye-lenses of the servitors promised no mercy to anyone caught in the killing box.

Uttam followed Tirtha and the soldiers towards a wide archway lined with las-mesh emitters, through which came the bass note of colossal generators and the actinic tang of powerful energy fields. Uttam passed beneath the arch, emerging into an enormous cavern, a kilometre wide at its narrowest part, with glistening walls and a dizzyingly high roof. The cavern had no floor, simply a bottomless pit that spanned its entire width. Uttam knew that such a term was hyperbole of the worst kind, but it was apt for all intents and purposes.

He stood on a wide platform built at the edge of cavern, in the shadow of a slender bridge of latticed steel that reared up like the body of an enormous crane. Tirtha stood at its control console, and Uttam watched as he manoeuvred the bridge towards an island of rock that floated in the centre of the cavern, suspended on a hazy cushion of invisible energy.

Enormous machines like vast engines were bolted around the circumference of the cavern walls and Uttam felt the hairs on the back of his neck stand to attention in the electro-statically charged air. At a moment's notice, these generators could be disengaged and the island would be allowed to plummet into the depths of the world. With such dangerous prisoners, no chances could be taken.

The bridge made contact with the floating island, and a host of automated gun pods mounted in the walls of the cavern swung long barrels to bear on the island. Thirty isolated cells stood on the floating rock, but only twelve housed inmates.

With the bridge in place, Uttam marched onto the bridge, with the soldiers and Tirtha following behind him. The bridge rang with the sound of his armoured boots, and he kept his gaze focussed firmly ahead of him. He unlimbered his guardian spear from the quick-release sheath on his back and rolled the muscles in his shoulder to loosen them in readiness.

'Expecting trouble?' asked Tirtha over the helmet vox.

'No,' replied Uttam. 'But I always feel better facing these bastards with a weapon in my hands.'

'I know what you mean,' said Tirtha. 'I almost hope one of them tries something.'

'Don't even joke about it,' warned Uttam as he reached the end of the bridge.

The first cell was a square block of triple-layered and ceramite-laced permacrete that gave little clue to the nature of the inmate within. Featureless aside from an alphanumeric designation stencilled on its side and a transparent door of armaglas normally found in the viewports of starships, it was a box that no one entered or exited without the say so of the Legio Custodes.

Uttam approached the door, feeling a familiar knot of tension in his gut: the flush of endorphins and battle stims that preceded a combat engagement. The sensation was welcome, even though he did not expect to fight here.

A single figure sat cross-legged in the centre of the cell, his muscular physique barely contained by the bright yellow of his prison-issue bodyglove. Long hair, dark as oil, spilled around a broad face with genetically spread features that should be ugly, but somehow combined in a handsome whole.

Though this prisoner was deadly beyond words, he had a smooth grace that was disarming. Uttam knew better than to underestimate Atharva simply because he came from a Legion of scholars. Where the others raged or spat biliously at their gaolers, Atharva appeared to accept his incarceration without rancour.

Atharva opened his eyes, one a glittering sapphire, the other a pale amber.

'Uttam Luna Hesh Udar,' said the warrior. 'You are interrupting my ascent into the Enumerations.'

'It is time for you to eat,' said Uttam, as the nutrition

dispenser was slotted home in the clear glass of the door. A cellulose bag of foodstuff dropped into the cell, and Atharva watched it fall with a mixture of distaste and resignation.

'Another day, another banquet,' said the Thousand Sons warrior.

'You are lucky we feed you at all,' said Uttam. 'I would let you starve.'

'Then you would become the villain of the piece,' said Atharva. 'And as the Emperor's praetorians that must never be the case, is that not so?'

'Do not say his name, you are not fit to speak it, traitor.'

'Tell me, Uttam, whom had I betrayed when I was brought here?' said Atharva, uncoiling from his seated position to stand in one smooth movement. 'When Yasu Nagasena led his three thousand into the Preceptory, who *exactly* had I betrayed? No one, yet here I am locked up in a cell with warriors whose Legions are rightly named oath-breakers.'

'When a group has a plague-carrier in its midst do you only remove those who are sick or do you quarantine the entire group?' asked Uttam.

'Allow me to counter your example,' said Atharva. 'If a man develops a tumour, do you selectively destroy it with treatment or do you simply kill the man?'

'The tumour dies either way.'

'Then let us be thankful you are not a medicae, Praetorian Uttam Luna Hesh Udar,' said Atharva.

THEY CAME BACK to him in the darkness, every face, every scream and every last, terrified breath. Kai lay on a hard stone bench that doubled for a bed, and curled in a foetal ball, rocking back and forth as he tried to forget the memories of pain they forced him to relive. A flyer had carried him from the Whispering Tower, high into the mountains, through starlit cloudbanks and moon-painted peaks of dizzying height.

That had been his ascent. Then had come the descent

into the lightless depths of a mountain that seemed somehow darker, somehow more threatening than any mountain had a right to be. As though it carried a weight of anguish borne by those taken into its depths.

Down corridors and through echoing passageways he was taken. Into rumbling elevators and pneumo-cars that carried him deeper and deeper into the unknown reaches of the sullen mountain until at last he was deposited in a bare cell, cut directly from the rock, with only the most basic human functions catered for. A rusted pipe in the corner of the room dribbled brackish water, and a circular pit in the opposite corner appeared to be a receptacle for bodily waste.

The walls were painted a faint bluish grey, glossy and hard-wearing. Previous occupants had scraped their presence into the walls with broken nails and whatever else could make an impression in the paint. Primitive, primal things, Kai couldn't make out what many of them were: random collections of lightning bolts and men with long spears for the most part. The carvings were little more than desperate pleas to be remembered by men now long forgotten and, presumably, long dead.

Kai wanted to add his own mark, but he had nothing with which to score the painted walls.

His captors had left him to sweat for an unknown period of time, letting the imagined horrors to be inflicted upon him do their work for them. Kai was not a brave man, and he had screamed that he would tell them what they wanted to know if he only knew what it was.

Though his mind was racing in a dozen different directions, Kai forced himself to sleep, knowing that whatever was to come would be more easily endured were he rested. He dreamed, but not of the Rub' al Khali, not of the great fortress of Arzashkun, but of a cold void, populated by the voices of the dead. He saw a blonde-haired girl with a blue bandanna he had known on the *Argo*. He knew her name, they had been friends of a sort, but his memory was hazy, too overwhelmed with the chattering voices of the dead.

They swarmed his dream-self, begging to know why he had been spared and they had been taken. Why the monsters of the deep had come for them with their brazen swords and chitinous claws that tore meat from bones and left gouging wounds that would never heal.

Kai had nothing to tell them, but still they demanded answers.

Why, on a ship of innocents, had he been one of only two to survive?

What gave him the right to live while they were condemned to eternal torment?

Kai wept in his sleep, reliving the horror of their deaths over and over again.

Only one voice was free of accusation, a soothing, cultured voice that spoke without words, but eased him from memories of pain with visions of a paradisiacal world of high mountains, verdant plains and beautiful cities of glittering pyramids constructed from crystalline glass.

When he woke, it was to find two people standing in his cell, a man and a woman, blandly attractive and dressed in crisp white tunics that had the look of lab coats and hazmat gear all in one. The man was the kind of handsome that comes from fashionable cosmetic sculpting, whereas the woman had lavished all her attention on her eyes. Pale emerald orbs, they were the most captivating eyes Kai had ever seen.

'You're awake,' said the man. Needlessly, thought Kai.

'It's time we found out what you know,' added the woman.

Kai rubbed his face, feeling the sagging skin of his jowls and a day's worth of stubble.

'I told you, I don't know anything,' said Kai. 'If I did, I promise I would tell you. I barely remember anything that happened in the mindhall.'

'Of course, we don't expect you to have any conscious

recall of the information implanted in you by Aniq
Sarashina,' said the woman, her expression plastic and
unchanging. 'But it is in you, that much is certain.'

'It's our job to remove that information,' said the man.

'Fine,' said Kai. 'Hook me up to a psi-caster and let's be
done with it.'

'I'm afraid it won't be quite that simple,' said the man.

'Or that painless,' added the woman.

'Who are you?' asked Kai. 'You're not part of the City of
Sight, so who do you work for?'

'My name is Adept Hiriko,' said the woman, 'and this
is Adept Scharff. We are neurolocutors, psi-augers if you
will. That's auger with an *e*.'

'As in a drill,' added Scharff. 'My role is to assist Adept
Hiriko in boring into your psyche and rooting out whatever information has been secreted within your mind.'

'Are you serious?'

'Quite serious,' said Scharff, as though puzzled as to
Kai's meaning. 'We are here at the behest of the Legio
Custodes. Our orders come with the highest authority, giving us carte blanche to achieve our goals by any
means necessary.'

'I'm afraid it is likely you will not survive the process,'
said Hiriko. 'But if you do it is more than probable that
you will be left in a permanent vegetative state.'

'This is insane!' cried Kai, backing away from these
monsters.

'If you think about it clearly, it's really the only option
open to us,' said Scharff.

'We anticipated you would be reluctant to help us,'
added Hiriko. 'How disappointing.'

KAI COULD NOT speak. A gum shield that prevented him
from biting off his tongue filled his mouth with a rubberised, antiseptic taste. An air pipe plunged down his
throat, and a leather headpiece studded with needles
and electrodes enveloped his head like a pilot's helmet.
A wealth of intravenous drips fed into his veins and the

blood vessels beneath his skull, while a lid-lock held his eyes open. Slender output jacks were plugged into the base of each orb, and bronze wires trailed to banks of ocular-visual recording equipment.

The interrogation chamber was horribly mundane, a simple metal box without windows or mirrors or anything in the way of character. Portable banks of monitoring equipment surrounded Kai as he lay back on a steel-framed gurney, each one telling a tale of his internal biorhythms.

A humming device like a gleaming scorpion's tail was bolted to the metallic floor behind him, arching overhead and festooned with dangling instruments that seemed designed to terrify as much as provide any function. Hiriko and Scharff busied themselves with monitoring the drugs flowing into his bloodstream, while the gold-armoured figure of Saturnalia stood at the far end of the chamber, his guardian spear held loosely in one hand.

'Are you ready to begin?' asked the Custodian.

'Almost,' replied Hiriko. 'This is a delicate procedure, and one doesn't want to rush.'

'The information you seek has been well hidden, Custodian,' added Scharff. 'We will have to go deep into his psyche, and such a journey requires faultless preparation.'

'We risk breaking his mind without due care and attention.'

The Custodian took a step towards the psi-augers, his fingers clenching tightly on his guardian spear.

'The Mistress of the Telepathica spoke of the Emperor,' said Saturnalia, 'and anything that concerns the Emperor is my business. Do not waste time in telling me of preparation and semantics. Find what she placed in his head, and find it now. Breaking his mind is a price that concerns me not at all.'

Kai wanted to rage at them, but his mouth couldn't form the words. He wanted to yell that he was a human being, an astropath of value to the Imperium. But he knew that even if he could make them hear, they would not care, Saturnalia because his duty to the Emperor overrode all other concerns, Hiriko and Scharff because they were simply doing a job.

He tried to struggle, but the restraints and drugs held him utterly immobile.

Hiriko sat beside him on a wheeled stool, and consulted a data slate hanging from the side of the gurney.

'Excellent,' she said. 'You're making wonderful progress, Kai. We should be ready in just a moment.'

Adept Scharff sat opposite Hiriko and Kai saw him insert a screw-plug into the back of his neck, where he could just see the gleam of implanted cognitive agumetics. He took the other end of the cable and plugged it into a featureless black box fitted to the side of the gurney. He smiled at Kai, unspooling a thin cable from the box and snap fastening it to a connective port on Kai's leather headpiece. His eyes lost their focus for a second, and Kai felt a stab of pressure in the frontal lobes of his brain.

'Are you in the umbra?' asked Hiriko.

'Yes,' answered Scharff, his voice distant. 'Ready for your insertion.'

'Good,' said Hiriko, and likewise wired herself up to the featureless black box. She too fastened the end of a cable to the apparatus covering Kai's skull and, once again, he felt the pressure of an invasive presence within his mind.

'Now,' said Hiriko. 'Let us begin.'

She depressed an orange stud on the side of the box, and Kai's mind filled with light.

THE LIGHT GREW to unbearable brightness, like the surface of a star viewed so close that it would burn his eyes away. Kai screamed, and the light faded until it became tolerable. He found himself standing in the middle of the desert, nothing around him for hundreds of kilometres in all directions. A hot wind feathered the lips of dunes around him, and the hammerblows of the searing sun were a welcome relief after the sterile environment beneath the mountain.

This was his place of safety, this was the Empty Quarter.

Whatever they had done to him hadn't worked.

Kai knew this wasn't real, knew it was an artificially conjured dreamscape, and in that realisation, he knew he should not have come here. This was what they wanted. They wanted him here, where his innermost thoughts were laid bare, and his deepest secrets might be revealed.

Though he had professed a desire to tell Hiriko and Scharff what they wanted to know, an unbidden imperative arose in his mind that warned him against that path of least resistance. His life depended on keeping what he had been given secret. Only the man with the golden eyes could be told what he knew, and only by keeping it safe from Hiriko and Scharff would that be possible.

No sooner had he given them names, than he felt their presence in his mind. He couldn't see them, but he knew they were there. Lurking, waiting for him to lead them to what they wanted to know.

A figure appeared on the sand beside him, a robed woman with long silver-grey hair with eyes that were kind and warm. He knew her, but not like this, not with eyes of flesh and blood. They were emerald green, sparkling and full of life. It seemed perverse to have willingly exchanged such beautiful eyes just to have gained protection from the creatures of the warp.

'Aniq,' he said. 'You're dead.'

'You should know better than that, Kai,' said Sarashina. 'No one is every really dead so long as someone remembers them. As the great poet said, "that which is imagined, need never be lost."'

'Sarashina told me that, but you are not Sarashina.'

'No, then who would you have me be?' said the woman, her features transforming in a heartbeat to those of his mother. Her eyes remained emerald green, but where before there was warmth, now there was only aching sadness.

Kai turned away from those eyes, remembering the looks of sorrow every time he and his father had left on another adventure across the globe. He fought to remain dispassionate, but it was difficult in the face of the woman who had raised him and helped shape him into the man he had become.

Except this wasn't her.

His mother was dead, just as Sarashina was dead.

'You are Adept Hiriko, aren't you?'

'Of course,' said his mother.

'Then look like you're supposed to,' snapped Kai. 'Don't hide behind disguises.'

'I wasn't hiding,' said Hiriko, assuming the form with which Kai was more familiar. 'I am simply trying to put you at your ease. This process will go much smoother if you don't fight us. I know you don't know what Sarashina told you, but I need to find it.'

'I don't know where it is.'

'I think you do.'

'I don't.'

Hiriko sighed and linked her arm with his, guiding him towards the gentle slope of a sand dune. 'Do you know how many psychic interrogations I've done? No, of course you don't, but it's a lot, and the subjects who fight us are always the ones who end up brain dead. Do you want that?'

'What kind of stupid question is that?'

She shrugged and continued as though he hadn't spoken. 'The human mind is a dizzyingly complex machine, a repository of billions of memories, inputs, outputs and autonomic functions. It's hard to break into it without causing irreparable damage.'

'So don't break in,' said Kai.

'I wish that were possible, I truly do,' said Hiriko with a smile. 'I like you, but I will tear the meat of your mind apart with my bare hands if I have to. Everyone yields their secrets in the end. Always. It's just a matter of how much damage they're prepared to live with at the end of it.'

They reached the top of the sand dune, and Kai found himself looking down at the shimmering fortress of Arzashkun. Its tallest towers wavered in the heat, and Kai shielded his eyes against the reflected glare of sunlight from its golden minarets.

'Impressive,' said Hiriko. 'But it won't keep me out. Don't think for a minute it will.'

Kai stopped and turned about, scanning the sands for some sign that they weren't alone. A suggestion of shadow moving under the sand on a far distant dune flickered at the corner of his vision.

'Where is Scharff?' he asked. 'Doesn't he join you?'

'He's here, but I'm leading this auger.'

Intuition surfaced in Kai's mind like a sunrise, and a slow smile creased his features.

'He's here to pull you out if this gets too dangerous, isn't he?'

A flash of irritation in her emerald eyes confirmed his insight.

'You don't know if you can do this, do you?' he said.

Hiriko's grip on his arm tightened. 'Trust me, I can do this. The only question is how hard you want it to go. I'll demolish that fortress in a heartbeat, tear down every fictive stone and brick. I'll break it down to dust and powder until you won't be able to tell its remains from the sand of the desert.'

She stretched out her hand, and the tallest tower of the fortress began unravelling. What had seemed solid only moments before was now dissolving into smoke and vapour. She clicked her fingers and another tower fell apart. Hiriko met his gaze as she undid in a heartbeat what had taken him years to perfect, but his eyes were on something far distant, something fashioned from dark memory and horror. It pushed through the sands towards them, the predator with the scent of blood in its nostrils.

Kai felt a spike of pressure behind his eyes and Hiriko turned in time to see the dark shape power to the surface of the sand. It came on a tide of blood, a subterranean river violently thrust to the surface of the desert. It roared, this river. It roared and screamed and filled the world with thousands of death cries and agonising last moments. Like a deluge of crimson oil it spilled over the desert, filling the depressions between the dunes with pools of stinking death fluids, washing up their slopes like an angry tide.

'Is this your doing?' demanded Hiriko.

'No,' said Kai.

'Stop it,' ordered Hiriko. 'Now.'

'I can't.'

'Of course you can, this is *your* mind. It bends to your will.'

Kai shrugged as the swelling lake of oily blood rose higher, its surface rippling with the motion of thousands of hands and faces pushing up from below. Until now, Kai had always feared this buried monster, its rages and its guilt, but now the sight of it was a blessed relief. The oozing tide rolled uphill in defiance of hydrodynamics, and gelatinous shapes at last broke the surface of its stinking substance. Tall and thin, with spindly limbs of red scale and volcanic breath, they folded themselves into existence with thin, screeching wails. Their distended skulls formed glossy and horned, their mouths ripped open with jagged fangs.

Creatures of memory to be sure, but no less dangerous for that in a place of dreams.

'What are you doing?' demanded Hiriko.

'I told you, it's not me,' said Kai. 'It's the *Argo*.'

The tide of night-skinned monsters roiled towards them, and Hiriko looked up to the sky.

'Get me out of here,' she said. 'Now.'

The adept vanished, and the tide of darkness that billowed and seethed like a living curtain of endless darkness spilled over the top of the dune, swallowing

Kai and plunging him into an abyss from which there could be no escape.

'WHAT JUST HAPPENED?' demanded Saturnalia.

Hiriko lay on the floor of the interrogation room, her eyes rolling back in their sockets, and blood running from her nose like a tap. Scharff propped up her head and administered a hypo of clear fluid via a canula on her forearm.

'I asked you a question,' said Saturnalia.

'Be silent!' said Scharff. 'I just extracted her from a hostile dreamspace without any of the proscribed decompressions. Her mind has gone into shock, and if I don't bring her back we might lose her completely.'

Saturnalia bristled with anger at being spoken to like a subordinate, but bit back his anger. Consequences for speaking out of turn to a warrior of the Legio Custodes could wait.

'What can I do?' he said.

'Nothing,' said Scharff. 'It's up to her now.'

Scharff continued to speak to Hiriko in low, soothing tones, stroking her cheek and holding her hand. Eventually, her eyes fluttered open and gained a clarity Saturnalia hadn't been sure she would ever know again.

'This is going to be harder than I thought,' said Hiriko.

ELEVEN

Erosion of the Self
An Open Door
Aeliana

TIME BECAME MEANINGLESS to Kai. Days, weeks and months passed in his dreamscapes, passages of time that bore no relation to the waking world. He recalled ceramic tiled rooms, rocky passageways and the glacier blue walls of his cell, but which of these experiences were real was beyond his ability to guess. The psi-sickness had gone from him, washed away in the daily exercises of his ability to enter a *nuncio*-receptive state.

He was fed and bathed, for he lost control of his bodily functions when severed from the routine cycles of existence. So much time was spent in realms of the senses beyond those endured by mortals blessed without psychic powers that Kai grew ever more disconnected from what was real and what was imagined.

He thought he saw his mother, standing at his cell door with a wistful expression. Her green eyes drew him in, but no sooner had he opened his mouth to speak to her than a black figure loomed behind her and drew a blade across her throat. An ocean of blood spilled from her ruined neck, a thousand voices screaming in the darkness.

Once, as he wandered a desolate plain of ashen grey, Kai thought he saw a shining figure armoured in red and ivory. The figure was calling to him in a language Kai did not know, but which faded in and out of clarity as a ghostly wind rose and fell. Kai wanted to run to the warrior, feeling that he represented some kind of salvation, but each time he turned towards him, the warrior retreated as though not yet ready to face him.

Time and time again, the neurolocutors went into Kai's mind. Sometimes Scharff, sometimes Hiriko, but each time they were cast out by the oily black thing and the howling revenants of the *Argo*. In the few moments of lucidity Kai grasped onto, he spat hatred and admiration at the late Aniq Sarashina. Hiding her message in his memories of that doomed vessel had been a masterstroke. As much progress as Kai had made, she knew he was not yet ready to face the horrors unleashed upon that ghost ship.

He could sense the growing frustration of his captors, and revelled in it.

They quickly abandoned such direct attacks on his psyche and changed tack to more subtle, less invasive approaches. While Scharff attempted to reason with him, Hiriko attempted seduction. Pleasure dreams, power dreams and a thousand gratified desires were paraded before Kai in myriad guises. Some masqueraded as reality, some as fantasy, but none could reach the buried secrets contained in the black horror of the *Argo*.

'We cannot remove it,' said Hiriko after a particularly gruelling session. Kai's face glistened with sweat, his body a husk of papery skin draped over a thin collection of bones, wasted muscle and sunken meat.

A giant loomed over Kai, and his augmetic eyes whirred as they shifted focus. Saturnalia's broad cheekbones and tapered jaw stared at him with contempt written all over his features.

'Why not?'

THE OUTCAST DEAD 215

'It is buried deep inside a memory he will not face,' said Scharff.

'The *Argo*?'

'Indeed,' said Hiriko. 'Sarashina, or whatever was acting through her, knew what she was doing. It is most aggrieving.'

'So if you can't get it out, who can?' demanded Saturnalia, and Kai could feel the man's urge just to kill him and be done with the matter.

'Only one person has the key to unlocking the information you require,' said Hiriko.

'Who?'

Hiriko placed a hand on Kai's shoulder. 'Kai himself.'

Kai laughed, but the gum shield in his mouth turned it into a gurgling sob.

THE CRUDITY OF their methods was what angered him the most. Like chirurgeons attempting brain surgery with a logger's saw and stonemason's chisel, they hacked into delicate aetheric structures of mental architecture without thought or hope of success. Atharva felt every brutal thrust of the psi-augers, their clumsy attempts to hack out the information they sought, and the childishly simple blandishments they hoped would seduce it to the surface of their captive's mind. Like a clawed gauntlet down a blackboard, the shrieking squalls of their brutish methods pained him on every level.

Like any true craftsman, amateurish work offended him, and though he was by no means certain that he could lift something evidently buried deep in the captive's mind, he would have a better chance than the two butchers they had working here.

He sat cross-legged in the centre of his cell, letting his mind wander the labyrinthine passages of Khangba Marwu, testing the boundaries of his confinement with casual ease. It amused him to let his gaolers think him confined to his cell, going slowly mad with the isolation like his brothers. It had been months since

Yasu Nagasena had come for them, and in that time the captive warriors of the Crusader Host had seen no one but the two Custodians and their woefully inadequate company of mortal soldiers.

Atharva had touched each and every mind within this subterranean prison, some lightly, others less gently. A mind was like a delicate lock, the tumblers of each psyche requiring the precise amount of pressure before it yielded all its secrets. The trick was in recognising the correct points to apply that pressure, the exact memories, desires or promises that would open a mind like a new blooming flower.

To an adept of the Athanaean cult, it was skill of no great consequence to lift thoughts from the surface of a mind. Far greater challenge was to be had in going down through the layers of a mortal consciousness, to plunge beyond the random surface clutter, past the basic desires and drives, beyond the secret vices and petty depravities lurking in the sewers of every individual to the heart of a person. This was where the truth could be found, the lightless place where the naked beast of existence lurked and every thought was exposed.

Reaching this place without detection was a talent few possessed, but one which Atharva had honed in his many years as a truth-seeker. Ever since the Crimson King had rescued the Legion from destruction, the truth-seekers had been the first to serve in the ranks, scouring the dormant minds of those who had been saved from the horror of the Flesh-Change for any latent signs of weakness.

Atharva knew his mortal gaolers better than they knew themselves. He knew their fears, their desires, their guilty secrets and their ambitions. He knew everything about them, and it amused him to know how simply their minds were assembled. How could any living thing that professed self-awareness function with such basic cognitive faculties?

Ah, but the Custodians…

Their minds were things of beauty, artfully-wrought arrangements of psychic engineering and genetic perfection. Like the most complex machines imaginable, they were like steel traps ready to snap shut on an unwary intruder. Like a cogitator protected from infiltration by a skilled infocyte, their minds were fully able to defend themselves from attack, and Atharva had not even attempted to do more than drift the outer edges of their brilliant consciousnesses.

Yet even though the Custodes were fascinating beyond measure, Atharva's thoughts were forever drawn to the mind the psi-augers were attacking. At first glance, there was little to distinguish this person from the hundreds of others incarcerated here, save the modicum of psychic ability and the glassy scarring left by the Soul Binding.

He understood the man's selfishness, the entitled conceit bred by years spent with Guilliman's Legion. Understandable, but not the man's true self. He was better than he knew, but it was going to take great hardship to strip that away, a process that had already begun, but would likely be left undone before his death.

Kai Zulane was the man's name, the man the Eye had spoken of, but it was a name unknown to Atharva. Even with all the man's memories laid bare, there was little to indicate what interest anyone could have in him. Yet there was something buried within him that not even Atharva could see, something wrapped in a black horror of raw aetheric rage and guilt that would be impossible to remove without the right tools.

Force was useless, this horror was stronger than any threat of violence. Likewise, it could not be appealed to by external reason or promises of gratification. This was an ordeal that could only be ended from the inside, yet what treasures might lurk within so heavily guarded a prison?

Atharva loathed mysteries, and this was one that demanded to be revealed. His scholar's brain had to unravel this secret. The Crimson King had taken an ill-advised step in coming to Terra, but his arrival had shown Atharva what needed to be done. Kai Zulane was vital to the future in ways no one could understand, but if there was anyone who would relish the chance to prise open his mind, it was a mystic of the Thousand Sons.

Atharva opened his eyes as a pack of guards moved past the glass door of his cell. All but one managed to avoid looking in his direction, and Atharva flicked a barb of his consciousness into the man's mind.

He was called Natraj, and Atharva smiled at the appropriateness of the name. Natraj was a soldier in the Uralian Stormlords, an elite drop-troop regiment that had served the Imperium since the early years of the wars of Unity alongside the gene-septs of the southern musters. His wife was raising their five sons in a hydro-farm collective on the slopes of Mount Arkad, and his brothers were all dead. Natraj was an honest man, a good man, but a man who no longer wished to serve in the Imperium's armies.

His devotion to his fellow soldiers and the oaths he had sworn before the regimental Ark of Wings bound him to his role as soldier and gaoler, but Natraj was nearing his fortieth year, and desired only to return home to his family and see his boys grow to men.

A simple desire. An understandable one.

An open door to an Athanaean.

KAI LAY ON the floor of his cell, sweat layering his skin and his heart racing as though he had sprinted the entire height of the Whispering Tower. His body ached and his eyes felt as though the sutures binding them to his skin were tearing loose. The bilious taste of vomit caked the inside of his mouth and his robes stank of urine and uncontrolled bowel movements.

Every portion of his anatomy ached, and micro-tremors in his muscles kept him from any form of rest. Bright light filled his cell and harsh static blared from an unseen vox grille. Kai wanted to pick himself up, to face

his interrogators with dignity and courage, but he had
nothing left in him for defiance.

His clawed hand scratched at the floor, and the ghost
of a smile creased Kai's face as he finally made a mark
of his own in the fabric of the cell. His parched tongue
rasped over his cracked lips and he blinked away the raw,
infected tissue gathering at the corner of his eyes.

Kai had no idea how long he had been lying here
in pools of his own ejected matter, and, in truth, had
stopped caring. He watched the patterns his breath made
in the vomit, like ripples on the surface of a vast lake that
sweltered beneath a glaring red sun.

Then, a change. A shiver of air movement. A door
opening.

Kai tried to move, but he could no longer move his
limbs. He saw a pair of boots, heeled and fashioned from
expensive materials available only to the moneyed and
influential of Terra. He heard a woman's voice, dull and
indistinct, then hands were under him, grabbing him
and hauling him upright. Kai flinched at their touch,
his body a morass of pain that shied away from human
contact. Dragged across the floor of the cell, he was
deposited on the edge of the bunk. Two figures in bulky
black armour, layered bands of what looked like leather
and bonded ceramite plate, took a step back from him
as the most exquisite woman Kai had ever seen appeared
between them.

Kai squinted through the glare of his cell's lights. His
visitor was unknown to him, a woman of undoubted
noble breeding and subtly judged cosmetic surgery. Her
eyes were vivid green, the surgically enhanced structure of her features framing them perfectly with high
cheekbones. She wore her blonde hair in an elfin bob,
asymmetrically cut and laced with amethyst beads.

A black bodyglove enclosed her lithe form, and a purple weave of shimmering fabric spiralled around her
body like a frozen whirlwind. She was dressed for one
of the grand Merican ballrooms, not a gaol beneath a

forgotten mountain, and Kai wondered what she could possibly want from him.

'Do you know who I am?' she asked.

Kai licked his lips with the little moisture left in his mouth.

'No,' he said, his voice a barely audible whisper. The dusty rattle of a desert corpse.

'And why should you? I move in circles far beyond your limited understanding,' said the woman, picking her way carefully through the matter on the cell floor and kneeling beside him. Her dress moved with her, slithering around her form like a snake and ensuring it never touched the ground.

She saw him notice and smiled. 'Nanofabric programmed to remain a fixed position and distance from my body at all times.'

'Expensive.'

'Monstrously,' she agreed.

'What do you want?'

The woman snapped a finger.

'Give the man a drink. I can barely hear him.'

One of the woman's protectors knelt beside Kai and offered him a plastic tube he detached from the shoulder of his armour. A droplet of moisture beaded the end of the tube, and Kai gratefully sucked cool liquid from the trooper's recyc-pack. That the water was reconstituted from the man's sweat and bodily waste did not bother Kai one iota. He felt it flowing through his body, along his limbs and revitalising him like a stimm shot.

Instantly, his thoughts sharpened and the sickness that plagued him abated.

'That's more like it,' said the woman. 'Now I don't have to get so close to you to hear what you're saying.'

'That wasn't water,' said Kai, indicating the trooper as he snapped the clear plastic pipe back to his shoulder plate.

'No, it wasn't, but you feel better, don't you?'

'Much better,' agreed Kai.

The woman cocked her head to one side and let her eyes roam his face. They were quite magnificent eyes, genuine and likely gene-tailored in utero. Kai's augmetic eyes saw the faint outline of an electoo just beneath the third dermal layer, and unconsciously brought it into clarity. Rendered in a familiar cursive, it was an italicised capital C, and Kai groaned as he touched the underside of his wrist, were an identical electoo had been applied.

'You are from House Castana,' he said.

'I *am* House Castana,' said the woman. 'I am Aeliana Septmia Verduchina Castana.'

'The Patriarch's daughter,' said Kai.

'Just so,' said Aeliana, lifting her fringe to reveal a bejewelled patch in the centre of her forehead concealing her third eye. 'And you are an embarrassment to my house, Kai Zulane.'

'I never meant to be, Domina,' said Kai, quickly averting his gaze and employing the formal means of address. To look into the eye of a navigator was death, and he had more than earned such a fate in the eyes of the Castana family of the Navis Nobilite.

'I am not here to kill you,' said Aeliana. 'Though Throne knows, that would solve a world of problems. I am here to give you a second chance. I am here to give you a chance to make amends for the loss of the *Argo* and the near-crippling loss of face my father has endured among the Conclave of Navigators.'

'Why would you do such a thing?'

'Because I dislike waste,' said Aeliana. 'For all the trouble you have caused, you are a skilled astropath and I would recoup the significant outlay my father incurred in securing your secondment to our House.'

'You can secure my release from this place?' asked Kai.

Aeliana smiled and shook her head as though amused at the naïve questioning of an infant.

'I am Navis Nobilite,' she said. 'I speak and the world listens.'

'Even the Legio Custodes?'

'Even the praetorians,' said Aeliana. 'On assurance that I never allow you to return to Terra. A small price to see an end to this... unpleasantness, I think you'll agree?'

Kai nodded. To never see the planet of his birth again would be no price at all.

'And you can take me out of here?' he said.

'I can, but first you have to do something for me.'

'What? Anything, Domina,' said Kai, reaching out to take Aeliana's hands.

Her skin was smooth, yet there was a hardness to it that spoke of subdermal haptic implants. Aeliana's eyes bored into his, and once again he was struck by the lambent green of her perfectly circular irises.

'I need you to look at me and understand that House Castana does not hold you responsible for what happened aboard the *Argo*. It was an old ship and well beyond its scheduled maintenance refit date. The vanes of its Geller field generators had been damaged in transit through the asteroid belt around Konor, and it was only a matter of time until they failed. It had nothing to do with you.'

'I was transmitting just before they failed,' said Kai, so softly he wasn't even sure he'd spoken aloud.

'What?'

'I was in a *nuncio* trance,' said Kai. 'I was sending a message to Terra when the shields failed. I was the way in for those... monsters... those *things* that live in the warp. The shields might have been cracked and ready to fail, but I was the hammer that finally broke them. The whole crew slaughtered and it's my fault!'

Aeliana gripped his hands tightly and looked him straight in the eye.

'It was *not* your fault,' she said. 'The creatures of the warp are dangerous, yes, but you are not to blame for what happened. I have seen the shipwright's report on the wreck that emerged from the warp, and it is a miracle the *Argo* made it back to realspace at all. You and Roxanne were all that brought it home at all.'

'Roxanne…' said Kai. 'Yes, that was her name… I remember. We knew each other. What became of her?'

'She is well,' said Aeliana, but Kai caught the hesitation before her answer. 'After a brief convalescence, she returned to her duties. As you must, but you need to tell the Custodians what Sarashina told you. There is no reason not to; you have my word as Mistress of House Castana that no harm will befall you, whatever words you speak to me.'

Kai tilted his head back and stared into the bright light filling his cell. He could see no source of illumination, yet the walls shone with reflected light. The grainy static noise swelled, and now he recognised it for what it was: a desert wind blowing through the valleys and troughs of a dune sea, reshaping the landscape with every gust.

'Very good,' he said. 'You almost had me.'

Aeliana's grip tightened, and the perfect cast of her bone structure wavered for the tiniest fraction of a second. But with awareness of its falsehood, the rest of the fiction fell away with increasing rapidity, and the walls of the cell fell away like the threadbare backcloth of a cheap playhouse.

In their place, the achingly empty expanse of the Rub' al Khali stretched out to the edge of the world. The armed troopers melted away like wind-blown sand sculptures and Kai found himself seated upon a shelf of rock overlooking the fortress of Arzashkun.

'What was my mistake?' said Adept Hiriko, the guise of Aeliana falling away from her.

'The eyes for starters,' said Kai. 'You can never change your eyes, and though I forget each time, you can never hide them.'

'That is all?'

'Well, no,' said Kai. 'You made one other mistake.'

'Oh, what was that?'

'Aeliana Castana is a complete bitch,' said Kai. 'She would never be so understanding to someone who had cost her house so dearly.'

Hiriko shrugged. 'I have heard that, but gambled on you never having met her.'

'I haven't, but word travels.'

Hiriko still held his hands and she leaned in to him. Her skin smelled of cheap herbal soap, and the sheer ordinariness of it made Kai want to weep. If only he could.

'Whether or not you believed the dreamscape is immaterial,' said Hiriko. 'The words I spoke with her lips are no less true. You were not to blame for what happened to the *Argo*. Only by accepting that will you be able to let go of what holds you here.'

'Maybe I don't want to let go of it. Maybe I feel I deserve to be punished just for surviving. Had you thought of that?'

'Why would you do something so self-destructive?' asked Hiriko. 'This augering is killing you every day. You must know that.'

Kai nodded. 'I know it.'

'Then why do it?'

'Aniq Sarashina bade me tell what I know to one person, and one person alone.'

'Who?'

'I don't know,' said Kai, scooping up a handful of sand and letting it spill between his open fingers. The wind snatched the falling grains, sending them out over the dunes to be lost among the endless desert. Kai imagined himself as one of those grains, carried away by the warm sirocco, to be lost beyond any hope of ever being found.

'That doesn't make any sense,' said Hiriko.

'It doesn't have to,' said Kai. 'But a promise is a promise.'

'Do you want to die here?'

Kai considered the question, wondering if death was truly what he wanted. A release from the nightmares and constant guilt at his survival would be welcome, but he was too much of a coward to let death claim him with such ease. Or was it strength that kept him struggling for life and the chance to give his survival meaning?

'No,' said Kai at last, as the answer came to him. 'I don't want to die here.'

'Telling me what Sarashina told you is the only way you will live,' promised Hiriko.

'You're wrong,' he said, without knowing how he could be so certain. 'I am going to pass on what I was told.'

Hiriko shook her head. 'Saturnalia will kill you first.'

THE BLEED WAS tempestuous, but what else could he have expected after so potent a psychic burst as the arrival of the Crimson King? Magnus himself had manifested on Terra from half a galaxy away, and Evander Gregoras could not even begin to imagine what an expenditure of power such a feat had cost him.

How had he done it?

Magnus was a primarch, true, but even a god-like being with such mastery of the psychic arts surely had limits. No psychic discipline of which Gregoras was aware could transport the physical body of an individual over so great a distance, so how had he done it? Legends told that the cognoscynths could open gateways through space and time, but even the most outlandish tales only spoke of travel from one side of the planet to another. To travel between worlds would require the greatest mind the galaxy had ever seen...

Gregoras had told Zulane that the cognoscynths were all gone, but might the Emperor have created another in the form of Magnus? Had that been the figure Zulane had met in his dream?

But to travel from Prospero to Terra!

Such a feat spoke of powerful sorcery, and it boded ill for the Imperium if Magnus had unlocked that forbidden door. As he had told Kai, there could only be one punishment for such blatant disregard for the Emperor's decree.

The Bleed roared and seethed like an atmospheric superstorm, raging with the distilled nightmares and

collected visions of thousands of traumatised astro-
telepaths. Hundreds had been killed in the psychic
shockwave that still echoed in the planet's aether, and
hundreds more would never regain full use of their abilities. At any time that would have been a calamity, but in
the midst of a full-scale civil war, it was nothing less than
catastrophic. The City of Sight was effectively blinded,
an irony not lost on Gregoras, but which Lord Dorn
found less than amusing.

To relive the nightmares of an entire city was no small
task, and the cryptaesthesians were suffering what their
fellows had suffered all over again. The whisper stones
ran red with incorporeal blood, fat with the bleak visions
and darkest fears of those they had saved from psychic
overload. The cascade of light from the dome's crystal
lattice was bleeding its horrors down onto Gregoras, and
no matter that he had steeled himself with rituals of isolation and mantras of protection, he still wept with every
fresh terror that cohered in the mists of psychic debris.

He saw loved ones ripped apart, nightmares of needles
and crawling things. Dreams of abandonment, nightmares of pain and fears of rejection. He saw childhood
traumas, relived pain and imagined terrors that had no
frame of reference. All this and more oozed from the
whisper stones like pus from a wound. Only by expel-
ling every last morsel of trauma would the City of Sight
be able to function again, and only the cryptaesthesians
had the skill to make it happen.

Nemo Zhi-Meng had personally tasked Gregoras with
purging the city of the power that had manifested within
the mindhall of Choir Primus.

'Make the nightmares go away,' had been his simple
instruction.

Simple to say, but difficult to obey.

The power within Aniq Sarashina that had destroyed
Choir Primus was so vast that elements of it had
insinuated their way into the collective psyche of the
Whispering Tower. Infinitesimally small fragments of

its purpose had lodged in the minds of all who heard its screaming siren song, and those fragments had been absorbed by the whisper stones.

And from there, it had bled into the shadowy realm of the cryptaesthesians.

To a mind not attuned to the secret pattern that underpinned the galaxy, such fragments would have been meaningless, a garbled hash of random images, absurd metaphors and mixed allegories.

Gregoras knew better and in every horrific image he lifted from the Bleed, he could see tiny references to the pattern, as though the madmen and prophets scattered throughout the galaxy had poured all their ravings and dreams into one mighty shout. The pattern was here, right in front of him, and the key to unlocking the mystery he had studied for the entirety of his adult life was secreted in Kai Zulane's mind.

Sarashina had said she was passing on a warning, but a warning to whom? And what kind of warning would not be best shouted from the highest rooftop instead of being hidden away in the mind of a broken telepath?

The truth of the matter was right here, in the nightmares of the tower's astropaths, and Gregoras was going to find it. The neurolocutors of the Legio Custodes were having no success in plucking Sarashina's legacy from Zulane's head, but the secret of whatever had come to the Whispering Tower was here in the Bleed, he was sure of it.

All he needed was time to find it.

TWELVE

The Enemy Within
The Fellowship of Vanity
A Promise Kept

THOUGH HIS ARMOUR insulated him from the cold beneath the mountains, Uttam Luna Hesh Udar felt an insidious chill creep into his bones as he watched the mortal soldiers manoeuvre the nutrition dispenser along the bridge towards the floating island at the heart of Khangba Marwu. A fine mist of rain drizzled from the darkened recesses of the cavern's roof, and droplets of moisture condensed on the blade of his guardian spear. They hissed as the energy field vaporised them instantly, sounding like snakes drifting through the air.

Its power would deplete quicker, but when there were enemies all around him, the seconds it would take to energise could cost him his life. Sumant Giri Phalguni Tirtha stood beside him, his guardian spear also fizzing in the moist air. He looked up, droplets rolling down the golden plates of his helm like tears.

'Rain beneath the mountains,' he said. 'I have never known the like.'

'Cold in the world above,' said Uttam. 'What does it matter?'

'The mountain weeps,' said Tirtha.

'What?'

Tirtha shrugged, as though embarrassed to continue.

'Spit it out,' said Uttam. 'What troubles you?'

'I have read the history of Khangba Marwu,' said Tirtha. 'It is said the mountain wept on the day Zamora escaped.'

'No one is escaping today,' said Uttam. 'Not on our watch.'

'As you say,' agreed Tirtha, and though his face was hidden behind his helm's visor, Uttam sensed a lingering unease in his body language.

'Come,' he said. 'Do not let a coincidence of subterranean precipitation keep the warriors of the Legio Custodes from their duties.'

'Of course,' said Tirtha, as the soldiers eased the nutrition dispenser onto the cell-island.

The bulky container slipped as its repulsor field interacted with a stray wave emanation from the mighty generators holding the cell-island afloat. A trooper in the grey tabard of the Uralian Stormlords cursed as the intersecting fields shocked him and he lost his grip.

'Watch what you're doing, damn it,' he snapped, directing his anger outwards.

'Hold your end properly and it won't slip,' said the man across from him, a veteran sergeant of the Gitanen Outriders, an elite unit of flyers based in the Baikonur crater aeries.

'I'm carrying half your weight,' said the man. His name was Natraj, and Uttam had, until now, thought him one of the steadier members of his detail.

'Be silent,' said Uttam. 'It is forbidden for you to speak while on duty.'

'Apologies, Custodian,' said Natraj. 'It will not happen again.'

'We are as one,' added the Outrider, but Uttam suspected that whatever ill-feeling existed between them would be taken up once they were beyond the confines of the mountain.

'When we are done here you will return to the surface and collect your dismissal papers. I have no use for men who cannot follow orders,' said Uttam.

'Custodian?' said Natraj.

'My lord, please–'

'Hold your tongues, both of you,' said Uttam. 'I do not tolerate dissent. You fail to understand what it is you do here, the danger of the prisoners you attend. Your commanding officers will hear of this lapse in discipline.'

Both men glared at him, and Uttam's stim glands swelled with trigger chemicals as his combat reflexes instinctively recognised anger and the threat of imminent violence. His grip tightened on his spear, but just as suddenly the anger had surfaced it vanished without trace, cut off as suddenly as though a switch had been thrown.

'Follow me,' said Uttam, turning and leading the soldiers between the cells. The lingering traces of combat stims danced in his veins, and Uttam scanned the spaces between the cells for enemies. The only enemies on the island were locked up, but the brief exchange between the mortals had disquieted him. He was no believer in omens, but taken together with the drizzling rain, it had set him on edge, combat ready and instinctive.

Not a good state to be in when caution and thoroughness was key.

'Which one first?' asked Tirtha.

'Tagore,' said Uttam, indicating a cellblock to his right.

Uttam despised Tagore, he had killed three hundred and fifty nine men before he had been subdued, and that made him almost as dangerous as a Custodian. The soldiers hauled the nutrition dispenser around as Uttam took position in front of the door.

The warrior inside paced the length and breadth of the cell like a caged raptor, tension knotting his muscles and keeping his jaw clenched like a rabid wolf. The prisoner's physique was enormous: a giant clad only in a tattered loincloth. It had once been a standard issue prison bodyglove, but the inmate had torn it to shreds. His body was a lattice of scars layered over gene-bulked muscle and ossified bone, while his flesh was a canvas of linked tattoos. Axes and swords mingled with skulls and jagged teeth that swallowed worlds whole.

The back of the man's head was a nightmare of metal plates embedded in furrowed grooves cut into the bone of his skull, and there was a demented look to the warrior that no amount of self-control could quite mask.

'Back away from the door, traitor,' ordered Uttam.

The warrior bared his teeth, flinching at the word *traitor*, but complied. His back was to the far wall, but his muscles were bunched in anticipation of violence. Tagore was a World Eater, and Uttam had never seen him in anything less than an attack posture. The others of his Legion were just the same, and Uttam wondered how they could stand to be so highly poised at all times. Some called the World Eaters undisciplined killers, psychopaths with tacit approval to be mindless butchers, but Uttam knew better. After all, what kind of discipline must it take to maintain such a level of aggression so close to the surface on so tight a leash?

The World Eaters were more dangerous than anyone gave them credit.

Tagore eyed him with a feral grin, but said nothing.

'You have something to say?' snapped Uttam.

Tagore nodded and said, 'One day I will kill you. Rip your spine out through your chest.'

'Empty threats?' said Uttam. 'I expected better from you.'

'You are more foolish than you look if you think I make empty threats,' said Tagore.

'And yet you are the one in confinement.'

'This?' said Tagore, as the nutrition dispenser dropped a pair of foodstuff bags into the cell. 'This won't hold me for long.'

Uttam smiled, amused despite himself by Tagore's posturing. 'Do you really believe that, or is it just that abomination hammered into your skull that makes you think so?'

'I am World Eater,' snarled Tagore proudly. 'I do not deal in abstracts, I deal in the reality of absolutes. And I know that I will kill you.'

Recognising the futility of further discussion, Uttam shook his head and moved deeper into the prison complex. The other inmates gave him cold glares or venomous hostility, but as always it was Atharva who perturbed Uttam the most.

The witch stood in the centre of his cell, hands straight down at his side and his chin tilted slightly up, as though he was waiting for something. His eyes were closed and his lips moved as though in silent supplication. The rain fell harder here, dripping from the hard permacrete edges of the cellblock. Uttam's eyes narrowed as the same chill he had felt upon entering the chamber grow stronger still. His combat instincts, already honed from the brief stim shunt drew in close as he sensed danger.

The spear spun in his hand as Atharva's eyes opened, and Uttam gasped as he saw they were no longer amber and blue, but the shimmering white of a winter sun.

'Pull back,' he ordered, moving away from the cell door. 'Evacuate immediately.'

'It's too late for that,' said Atharva.

'Tirtha!' shouted Uttam. 'Danger threatens!'

A blast of superheated air sounded like the crack of a whip, and Uttam spun on his heel. Natraj of the Ural-ian Stormlords held his plasma gun pulled in tight to his shoulder, the vents along its barrel drooling exhaust gasses.

Custodian Sumant Giri Phalguni Tirtha fell to his knees with a smoking hole burned through the centre of his stomach.

'The mountain weeps,' he said, before pitching onto his front.

* * *

THE INTERROGATION CHAMBER was cold, as it always was, but Kai sensed a strained atmosphere that had nothing to do with Scharff and Hiriko's continued failure to reach the information Sarashina had placed within him. Though Kai's physical frailty made restraints unnecessary, he was still strapped into the contoured chair in the centre of the chamber. Adept Hiriko sat opposite him, and Kai saw dark smudges under her eyes that hadn't been there the last time they had met in the waking world. The process of interrogation was draining her almost as much as it was draining him.

Kai said, 'Please, do we have to do this again? I can't give you what you want.'

'I believe you, Kai, I really do,' said Hiriko, 'but if the Legio Custodes cannot have the secrets in your head, they will settle for you dead. They are an unforgiving organisation. And if you won't give me what I want willingly, then I have no choice but to tear it out of you.'

'What does that mean?'

Hiriko fixed him with a stare that was part melancholy, part exasperated. 'It means exactly what you think it means, Kai. You won't survive this.'

'Please,' said Kai. 'I don't want to die. I don't want to die like this.'

'That doesn't matter anymore,' said Hiriko. 'Others have decided that you must, but it if it is any comfort, know that you will soon be unconscious and won't feel a thing.'

The door to the interrogation chamber opened before Kai could answer. Adept Scharff entered, looking as though he had been deprived of rest for weeks. The man gave Kai a weak smile and Hiriko looked up with a concerned glance.

'You are late,' she said. 'You're never late.'

'I slept badly. I dreamed of a figure armoured in crimson and ivory,' said Scharff, and something about that description tugged on a thread in Kai's mind. 'He was calling to me.'

'What was he saying?' asked Hiriko.

'I do not know, I could hear nothing of his words.'

'Residue from the umbra perhaps?' asked Hiriko. 'Should I be vexed?'

Scharff shook his head. 'No, I believe it to be bleed off from the psychic trauma caused by the arrival of Primarch Magnus. The crimson and ivory of the figure's armour suggests a link to the Thousand Sons after all.'

Hiriko nodded. 'That appears likely.'

Scharff took a seat beside Kai and sifted through the many chem-shunts and canula needles piercing his pallid skin. Kai couldn't move his head to see what he was doing, but his peripheral vision was almost as clear as his binocular vision. Scharff's eyes were ever so slightly unfocused, like a sleeper suddenly awoken from a deep slumber. The man's hands were out of sight, but Kai heard a soft hiss as one of the drug dispensers introduced yet another foreign substance into his bloodstream.

Expecting unconsciousness, Kai was mildly surprised to feel tingling at the extremities of his limbs. His eyes flicked to Hiriko, but her beautiful green eyes were perusing lines of text scrolling down the face of a data slate. Kai looked over to Scharff, now able to move his head as whatever chemical Scharff was feeding him began to fully counteract the muscle relaxants and anaesthesias keeping him docile.

Kai bit his lip as control returned to his body. His limbs were his own again, but it was more than that. This was rejuvenation, a stimulus that was restoring his body with vitality. He wanted to ask Scharff what he was doing, but an instinct for danger warned him to keep his mouth shut. His actions couldn't escape Hiriko's notice for long, and the machines monitoring Kai's vital signs registered his increased brain activity and elevated heart rate.

Hiriko glanced over at the bio-readouts with twin lines creasing the smooth skin at the bridge of her nose. Her eyes darted from readout to readout, taking in at a glance Kai's return from the brink of dormancy.

'Scharff? Have you seen these readings?' she asked, putting aside the data slate and rising to her feet. When her companion didn't answer, she finally turned to face him and the surprise in her face was compounded with irritation.

'Sharff? What are you doing? We need Kai unconscious for this procedure.'

'No,' said Scharff.

'No?' replied Hiriko. 'Have you lost your mind? Stop whatever it is you're doing.'

'I can't do that, Adept Hiriko,' said Scharff, in a voice that suggested he very much wished he could. Scharff's hands danced over an exposed keypad on the black box that had been the source of so many of Kai's nightmares recently. Hiriko circled the chair and took hold of Scharff's arm. Kai saw her register what he had understood only moments before.

'Adept Scharff,' snapped Hiriko. 'Back away from the prisoner immediately. I believe your mind to be compromised.'

Scharff shook his head, and the veins at his temples throbbed like a heart on the verge of cardiac arrest. 'The subject must be conscious and motile if he is to leave the facility.'

'He's not leaving, Scharff,' insisted Hiriko.

Kai felt the metal restraints that bound him to the chair release with a pneumatic hiss as the blare of alarm klaxons sounded throughout Khangba Marwu.

'Oh, but he is,' said Scharff in a voice that was not his own.

NATRAJ WAS DEAD before Tirtha hit the ground. Uttam's guardian spear spat a bolt from the weapon beneath the blade and the man's body blew apart into vaporised blood and bone shrapnel. Two of the nearest soldiers went down with the force of the explosion, but Uttam was already moving as alarm klaxons and warning bells filled the cavern with noise. Natraj had been compromised, and the loyalty of his fellows was likewise in doubt. For that, all would have to die.

Uttam swayed aside from a hellgun shot and rammed his spear through the chest plate of a soldier armoured in crimson battle plate. Blood sprayed the golden visor of his helm as he was cloven from hip to collarbone. A rifle barked to the side, deflected by Uttam's shoulder guard. He spun low, his spear sweeping in a low arc that sliced through the knees of four of his attackers. A searing blast of plasma blinded him momentarily as it flashed past his helmet and he dropped into a defensive crouch, sweeping his spear around him in a spinning blur of silver and adamantium.

Shots ricocheted from the blade, but none penetrated his defences. His sight returned a moment later, and Uttam pulled his spear in tight to his body. Diving forward he rolled to his feet and another shot punched a warrior armoured in mirror-black armour from his feet. The pulped remains slammed into the wall of the nearest cellblock.

Threat protocols picked out the dangers.

Uralian Stormlord with a hellgun. Minimal threat.

Two Vitruvian Commissars, one with an ion breaker the other with a grenade launcher. Moderate threat.

Three Crimson Dragoons: webber, plasma carbine and a mass crusher. Immediate threat.

They were firing and moving, working better as attackers than they ever had as gaolers, but even six highly trained mortals with advanced weaponry were no match for a warrior of the Legio Custodes. Uttam swung his spear around and killed the dragoon armed with the mass crusher, taking his head off with a neat cut that cauterised the wound even as it decapitated. The plasma carbine fired again. Uttam deflected the shot with a horizontal slash, sending the superhot bolt into the chest of the Commissar with the grenade launcher. He fell with a strangled scream that changed to a shrill howl as the air in his lungs ignited.

A hellgun shot impacted on the side of his helmet, and Uttam spun to face the shooter, but the two surviving dragoons obscured his aim. They fired at the same time, but Uttam was already among them. His blade sliced the first soldier's arm from his body, and the return stroke of the haft shattered every rib in his chest.

A warm mist of sticky mucus-like liquid enveloped Uttam, and he felt the rapidly solidifying web gel hardening around his armour. Anyone not blessed with the preternaturally swift reflexes of the genhanced would have been trapped completely by the web's ultra-rapid setting, but Uttam pulled clear before the worst of the gel had done its work. His spear arm was gummed with sticky strands of the stuff, but his left was still free and lethal.

A pistoning jab caved in the front half of the web gunner's face and a following elbow broke the neck of the plasma gunner even as he brought his recharged weapon to bear once more. That just left the grey-clad Stormlord, and Uttam jogged in the direction the man had run, shaking the last strands of dissolving web gel from his arm.

'You have to die now,' said Uttam, rounding the corner of the cellblock.

Shock and horror pulled him up short as he saw the Uralian Stormlord standing before an opened cell with Sumant Giri Phalguni Tirtha's bloodstained signifier ring pressed to the locking panel. A towering figure of rage and scar tissue stood by the opened door, pumping muscles bunched and writhing beneath his tattooed skin.

'I am going to kill you,' said Tagore of the World Eaters. 'Rip your spine out through your chest.'

From a cross-legged position, Atharva watched the dance of his puppets with a satisfied smile. A tug of thought brought the Uralian Stormlord running towards his cell while Tagore and Custodian Uttam faced off against one another. Time was critical. He couldn't let the World Eater kill the Custodian or this escape would be over before it began.

His other thrall was already rousing Kai Zulane, though it was proving difficult to maintain his control over Scharff. The man had some training in resisting mental intrusion, basic training compared to that endured by adepts of the Thousand Sons, but he had natural talents that ensured his will was a slippery thing. His attempts to break Atharva's control were amusingly naïve, but he had help from his compatriot, and she was a sly little fox.

Beads of sweat trickled down Atharva's face like tears. Though it was an uncomplicated matter to exert control over mortals, maintaining it through psychically warded permacrete and without being able to *see* his thralls took great effort.

A shape appeared at the door to his cell, a man in a grey tabard marked with lightning bolts and a crude representation of a diving raptor. The soldier's face was pale and he wept even as his hand shuddered with the effort of trying to resist Atharva's control.

'Don't try to fight it, Tejas,' said Atharva. 'You don't have the strength.'

Tejas Doznya had served with the Uralian Stormlords for six years, and had been passed over for promotion three times. Too reckless, his superiors said, which, in a regiment renowned for leaping from perfectly good aircraft with nothing but a flimsy grav-chute to prevent gravity working its inevitable end result on their fragile bodies, was saying something. This secondment to the Legio Custodes was intended to temper his reckless streak with the discipline of the Emperor's praetorians, but his resentment at being sidelined had only festered until it was practically begging to be used as leverage to open his mind to control.

With a cry of impotence, Tejas placed the Custodian's signifier ring against the lock plate and the door slid into the walls of the cell. Cut from the hand of a dead man, the ring's skeleton key properties spoke to the arrogance of the Legio Custodes that they had never considered the possibility of one of their precious rings falling into enemy hands.

Atharva stood in a fluid, uncoiling motion, like a rearing snake poised to strike down its victim. He stepped from the cell, gasping in remembered pleasure as he felt the power of the Great Ocean swell around him. The psi-damping collar around his neck cracked and broke apart as though twisted by invisible hands. Its remains clattered to the ground and Atharva laughed as he felt the currents and tides of the Great Ocean rush to fill his body.

'Tejas, the ring if you please,' said Atharva, extending his hand.

The horrified Tejas dropped the ring onto the plateau of Atharva's palm, and he lifted it to his lips, as if to kiss it. His tongue flicked out to clean it of blood, and the rich gene-rich flavour of the Custodian's essence flooded his senses, an ambrosia of genetic mastery.

'Oh, this is a wonder indeed, Tejas,' said Atharva. 'What secrets might be unlocked by its study? What wonders and miracles might a master like Hathor Maat work with such a palette of genius?'

Tejas didn't answer and Atharva handed the pristine ring back to him. He placed one oversized hand upon his thrall's shoulder, placing the images of five warriors in the forefront of his mind. Five. All that would be useful from twelve. What a waste.

'Tejas, I want you to release these men, and these men only,' said Atharva.

The man nodded, his mind bursting with the need to do Atharva's bidding and the horror of what he was doing. Though every fibre of the man's willpower was trying to fight off his control, he was a leaf in the face of a hurricane. Atharva watched him run towards the other cells, and let his mind float into the mid-level heights of the Enumerations that would better enhance his skills in bio-manipulation. Sense organs at the back of his throat struggled to assess the content of the Custodian's blood, though they could not hope to unravel something so exquisitely constructed. Yet what understanding they could glean might be enough.

Though Atharva's skills as a Pavoni were not the equal of Hathor Maat, he had mastered enough of the vain Fellowship's arts to achieve what would be required to leave this place of confinement.

So long as Tagore didn't kill Uttam Luna Hesh Udar too soon.

FISTS AND ELBOWS, knees and feet. They fought in a blur of thundering punches, bone-breaking kicks and titanic impacts. Two warriors, crafted to be the pinnacles of fighting men, flew at each other with rage and neuro-cortical implants and the finest genetic manipulation on either side of loyalty.

Tagore fought with teeth bared, eyes bulging madness. He fought without heed or thought of restraint, with no care for injury or death. Uttam Luna Hesh Udar fought with precision, grace and exacting killing blows straight from the combat forges of the Legio Custodes.

Two warriors of extremes, two warriors primed to deal death in completely different ways.

Uttam was armoured, Tagore was bare-skinned and bleeding.

The Custodian's guardian spear lay broken between them, its haft snapped like matchwood in Tagore's grip. Its blade fizzed and spat in the moisture drizzling from the cavern's roof. Tagore spun around Uttam, kicking his heel into the back of the Custodian's knee. Uttam went down with a grunt, catching the follow-up knee to the face in his blocking gauntlets. Uttam twisted his grip, spinning Tagore from his feet. He followed up, foot thundering down to crush the World Eater's head.

Tagore rolled, came up, and punched the side of

Uttam's thigh. Plates cracked and the paralyzing nerve-impact dropped him to one knee. A right cross tore his helmet off and an uppercut threw him onto his back. Tagore scissored himself to his feet and hurled himself at the fallen Custodian. Uttam met his flying leap with a downward-bludgeoning fist that drove Tagore into the ground like a downed Stormbird. Tagore rolled aside from the inevitable head-crushing elbow and sprang to his feet in time to meet the Custodian's charge.

They grappled like street brawlers. Rabbit-punching kidneys, legs locking and unlocking as each warrior sought a hold that would drop their opponent. The iron plates bolted to Tagore's head spat fat red sparks as it pumped chem-stims and rage boosters into his bloodstream and electrical impulses to the anger centres of his brain. His fury had been building to critical mass ever since his incarceration, and this was just the fight to unleash it.

The first advantage went to Uttam. Every blow Tagore struck was against artificer-forged plate, hand shaped in the armouries beneath the Anatolian peaks, where Uttam hammered unprotected flesh. Pure concussive force cracked the bone shield in Tagore's chest, and he grunted as a piledriver of an uppercut drove up into his gut. The briefest flinch, but an opening nonetheless.

Uttam twisted and slammed his elbow into Tagore's jaw. Blood and teeth flew from the World Eater's jaw. Uttam closed for the killing blow, but pain was just another stimulus to a killer like Tagore. The World Eater spat a tooth, and caught Uttam's fist in one raw meat palm. He caught the other fist mid-punch and smashed his forehead into Uttam's face. The Custodian's nose broke, and both cheekbones shattered. Blood blinded him for an instant before he shook his eyes clear of it, but an instant was all Tagore needed.

His blooded fist hammered into Uttam's chest, driven by rage and betrayal.

Ceramite shattered, adamantium buckled and bone broke.

Tagore bellowed in atavistic triumph as his power, momentum and strength drove his fist deep into the Custodian's chest. Meat and blood parted before his digging hand until his fingers closed on iron-hard bone.

The Custodian's eyes were wide with agony, his body still fighting for life even as Tagore ripped it out of him. Tagore spat blood in his face, grinning a manic skull's grin.

'Still think I make empty threats, Custodian?' he snarled.

Uttam tried to respond, but only managed a horrid sucking noise from his gored chest cavity. Tagore felt bone buckle, crushed beneath his implacable grip. Strong and tough, but not as strong or tough as a sergeant of the World Eaters.

A figure appeared at his back, tall and reeking of cold metal and ice.

'Damn you, Tagore, I need him alive,' said a voice that could only belong to Atharva of the Thousand Sons. 'He can still survive this, Tagore. Don't kill him.'

'Only Angron and his captains can tell me what to do,' hissed Tagore. 'One of Magnus's bastards does not.'

With an awful cracking sound that seemed to go on and on, Tagore twisted his grip and wrenched his arm from Uttam's chest. Crimson past the elbow, nubs of broken bone protruded from either side of his fist. Glistening mucus-like blood and spinal fluid dripped from the ruptured bone, and in the last seconds of life left to Uttam, he realised he was looking at a portion of his own spine.

'Rip your spine out through your chest!' yelled Tagore, hurling the wreckage of Uttam's bone to the ground. 'And what I say I will kill, I kill.'

The Custodian toppled onto his side, his body still trying to fight the inevitibility of his death. But even the formidable endurance wrought into so magnificent a body could not survive such a grievous wound, and Uttam Luna Hesh Udar's life ended in a shimmering pool of his own blood at the feet of a warrior to whom each opponent bested was a badge of honour.

'By the Eye, Tagore,' snapped Atharva, dropping to one knee beside the slain Custodian. 'Do you realise what you've done?'

'Killed a powerful foe, one worthy of remembrance,' said the World Eater.

Atharva waved away Tagore's words.

'Irrelevant,' he said, looking up at the cavern's ceiling and walls as nearly a hundred blister-turrets unmasked in readiness to cleanse this floating island of life. Both warriors knew they could not survive such weight of fire.

'The Crimson Path before the Iron Fetter!' bellowed Tagore, lifting his arms to meet death head on.

Atharva laughed in the face of such a wantonly self-destructive code of honour, knowing there was only one way they were going to live through the next few seconds.

'My apologies for this desecration, Uttam Luna Hesh Udar, but my need is greater than yours,' said Atharva, tearing the dead Custodian's head from his shoulders.

THIRTEEN

The Crusader Host
Freedom
If You Want To Live

WITH THE POWER of the Great Ocean at his disposal, there was little beyond the reach of an Adept Exemptus of the Thousand Sons, but even Phosis T'kar would have been hard pressed to create a kine shield capable of withstanding so many guns. Atharva could protect himself with such a shield, but the rest of the Crusader Host would surely be killed, and – for the moment – he needed them alive.

Freed from the limiting confines of his cell, Atharva's power flowed back into his body. He wanted to savour this moment, to revel in the return of his full gamut of abilities and the clarity of thought that was his to command, but time was now his enemy and the Eye had work for him.

Custodian Uttam's blood flowed from the ruined stump of his neck, spilling over Atharva's hand and streaming down his arm. The cracked tip of a crushed vertebra jutted from the wound and the grey matter within would beyond use in a few moments.

But a few moments was less time than he had.

The guns on the cavern walls opened fire and a cascade

of lasers and solid rounds drowned the din of alarms. Thousands of shells bombarded the floating island in a blitzing storm of fire. Atharva dived inside the cell that had recently housed Tagore, but the World Eater sergeant flattened himself against its outer walls, too stupid or too proud to take refuge within its confines.

'Can you stop this?' bellowed Tagore, his voice almost lost in the crescendo of gunfire. Acrid propellant smoke and billowing clouds of pulverised permacrete filled the air as the solid rounds smacked into the cells and chewed them apart like necrotic viral strains attacking healthy cells.

'That remains to be seen,' shouted Atharva in response, pushing his consciousness into the Custodian's head, directing the living power of the warp into the myriad dying blood vessels in an effort to keep brain death at bay.

A breath sighed from the head as the mouth fell open in a silent scream. Atharva felt the crackle of neural activity in the fitfully sparking synapses, and meshed his mind with the dying brain. He goaded it back to life with immaterial energy, letting the power of the Great Ocean reanimate cells that had been on the brink of disintegration. Atharva felt Uttam's horror pricking the edge of his perception, and briefly wondered what manner of awareness the dead Custodian might yet be experiencing.

As more of Uttam's brain returned to life, the stronger the maddened horror became, but Atharva kept it at bay for now. With his mental architecture attuned to the rhythms of the Pavoni in the sixth Enumeration, Atharva let his body's newfound familiarity with Legio Custodes blood restructure itself, altering his biometrics to more closely match those of his erstwhile gaoler. Though Atharva's body did not change outwardly, his inner flesh took on the guise of Uttam Luna Hesh Udar at the cellular level. A crude deception, conceived in haste, that would not fool any gene-sampler for long, but perhaps long enough.

Much of what the Custodian knew was Atharva's to know: the layout of Khangba Marwu, its security protocols, its roster of forces and, most importantly, its entrances and exits. Though in the current situation, the disabling codes for the cavern guns was top of Atharva's list of information to pluck from the dead man's skull.

Taking a deep breath, Atharva cowled himself in the crudest of kine shields and stepped from the cell. A storm of shells battered him, enough to saw through an entire company of Imperial Army troopers in an instant, but the shield held firm for now. It seemed as though every gun on the cavern walls was aimed right at him, and Atharva knew he would not have much time to make this work.

'All guns disengage and power down,' he shouted, his voice so perfect an imitation of Uttam Luna Hesh Udar that no vox-sampler ever made would dispute the authenticity of the speaker. 'Authorisation Omega Omicron Nine Three Primus.'

The deafening barrage of fire ceased in an instant as every gun retracted into an armoured housing and shut down. Smoke and dust drifted on the wind currents created by the sudden heat and passage of tens of thousands of expended rounds. The howling alarms seemed almost quiet by comparison.

Atharva dropped his kine shield and let out a relieved breath as shapes emerged from the choking dust clouds. Five of them, all bulked by unimaginably complex science to a size far beyond human, yet moving with a gait that was clearly authored from the template of homo sapiens. The twins were the first to emerge from the dust, Subha and Asubha, the butcher and the assassin. World Eaters and killers, neither bore the nightmarish augmetics of Tagore, but like their brother sergeant, their bodies were pitched in a posture of taut aggression.

Gythua followed them, a warrior from Mortarion's Legion whose bulk and solidity had made others in the Crusader Host give him the epithet of 'Goliath', a giant from ancient myth. Argentus Kiron, the tall, broad-shouldered swordsman, jogged alongside him. The pair shared an unlikely friendship, for who would have thought warriors of the Emperor's Children and Death Guard might find much in the way of common ground?

Lastly came Severian, dubbed the Wolf by his fellows for the secretive and lonely path he trod. Atharva barely knew him, but as a warrior from the Legion of Horus Lupercal, he held a unique position amongst the warriors of the Crusader Host.

Crusader Host…? The name was a joke now…

The three World Eaters greeted each other with clenched fists and primal displays of their strength, though Atharva saw the subtle dance of superiority in its ritualistic displays of prowess. Alpha male and subordinates were clearly defined in the tilt of their heads and the baring of necks. It made Atharva want to smile, but Tagore would take a dim view of any such analysis of his warriors.

Tagore swept up the guardian spear of the first Custodian to die, testing the edge of the blade with a satisfied grunt. He snapped the haft just below the cutting edge, making what was left look more like a long-bladed cleaver as Subha took up the spear blade Tagore had broken in his battle with Uttam.

'How are we free?' asked Kiron, picking up a fallen plasma carbine. The weapon looked absurdly tiny in his hands, but with a snap of a trigger guard, the weapon became useable. 'Is this your doing, Atharva?'

Neither Gythua or Asubha deigned to pick up a mortal weapon, but Severian slid a blade from the shoulder scabbard of a dead soldier clad in crimson plate. In the dead man's hands it would have been a monstrous blade, a two-handed hewer of men, but to the Luna Wolf it was little more than a gladius.

'It is indeed my doing,' replied Atharva, already jogging towards the bridge that led from the island. 'But explanations can wait until we are free of the mountain.'

Tagore ran alongside him, glancing warily at the silent guns.

'How did you do that?' he demanded, his words still slurred with the after-effects of combat drugs and the stress of his battle with the Custodian.

Atharva shook his head. 'It would take too long to explain.'

The World Eater took his arm in a powerful grip. 'I am not a fool, Atharva. Tell me.'

Atharva wondered for a moment how he could possibly explain the intricacies of bio-psychic engineering to a warrior of the World Eaters. It would be as futile as attempting to elaborate upon the shortcomings of Pandorus Zheng as a scholar relative to the achievements of Ahzek Ahriman to an amoeba.

He held up the severed head and said, 'I was able to extract the deactivation codes from the Custodian's brain before it ceased to function.'

Tagore eyed the head of the man he had killed with grim fascination.

'You sounded like him,' he said.

Not quite the barbarian then…

'I am a talented mimic,' said Atharva, once again using a flicker of his powers to alter the density and length of his vocal chords to match those of Custodian Uttam.

The bridge rang to the sound of heavy Space Marine treads as they crossed to the spur of rock at the edge of the depthless chasm. The warriors paused as they stepped from the bridge, all recognising the significance of the moment. They were clear of their cells, but there was fighting yet to be done if they were to truly call themselves free.

Atharva felt Kiron's eyes upon him.

'Is that head still alive?' asked the warrior of the Emperor's Children, with a grimace of distaste. Artificial colour in the warrior's hair had made him an albino while they had been honoured as representatives of the conquering Legions, but deprived of his dyes as a prisoner, dark roots were showing at his temples.

'After a fashion,' said Atharva, 'I can use it to get us past the guns, but we will have to hurry before the synapse connections degrade beyond the point where I can sustain them.'

'You dishonour a fallen enemy,' said Subha, pushing into Atharva's face.

Atharva sent an exasperated glance in Tagore's direction, and though the World Eater sergeant clearly shared Subha's feelings towards violating a fallen enemy's body, he nodded in understanding. Tagore thumped a fist against his chest, an old Unity salute that seemed more in keeping with their status as captives than the Aquila.

'We are World Eaters, Subha,' said Tagore. 'You were there at the great breaking of the chains. We swore to be no man's slaves, remember?'

'I remember,' said Subha with a feral snarl, his fists clenched.

'We all remember,' added his twin. 'The Crimson Path before the Iron Fetter.'

'Good words,' said Tagore, gesturing beyond the stone archway before them. 'Words to live by. Words of meaning.'

'Angron's words,' said Subha, as though that settled the matter, but Atharva didn't miss the uneasy glance shared by Asubha and Tagore.

'Beyond that arch lies freedom, but that freedom has to be won in blood,' said Tagore, brandishing the spear blade. 'We will show our enemies what it means to put chains on a World Eater.'

'We're wasting time,' said Severian. 'We should go. Now.'

'First sensible thing anyone's said,' grunted Gythua. 'Like as not we'll all die trying to get out of this place, but at least it'll be on our feet and facing our enemies.'

'Die?' said Kiron. 'What force could lay low the Goliath? You are too big and stubborn to die, my friend.'

'We can all die, Kiron,' said Gythua. 'Even me.'

* * *

KAI SPRANG FROM the chair as alarm klaxons echoed from far away. It didn't take a psychic to figure out that something terrible was happening, something that had never happened in the gaol of the Custodians. Scharff's inexplicable behaviour and the alarms could mean only one thing. Someone was escaping from the mountain, and though he didn't know whom or how, Kai knew he was somehow included in this prison break.

He wrenched the canula and drips from his body, crying out as the needles ripped his skin. Blood ran down his arm and clear plastic piping drooled coloured fluids to the tile floor of the interrogation room. The chemical stink of them was pungent, and Kai recoiled from the idea that he had been subjected to their effects.

Kai backed away from Adept Hiriko, putting the chair between them. The extremities of his limbs were still tingling, and there was a clearness to his thinking that could only have come from the stimulants Scharff had fed him. His body was dreadfully weakened from the psychic abuses Hiriko had heaped upon him, and Kai had no idea how long he would be able to function before this new state of physical and mental clarity began to fade.

'Get back on the chair,' ordered Hiriko, and Kai laughed.

'Seriously? You want me to get back into a chair for a procedure that's going to kill me?'

'More lives than yours are at stake,' said Hiriko, her green eyes boring into his. 'Lives more important than yours.'

'Not a chance,' said Kai.

'The Emperor's life,' said Hiriko.

That gave Kai pause, for he was still a loyal servant of the Imperium.

'You can't ask me to make that sacrifice,' said Kai, his voice pleading.

'Why not?' said Hiriko, circling the chair. 'You already gave up your eyes. Listen, Kai, everyone makes sacrifices for the Emperor: the soldiers of the Imperial Army, the warriors of the Legiones Astartes, all the astro-telepaths who died in the Whispering Tower. Why should you be any different? All these sacrifices mean something, and you can make yours mean something too, something infinitely greater than you can imagine. You would be a hero.'

Kai shook his head as a wave of dizziness washed over him. 'I'm not a hero,' he said. 'I can't do something that's going to kill me. I don't have the courage.'

'Of course you can,' said Hiriko. 'You think heroes aren't afraid? Of course they are. That's why they are heroes. They faced their fear and they overcame it. They did the right thing even though it meant the end of their lives.'

The tingling in Kai's limbs began to fade, and an icy numbness replaced it. He glanced over at Scharff, but the man simply stood there with the dead-eyed stare of a mannequin. There would be no help from that quarter.

Hiriko lifted a long, sharp-tipped hypodermic from the silver tray attached to the chair and stabbed the needle into a bottle filled with clear liquid. She drew a measure of the fluid into the body of the injector and tapped it to remove any lingering air bubbles.

'Very well, Kai,' she said, as a droplet of liquid beaded at the sharp tip of the needle. 'If you can't be a hero yourself, then I'll make you into one.'

INTO THE CORRIDOR that led from the island. Bright lumen strips banished shadows as Atharva led the way down the rock-hewn passageway. Subha and Ashuba flanked their sergeant, while Kiron and Gythua ran side by side, with Severian at the rear of their ad hoc formation. Ahead, two servitor-crewed turrets spun around to face them, servos whining as multiple barrels rotated and auto-loaders slammed shells into breeches.

Red-eyed targeter lenses bored into Atharva like the eyes of a daemon.

'Atharva,' said Tagore.

'I see them,' he answered, holding the disembodied head before him and allowing the targeting cogitators to scan its contours and electrical activity. He fed the dying cells within the brain, keeping them alive like a medicae fighting to save a patient he knows will not survive his wounds.

'Uttam Luna Hesh Udar,' said Atharva, once again using his Pavoni arts to replicate the dead Custodian's voice.

'It's not working,' said Kiron, pressing himself against the side of the passageway as the barrels continued to spin.

'It's working,' said Atharva through clenched teeth. The Custodians used advanced biometric readers in their automated weaponry, but hopefully not ones that could tell the difference between a warm body and one kept alive by psychic means. Atharva felt the machines scan the head again, before remembering – though the memory was not his own – that the greenskin toxin that had taken Uttam out of the front line made it more difficult for the signifiers to read him.

'Uttam Luna Hesh Udar,' he repeated with confidence, and this time the weapons accepted that one of their masters was standing before them. The barrels slowed and the eyes of the servitors changed from red to green.

'Take them,' said Atharva.

The three World Eaters sprang forward like hunting dogs loosed from their chains.

Ashuba sprinted towards the gun on the left and vaulted onto the rungs of the maintenance ladder bolted to its side. His hand speared out, fingers rigid, and the servitor's head was severed from its neck as cleanly as though cut with an energised blade.

His twin and Tagore sprang onto the turret on the right, their blades hacking deep into the servitor's body in a flurry of rapid, punching blows. In seconds, nothing even remotely human was left of the cybernetic creature, just slopping chunks of carved meat that fell from the turret with a series of moist slaps. Yet for all the butchery of the slaying, there was no frenzy to the attack, each blow precise and controlled without any wasted effort.

'Let's move,' said Tagore, dropping to the ground.

Atharva moved past the turrets, impressed despite himself at the thoroughness and speed of the World Eaters' attack. Kiron, Gythua and Severian followed at his heels, and Atharva felt their admiration for their fellows' speed.

At the end of the passageway, a heavily armoured door blocked further progress, its impenetrable facings painted black and gold and marked with numeric codes that told Atharva exactly where they were in the prison complex. Gythua braced himself on the door and closed his eyes. Surely he didn't think to break the door open on his own?

'Two metres thick at least,' said Gythua, the muscles at his shoulders and biceps flexing like inflating fuel bladders. 'If I had time and leverage I could open it.'

'Which you don't,' pointed out Kiron, aiming the plasma carbine at the door.

'That won't even scratch the paintwork,' said Gythua with a disdainful glance.

'Not even the combined strength of all seven of us will be able to break it down,' said Asubha. 'Atharva, is there any life left in that head of yours? Can it open this door?'

'It better, or this is going to be a damn short escape attempt,' said Subha.

Atharva ignored them and lifted the head towards the black slate of the signifier mounted above the door. His hand was sticky with blood, and he felt the weight of death dragging the struggling synapses of the Custodian's consciousness down into oblivion.

'One last favour I must ask of you, Custodian Uttam,' said Atharva as he held the severed head up towards the signifier. His breath came in short hikes as he poured the power of the Great Ocean into the dying organ within the

severed skull. Such energies were creation unbound, but
what was dead was dead, and there could be no return from
that black abyss. All Atharva could hope was that Uttam
Luna Hesh Udar had not fallen too far into its embrace.
Every scrap of his skill went into honing his deception, his
genes donning the mask of another and his muscle density
altering to match the body mass of the Custodian.

The signifier clicked as the machine brain behind the
blank slate considered the living creature before it.

'It's not working,' he heard Kiron say. 'Why would you
break us out if you didn't have a plan to get us beyond
the first damn door? I thought you Thousand Sons were
supposed to be clever?'

'Be silent,' hissed Severian.

'I'll speak my mind as I please, Wolf,' said Kiron with
a poisonous glare.

'Enough,' hissed Asubha. 'Give it a chance to work
before admitting failure.'

The hiss and thump of disengaging locks answered
before Kiron could take issue with Asubha's words, and
Atharva sagged against the walls of the passageway as the
door swung slowly open on greased hinges. The Great
Ocean was a powerful tool to achieve impossible ends,
but it was also a demanding master. No sooner had the
door opened enough to allow passage than Severian
ghosted through the gap.

Tagore bent down to look Atharva in the eye.

'Can you continue?' he asked.

Atharva nodded and took a deep breath as he pushed
himself upright. 'I can continue.'

'Good,' said Tagore. 'I don't want to die here when the
open sky is so close.'

'You would stay here and die with me?' said Atharva.
Tagore was a killer, but at least he was a loyal killer, like
a faithful war hound that would fight and die beside its
master.

Tagore regarded him strangely, as though the question
was beneath him. 'I do not like you, Atharva, and there

is yet a reckoning to be had between us, but you are a brother of the Legiones Astartes. We fight and die as one.'

Atharva doubted the rest of their group felt as strongly, but kept that thought to himself.

'Besides,' added Tagore, gesturing to the severed head Atharva carried, 'you are the only one who knows the way out.'

'About that,' said Atharva. 'We need to make a detour before we get to the surface.'

'A detour? What are you talking about?'

Atharva dropped Custodian Uttam's head and wiped frosty sweat from his brow.

'There is another prisoner we have to free before we leave this place of incarceration.'

'More soldiers are coming,' said Tagore. 'We do not have time for fool's errands.'

'This is no fool's errand,' snapped Atharva. 'We free this prisoner or else we may as well surrender now.'

'Who is this prisoner? What is he to us?' demanded Tagore.

'Someone more important than you can possibly imagine,' said Atharva. 'Someone upon whom all our fates may rest.'

KAI COULD NOT take his eyes from the droplet on the end of the needle. The label on the bottle from which it had been drawn was turned away from him, but he had no doubt that it was a powerful sedative. The hypodermic contained enough to put him out in moments or perhaps even kill him.

'Adept Scharff or whoever you are,' said Kai. 'Are you just going to let her do this?'

Sharff flinched at the mention of his name, but did not move or otherwise acknowledge Kai's words. Whatever notion had possessed Scharff to help him had clearly passed, but neither had he shown any inclination to help his former colleague.

'This is Adept Hiriko, immediate assistance required,'

said Hiriko, speaking into a vox-bead at her collar. 'Interrogation cell four seven, primus zero.'

She smiled and said, 'In moments there will be a squad or more of soldiers here, perhaps even a Custodian, so you might as well surrender now.'

'I'll take my chances,' said Kai, lunging for the door. He pressed the opening mechanism, but the door stayed resolutely closed. It had been a forlorn hope to imagine the door wouldn't be locked, but it was all he had.

He turned just as Hiriko lunged at him with the needle extended before her. He raised his hands to fend her off, and more by luck than judgement managed to grip her forearms with the needle less than a hand span from piercing the pulsing vein at his neck. Though she was short and slender, Hiriko was stronger than she looked, and the needle inched towards his skin. Whatever Scharff had given him to counteract the soporific drugs that had kept him placid was clearly wearing off.

Kai found himself staring into Hiriko's lambent green eyes and had a brief moment to reflect that if he was going to die here, at least it would be while staring at something beautiful.

He felt the needle depress the surface of his skin, but before it could draw blood, Adept Scharff had his hands wrapped around Hiriko's shoulders. He yanked her off her feet and hurled her against the chair that had held Kai prisoner for so many nightmarish sessions of psychic interrogation.

'Scharff!' yelled Hiriko. 'Whatever is in you, fight it!'

Her attacker paid no heed to her words and Kai slid down the wall beside the door as he punched her square in the face. Hiriko reeled from the blow and sagged against the chair. Scharff leapt upon Hiriko and wrapped his hands around her neck, throttling the life out of her even as his face purpled with the effort of resisting the force that impelled him to murder.

Kai knew he should join this struggle, but his limbs were filling with ice water and lead.

Scharff's hands were crushing the life from Hiriko, and the restraint she had shown towards her fellow neurolocutor was forgotten as she accepted that the force controlling Scharff was too strong for him to defy.

Kai saw the needle glint in the harsh overhead lights, and watched as it described a short arc that saw it thrust into Adept Scharff's eye. The man howled and his back arched in pain. Scharff hurled himself away from Hiriko, as though distance from the source of his hurt could somehow lessen it. Viscous fluids drooled down Scharff's cheek and he flopped onto his back as the chemicals raced to his brain.

His body convulsed as rogue electrical impulses sent his muscles into spasm. Spittle flew from his mouth and a hideous wet gurgling bubbled up from his lungs with bile-flecked foam. Scharff beat his heels on the floor and scrabbled with clawed hands, tearing out his fingernails and leaving bloody tracks on the tiles.

Hiriko slumped to the floor as Scharff's body twitched with what remained of his life, and Kai felt sick to his stomach at the sight. He had watched the astropaths of Choir Primus die, had felt Sarashina's blood on him, and had listened to the entire crew of the *Argo* die, but to see a man die so painfully right in front of him was a truly horrific sight.

The interrogation chamber was silent save for the soft chiming of the bio-monitoring equipment, Hiriko's laboured breathing and the dripping of noxious saliva from Scharff's gaping mouth.

Kai let out a terrified breath, knowing he had only a few precious moments to make the most of the opportunity Scharff had given him. Before he could do more than recognise that fact, a booming impact struck the door of the interrogation chamber. Another swiftly followed, and Hiriko smiled as she slid down onto her side.

'They're coming for you,' she said, her words coming out in a hoarse rasp.

Another impact shook the door, and this time it

buckled inwards, the locks holding it closed shattered by the force assaulting them. One further blow tore the door from its housing, and it landed of the tiles with a booming clang. A towering shape in a form-fitting yellow bodyglove ducked through the doorway, and Kai backed away from this latest terror.

Long black hair framed a face of thick, flattened features that nevertheless combined in a handsome whole, and Kai smelled a pungent reek emanating from the warrior's skin as he extended a hand towards him.

'Kai Zulane, I am Atharva of the Thousand Sons,' said the giant. 'Come with me.'

FOURTEEN

Flight and Fight

THE GIANT'S WORDS took a moment to sink in, and even then Kai couldn't process their meaning. There could be no question that this figure was a Legiones Astartes warrior: his bulk and unspoken threat was undeniable, but there was more to it than that. Kai saw the world through artificial eyes, and every sweep, curve and angle of the giant's face seemed somehow more solid than any other living soul he had seen.

'You are Legiones Astartes,' said Kai, his words slurred and little more than a whisper.

'I already said that,' stated the giant, taking hold of Kai's shoulder and hauling him to his feet as though he weighed nothing at all. Atharva was enormous, as tall as Saturnalia, but broader and more powerfully built.

'Why?' said Kai.

'I have little time for questions, and no patience for ones so ambiguously formed,' said Atharva. 'Our escape has not gone unnoticed, and warriors we cannot face will be on their way. Now we must hurry.'

Kai stumbled through the buckled doorway of the interrogation chamber. He glanced over his shoulder at the recumbent form of Adept Hiriko, wondering if she were alive or dead. Despite all that she had subjected him to, Kai hoped she still lived.

Six figures filled the vestibule beyond the chamber in which he'd spent an unknown amount of time, six warriors of enormous bulk and distinct character that was immediately apparent even if they hadn't sported tattoos and Legion markings on engorged biceps, mountain-ridge shoulders and forearms larger than Kai's thighs. Instantly, he knew who had rescued him from his cell.

'You are the Crusader Host,' he said.

'What is left of it,' said a warrior with hair that was a dirty mix of pale white and dark roots. 'You do not see us at our best.'

'That name is meaningless to us now,' said another with a bare chest that rippled with muscles and crudely-inked tattoos of weapons and teeth. 'We are dead to the Imperium.'

'We are outcast,' spat the warrior next to him, and Kai saw a resemblance between the two that went beyond their shared genhancements.

'The Outcast Dead,' said Atharva, with a sly twist of a grin. 'If you knew what that meant in ages past, you would appreciate the irony of that.'

'The Outcast Dead,' repeated a grim-faced warrior who was a giant even in the company of giants. 'A dishonourable name for warriors, but a more fitting one than the last we bore.'

'What's happening here? I don't understand what's going on,' said Kai.

'What is to understand?' said a brute with half his head encased in hammered pig iron and plugged with copper-wound wires. 'We are fighting to be free. You are coming with us.'

'Why?'

'Again with the vaguely-worded questions,' said Atharva, shaking his head. 'Tagore, Asubha and Subha are World Eaters, Kiron is Emperor's Children, Severian a Luna Wolf and that hulking brute with the shaved skull is Gythua, a true son of Mortarion. We were incarcerated, as were you. And as Tagore says, we are fighting to be free, a situation that would be made a great deal easier if you were to save your questions until later. Understood?'

Kai nodded, and Atharva gestured to the corridor behind the warrior he had named as Kiron. Severian ghosted down its length, far faster and quieter than a man of such bulk had any right to move.

Atharva turned to one of the World Eaters and said, 'Subha, keep this one safe.'

'I am not your lapdog, sorcerer,' snapped the warrior.

'And yet you will do it,' said Atharva with a firm, demanding tone. Kai sensed a brief flare of psychic energy, but said nothing as Subha nodded and took hold of him. The warrior's fingers easily encircled Kai's upper arm, and he winced at the strength of the grip.

Atharva gave him a smile that was part conspiratorial, part shared secret, and set off after Severian. The rest of the group fell in behind them, moving with a familiarity that spoke of decades of training.

He had seen warriors of the Legiones Astartes many times before aboard the ships of the XIII Legion, but where the Battle Kings of Macragge were honourable paragons of all that it meant to be noble, these warriors were more like corsairs or mercenaries.

Or traitors, thought Kai, remembering why they had been held captive in the first place.

He was in the company of traitors, so what did that make him?

THE PACE WAS brutal, and Kai wasn't so much walking behind the Space Marines as being dragged by them. Tunnels of rock, corridors of antiseptic sterility and bare stone passageways passed in a blur until Kai lost all sense of direction.

'Enemies,' came a voice from ahead. Little more than a whisper, yet sounding as though the speaker were right in front of him. Kai saw Severian at a cross junction, making a chopping motion with his hand along a corridor at right angles to their route.

'Tagore,' said Atharva.

'On it. Asubha, low and fast.'

'Me first,' said Kiron, rolling around the corner with a rifle that looked absurdly tiny in his fist. He fired two blisteringly bright shots in quick succession, before ducking back into cover.

'Go,' he said.

Tagore bared his teeth and ran around the corner with Asubha at his side. Kai heard the pounding of feet and a feral roar that sounded inhuman in its ferocity. The grip on his arm tightened, and Kai let out a muffled grunt of pain.

'My arm, you're hurting me,' he said.

Subha looked down at him, as though offended he was even talking to him.

'My brothers kill, yet I am nursemaid to a mortal,' he hissed, but the grip on Kai's arm relaxed a fraction. Screams of pain and fear echoed from the walls, and Kai jumped in fright.

'The way is clear,' said Atharva, rounding the corner and gesturing for the others to follow. Kai was dragged along with the Space Marines, and the scene of carnage he faced at the end of the corridor was so utterly horrific that he retched until his throat was raw.

A host of bodies – it was impossible to say how many – lay in dismembered abandon at yet another cross-junction. Broken limbs, caved-in skulls and ruptured torsos lay scattered like the leavings of a slaughterhouse and wild arcs of blood looped over the walls in scarlet arches. That Space Marines were killers of men was a fact Kai understood on a very basic level, but to see the reality of their unleashed power was a shocking, sobering moment.

Kai had done nothing wrong, but these warrior's Legions had betrayed the Emperor. Just by talking to them he would be considered no better than a betrayer. Yet they had saved him from death and were killing these men for reasons he could not even begin to fathom. Though this scene of butchery sickened him, Kai had sense enough to know that any chance of life was better than the death he was certain to face had he remained here.

Only two bodies had escaped the attention of the butchers that had made a ruin of more than a dozen men in a few seconds. These two soldiers had been armed with large-calibre energy weapons, and both were headless, their necks ending in cauterised stumps.

'You shoot well,' said Atharva as Kiron moved up the corridor.

'Marksman first class,' said Kiron, tapping his shoulder. 'Only Vespasian ever outshot me in tourneys'

'Tourneys?' spat Tagore. 'Why waste time on play when there are wars to be won?'

'To hone one's skills, Tagore,' said Kiron, as though offended. 'Perfected skill beats raw violence every time.'

Tagore clenched his fists over the broken stub of his spear blade. 'Another time and I would show you the error of that belief.'

'Pissing contests? Now? Are you insane?' demanded Gythua.

Tagore laughed and slapped a hand on Kiron's shoulder with enough force to draw a scowl of displeasure from the Emperor's Children warrior.

'Another time,' repeated Tagore.

Kai let out a pent up breath, feeling the horrible tension that had built up in that fleeting confrontation. Their prowess as warriors gave meaning to each Space Marine, and to impugn that was the gravest of insults. In a brotherhood of equals, such posturing was friendly rivalry, but among warriors who shared no bond other than that forced upon them, it could be deadly.

'Where to now?' said Tagore. 'The net will be closing.'

'This way,' said Severian, taking a passageway that led upwards.

'You knew the Custodian's mind,' said Tagore. 'Is the Wolf right?'

'He is,' confirmed Atharva. 'Severian's awareness serves him well.'

Again they set off, and each time the Space Marines met resistance, they demolished it with efficiency that would have been cruel had it not been achieved with such clinical precision. Only the three World Eaters seemed to take any pleasure in the violence, but even that was more about the display of prowess than any base enjoyment of slaughter.

Onwards and ever upwards they pushed, sometimes fighting their enemies, sometimes avoiding them. Severian and Atharva had knowledge of this prison that was more than the equal of the soldiers tasked with preventing their escape, though Kai could not imagine how they could have come by such information.

'Where are the Legio Custodes?' asked Kai, in a moment between desperate flight and visceral bloodshed. None of the Space Marines had an answer for him, though he saw the same question had occurred to them all.

'They are not here,' said Gythua. 'That is all that matters.'

'They are heading to Prospero,' said Atharva. 'If they are not there already.'

'Prospero?' said Kiron. 'Why?'

'To slay my primarch,' said Atharva, and Kai heard the resignation in his voice.

Even Tagore had no reply to that, and Kai sensed their shock at so bald an assertion. Clearly there was little love lost between these warriors, but to hear so terrible a thing spoken aloud reminded them of what they had lost by being brought here.

'Is such a thing even possible?' asked Kai.

Atharva looked at him as though he had said something profoundly stupid, but the moment passed. 'Regrettably, it is entirely possible. We are all wrought from the raw matter of stars and the Great Ocean, but even stars can die and oceans turn to dust.'

'How do you know this?' asked Asubha.

'I know it because Primarch Magnus knows it,' said Atharva.

No more was said on the matter, and their brutal, bloody ascent to the surface of the world continued. Where ambushes were laid, Severian would strike from the shadows. Where attacks came upon them without warning, Tagore and Asubha would counterattack with furious strength. Where men with guns filled the passages with fire, Kiron would drop them with pinpoint shots that boiled brains within skulls before bursting them like overfilled balloons of blood and brain matter.

When barriers were erected to bar their path, Gythua would wade through hails of gunfire to batter them down, shrugging off the shots of his enemies as though they were of no more consequence than insect bites. Dried blood slathered the Death Guard's chest, and a charred crater the size of Kai's fist had been bored in his side. Armoured doors presented no obstacle to them, for Atharva possessed a golden ring, like that worn by Saturnalia, which unlocked every portal closed against them.

As the last such shutter was opened, Kai was bathed in the most beautiful illumination he had ever seen, a light he thought he had forgotten, the light of Terra's sun. Kai's augmetics recognised the filtering effect of an integrity field on the sunlight and realised they were in a mountainside embarkation bay. A row of gold-trimmed shuttles and landers lined one of the cavern's walls, and a number of less ornate craft hissed and vented pressurised gasses as servitors and loaders cleared their cargo holds and stowage bays.

'Move,' said Severian, looking back the way they had come. 'They know where we are now, and aerial units will be scrambling soon.'

Half carried, half dragged by Subha, Kai and the others ran into the hangar. Surprised faces turned towards them, ground crew, tech-priests and menials. None of them dared challenge the intruders in their midst, for it was clear that these bloodied daemons were butchers of men.

Gythua led the way, a limping mass of bloodied muscle and scar tissue. He growled with a mixture of pain and anger, leaving a spotty trail of sticky droplets in his wake. Kiron ran alongside him, ready to help his friend should he falter yet keeping his hands to himself lest the proud Gythua take offence. Severian followed and Tagore went with him. Asubha ran to the nearest craft, a sleek cutter that had not long touched down by the heat haze rippling around its engine vanes.

'Can you fly it, brother?' shouted Subha.

'This thing? In my sleep,' replied his twin.

A tech-priest in crimson robes with a rotating series of eye lenses attached to a radial disc attempted to intervene, but Subha put him down with a casual swipe of his spear. Even as the shorn halves of the Martian fell, the body's upper half continued to harangue the World Eater as a burst of panicked binary static screeched from his shoulder-mounted augmitters.

Alarms shrieked from above, and an armoured blast door began rumbling across the wide rectangle of open space visible through the integrity field. Spinning warning lights threw stark shadows and a hellish orange glow through the hangar as the ground crew who could flee took to their heels.

'Get on!' shouted Kiron. 'Hurry, the close-in defence guns are coming online!'

Subha dispensed with any pretence of courtesy and picked Kai up as though he were a recalcitrant child. The World Eater sprinted towards the open hatchway as the rest of the Outcast Dead climbed aboard.

'Atharva!' shouted Subha. 'Catch.'

Kai yelled as he sailed through the air, but Atharva caught him without difficulty and swung him around to plant him in a crew seat bolted to the fuselage. Kai felt as though every single bone in his body had been battered, and bit back a vulgar insult as Atharva pressed him into his seat.

'Don't move,' he said. 'This will not be a smooth ride.'

Subha threw himself on board as Asubha feathered the engines of the craft with a sudden shriek of power injection. The cutter leapt into the air and spun around as the crew door slid shut with a pressurising hiss of pneumatics.

'Go!' shouted Kiron. 'Get us out of here, World Eater.'

The cutter leapt forward like an unleashed colt, and but for Atharva's restraining hand, Kai would have been hurled down the length of the compartment. The craft lurched and he heard hammering blows on the aircraft's hull.

'Are they firing on us?' he yelled over the screaming engines and battering impacts.

Atharva nodded, bracing himself with his free hand on the ceiling of the cutter's crew compartment. Gythua slumped against the bulkhead, as Kiron held a stanchion beside him. Subha lay prone on the metal decking, and Tagore clung to the bulkhead at the entrance to the cockpit while Severian simply stood in the centre of the compartment as though this was just a routine lift off.

Kai screamed as the cutter rolled sharply and Asubha pushed the throttle out. The trailing edge of the cutter's left wing clipped the edge of the closing blast door, sending it into a wild spin. Centrifugal force pressed Kai into his seat, and he lost all sense of spatial awareness as the cutter boomeranged out into the open air.

Up was down and down was up. Kai lost all sense of whether they were falling or climbing as the walls and floor spun crazily. Sky and mountain flipped sickeningly through the toughened view ports, and Kai closed his eyes. At any moment they would be dashed to a million pieces against the rocks, their shredded remains spread over hundreds of square kilometres of the mountainside.

Warning lights flashed and alarms from the cockpit echoed down the fuselage. Kai heard Asubha yelling obscenities at the controls and avionic cogitator.

'I'm sorry, I'm sorry...' said Kai through gritted teeth,

repeating the words over and over again as they tumbled through the air like a dying bird until he felt the pressure of Atharva's restraining hand lift.

'To whom are you apologising?' asked Atharva.

Kai opened his eyes as his lurching senses told him they were flying level again. Hope and amazement vied for centre space in his mind as he saw tall spires of gold and the rugged flanks of the mountain sweeping past through the view ports.

'The dead,' said Kai without thinking.

'The dead need no one to apologise for them,' said Atharva. 'It is the living who need forgiveness.'

Though the words were said lightly, Kai sensed the bitterness behind them. Atharva had the bearing of a scholar trapped in a warrior's body, but there was no mistaking the potential for violence that swelled within his breast.

'Good flying, Asubha,' shouted Tagore.

'We're not done yet,' said Asubha. 'Incoming fighters vectoring in on our position. Firelances by the speed of them.'

'How far?' called Atharva.

'One hundred and eighty kilometres and closing fast.'

'Fly nap of the earth and hold your course,' ordered Atharva.

'That won't hide us,' Asubha warned him.

'I know, but I have wiles beyond your understanding,' said Atharva, closing his eyes.

FLIGHT LEADER PTELOS Requer eased up on the afterburner, letting *Eastern Light* flatten out the steep curve of its ascent from Srinagar Station. The roar of the Firelance's engine was like the bellow of a giant beast, and the force of acceleration was like being kicked in the back by one of the *migou* labourers that worked in the camps before the palace walls.

Tobias Moshar flew *Promethean Ark* just off his right wing, and Osirin Falk captained *Twilight's Fade* on his left, three flyers with a combined kill count of over two hundred enemy aircraft. Most of their combat flying had been done over two centuries ago, but the pilots remembered and their enhanced cognitive recall had lived those fights scores of times.

Requer was a natural flyer, a man who felt ill at ease when not able to take a warplane into the sky, a man who regarded a life lived on the ground as a waste of potential. The majority of sorties he flew these days were nothing more than routine intercepts of privateers bringing contraband into the mountains aboard prop-driven aircraft that predated the beginning of the wars of Unity.

This flight promised to be different.

A red-ball alert had come down from on high, and Requer had been first to the flight line, running though his pre-flight check in the shortest time before waving away the ground crew and punching the lifter-jet to get him airborne. Operations had vectored them to the target, and checking the readings on the slate before him, Requer felt his initial exhilaration bleed away as he saw how slowly the target was moving.

'Do you have the contact, Torchlight?' came the voice of Operations.

'Got it,' answered Requer. 'Bearing two-seven-nine, one hundred and sixty-seven kilometres out, altitude one thousand metres.'

'That's it, Torchlight,' confirmed Operations. 'Your orders are to close and destroy the target. Visual confirmation of destruction is required.'

'Understood, operations,' said Requer. 'What is the nature of the target?'

'As I have it, the target is a Cargo 9 escort cutter.'

'An escort cutter?'

'That's what I have here,' said Operations. 'Its destruction comes with the highest authority prefix.'

'I think we can handle an escort cutter,' said Requer.

'Understood,' said Operations. 'Good hunting.'

Requer shut off the link and opened the vox to his fellow flyers.

'You all heard that?' he asked.

'Someone *really* wants that cutter brought down,' said Moshar.

'Who do you think is aboard?' asked Falk.

Requer plotted a reverse vector for the cutter and let out a whistling breath of surprise.

'Looks like it's come from Khangba Marwu, so I'm thinking there must be some escapees on board,' answered Requer. 'Must be some very bad men aboard that cutter, so let's get this done right. We're coming up on the initial point, so climb to Angels minus two thousand on my mark.'

Moshar and Falk acknowledged his command with a click on the vox and Requer turned his attention to the countdown unfolding on the ranging scope. When the number reached zero, he pulled back on the stick and pulled the Firelance into a steep climb. Their closure rate would put them in missile range inside two minutes, but Requer wasn't about to launch until he had a visual on the fleeing cutter.

The mountains flashed past to his right, a blur of icy rock that moved too fast to make out any detail. Despite the novelty of escapees from Khangba Marwu, this mission looked like it would be as routine as any other. After all, a Cargo 9 was no match for even one Firelance, so three was overkill. The structures of the palace below were a blur, a streaking tapestry of gold, silver and white marble. Requer had flown the length, breadth and circumference of the palace a hundred times or more, and every time he found some new wonder at which to marvel. Yet he had no eyes for its magnificence on this flight, he was on a war footing and all his attention was claimed by his target.

The range marker was slipping closer to the centre of his display, and Requer looked down as he saw a flash of silver against the black rock of the mountains. The cutter was jinking left and right, hugging the side of the mountain in the false hope that such manoeuvres would keep it safe from a hunting Firelance. The pilot had skill, weaving in and out of natural rock formations at high speed to keep his pursuer from obtaining missile lock, but it would take more than that to evade Ptelos Requer.

He checked his scopes one last time. The direction was right, and the returns were solid. He craned his neck, twisting left and right to make sure there was nothing else in the air with them. The last thing he needed was an accidental shoot down of some civilian craft straying too close to an engagement zone.

Satisfied this craft below him was the Cargo 9 he had been ordered to kill, Ptelos Requer armed the weapons systems and almost immediately his helmet was filled with the harsh buzzing of a missile lock.

He eased the stick forward, pushing *Eastern Light* into a shallow attack dive.

'Target acquired,' said Requer, flipping up the trigger guard on his control column.

KAI LOOKED UP at Atharva, feeling a build up of psychic power that filled the air with an actinic chill and the bilious taste of metal. The *nuncio* was nothing compared to this, and even the *vatic* and the *er* employed no abilities of this magnitude. Atharva was a battle psychic, a warrior-mystic who wielded his powers for destruction and violence, and Kai had tasted its like only once before, in the mindhall of Choir Primus.

Without thinking, Kai opened himself a fraction to that power, feeling himself dragged along with Atharva's abilities, seeing the mountainside flash past as though he were a bird flying at impossible speed through the air. He saw the majesty of the palace below them, ten thousand towers and domes, a multitude of grand colonnades and the palatial demesnes that housed the billions of loyal servants of the Administratum.

Kai was a comet, a shooting star of thought and purpose. Incandescent, he raced through the sky until he saw three bat-winged specks that arced over the mountains towards them. The shapes grew larger until Kai saw the fighter aircraft clearly, the Firelances Asubha had spoken of: graceful war machines that could jink and spin through the air like dancers.

Their combined essence entered the mind of the lead pilot, and Kai's thoughts were immediately filled with trajectories, approach vectors and deflection values. It meant nothing to him, but the dominating presence of Atharva absorbed it in a second.

Kai looked through the pilot's eyes, seeing the ghostly green of a projected display and feeling the constricting grip of his pressurised flight suit. He felt the heaviness of his helm and the exhilaration of making an enemy kill. A warbling tone in his ear told him the missile pods slung beneath the wings had a target lock, and his thumb hovered over the firing trigger.

Before the pilot could fire, a conflicting impulse arose in his mind.

PTELOS REQUER FELT a sudden conviction that the aircraft on which he was about to fire was not an enemy craft at all, but an Imperial one. His thumb slid away from the trigger and he re-engaged the safeties on his missiles.

He blinked in confusion, pulling out of his attack dive and flying over the target. His breathing was laboured and his flight suit hissed as it compensated for his elevated heart rate and increased blood pressure.

'Requer? What happened?' asked Moshar. 'Do you have a weapons failure?'

He tried to answer, but he couldn't remember what had happened, only that he had an undeniable urge not to fire. A grey fog filled his head, making it impossible to think clearly. Flickering images of things he didn't understand flashed in his mind, painful and intrusive.

'Ptelos?' said Falk. 'Talk to me, what happened?'

Requer shook his head, trying to push the cacophony

of thoughts from his head. He banged the side of his helmet in an attempt to clear his head, but the images kept coming.

'I'm fine,' he said, but the fug of confusion pressed even deeper into his thoughts. 'I had a fire control glitch. Coming around for another pass. Hold station.'

He rolled his Firelance and pulled into a wide turn that brought him in behind the Cargo 9 once more. *Promethean Ark* and *Twilight's Fade* followed the cutter, their blue hot engines burning like bright pulsars in the early evening sky. Their light was so bright he had trouble focusing, and his mouth dropped open as the blood drained from his head.

Requer checked his scopes again, and let out a breath two threat icons appeared on his scope, enemy aircraft right in front of him. He was right on top of the enemy and they hadn't seen him! His wingmen were gone, shot down in all likelihood, and he had the drop on the enemy aircraft that had blown them from the sky.

With calm, methodical precision, Requer tagged all three contacts in front of him – the two new ones and the Cargo 9 – and once again armed his missiles.

'Requer! What are you doing?' yelled a garbled voice that sounded familiar yet completely alien to him. An enemy trick, no doubt.

'I have good tone,' he said as the trill of a target lock sounded in his helmet.

'Ptelos, your weapons are glitching again!' shouted Moshar, pulling away and climbing.

'Requer, stand down!' shouted another voice that was unknown to him.

Three missiles leapt from the rails in a bloom of smoke and peeled off in search of their targets. The first sliced up on a perfect trajectory and flew right into the engine of *Promethean Ark*. The warhead exploded deep in the guts of the Firelance and blew it apart in a spinning fireball of orange flame and silver wreckage. The remains of the blazing fuselage spun down towards the mountain, trailing thick black smoke and blisteringly bright flares of exploding munitions.

The second enemy pilot cut in his afterburners, but against missiles launched at such close range, he had no chance to evade. Every jink and roll was met and countered by the missile's seeker head until the aircraft could run no more. The pilot cut his burners and threw out the air brakes in an attempt to cause an overshoot, but the missile was already too close and its proximity fuse detonated less than ten metres from its yawning air intakes.

Flames and thousands of razor-sharp pieces of spinning shrapnel were sucked into the aircraft's engines, tearing them apart in a thunderous, chugging explosion that ripped the aircraft in two. The sight of an enemy craft so comprehensively destroyed would normally have sent a surging thrill of adrenaline through Requer's body, but he felt nothing as he watched the burning remains of his victim plummeting downwards.

Requer released his control column as he searched his scope for the third contact. Had his missile downed it already? He couldn't see it, but it had been close to where his second kill had gone down. Requer knew he should make a visual check for the third target, but it was all he could do to keep his eyes focused on the landscape around him. The idea that an enemy craft might be lining up a shot on him concerned him not at all, and a vacant smile spread across his face. The grey fog that filled his mind soothed him and kept any thoughts of the aircraft he had shot down at bay.

That contented smile never left Ptelos Requer's face as he flew his Firelance into the side of the mountain.

FIRE AND SMOKE filled the crew compartment, and Kai gagged, his consciousness returning to his body with a violent jolt. His flesh felt suddenly heavy, and he let out a cold breath as he looked up into Atharva's eyes. Flecks of winter white danced in his pupils, fading like a dream as their natural colours restored themselves.

A long tear in the aircraft's fuselage billowed smoke and Kai saw the jagged stub of the cutter's wing hanging by a collection of thick cables and dangling struts. The heavy cutter shuddered and lurched like a dying bird, dropping through the sky at high speed towards an unforgiving ground. The breath was snatched from Kai's throat and the cold of the mountains hit him like a physical blow. Roaring winds tore through the crew compartment, fanning the flames and doing its best to sweep its occupants from within.

Kiron and Gythua clung onto broken stanchions, and Severian pressed himself to the side of the aircraft. Tagore and Subha were braced against the aircraft's interior, while Atharva stood before him. The Thousand Sons warrior held onto the stowage racks above him and pressed himself against Kai to keep him from being snatched away by the wind.

'I can't hold her in the air!' shouted Asubha from the cockpit. 'We're going down!'

'How did you do that?' shouted Kai over the deafening howl of the wind.

Atharva ignored the question and said, 'Do not do that again. You could have stranded both our consciousnesses out there in that pilot's skull when he hit the mountain.'

'You made that pilot shoot down his own aircraft.'

Atharva shook his head. 'No, all I did was show him something that more closely matched his parameters of an enemy target and let him make the decision. I altered nothing of his own essential thought processes. I am powerful, but I am not *that* powerful.'

Kai thought back to what Evander Gregoras had told him of the cognoscynths, but realised that Atharva's abilities had only *steered* the pilot's thought processes, not altered them.

A subtle, but important difference.

Right now it seemed irrelevant, as the ground rushed to meet them with terrible inevitability. Towers that seemed tiny and distant from the air were now horribly close, and Kai could see a rushing collage of ramshackle structures speeding below them, close enough to make out individual buildings and streets as Asubha fought to control their descent.

The cutter made a last ditch effort to evade gravity's clutches, but that was a fight it could never win. With one wing missing and a hole blown in its side, the cutter slammed into the ground with a thunderous impact of splintering metal that seemed to go on for ever and ever.

FIFTEEN

The Hunters Assemble
Reluctant Petitioners
The Clan Lord

YASU NAGASENA IS well known in this city, and no one challenges him when he passes beneath the Obsidian Arch on his way towards the tower at its heart. It has been a long time since he trod its empty boulevards and gazed in admiration at the sublime constructions that no one beyond its walls even knows exists. The palace masons, perhaps knowing that the City of Sight's inhabitants seldom venture beyond the walls of their prison, spared no expense and employed every subtlety of their art to render a city as beautiful and harmonious as it was isolated.

'I wonder who named this place,' muses Nagasena, looking up at the gilded capitals and ornamented pediment of the Emerald Ossuary. The bones of Terra's astro-telepaths are interred within, together with those who did not survive the final rituals to render them fully capable of service. It is a place of sadness rendered in joyous architecture.

'The Ossuary?' asks Kartono.

'No, the City of Sight.'

'Someone with a perverse sense of humour.'

'Perhaps,' replies Nagasena. 'Or perhaps someone who appreciated the true value of what these poor, blind souls do here.'

Kartono shrugs, uncaring and uncomfortable at being here. Nagasena does not blame him. To his bondsman, this place is anathema. Kartono is hated by most people, for reasons they can never fully articulate, but in this place, those who encounter him hate him and know exactly why.

Kartono makes them truly blind.

The streets are deserted. Everyone in the City of Sight knows they here, sensing the empty hole in the constant chatter that throngs the air with invisible voices. They are a silence in a city of voices, and they do not pass unnoticed.

Nagasena sees them first, but it is Kartono that gives them name.

'Black Sentinels,' he says, watching the armoured squad marching towards them with rifles held at their shoulders. 'Golovko's men.'

'Led by the man himself,' says Nagasena, spotting the bulky form of Maxim Golovko at their head. 'We are honoured.'

'Honours like this I could do without.'

'Maxim has his uses,' says Nagasena. 'Some hunts require stealth, others require the hunters to flush their prey into the open with… less subtle means.'

Kartono nods, and falls in behind Nagasena as Golovko brings his men to halt before them with a crash of boots stamping the ground in unison. They are formidable soldiers, well trained, disciplined and without mercy, yet they are blunt instruments compared to the needle-precision of Nagasena.

'Maxim,' says Nagasena with a bow deep enough to indicate respect, but shallow enough to convey his superiority. It is a petty gesture, but it amuses Kartono, and Maxim will never realise its significance.

'Nagasena,' replies Golovko. 'Why are you here?'

'I am here for the hunt.'

'You received a summons?'

Nagasena shakes his head. 'No, but I am needed, yes?'

'We can catch these traitors without your help,' states Golovko. 'I'm assembling a team right now, and this will all be over by day's end.'

Nagasena looks up as a long cloudbank covers the sun.

'Show me this team,' he says.

THERE ARE THREE of them of note, and Nagasena considers them all.

Saturnalia is Legio Custodes, and his anger is matched only by his shame. The astropath, Kai Zulane, and the warriors of the Crusader Host escaped from his gaol, and such a grievous lapse can only be erased by their immediate recapture. He is angry, but he is steady. Nagasena knows he can count on a Custodian to follow instructions and Saturnalia will be the only one who stands a chance against the hunted warriors if they turn and fight.

Adept Hiriko is uncomfortable here, and Nagasena knows why. Her neck is bruised and her eyes are dotted with red pinpricks of blood where her former colleague attempted to strangle her. Though she feigns indifference, Nagasena sees his death has affected her more deeply than she will admit. She is no hunter and has only one skill that will be of use in the hunt. Hiriko is a psychic extractor, and she believes she can remove the secrets that make Kai Zulane so valuable.

Athena Diyos is a crippled astropath whose presence on such a hunt Nagasena would not normally countenance. Her body is broken, and her life-sustaining chair will only slow them down, but she has been into Kai Zulane's mind and that gives her a unique insight. She can guide them to him when he is near, and though she is an unwilling participant in this hunt, she knows she has little say in the matter.

They are gathered in the chambers of the Choirmaster, and Nemo Zhi-Meng paces the length of his sumptuous chambers with nervous energy, his white robes flapping around him like the wings of a panicked bird.

'You must get him back, Yasu,' he says, pausing in his pacing long enough to address Nagasena. His white hair is unbound and his beard is ragged. The last few days have taken a heavy toll on him, and the strain of holding an inter-galactic communications network together is visible in every strained gesture and barked utterance.

'I will, Nemo,' promises Nagasena with a bow of deep respect. 'Now tell me why this man is so important. Why did seven Space Marines put their own escape at risk by bringing him with them? There was no need for them to do such a thing.'

Zhi-Meng hesitates before answering and Nagasena tries not to read too much into that pause. 'Before the loss of the *Argo*, Kai Zulane was one of our finest operatives,' says the Choirmaster. 'He has the synesthesia codes for our highest tiers of communication. If he sends that information to traitors in service to Horus Lupercal then our entire network is compromised.'

'Zulane's record indicates he is defective as an astropath,' says Nagasena, sensing that the Choirmaster's explanation is a lie. His fingers tighten on the grip of *Shoujiki*. The blade is his touchstone to honesty, and though Nagasena does not always need to know *why* he is hunting, he dislikes hunting for the wrong reasons.

'He was,' says Zhi-Meng. 'But Mistress Diyos was working to restore his abilities.'

Nagasena turns to Athena Diyos and kneels beside her, sweeping his robes out behind him. She cannot see him with her eyes, but he knows she feels his presence.

'And how successful had you been? Can Kai Zulane send anything off world?'

Athena Diyos takes her time before answering, but Nagasena believes she is truthful. 'No. Not yet. He is recovering, but I think he is still too afraid to cast his mind into the warp.'

'That may not matter if he is in the company of

Atharva,' says Saturnalia. 'Sorcery may be able to pluck the codes from his mind.'

'Is he capable of that?' asks Nagasena, turning back to Nemo Zhi-Meng.

'Little is known of the abilities possessed by Magnus's warriors,' admits Zhi-Meng, 'but I wouldn't count it beyond the realms of possibility.'

'Then we must apprehend Kai Zulane swiftly,' says Nagasena.

'Can't you just change the codes?' asks Kartono.

'Do you have any idea what that involves?' snaps Zhi-Meng. 'Developing new ciphers for a galaxy-wide network requires decades of preparation and attempting such a task in the midst of a rebellion would be madness. No, we must find Kai Zulane before the traitor Space Marines wring the information from him.'

'If they haven't already,' says Saturnalia.

'Of all the places they had to crash,' says Golovko. 'It had to be the damn Petitioner's City. There's no maps, no plan and a thousand places they could go to ground.'

'An astropath and seven Space Marines will find it hard to stay out of sight, even in a warren like the Petitioner's City,' points out Nagasena.

'We need to get to that crash site,' says Golovko. 'Pick up the trail from there.'

'Agreed, but to hunt with success, we must first understand our prey,' says Nagasena. 'We are hunting an astropath and seven Space Marines. What I want to know is why only seven? Why did they not free everyone before they fled?'

'Does it matter?' asks Saturnalia. 'Seven traitors at liberty on Terra is seven too many.'

'Everything matters,' states Nagasena. 'Only warriors from the Legions that have sided with Horus Lupercal were freed. I believe Atharva is the leader of these warriors, and he knew enough to recognise which of the imprisoned warriors would follow him. The question then becomes, why did a warrior of the Thousand Sons engineer such a break out? His Legion is still counted as loyal to the Throne is it not?'

Saturnalia steps forward and grips his spear in both hands. 'No, it is not.'

Hiriko and Diyos gasp in shock, and even Kartono lets out a surprised breath.

'Would you care to elaborate on that?' asks Nagasena.

'The Emperor has pronounced judgement on the Thousand Sons and its Primarch,' says Saturnalia. 'Even now, my fellow Custodians draw near Prospero in the company of Russ and his warriors. Primarch Magnus is to be brought to Terra in chains.'

'Why?' asks Nagasena.

'For breaking the edicts of Nikaea and employing sorceries forbidden by the Emperor himself,' says Saturnalia. 'Valdor himself has unsheathed his blade.'

'Then Magnus will be lucky to leave Prospero alive,' says Nagasena, and he sees Saturnalia wonder if he is insulting the master of the Custodians.

'We're wasting time,' says Golovko. 'I can fill the Petitioner's City with Black Sentinels in thirty minutes. We'll take that shithole apart, brick by shitting brick until we find them.'

Nagasena shakes his head, already irritated at Golovko's lack of subtlety.

'Choose thirty of your best men, Maxim,' he says. 'More will only hinder us.'

'Thirty? You saw how badly they mauled us when we first came for them.'

'This time will be different,' says Nagasena.

'How so?'

'This time they care if they live or die,' he says.

AN HOUR EARLIER, Kai had woken in agony in a flaming steel coffin. His body felt broken, and he struggled to draw breath as something heavy pressed down on his chest. He coughed as acrid smoke drifted in a soft wind, and he heard the creak of twisted metal and sparking of ruptured cables over the crackle of flames.

He turned his head, even this small movement painful, to survey his surroundings.

The interior of the cutter had flattened on impact and the hull was an oval tube laced with broken spars of metal and hung with ribbed piping that spat hissing gasses or drooled hydraulic fluid. Atharva lay next to him, and Kai saw it was his arm that lay across his chest and pinned him to the ground.

Smoke-filtered light filled the cabin, the heavy fuselage torn open down the entire length of the cutter, and Kai was amazed he had survived so ferocious an impact. Across from him, a figure with dirty white hair picked himself up from the wreckage and shook his head.

'That's what you World Eaters call a landing,' said Argentus Kiron.

A blackened shape at the front of the craft pulled itself from a heap of broken panels and coils of spitting wiring.

'Any landing you walk away from is a good one,' said Asubha with a wide grin. It looked to Kai as though he had enjoyed crashing the cutter.

'Does it still count if you can only crawl?' asked Subha, pushing himself to his knees and spitting a wad of teeth.

'You are alive,' said Tagore, wiping blood from a series of deep gashes on his chest and smearing it over his shoulders and face like tribal war paint. Kai tried to push Atharva's arm from his chest, but he was still too weak and the warrior's arm was too heavy. The cold-eyed features of Severian appeared above him, regarding him as a hunter might study a snared animal.

'I'm trapped,' said Kai, and Severian lifted Atharva's arm from his chest. He moved on before Kai could thank him. The movement stirred Atharva, and he rolled onto his side with a groan of pain. Blood was coagulating on his face and arms, and he pulled a shard of metal the size of a dagger from his side.

A sudden cry of alarm made Kai jump and he smacked

his head on the buckled side of the cutter. He saw Kiron
kneel at the edge of the hole torn in the side of the cutter, presumably by a missile impact or the crash itself. He
clambered over the crumpled interior of the cutter to the
light and saw Gythua sitting upright in a pool of blood
with torn spars of metal jutting from the centre of his
stomach and chest.

'Looks like the Goliath was right,' said Subha. 'He *can*
die.'

'Don't say that!' snapped Kiron with a venomous glare.

Severian knelt beside the Death Guard warrior and
probed the bloody mess of his guts.

'The wound is mortal,' he said. 'We should leave him.'

'He's right,' said Gythua with a grimace of pain.

'I'm not abandoning you,' said Kiron.

'I meant about the wound being mortal,' said the
Death Guard. 'I'm dying, but you're not going to bloody
leave me here for the hunters.'

'We leave no one behind for the hunters,' agreed
Tagore.

Kai was surprised to hear such a sentiment from a
World Eater. From all he had heard, Kai had assumed
Angron's warriors to be brutal killers, without compassion or mercy. It was hard to believe a warrior that
looked so feral and brutal could have any mercy in
him, but the steel in Tagore's voice brooked no disa-
greement.

Severian saw the same thing and gave a small shrug of
acceptance.

'Then we need to get him off these spikes of metal,' he
said.

'Lift him clear,' said Tagore, waving Asubha and his
twin forward. Kai turned away as they bent down to pull
Gythua free.

'Do it quickly, World Eaters,' said Gythua.

'Don't you worry about us,' Subha told him. 'You just
mind your own self.'

Kai put his hands over his ears, but could still hear the

terrible scraping of metal on bone, the awful suction of
pierced flesh. The World Eaters strained with the effort
of pulling Gythua clear, but to the Death Guard's credit,
no more than a grunt of pain escaped his lips as he came
free of the metal spars.

Kai felt pressure on his arm, and let himself be guided
from the wreckage. Gythua gave out great shuddering
breaths as his body tried to fight the inevitable, and Kai
let out an involuntary cry of horror as he saw the monstrously bloody ruin of Gythua's body.

'Don't know what you've got to be bothered about,'
said Gythua, climbing to his feet with help from Kiron.
'It's me with the hole right through me.'

'Sorry,' said Kai, stepping from the remains of the
crashed cutter.

Kai blinked his augmetic eyes, and he smiled at the
simple pleasure of sunlight on his skin. The cutter had
come down in a wide courtyard space between a series
of abandoned structures that might once have been
warehouses. The ground was hard-packed earth and
bare rock, the buildings that clustered close like curious
onlookers at the scene of an accident.

No two were the same, constructed from sheets of
corrugated metal and crudely shaped stone. Even over
the reek of scorched iron and burning fuel, Kai could
smell the wretched aroma of human waste, sweat and
bad meat. How far had they travelled from the gaol? This
surely could not be part of the Emperor's palace.

'Where are we?' he asked, as Atharva joined him.

'My guess would be the Petitioner's City.'

'It's awful,' said Kai. 'People actually live here?'

Atharva nodded. 'A great many of them.'

'A good place to stay hidden,' said Severian, moving
to the edge of the courtyard in which they had crashed.

'Hide?' said Tagore. 'I don't plan on hiding from anyone.'

'No? Then what *is* your plan?'

'We make our way to the nearest port facility and

capture another flyer, one capable of getting into orbit without getting its arse shot off.'

'And then what?' asked Severian.

Tagore shrugged. 'We have an astropath,' he said. 'We get him to send for our brothers.'

'You make it all sound so simple,' said Severian with a wry grin. 'And I was worried for a moment that it would be difficult to escape from Terra.'

'I am World Eater,' said Tagore, a warning in his tone. 'Do not mistake simple for stupid.'

Severian nodded and turned away as Subha and Asubha helped Gythua from the cutter. Kiron emerged from the wreckage with his upper body now bared to the elements, and Kai was reminded of the marble statues with perfect physiques that flanked the steps of the Circus Athletica on the island crag of Aegina. Where the other Space Marines were bulky to the point of being ungainly and grotesque, Kiron was more akin to the proportions of a mortal, albeit one whose body was shaped to an idealised form. The torn fabric of his bodyglove now plugged the hole in Gythua's stomach, and Kai saw the yellow cloth was already stained crimson.

The Death Guard warrior had an arm around the twins' shoulders, and he took in their surroundings with a stoic shrug.

'So this is the Petitioner's City,' he grunted. 'Don't suppose there's much chance of finding a Legion apothecary around here?'

THEY TORCHED THE wrecked cutter with three blasts from Kiron's plasma carbine and moved into the winding streets of the city. Severian led the way, putting as much distance between them and the crash as was possible, given that the wounded Gythua limited their speed. They kept to the shadows and the farther they travelled into the city, the more Kai lost track of the age in which he lived.

The lanes were dark, cool and filled with shadow,

the buildings between which they travelled ancient
and dilapidated, stone facades crumbling and grimed,
patched with ad-hoc repairs and haphazard necessity.
Wirework traceries of cabling skeined the surfaces and
roofs of the buildings, a fragile network of illicit power
that looked as fragile as silken cobwebs.

Between the wires, the sky diminished to a thin brush
stroke of deepening blue.

All signs of technology began to vanish, and the air
grew sharper with spices and perfumes and sweat, undi-
minished by the stale, metallic smell of the Imperium.
The sounds changed too: echoing noises of children
reciting nonsense verse, the hectoring voice of a man
sounding like he was preaching, the buzz and whirr of
stone on stone, knife sharpeners and a hundred other
hawkers.

They turned into older streets, so narrow that the
Space Marines had trouble moving two abreast. Ragged
awnings and sagging balconies jutted into the passageways, making it difficult for Kai to see more than a few
meters in any direction. His mental map spun, flipped
around and turned inside out. Everything around him
looked so different, but, perversely, it all began to blur
together until he had no idea in which direction they
were heading.

Those few people who saw them stared in wonder at
the giants, and pressed themselves to the sides of the
ramshackle buildings or turned and ran for their lives.
Children in bright robes and tattooed faces gawped at
them as women in orange shawls hurried them away.
A multitude of skin tones dwelled here, from the exotic
to the mundane, and he saw styles of dress from every
corner of the globe: turbans, baggy silk pantaloon, all-
enclosing robes that left only the eyes open to the world,
labourers' clothes and clothes that looked fit for any
royal palace. Kai wondered what these people thought
to see warriors in their midst, towering figures of heroic
might that now passed through their slums.

Did they fear them as much as he did?

Kai stumbled after Severian in a daze, losing track of his surroundings. He had been psychically mauled and chemically subdued by his captors, both of which had weakened his body to the point of ruination. Kai's body felt like one enormous wound, and he put one foot in front of the other mechanically, too exhausted to care where they were going or what they were going to do when they got there.

Tagore expected to send an astropathic message to his brothers off-world, but he was going to be disappointed if he thought Kai could be that messenger. By the last test Athena had set him, Kai could barely manage to reach a receiving astropath one tower distant. What chance did he have of reaching one on a far-distant world? The World Eater did not look like the kind of warrior who would take disappointment well, and Kai felt a numbing dread take hold of him at the thought of his anger when he discovered Kai's limitations.

How had his life taken such a strange turn?

Kai had been honoured to serve the XIII Legion, happy to be part of so vast an undertaking as the conquest of the galaxy, and content in the knowledge that there was no better astropath in the service of the Adeptus Astra Telepathica. Now he was a hunted man, shorn of his abilities and travelling in the company of warriors the Imperium counted as base traitors.

He thought back to when this had all begun, the moment his life had turned to shit.

'The *Argo*,' he said.

'A helot vessel of the Ultramarines,' said Atharva. 'Its keel was struck in the shipyards of Calth a hundred and fifty six years ago.'

'What?' said Kai, unaware he had spoken aloud.

'The *Argo*,' said Atharva. 'You served on her for eleven years.'

'How do you know that?'

'I know a great deal about you, Kai Zulane,' said

Atharva, tapping the side of his head.

'You read my mind?

'No,' said Atharva. 'My primarch told me of you.'

Kai searched Atharva's face for any sign of mockery, but it was hard to read his features with any degree of accuracy. Though Kai and Atharva shared the same basic physiognomy, the features of the Space Marines were subtly different from those of mortals and the same visual cues did not quite hold true between the two branches of humanity.

'Really? The Crimson King told you of me?'

'He did,' agreed Atharva. 'How else did I know to come for you? How else would I know that you were aboard the *Argo* when it suffered a critical failure of its Geller field, allowing a host of warp entities to rampage through its halls to slaughter the crew, leaving you and Roxanne Larysa Joyanni Castana as the only survivors.'

Kai felt sick to his stomach at the mention of the massacre aboard the *Argo*, and he reached out to steady himself on the wall of a nearby building. His stomach flipped and though he couldn't remember the last time he had eaten anything solid, he felt as though whatever was in his stomach was about to be ejected.

'Please,' he gasped. 'Please don't talk about the *Argo*.'

Atharva held him upright and said, 'Trust me, Kai, I know the dangers of the Great Ocean better than most, and believe me when I say that the loss of that vessel was not your fault.'

'You can't know that,' said Kai.

'Oh, but I can,' said Atharva. 'My subtle body has flown the farthest immaterial tides and plunged to the warp's most secret dreamings. I know its limitless potential and I have fought the creatures that dwell in its darkest places. They are dangerous beyond your understanding, but to think that you alone could have doomed an entire ship is laughable. You credit yourself with too much.'

'Is that supposed to make me feel better?'

Atharva frowned. 'It was a statement of fact. Whether it

makes you feel better or not is irrelevant.'

Kai sank to his haunches and rubbed a hand across his brow. His skin was greasy with sweat and the roiling sensation in his stomach was continuing unabated. He retched up a thick rope of acrid saliva and spat it to the ground.

'Please,' he said. 'I need to stop. I can't go on like this.'

'No, you cannot,' replied Atharva. 'Pause a moment here.'

Kai took a deep breath and fought to quell the sickness in his belly. After a few minutes he began to feel better and looked up. Severian and Tagore were arguing, but he couldn't hear their words. Asubha supported Gythua, whose features were ashen and corpse-like. Blood stained his thighs and even Kai could see he was living on borrowed time. Kiron kept watch on the rooflines with his rifle while Subha examined the Death Guard's wound.

Of all the Legions, Kai imagined the World Eaters must know the most of battlefield injuries, that those who understood the mechanics of taking bodies apart should also understand the most about putting them back together.

'He's going to die, isn't he?' said Kai.

Atharva nodded. 'Yes, he is.'

SMOKE AND THE smell of roasting meet filled the warehouse, gathering in a layer below the roof and wreathing the iron girders in a misty fog. The walls were hung with long strips of cloth and panelled with sheets of layered metal and ash. A long fire of glowing coals burned low in a trench in the centre of the space, and spits of questionable meat turned as the skins cracked and drizzled fat.

Hard men filled the warehouse, sitting on rough wooden benches or cleaning weapons and speaking in low voices. Each one was a broad-shouldered brute, made huge by unnatural muscle growth and a rigorous regime of fighting and tests of strength that would

not have been out of place in the training halls of the
Legiones Astartes. They dwarfed the slaves that served
them, though none of the wretched individuals bound
to the Dhakal clan were particularly diminutive.

Most of these hard men bore heavy-calibre pistols,
and long, factory-stamped blades hung from their belts.
The biggest carried weapons of a bygone age: leaf-bladed
axes, long-hafted falchions and chain-length flails. Like
the warriors who once roamed the wastelands of Old
Earth, they were an anachronism in this golden age of
scientific advancement and progress, but here in the
heart of the Petitioner's City, they ruled with the iron
fist of might.

Weapon racks lined one wall and sheets of iron beaten
into the shape of kite shields ringed a shallow pit at one
end of the hall. It had the appearance of an arena, and
the dark earth was stained a deep, muddy brown from
the hundreds of frightened men and women who had
been thrown in to die for the amusement of the hard
men and their master.

Nor was this fighting pit the only indication that the
occupants of the warehouse were bloodthirsty beyond
imagining. A dozen long chains attached to windlass
mechanisms of black iron descended from the roof,
and mounted on each was a blackened corpse, pierced
through by a hook intended for a meat-vendor to hang
his butchered carcasses upon. The corpses reeked of
putrefaction, but no one in the hall appeared to care or
even notice them. In time they would be thrown out for
the city's feral dogs to devour, but there would always be
fresh meat to fill an empty hook.

The master of this hall sat at the other end, upon a vast
throne of beaten iron, though none of the hall's occupants dared turn their gaze upon him.

To look upon the clan lord without permission was
death, and everyone knew it.

Dim light penetrated the gloom of the warehouse as a
shutter door in the centre of one wall rumbled open. The

hard men barely looked up, knowing that no one would
be foolish enough to come to this place with violence in
mind. Even the arbitrators of the Emperor's law did not
come here.

A few heads nodded in greeting as the towering figure of Ghota entered, dragging a weeping man clad
in rough, workman's clothes. Ghota's meaty fist was
wrapped around the man's neck, and though he was a
stocky-built labourer, the clan lord's chief enforcer carried his as easily as a man might hoist a wayward child.

Ghota was clad in a heavy bear pelt cloak and padded
overalls unzipped to his muscled belly, and the crossed
bandoliers of blades glittered in the red glow of the
coals. His flesh shone with ruddy light that almost, but
not entirely, gave his pallid complexion a more natural
tone.

The tattoos cut into his flesh bunched and writhed as
he approached the iron throne, and he spat a wad of
gristly phlegm to the floor. Men avoided his gaze, for
Ghota was a man of unpredictable moods, quick temper
and psychotic rages. His blood red eyes were impossible
to read, and to speak with Ghota at all was to dance with
death.

Ghota halted before the throne and beat a barb-
wrapped fist against his breast.

'What do you bring me, Ghota?' said the figure on
the throne in a voice wet with the gristle of cancerous
tumours. None of the dim light from the fire trench
reached the speaker, as though understanding that some
things were better left to the shadows.

Ghota hurled the labourer to the floor in front of the
iron throne.

'This one speaks of warriors drawing near, my subedar,'
he said.

'Warriors? Really? Has the palace grown bold, I wonder…'

'No ordinary warriors these,' added Ghota, delivering
a heavy boot to the labourers gut. The man screamed

in pain and rolled onto his side, coughing blood and screwing his eyes shut. Ghota's kick had ruptured something inside him, and even if the hard men didn't kill him out of hand or toss him into the pit for a moment's amusement, he would be dead by sunrise.

'Speak, wretch,' ordered the master of this hall, leaning forward so that the barest hint of light shone from a shaven scalp and glittered on six golden studs set in his thunderous brow. 'Tell me of these warriors.'

The man sobbed and pushed himself up onto one elbow. He could barely breathe, and spoke in wheezing gasps.

'Saw them out by the empty ranges to the east,' he said. 'Fell outta the sky and smashed down in a wrecked lifter. Cargo 9 by the looks of it.'

'They crashed, and yet they walked away unhurt?'

The labourer shook his head. 'One of 'em was bloody and they had to carry him. A big man, bigger than any man I ever seen.'

'Bigger than my Ghota here?' asked the shadowed figure on the throne.

'Aye, bigger than him, they all were. Like the Space Marines on the Petitioner's Gate.'

'Intriguing. And how many of these giants were there?'

The man coughed a wad of bright, arterial blood and shook his head. 'Six, seven, I ain't sure, but they had a scrawny fella with them too. Didn't look like much, but one of the big men was making special sure he took care of that one.'

'Where are these men now?'

'I don't know, they could be anywhere now!'

'Ghota...'

Ghota leaned down and hauled the man upright until his feet were dangling just above the floor. His arm was fully extended, but he gave no sign that this feat of strength was any effort whatsoever. With his free hand, Ghota drew an enormous pistol from his holster, a weapon that bore an eagle stamped onto its foreshortened barrel.

'I believe you. After all, why would you speak false when you know you are going to die anyway?'

'Last I saw they was heading towards the Crow's Court, I swear!'

'The Crow's Court? What draws them in that direction, I wonder?'

'I don't know, please!' sobbed the labourer. 'Maybe they're taking the wounded one to Antioch.'

'That old fool?' laughed the wet voice. 'What would he know of the miraculous anatomy of the vaunted Legiones Astartes?'

'Anyone desperate enough to crash here might risk it,' said Ghota.

'They might indeed,' agreed the figure on the throne. 'And I have to ask what brings warriors like that to my city.'

The figure stood and took a step down from his throne. The labourer whimpered in fear at the sight of the man, a grossly misshapen giant with a physique so enormous he was more powerful than Ghota. Muscles like mountains clung to his body, barely contained by curved plates of beaten iron and ceramite strapped to his body in imitation of the battle plate worn by the Legiones Astartes.

Babu Dhakal approached the sobbing labourer and bent down until their faces were centimetres apart: one a blandly unremarkable face worn thin by a lifetime of work, the other a pallid corpse face of dry, desiccated skin pierced by numerous gurgling tubes and criss-crossed by metal sutures holding the cancerous flesh in place. A thin Mohawk of hair ran in a widow's peak from the clan lord's studded forehead to the nape of his neck, and jagged lightning bolt tattoos radiated from this centreline in a jagged arc to his shoulders.

Like Ghota, his eyes were a nightmare of petechial haemorrhages, red with ruptured blood vessels and utterly devoid of human compassion or understanding. These were the eyes of a killer, the eyes of a warrior who had fought from one side of the world to the other and slaughtered any man who stood in his way. Armies had quailed before this man's gaze, cities had opened their gates to him and great heroes had been humbled before his might.

A sword as tall as a mortal man was strapped to his back and he drew it slowly and with great care, like a chirurgeon preparing to open a patient.

Or a torturer readying an instrument of excruciation.

Babu Dhakal nodded and Ghota released his grip on the man.

The sword swept out, a blur of steel and red, and a vast gout of crimson splashed to the floor of the warehouse. It hissed and bubbled as it landed on the coals, filling the air with the scent of burned blood. The labourer was dead before he felt the impact of the blade, carved in a neat line from crown to crotch like a side of beef. The shorn halves of the man crumpled to the floor, and Babu Dhakal cleaned his blade on Ghota's bear-pelt cloak.

'Hang those up,' he said, gesturing to the lifeless sides of meat splayed on the floor as he sheathed his sword over his shoulder. Babu Dhakal returned to his throne and lifted an enormous weapon from a hook welded to its side.

It gleamed with all the love and care that had been lavished upon it, a hand-finished assault rifle crafted in one of the first manufactories to produce such weapons. It bore a carven eagle upon its barrel, and though it was much larger than the pistol borne by Ghota, it clearly belonged to the same class of firearm.

It was a boltgun, but no warrior of the Legiones Astartes had borne a weapon of such brutal, archaic design since the union of Terra and Mars.

'Ghota,' said Babu Dhakal with undisguised hunger. 'Find these warriors and bring them to me.'

'It shall be done,' said Ghota, hammering a fist to his chest.

'And Ghota…'

'Yes, my subedar?'

'I want them alive. The gene-seed is no use to me in corpses.'

SIXTEEN

A Different Drum
Mechlairvoycance
Blind

SEVERIAN LED THEM past to the ruined shell of what had once been a haphazardly built tenement block, but which had collapsed after one too many floors had been added to an already unstable and poorly built structure. Atharva sensed the lingering anger of those who had died here, the psychic echoes that had not yet been dispersed and reabsorbed by the Great Ocean.

Sadness dwelled here, and even those without sensitivity to the workings of the aether stayed away. In a city of millions, Severian managed to find them a deserted corner in which to take refuge and catch their breath. The Luna Wolf claimed they had come here unseen, though Atharva found it hard to imagine that their passing had gone completely unnoticed.

Water fell in runnels from the cracked floors above them, a zigzagging collection of sheet metal and timber that looked horribly unsafe, but which Gythua claimed was in no danger of imminent collapse. The Death Guard was sitting propped up against one wall with Kiron speaking to him in low tones, while the World Eater twins were examining the two blades they had taken from the dead Custodians. The power cell housings were open and it seemed they were attempting to get the energy fields working again.

Severian knelt by the largest opening in the buckled wall, scanning the approaches to their refuge for any signs of the hunt that must surely be closing in on them. Kai lay sprawled on his side in the driest part of the structure, his chest rising and falling in the gentle rhythm of sleep. The mortal was exhausted, his mind and body on the verge of complete collapse, but Atharva knew he would go on. The power that had touched his mind would not allow him to fail, and Atharva had to know what that was. Like all in his Legion, he abhorred ignorance, viewing it as a failure of effort and determination. Whatever was in Kai's mind had been deemed vital enough that the Legio Custodes had brought in psychic interrogators, and that made it a personal challenge that he be the one to extract it.

Atharva closed his eyes and let his subtle body drift from his flesh, feeling the lightness of being that came with loosening the bonds of corporeal confinement. He could not remain parted from his body for long, as their hunters would be sure to have psi-hounds in their midst, and a subtle body would be a shining beacon to them.

The mental noise of the Petitioner's City washed over Atharva, a background haze of a million people's thoughts. Banal and irrelevant, he filtered out their hopes of one day being admitted within the walls of the palace, their fear of the gangs, their despair and their numbness. Here and there, he felt the unmistakable hint of a latent psyker, a talented individual with the potential to develop their abilities into something wondrous.

It saddened him that these gifted ones would never have that chance on Terra. Had they been born on Prospero, their abilities would have been nurtured and developed. The great work begun by the Crimson King before the betrayal of Nikaea had offered blinkered humanity a chance to unlock the full potential of their brilliant minds, but Atharva knew that fragile moment when dreams take flight had been shattered forever and could never be remade.

Yet even as the thoughts of the city faded, Atharva sensed another presence hidden within its depths, something powerful and alien. His subtle body felt its nearness and he fought the urge to fly the aether towards it. Somewhere close, something had found a way through the veil that separated this world from the Great Ocean, a passage that had escaped the notice of the material world's inhabitants.

And as Atharva became aware of this intelligence, it too became aware of him and shrank back into whatever shell currently hosted its form. He could still sense it; something that powerful could not completely conceal its presence, it was a thorn in the flesh of the world that would never completely heal.

Atharva dismissed it for now and turned his thoughts to Kai Zulane. He let his body of light drift into the upper reaches of the astropath's mind, sifting through the clutter of his waking thoughts and the panic and fear of his last few weeks. The savage scarring left by the neurolocutors angered him, and Kai shifted in his dreams as that anger bled into his thoughts.

Atharva saw fleeting images of a vast desert and a towering fortress he recognised as the long-vanished Urartu fortress of Arzashkun. A dry, but informative text of Primarch Guilliman had described it, and a copy of that work resided in the Corvidae library in Tizca. Why would Kai Zulane be dreaming of such a place? True, he had served with the XIII Legion, and it was not beyond the realms of possibility that he might have seen the original work somewhere in Ultramar, but why would he have need to dream of it?

Pushing deeper into that dream, Atharva smelled the aroma of the souk, the fragrance of hookah smoke and the spiced flavour of a dead culture. He had no frame of reference for these sensations, but he sensed their importance to whatever secret Kai held within his mind.

What did the Eye want with this mortal? What could be so important that it would be placed within such a fragile vessel instead of someone worthy of its protection?

Atharva smiled as he recognised a hint of jealousy in his thoughts.

He pressed harder against the edge of Kai's dreams, employing skills beyond the imaginations of the simpletons who had tried to open his mind. He saw the desert and the vast emptiness it represented. He recognised the significance of the great fortress and the prowling shadow that circled it with a predator's patience. This was Kai's refuge, but it would prove wholly inadequate to keep a truth-seeker of Atharva's skill from eventually breaching its defences.

With a thought, Atharva was at Arzashkun's mighty gates and he looked up at the brilliant whiteness of the fortress's many towers and gilded rooftops. Portions of its silhouette were missing, and he could picture the neurolocutors disassembling its structure in an effort to intimidate their captive.

'You only drove him deeper in,' said Atharva.

He extended his hand towards the great defensive gates and willed them to open. When nothing happened, he repeated the gesture. Again the gates remained stubbornly closed to him, and Atharva felt a prescient sensation of warning as the sand around him erupted with black streamers of oozing menace. Screams of the dying enveloped him and grasping, clawed hands of glistening black matter pulled at his subtle body, tearing shards of light from his immaterial form that would leave black repercussions on his physical body.

Atharva rose up from the cloying morass of horror and fear, irritated that he had allowed himself to be surprised by such base emotions. His body floated high above Arzashkun, but the black ooze rose up like creepers climbing an invisible building towards him. Atharva had the strongest sensation that Kai's own guilt was shielding the secret within him, and he smiled in admiration for whoever had placed it there.

'Very clever,' he said. 'The defences can only ever be opened from the inside.'

ATHARVA OPENED HIS eyes and groaned as he allowed his subtle body to return to his flesh abode in the material world. The quality of light in their hiding place had changed, the sun drawing close to the western horizon as night drew in on the mountains.

'Where did you go?' said Tagore, and Atharva flinched as he realised the World Eater was right beside him.

'Nowhere,' said Atharva.

Tagore laughed. 'For someone supposed to be clever, you are a terrible liar.'

Atharva had to concede the point. 'I am a scholar, Tagore. I deal in facts and facts are always true. Lies are for lesser minds who cannot face the truth.'

'You are a warrior, Atharva,' said Tagore. 'First and foremost, that is what you were created to be. Do not forget the truth of *that* fact.'

'I have fought my share of wars, Tagore,' said Atharva. 'But it is always such a brutal business that teaches nothing except how to destroy. Knowledge can only ever be lost in war, and such loss is abhorrent to me.'

Tagore considered this and jerked a thumb in Kai's direction.

'So we broke him out and he's still alive. Are you going to tell me what's so important about him and why we risked our lives for him?'

'I am not sure yet,' said Atharva. 'I was attempting to go into his mind to find out what the Legio Custodes wanted from him, but it is hidden deep.'

'Something to do with the Emperor,' said Tagore. 'That's the only reason for the Custodians to get involved.'

'You could be right,' agreed Atharva.

'Now you will tell me why you spoke with the hunter on the steps of the Preceptory.'

Atharva had been waiting for this. There was no mistaking the vibrating chord of anger within the World Eater sergeant, and for all Tagore's lack of subtlety, he would be swift to spot any falsehood.

'It is hard to explain,' Atharva began, holding up a hand to forestall Tagore's ire, 'but I do not say that to evade an answer. My Legion has many of its warriors dedicated to the arts of divination, sifting the currents of the Great Ocean – the warp as some know it – for threads that link past, present and future. Everything that ever was and ever will be can be read in its depths, but sorting what *will* be from what *could* be requires decades of study, and even then it is an imprecise art.'

Atharva smiled, wondering what Chief Librarian Ahriman would make of that.

'Are you one of these seers?' asked Kiron, moving away from the recumbent form of the unconscious Gythua. 'Can you see the future?'

'I am Adeptus Exemptus, a high-ranking member of my fellowship, and I have trained in all the arts of my Legion, but I am not skilled enough to future-see with any degree of certainty.'

'But you saw something that day, didn't you?' asked Asubha, the blade in his hand crackling with power. 'Something that made you stand aside when you could have warned us of the approach of our attackers.'

'I did,' said Atharva. 'I saw the galaxy overturned, and moving to the beat of a different drum. I saw us as guardians of a secret that could alter the outcome of this rebellion of Horus Lupercal.'

'Enough riddles,' snapped Subha. 'Speak plainly of what you saw.'

'I can speak only in possibilities, for that is all I have,' said Atharva. 'For reasons none of us can guess, Horus has turned on his father, and three of his brothers have turned with him. Lords Angron, Fulgrim and Mortarion have joined Horus in rebellion, but I do not believe they will be the only ones.'

'Why not?' asked Tagore.

'Because Horus is no fool, and he would not risk everything in one gamble on the sands of a dead world. No, Isstvan V is just the beginning of the Lupercal's plan, and there are players yet to reveal their faces.'

'So what does this have to do with him?' asked Kiron, jerking his thumb at Kai.

'I believe that Kai Zulane knows the outcome of Horus's grand plan,' said Atharva.

He paused to let the implications of that sink in, letting each man reach the inevitable question in their own time. In the end it was Asubha who gave it voice.

'So what happens? Does Horus defeat the Emperor?'

'I do not know,' answered Atharva, 'but either way, Kai Zulane is now the most important man in the galaxy. His life is worth more than any of ours, and *that* is why I had us break him from captivity.'

'But you say the information is locked inside him,' said Tagore. 'How do you get it out?'

Atharva sighed. 'I am not sure I can,' he said. 'The information was hidden in the deepest recesses of his guilt, and such an emotion is powerful enough to defeat any interrogation.'

'Then what use is he?' demanded Subha. 'We should kill him and be done with it. All he'll do is slow us down and get us killed.'

'There is merit in what Subha says,' pointed out Kiron. 'If the future is predestined, what does it matter whether the astropath lives or dies? The outcome will be the same.'

'I do not believe in predestination,' said Atharva. 'By gaining knowledge of the future, we inherit the ability to change it, and I will not allow the future to pass me by and know that I had a chance to shape it.'

'That smacks of arrogance,' said Severian, turning from his vigil at the entrance.

Atharva shook his head. 'Does it? Is it arrogant to want to change the course of a war that will claim hundreds of thousands, if not millions, of lives? Imagine the power of an army that marched to war knowing with *absolute* certainty that it could not lose. Now imagine that same army learning that *no matter what* they could not win. Knowledge is power, the Mechanicum know this, and my Legion knows it too. Whoever holds the truth that hides in this astropath's head, will be the victor in this war.'

'So what do we do with him?' asked Kiron.

'We take him to Isstvan V,' said Subha. 'Isn't it obvious? Our place is with our Legions, and if the Red Angel has thrown in his lot with Horus, then he clearly had a good reason.'

Tagore nodded in agreement and Atharva saw that Kiron believed the idea had merit too. Asubha remained impassive and Severian did not look up. Atharva took a deep breath, knowing that what he was about to say was dangerous.

'But by the same token, if the Emperor has named them traitors, might he too have had a good reason? Perhaps your Legions are not worthy of your loyalty.'

Tagore surged to his feet, blade in hand.

'The Legio Custodes call me traitor, and now you too? I should kill you where you sit.'

'The Phoenician a traitor?' said Kiron, aiming his plasma carbine at Atharva's head. 'I'll thank you to choose your words with more care, sorcerer.'

Atharva knew he could not back down, but nor could he so baldly assert the facts in the face of such emotional response.

'How can any of you say for sure what has happened to any of our Legions? When was the last time any of us spent any time alongside our battle brothers? Fifty years? A century? Who can say for sure what their Legion has become in that time? I have not laid eyes upon the Crimson King in over seventy years, and Tagore, it has been over a century since you knelt before Angron.

'We were locked in Terra's deepest gaol simply for the insignia on our armour, not the truth in our hearts, so who is to say where our loyalty lies now? Our first loyalty is to the Imperium, is it not?'

'Any master that puts me in chains is not worthy of my loyalty,' said Tagore.

'Perhaps not, but what of our brother Legionaries? What can break such bonds of brotherhood as are forged in war? Is our loyalty now to them alone? Or is it to this fledgling band of brothers we now find ourselves within? Consider this, we have been given a unique chance, a chance to decide for ourselves the master to whom we will swear our loyalty.'

'A pretty speech,' said Tagore, tapping the side of his head. 'But I know where my loyalty lies, it is to the pri-march whose words and deeds I have followed into the fires of battle and who granted me the gift of rage bound by steel.'

'I expected as much from you, Tagore, you fought alongside Angron from the last days of the War Hounds, ever since Desh'ea, but what about you two?' asked Atharva, nodding towards Asubha and Subha. 'Neither of you have yet been augmented like Tagore. What do you say?'

'I agree with Tagore,' said Subha, an answer Atharva had expected.

'And you?'

Subha's twin met Atharva's unblinking stare with one of his own. His face was thoughtful, measured, and Atharva liked that he took time to consider the question properly.

'I believe we do not have enough facts to make a deci-sion as important as this,' he said.

'A coward's answer,' snapped Tagore, and Atharva saw the undercurrent of anger in Asubha's face. Tagore was his sergeant and deserved his respect, but they were far from the strictures of their Legion, and it was never wise to use such pejorative words amongst warriors of such notorious violence.

'You mistake prudence for cowardice, Tagore,' said Asubha. 'It may be that Horus Lupercal and our primarchs have just cause for rebellion, but Atharva speaks truly when he says that none of us know our Legions any more. Perhaps they have fallen to petty jealousies or allowed ambition to blind them to their oaths of loyalty, who can say?'

'Loyalty is all I need,' said Subha, moving away from his brother. 'I will find a way to rejoin the Legion and fight by my primarch's side.'

'Spoken like a true World Eater,' said Tagore, clapping a hand on Subha's shoulder. 'We should all rejoin our Legions. If you want to stay on Terra, Atharva, that is your business, but I will find a way to return to my primarch. I have my strength and battle brothers to guard my flanks. I *will* find a way off Terra. It may be that I will walk the Crimson Path before I get to Isstvan V, but this is a road I intend to travel.'

'And what then?' asked Atharva. 'What if you manage to reach Angron's side only to discover he is a corrupt traitor who does not deserve your loyalty?'

'Then I will take up my sword and die trying to kill him.'

'Are you hearing all this?' asks Saturnalia. 'The madness of it astounds me.'

'I hear it,' says Nagasena, 'and the sadness of it almost breaks my heart.'

Saturnalia looks up at him, unable to read his face, and Nagasena knows he is trying to decide whether he is joking or being disloyal.

'Choose your words carefully, hunter,' says the giant Custodian, 'lest you find yourself dragged back to Khangba Marwu alongside these traitors.'

'You misunderstand me, friend Saturnalia,' says Nagasena. 'I will hunt these men until the ends of Terra.

Without mercy and without pause, but to hear their fear and confusion is to know that, but for an accident of genetics, they could have fought at our side. They are lost and do not know what to do.'

'I don't know what feed you were listening to,' says Golovko, looking up from the data slate carried by Kartono. 'but I heard them say that they were going to try and get off-world to rejoin their Legions. We have to stop them.'

'Agreed,' replies Nagasena with a nod, staring hard into the grainy image flickering on the data slate. The signal is weak and distorted by all the metal and illegal antennae that cluster like wire-weed on the roofs of nearby buildings, but it is clear enough to give the hunters their first glimpse of their quarry.

Behind Nagasena, the burned remains of the Cargo 9 smoulders in the purple glow of evening, surrounded by Black Sentinels with their weapons primed and held to their shoulders. Night is drawing in, and the Petitioner's City is a dangerous place in darkness, but they have no choice but to continue onwards. Much of the shuttle has been picked clean by scavengers, its wings cut free with acetylene torches and the metal ribs of its internal structure stripped to form supporting columns or girders.

Some of the salvagers fought them, believing them to be rivals for these valuable parts, but they are now dead, shot down by the Black Sentinels as they swept in from the landing site, two hundred metres back. Saturnalia and Golovko wasted valuable time in searching the wreckage, but Nagasena knew they would find nothing.

Severian had made sure of that, and Nagasena knows he will be the most formidable of the renegades to catch. That one is a wolf, a loner who will not hesitate to abandon his fellows when he feels the breath of the hunters at his neck. Adept Hiriko stands by the crushed fuselage, running her palm over the warm metal and attempting to draw out any latent psi-traces of their targets. It is a hopeless task. Too many have travelled in this craft and too many have touched it since it crashed for any real trace to be left, but every avenue must be explored, every element considered.

Saturnalia is impatient to begin the hunt again, but Nagasena knows their prey is not going anywhere in the immediate future, and there is much that can be learned by simply observing them for a time. While the escaped Space Marines debate their future, unaware that their every move is being watched – thanks to the coerced co-operation of House Castana and Kartono's technical ability – they will gradually reveal their strengths and weaknesses, making the hunt's outcome inevitable. It is the way Nagasena trained to hunt, the way he has worked for many years, and no amount of pressure from Saturnalia or Golovko will change that.

Saturnalia turns to Kartono, his manner brusque and irritated.

'Can you identify their location from this feed?'

Kartono looks over at Nagasena, and nods slowly before answering. 'Not precisely, but maybe to within a few hundred metres.'

Saturnalia then addresses Athena Diyos. 'And if you are that close, can you establish a more precise location?'

Athena Diyos does not want to be here, but she knows she has little choice. From what Nagasena has learned of her, he knows her to be an unforgiving tutor, but a staunch friend of those who earn her trust. It is not hard to see why she should feel protective of Kai Zulane.

'I think so,' she says.

'Then we need to move,' says the Custodian.

Nagasena steps to Saturnalia, blocking his path. 'Be mindful, Custodian,' he says. 'This is my hunt, and I set the pace. You underestimate these men at your peril. In any scenario they are dangerous beyond belief. Corner them and they will fight like Thunder Warriors of old.'

'There's only seven of them, and I doubt the Death Guard will see the sunrise,' sneers Golovko. 'Throne only knows what you think you gain by waiting.'

'I gain understanding of the truth,' says Nagasena, rest-ing his right hand on the pommel stone of his sword. 'And that is the most important thing.'

'Truth?' asks Saturnalia. 'What truth do you think to learn from traitors?'

Nagasena hesitates before answering, but he will not lie to Saturnalia, for a lie would diminish him.

'I hope to learn whether I should catch these men at all,' he says.

KAI WOKE FROM a terrible dream in which his head was being slowly encased in clay that hardened around him with each breath. Like being bricked up in a suf-focating cave the exact dimensions of his body, each breath came shorter and more forced than the last. As awareness of his surroundings returned to Kai, his fatigue crashed down upon him as though he had not rested at all.

His eyes hurt and he rubbed the skin around them. His skull felt as though it was vibrating from the inside, and the interrogation clamps that had widened the orbits of his eye sockets to allow the insertion of ocular-recording equipment had badly bruised his cheeks and forehead. He scratched his eyes, feeling like there was an itch beneath his skin he couldn't reach.

Kai felt the eyes of the Outcast Dead upon him and took a deep breath as he saw the sky beyond the entrance of their hiding place was a yellowed purple, like an intensely livid bruise.

'What's happening?' he asked, sensing the tension in the warriors before him. 'Are we in trouble?'

Severian chuckled and the World Eaters grinned broadly.

'We are branded as traitors and are being hunted by our enemies,' said Tagore. 'It's fair to say we are going to be in trouble for some time.'

'That's not what I meant,' said Kai.

'We are deciding what is to be done with you,' said

Atharva, and Kai felt a tremor of fear at the casual nature of his words.

'Oh,' he said, scratching the skin beneath his eyes. 'Did you reach a decision?'

'Not yet,' admitted Atharva. 'Some of our number want to escape Terra and take you to Horus Lupercal, while others want to just kill you.'

'Kill me? Why?' gasped Kai.

'You represent a very real danger, Kai,' said Kiron, putting a hand on his shoulder, and Kai felt the killing power in that grip. The Space Marine's hand was so enormous it cupped his entire shoulder, from clavicle to scapula. With only the slightest increase of pressure, Kiron could break every bone without even thinking about it.

'Danger, what danger?'

'I suspect the information you carry is knowledge of the future,' said Atharva. 'And truth is the most dangerous weapon in any war.'

'But I don't know anything,' protested Kai. 'I told them that!'

'You do,' said Kiron, pressing hard enough to make Kai wince in pain. 'You just don't know you do. The army that carries truth as its banner cannot falter. Picture a perfect war, waged by warriors who know they cannot lose. That is the promise you carry within you, and to possess that knowledge, great and good men will do anything to make you their banner.'

'We will fight our way off this world, and you will help us,' said Tagore.

'Leave Terra?' said Kai, baring his teeth and rubbing his temples with the heels of his palms. 'Throne, it feels like my eyes are on fire.'

'What is wrong with him?' asked Subha.

Asubha knelt beside Kai and took his head in his hands. The World Eater turned Kai's head and peeled back the skin at the juncture of his augmetics. A tear of blood ran down Kai's cheek.

'Angron's blood,' swore Asubha. 'Be silent all of you, they are watching and listening.'

Kai struggled in the World Eater's grip, but it was utterly implacable. He could no more move his head than he could move his shoulder. Asubha stared straight into Kai's eyes and had he been able to move, he would have flinched at the venom he saw there.

'Clever,' said Asubha, resting his fingertips on Kai's cheeks, 'but this is where it ends.'

'What are you talking about?' gasped Kai.

'What are you doing?' said Atharva.

'Covering our trail,' said Asubha, digging his thumbs into the meat of Kai's skull and gouging out his eyes in a welter of blood and cabling.

SEVENTEEN

Death is Coming
A Snare Slipped
Antioch

KAI WORE A mask of blood and oil and coolant fluids. Subha held him up as they plunged deeper into the city, moving as fast as the wounded Gythua allowed. Tagore and Kiron supported the wounded Space Marine, and no amount of his demands to be left to die would make them drop him. Kai had given up screaming. The pain was shocking, and showed no sign of fading. He didn't think that was a good sign.

Wires flopped on his cheeks, and though he was suddenly plunged into the world most astropaths lived in daily, he was finding it hard to adjust after such a sharp trauma. Yet for such an apparently senseless and brutal act, the removal of Kai's eyes was as precise as any augmetic specialist could have managed.

Blurred lines of smudged light flashed past Kai as his blindsight struggled to reorient itself to being his primary mode of perception. He travelled in a world of sound and smell, of taste and touch. He felt the rough cobbles beneath his feet, and the cold air of night on his skin. The smell of cooking fats and precious woodsmoke drifted through covered alleyways, and the warm reek of

315

close-packed humanity was a pervasive odour that overlaid every other ingredient.

'Why did he do that?' hissed Kai between strangled
sobs and pained gasps as Severian halted them at a junction of three streets.

'What?' said Subha. 'Who?'

'Your twin, why did he take my eyes?'

Subha was visible as an angry blur of red and gold, a
confused jumble of sharp edges and confusion, his aura
rippling with almost crippling sense of isolation. Subha
missed the brotherhood of his Legion, and that weakness was killing him inside.

'You were a spy,' said the warrior.

'What? No! I wasn't. I don't understand.'

'Your eyes,' explained Subha. 'The people hunting us
were using your eyes to watch us. They heard and saw
everything in that ruined place.'

He took a breath and forced the pain down to a manageable place.

'How could they do that?' he asked.

Subha shrugged. 'I don't know. Asubha's the clever
one, not me. He was going to be sent to Mars to train as
a Techmarine before we got posted to Terra.'

'Your augmetics were provided by the Telepathica?'
asked Atharva, taking hold of his head and peering into
the caverns of his eye sockets. Kai wanted to close his
eyes, but he had no lids to close, and he could not turn
away from the golden brightness of Atharva's outline.
Where the rest of the world was subtly out of focus, the
warrior of the Thousand Sons was a crystal clear silhouette of shimmering light and wonder. So *real* was Atharva
that it set off a roiling nausea in Kai's belly.

'No,' said Kai. 'House Castana arranged the implants.'

'The Navigator House?'

'Yes,' nodded Kai, and instantly regretted it as the
motion made him sick to his stomach. He grabbed
onto Subha's arm, feeling the colours and light of the
world swirl around him like a shimmering rainbow

whirlpool. His legs gave out and he retched glistening wads of bile.

Subha lowered him to the ground and let him heave until there was nothing left to come up. Kai felt as weak as a newborn, the strength that had sustained him until now pouring from him in each expulsion. Atharva knelt beside him.

'Our hunters are cunning,' he said. 'They must have been given the specifications for your augmetics from House Castana and acquired the feed from your optic conduits. The Eye alone knows how much they heard and saw, but we must assume they are close.'

Kai felt himself lowered to the ground and propped up against a rough wall of poorly-formed adobe bricks. The texture was rough, but simply to pause for a moment was the most sublime sensation. He rested his head on the bricks, feeling the pulse of life behind it. This was a dwelling place, a home where people lived, loved and dreamed. Kai missed his clifftop home, perched on the smooth rock of what had once been an ancient king's brow. He missed the sad smile of his mother and the warm embrace of the very notion of home.

'I want to go home,' he said, as a welcome peace settled upon him. 'I miss my home... it was a nice home. You would have liked it, Athena. It had floors of pearl-smoked marble and domed ceilings painted with replicas of Isandula Verona's work.'

'What's he talking about?' asked a gruff voice he felt sure he should know. 'Who is this Athena he's talking to?'

A hand touched his brow, rough and callused from a life of hard work. It was a large hand, too large for any normal man's hand.

'His body is giving out,' said another voice. 'He was virtually dead by the time we got to him, and the crash and Asubha's *surgery* has almost finished the job. He needs medical attention.'

'What do any of us know about mortal bodies?' asked

a silver voice with a petulant edge to its vowels. 'None of us are apothecaries.'

'There will be one in this city, several probably.'

'And you know where to find one?'

'No, but someone here will.'

'Someone who can heal Gythua too?'

'Don't be foolish,' rasped the blunt edged voice of a chained angel in red. 'Gythua is on the Crimson Path, and no one in this city can turn him from its end.'

Kai heard the voices, but it seemed they belonged to shimmering ghosts that gathered around him like angels of legend. He remembered tales carved into the pillars of a sunken hall discovered by agents of the Conservatory in the fjord-beds of Scandia that spoke of warrior maidens who carried the souls of the dead to a heroic afterlife of battle and feasting.

He laughed at the idea of warrior maidens coming for him. What had he done to deserve such a gathering? Warm wetness gathered on his cheeks and he reached up to one of the figures, a golden giant limned in a halo of shimmering light.

'I saw you…' he said. 'In Arzashkun. You were in my dreamscape…'

'I was?'

'Yes, I mean, I think it was you,' said Kai, his voice trailing into a whisper as the abuses heaped upon his already weakened body took their toll. 'I remember thinking you must have a thousand more important things to do than talk to me.'

'You spoke to me?' asked the golden figure, his form leaning close.

Kai nodded. 'You said you wanted to know your future, and that I was the key to understanding it…'

'You are,' said the voice, with undisguised interest. 'And you can tell me of it whenever you are ready.'

'I will,' promised Kai, feeling as though his body was becoming lighter by second. He wondered if that was what these beings were waiting for. Perhaps it was easier to carry him away if he shed his mortal flesh. But there was one thing he wanted to know before they took him up.

'Why the Outcast Dead?' he asked. 'Why did he say it was an appropriate name…?'

Kai felt the golden giant's amusement and was content to know he had managed to please him.

'When this was a world of gods, men believed that if they prayed hard enough and lived their lives according to laws handed down by mad prophets they would go to a wonderful afterlife upon their death. They would be buried in ground deemed sacred, and at the appointed hour they would rise up to take their place in this miraculous dimension. But those who these prophets deemed outcast were not afforded such bounty, and the bodies of the unwanted, the forgotten and the invisible were sunk in the liminal spaces of the world. No markers. No headstones. Quicklime and a shallow pit. Forgotten and discarded. They were the Outcast Dead, and so are we.'

'I see…' said Kai, happy to have learned this last fact.

Another shape appeared beside the golden angel, and his aura was like a shadow, half-glimpsed and elusive. To Kai's fading senses it was beautiful, more akin to something animal instead of a man.

'Can he continue?' asked this lupine shape.

'No,' answered Kai. 'I think I'm done.'

Fresh wetness rolled down his cheeks, and a finger gently pressed it away.

'Am I crying?' asked Kai.

'No,' said the lonely warrior. 'You are dying.'

THE HUNTERS FAN out through the ruined tenement block, searching for any sign of where the escapees might have gone. Golovko paces like an angry bear, cursing the World Eater for realising they were observing them, while his Black Sentinels overturn broken pieces of furniture and ragged bundles of sodden cloth.

Saturnalia kneels beside a wet patch of cracked

permacrete and dabs his fingers in it, his golden armour glistening with moisture and the red horsehair plume of his helm hanging limply at his shoulder.

'They were here, damn it,' snarls Golovko. 'We just missed them. Someone must have seen them, so we need to get out there and break some heads until someone starts talking.'

Saturnalia and Nagasena share a wordless glance that says all that needs to be said of Golovko's outburst. Water cascades through the cracked slabs, and the sound is soothing as Nagasena moves through the space as though stalking a prey creature. His legs are slightly bent, his head cocked to one side as if listening for a telltale crackle of a breaking twig or the rustle of leaves.

Nagasena looks towards the torn entrance to the block, sliding down to sit with his back to the wall. He leans to the side and rests his head on the floor, feeling the last lingering trace of warmth from a human body.

'We're on a damn hunt, and you're lying down,' snaps Golovko. 'They were just here, and we need to get out there to find them.'

Nagasena ignores him and the Black Sentinel moves towards him.

'Are you listening to me?' says Golovko.

Kartono steps between them, and Golovko's face crumples in disgust. 'Get away from me, freak,' he says.

'Call him that again and I will let him take you to task for your rudeness,' says Nagasena.

'I'd like to see him try.'

'Ulis Kartono was trained by the Clade Masters of the Culexus,' says Saturnalia, as though speaking to a child. 'You would be dead before you could raise your rifle, Maxim Golovko.'

Golovko spits a wad of saliva, but turns away, unwilling to rise to Saturnalia's challenge.

The Custodian kneels beside Nagasena and follows the direction of his gaze.

'Kai Zulane lay here?' he asks.

'Yes,' agrees Nagasena.

Saturnalia nods. 'I found blood by the entrance. Mortal blood, still wet.'

'It is Zulane's,' says Nagasena, reaching beneath a pile of tumbled blocks of permacrete that fell from the roof an indeterminate time ago. His fingers encounter crushed fragments of stone and dust, but then he feels the cold touch of metal and smooth glass and pulls out the still-wet remains of a pair of augmetic eyes.

Saturnalia smiles as Nagasena holds them up, the thin cables dripping with bio-oils and optical fluids.

'How did you know?'

'Asubha tore out Zulane's eyes here, and he is left handed,' says Nagasena. 'It seemed logical he would discard them in this direction.'

'So you have his eyes,' asks Saturnalia. 'Does that help us find him?'

Nagasena stands pats his robes free of grey dust. 'Possibly. It is a breadcrumb that neither you nor I can follow, but perhaps others can.'

'The telepaths?'

'Just so,' says Nagasena, as Saturnalia beckons Athena Diyos and Adept Hiriko to enter the ruined tenement block. Both women are frightened, and they do not want to be here: on the hunt or in the Petitioner's City. It is an environment that is utterly alien to them, and Nagasena wonders if he will have to coerce their co-operation.

Athena Diyos looks up at the sagging roof, imagining it looks ready to collapse, while Adept Hiriko stares straight ahead, moving like an automaton. The death of her fellow neurolocutor hangs around her neck like a lead weight, but this hunt has no time for compassion. Nagasena hands the torn augmetics to Hiriko and she grimaces in revulsion.

'Are those Kai's?' asks Athena Diyos.

'They are,' says Nagasena, and Hiriko places them in Athena's outstretched manipulator arm as though they are poisonous serpents. The astropath brings the torn augmetics closer to her face, studying them intently.

'And what do you expect us to do with them?'

'I had hoped you would be able to use them in locating Kai Zulane,' says Nagasena. 'I understand from your file that you do not specialise in the arts of the *metron*, but you have some talent in that regard.'

'Once maybe,' says Athena. 'But ever since the destruction of *Phoenician* I haven't been able to read things like I used to. You'd be better off getting one of the *metron* from the City.'

Nagasena cannot tell for sure if she is lying, the corrugated scar tissue of her face contorts her features in unusual ways that conceal the usual telltales of a liar. He decides she is bluffing and says, 'You will attempt to make a reading on those augmetics or there will be dire consequences.'

'If you've read my file then you know my psychological profile says I don't respond well to threats.'

'I did not mean for you,' says Nagasena. 'I meant the Imperium.'

'You're being melodramatic,' she says, but Nagasena sees the crack in her reluctance.

He kneels beside her silver chair and places his hand over hers. The skin does not feel like skin, it has the unpleasant hairless texture of artificially grown flesh.

'Do you think we are hunting Kai Zulane?' he says. 'We are not. We are hunting seven of the most dangerous men imaginable. Men who have killed hundreds of loyal soldiers of the Imperium. Kai is their prisoner, and they mean to take him to Horus Lupercal. You understand? Whatever it is that Kai knows, the Warmaster will know. None of us know for sure what Mistress Sarashina placed within Kai's mind, but do you really want to risk it falling into hands of our greatest enemy?'

'Is that really true?'

Nagasena stands and draws his sword in one smooth motion. The blade glitters in the half-light of the ruined tenement, the blade an arc of polished silver and its black and gold wrapped handle wound in soft leather and copper wire. Athena and Hiriko's eyes widen at the sight of the weapon, but Nagasena has not drawn it with violence in mind.

'This is *Shoujiki*,' he says. 'Master Nagamitsu crafted it for me many years ago, and its name means honesty in a dead tongue of a long lost land. Before this sword came to me, I was a fool and a braggart, a man of low morals and wicked temperament. But when Master Nagamitsu presented this blade to me, its truth became part of me, and I have never spoken falsely or dishonoured its name since. I do not do so now, Mistress Diyos.'

He sees the acceptance of his words as she nods slowly and transfers the eyes from her augmetic arm to her other hand.

'Hiriko,' she says. 'I'll need your help.'

'Of course,' says the neurolocutor. 'What do you need me to do?'

'Place your hands at my temples and focus your mind on everything you learned from Kai, every dream you shared, every word you spoke. All of it.'

Hiriko nods and does as Athena says, standing behind her and placing a hand on either side of her head. Athena's fingers close over Kai's plucked eyes and she rolls the glassy orbs dextrously around in her palm like a conjurer. Dried spots of blood smear her skin, and Nagasena wonders if that will help her divine Kai Zulane's location.

'How long will this take?' asks Saturnalia.

'As long as it takes,' says Athena. 'Or perhaps you would like to try?'

Saturnalia does not reply and Athena's head sinks to her chest as she enters a *nuncio* trance. Her breathing deepens, and Nagasena moves away, feeling a sudden chill as her mind reaches out into invisible realms he cannot even begin to understand.

While Golovko's men kick down nearby doors and barrage any inhabitants they find with questions,

Nagasena casts his eyes around this squalid refuge, and feels nothing but remorse for the fate that has seen these men condemned as traitors.

Nagasena scabbards his sword as Saturnalia approaches. Though their goals are aligned, it is never wise to bear an unsheathed blade in the presence of a Custodian.

'How could the World Eater have known they were being observed?'

Nagasena shakes his head. 'I do not know, but in the end it is irrelevant. These men are Space Marines and I am coming to realise that we have underestimated them.'

'How so?'

'They were created to be the ultimate warriors, and it is easy to assume they are nothing more than gene-bred slayers whose only purpose is to kill and destroy. But they are far more than that. Their minds have been enhanced beyond mortal comprehension and their brains work in ways I will never be able to replicate.'

'Are you saying you cannot hunt them?' asks Saturnalia.

Nagasena allows himself a small smile. 'No, nothing of the sort. For all their genhancements and physical superiority, they are still men at heart.'

'What do you mean?'

'What is the biggest factor slowing their escape?' asks Nagasena.

'They are carrying a wounded man,' replies Saturnalia. 'The Death Guard will not survive much longer. They should have left him at the crash site. To risk everything by keeping him with them is illogical.'

'Would you leave an injured Custodian behind?' asks Nagasena.

'No,' admits Saturnalia.

'They are still bound by their oaths of brotherhood,' says Nagasena sadly. 'They are acting with honour. Not behaviour I would expect from traitors.'

'What are you saying?'

'And you were mistaken,' says Nagasena, ignoring Saturnalia's question and pointing to the spattered trail of
blood on the ground. 'They are carrying *two* wounded
men.'

ATHARVA BATTERED A fist on the painted metal door and
waited for an answer. The building was a ragged lean-to
built at one end of a refuse-cloaked square partially sheltered by tattered canvas awnings. A number of narrow
streets led here, and ironwork crows were perched on
many of the surrounding buildings, staring impassively
down into the square like mute observers. Though they
remained out of sight, Atharva knew at least a hundred
pairs of eyes were upon them.

'Just kick the damn door down,' snapped Tagore, and
Atharva saw the pulse of the veins at the side of his head.
The neural-implants grafted to his skull fizzed in the cold
air, and Atharva wondered what damage it was wreaking
in the delicate mechanisms of his brain.

'We need this chirurgeon to help us,' said Atharva.
'How well disposed towards us do you think he will be if
we break down his door?'

'You say that like I give a damn,' replied Tagore, plant-
ing a foot in the centre of the shutter and battering it
down with a single kick. The door crashed down inside a
room dimly lit by a low-burning lantern of crude oil and
animal grease. The smell of chemicals, hung herbs and
spoiled meat that wafted out was potent.

Asubha and Kiron dragged Gythua inside and deposited him on a wide cot bed that groaned in protest at his
weight. Subha carried Kai over one shoulder, the astropath's body looking limp and already dead. His aura was
dull and listless, but Kai was not beyond saving and it
would blaze fully once again.

'Put him there,' said Atharva, indicating a wooden
bench pushed up against one wall.

Subha gently lowered Kai to the bench and Atharva
took a moment to survey their surroundings more fully.

The room was made small by their presence, yet from what Atharva had seen of the Petitioner's City, he suspected it would be considered expansive.

The walls were hung with bundles of dried herbs, mouldering shanks of salted meat and curling sheets of paper depicting chemical structures and anatomical references. A number of tables sagged under the weight of heavy books and trays of rusting surgical equipment. Cupboards with cracked glass fronts contained hundreds of unmarked bottles of fluids, powders and crushed tablets. A bank of bio-monitors sat in the corner next to a petrochemical generator, though Atharva doubted any of them still worked.

'Are you sure this is the place?' demanded Tagore. 'Looks like just another shitty house to me. You really think a chirurgeon lives here?'

'The signs all pointed to this place,' said Atharva, lifting a dusty copy of *The Book of Prognostics* from a nearby table. He saw other works by Hippocrates, scattered without thought for any system he could discern, amongst the writings of Galen of Pergamon, Abscantus and Menodotus. These were ancient texts and priceless beyond imagining, though woefully outdated.

'What signs?' asked Kiron, wiping a smear of resin from his shoulder. 'How can people live like this?'

'People live how they must,' said Atharva. 'And the signs were there for anyone with eyes to see them. This is a Serpent House.'

'A what?' said Subha.

'A place of healing,' explained Atharva, pointing to a mural on the door Tagore had kicked down. The door was in two pieces, but it was still possible to make out the image of a bearded man clad in a long toga who bore a staff with a coiled snake entwined along its length.

'Who is that supposed to be?' asked Kiron.

'He is Aesculapius,' said a hoary old voice from the shadows. 'An ancient deity of the Grekians. Or at least he was until your ugly bastard friend put his bloody foot through him.'

A lumpen shape rolled from a previously unseen bed at the back of the room, and Atharva now picked out the reek of the man's unwashed body and sweat from the cocktail of chemicals hanging in the air. Tagore was on the man in an instant, lifting him up by the neck and pinning him against the wall. Killing fury lit his eyes as his fist pulled back to strike.

'Don't kill him, Tagore!' cried Atharva.

Tagore's fist slammed into the wall, breaking it apart and sending a cloud of brick dust and fragments falling to the floor.

'Who are you?' he demanded.

'You're in my house,' snapped the man. 'I'm the chirurgeon, who do you think I am?'

'Tagore, let him go,' said Atharva. 'We need him.'

Reluctantly, Tagore lowered the man and pushed him towards Atharva.

'My apologies, medicae,' said Atharva. 'We mean you no harm.'

'Are you sure *he* knows that?' said the man glaring at the World Eater and rubbing his neck. 'And who in the name of the Emperor's balls are you?'

Wearing only a thin nightshirt, the medicae was an unimpressive sight. From the smell of him and the look of his eyes, he was a drunk and an imbiber of narcotics, but the signs had led them to this place, and there was likely to be no other practitioner of the healing arts close enough to be any use.

'I am Atharva, and we need your help. What is your name, friend?'

'I am Antioch, and I'm not your friend,' said the chirurgeon. 'It's too bloody late for this kind of thing, so what are you doing here, breaking my door down and insulting my housekeeping? I'm too drunk and messed up to do anything for you just now.'

'This is a matter of life and death,' said Atharva.

'That's what they all say,' snapped Antioch.

'He meant yours,' said Tagore, looming over Antioch's shoulder.

'Threatening me?' said Antioch. 'Good one. *That's* the way to get my help.'

Atharva took the diminutive chirurgeon's shoulder and led him towards the bench and table where Gythua and Kai were laid out.

'What's wrong with them?' asked Antioch, barely looking at them.

'I thought you were the chirurgeon,' snapped Kiron. 'Can't you tell?'

Antioch sighed and said, 'Listen, tell Babu Dhakal if he wants to keep injecting his men with growth hormones and messing with their gene-code then he can count me out of helping him get them back on their feet. He's going too far now.'

'Babu Dhakal? I don't know who that is,' said Atharva.

Antioch snorted and looked up at him sharply, as though seeing him clearly for the first time. He peered from beneath bushy eyebrows and through rheumy eyes, studying Atharva and the warriors around him intently.

'You're not from the Babu?'

'No,' agreed Atharva. 'We are not.'

Antioch came closer and craned his head upwards, the reality of his situation now penetrating the fug of whatever narcotic haze was enveloping his brain. He rubbed his eyes with a stained sleeve and blinked furiously as though clearing it of grit.

'You are of the Legiones Astartes…' he breathed, looking from warrior to warrior.

'We are,' said Atharva, guiding him towards Kai. 'And he needs your help.'

'Help Gythua first,' said Kiron.

'No,' stated Atharva. 'Gythua can wait, Kai cannot.'

'Gythua is a Legionary,' protested Kiron. 'You would put a mortal above him?'

'I would put him above you *all*,' said Atharva, before turning to Antioch. 'Now heal him.'

Antioch nodded, and Atharva almost felt sorry for the man, woken from a stupor to find angry giants demanding that he save two lives that hung by the slenderest of threads. Even a man as disoriented at Antioch could sense that his life hung on those same threads.

To his credit, the chirurgeon rallied well, taking a deep breath and fetching a tray of surgical instruments that probably harboured more bacteria than a Biologis gene lab from the table opposite. He bent over and began to examine Kai's bloody eye sockets.

'Augmetic scarring. Input jacks torn out, and bruising around the ocular cavity,' said Antioch, dabbing away the sticky blood on Kai's cheeks with the sleeve of his nightshirt. He removed a sealed package from a bottle filled cupboard and tore the sterile lining to expose its contents. Without looking up from his work, Antioch laid a number of smaller packets on Kai's chest and with care and precision Atharva hadn't expected began to apply counterseptic gel to the inside of Kai's eye sockets before packing them with what smelled like a mix of saline and petroleum gauze.

'How did this happen?' asked Antioch. 'It's wasn't surgical, but it's neat.'

'I pulled his eyes out,' said Asubha.

Antioch glanced up, as though trying to work out whether Asubha was joking.

He shook his head and sighed. 'I won't ask why. I get the feeling I won't like the answer.'

'The people hunting us were using them to spy on us,' said Subha.

Antioch paused and bit his lip. 'So who hunts seven warriors of the Legiones Astartes?' He held his hand up before Subha could answer. 'That's a rhetorical question, by the way, I *definitely* won't like that answer. Now be quiet all of you if you want this man to live.'

Opening a suture kit, Antioch began sealing Kai's

sockets with deft strokes of the needle, working swiftly and methodically on each eye. Sweat like bullets popped on his forehead, and Atharva could see the effort it was taking for the chirurgeon to maintain his composure and steady hand. With the sutures complete, Antioch wrapped a bandage around Kai's head that, miraculously, appeared to be free of stains.

'How is it a man of your skill comes to live in a place like this?' asked Atharva as Antioch tied the bandages off and stood upright with a groan of relief.

'None of your damn business,' was the curt answer. 'So, are you going to tell me what else is wrong with him or do I have to guess?'

'He was drugged and repeatedly psychically interrogated by skilled neurolocutors.'

'Of course he was,' sighed Antioch, wiping his hands on his chest. 'And I suppose that helping you with these men makes me an accomplice in whatever it is you're mixed up in, yes?'

'Perhaps,' said Atharva. 'That depends. Save their lives and we will be gone. No one will ever know we were here.'

Antioch gave a bitter bark of a laugh. 'Half the city will already know you are here, and the other half will know by morning. You think seven warriors like you can move through a city like this without attracting notice? However superhuman you are, you're not *that* skilled.'

'He's right,' said Tagore. 'We should not linger here.'

'We're not leaving before he treats Gythua,' said Kiron.

'I didn't say that,' snapped Tagore angrily. 'Don't put words in my mouth.'

Antioch ignored the altercation and rummaged through his cupboards to concoct a hybrid potion of chemicals from a series of unmarked bottles. He filled a cracked hypo with the end result and pressed the needle against the loose flesh of Kai's arm. Before depressing the injector trigger, the wiry chirurgeon looked up at Atharva.

'You're a son of a bitch, you know that?' said Antioch.

Atharva chuckled. 'I have fought alongside the *Vlka Fenryka*,' he said. 'You are going to have to do better than that if you are trying to offend me.'

'I'll keep that in mind,' he said, and depressed the trigger.

Kai drew in a sucking lungful of air and his back arched with an audible crack. His muscles spasmed and a geyser of noxious fluids erupted from his mouth. Kai danced the dance of the hanged man on the bench, his heels rattling on the wood as his body evacuated itself from every orifice.

'I'd turn him on his side if I were you,' said Antioch, stepping away from the convulsing astropath. 'There's some clean-ish clothes in the back he can have once he's done shitting and puking. He's going to need them.'

Tagore grabbed Antioch and said, 'The astropath will live, yes?'

Antioch's face crumpled in pain at the World Eater's grip. 'The chem-purgatives should clean out his system, yes, but he's so exhausted and worn thin it's a miracle he's still alive.'

'Good enough,' said Tagore pushing Antioch towards the Death Guard. 'Now do the same for our brother.'

Gythua was barely breathing, his body having suspended most of its surface functions to divert its energies into restoring itself. Atharva had seen Space Marines survive wounds more hideous than these, but without the facilities of an apothecarion to hand, he suspected Gythua had been broken beyond repair.

Antioch bent over Gythua and, using the same instruments with which he had examined Kai's wounds, he made a thorough inspection of the bloody craters and valleys torn in the Death Guard's pallid flesh. From his expression, Atharva's worst suspicions were confirmed.

'This man should be dead,' said Antioch at last. 'For starters, this wound here looks like its ruptured his heart, and I think both his lungs have collapsed. And I don't even recognise the organ this wound's damaged. He's been shot by energy weapons and there's enough bullets in him to equip an entire squad of Army grunts.'

'Are you saying you can't save him?' demanded Kiron.

'I'm saying I can't even begin to guess at the anatomy beneath what's left of his skin,' said Antioch. 'He's beyond my help. Beyond anyone's help would be my guess, but I think you all know that.'

'Damn you,' said Kiron, pressing the chirurgeon against the wall of his home. 'You have to do something. Do you realise who this is? This is Gythua of the XIV Legion. He was the first Lantern Bearer, one of the original Seven! This man saved my life when we drove the Ringers from the equatorial ridges of Iapetus. He carried the Emperor's banner and planted it in the dark heart of *Cassini Regio* at the fall of Saturn. Do you understand?'

Atharva and Asubha prised Kiron's fingers from the chirurgeon's neck before his anger and grief overcame his intellect.

'Kiron, let go,' said Atharva. 'Killing him won't help Gythua.'

'He has to save him!'

'Nothing can save Gythua now,' said Asubha. 'He has walked the Crimson Path.'

Kiron stepped away from Antioch, his fists balled and a perfect rage boiling behind his grey eyes. He stared in hatred at the cowering chirurgeon, but even as the need to break something threatened to turn his anger into murder, Severian called out a warning from his watchful position at the doorway.

'Save your anger, brothers,' he said. 'A better target for it comes this way.'

'Our hunters?' demanded Tagore. 'Who is it, Imperial Fists or Legio Custodes?'

The Luna Wolf shook his head.

'I don't know who they are,' replied Severian, looking back out the door into the square beyond, 'but they are armed and they are definitely *not* Imperial.'

EIGHTEEN

Dark Imperium
The Battle of Crow's Court

ALL OF IT was here, all of the echoes of truth retraced, all the wasting light and the garbled words of a million madmen. It seethed in the whisper stones, swirling around the length of the tower like caged electricity that must soon earth or else burn away the fool who has summoned it into being.

Evander Gregoras swayed on the point of exhaustion, his body wasted and his flesh drained of life and vitality. He had not eaten or slept in days, the obsession to unlock the truth of what had come to this tower driving him to that liminal space between devotion and madness. A lifetime's worth of text in touch-script filled the air, a static explosion in a library held aloft in the aetheric energy that engulfed the chamber.

His books, his scrolls and every single note he had ever assembled on the Pattern was here, and the letters shimmered as though embossed with luminous gold script. The walls of the chamber oozed light into the motionless forest of pages, and as each word bled into the air it was lifted from the page before dissipating into the aether.

As each one vanished, Gregoras subsumed its meaning

and assimilated it into his understanding of the Bleed. He knew that his greatest work was dying around him, but it was a small sacrifice to unlock the elusive meaning that danced around him.

The lattice above him pulsed with light, but it was light that neither illuminated nor warmed the skin. It was a gateway to the nightmares of a city of telepaths, stored and tapped and dissected like an anatomist with a hitherto unknown form of life. The worst of the nightmares were gone, purged by the diligent and methodical work of his cryptaesthesians, but the core of it... ah, the heart of the nightmare... he had kept that here, wrapped in such complex allegory, tangential metaphors and obscure symbolism that only one as versed in the Pattern as he would ever know it for what it was.

This was what Kai Zulane knew, this was the secret he carried within him that only he could understand. *This* was what Sarashina had thought was so important that it could be trusted to no one else. Nothing of such power could pass through the Whispering Tower without leaving a bruise, and if you knew how and where to look you could reform the source of that impact.

Like a forensic chirurgeon reconstructing a murder weapon from the damage done to the victim, so too was Evander Gregoras assembling the billion fragments of information that had been hidden within the mind of the tower's greatest failure.

Its pieces were cohering, but too slowly...

He had seen tantalising hints... word shapes, expressions that meant nothing to him, but which were redolent with the promise of grim darkness in a far future...

An age of war in a lightless millennium...

Great Devourer...

Apostasy...

The Blood of Martyrs...

The Beast Arises...

Bloodtides...

Times of Ending...

Over everything, he heard the dolorous sound of
marching feet, of armies going to war in an endless
parade of slaughter and mayhem that could only end
with the extinction of all things. These armies would
never surrender, never forgive and would only ever lay
down their weapons when death claimed them at the
end of war itself.

Was Kai foreseeing the end of the Imperium? Had he
seen the ultimate victory of Horus Lupercal? Gregoras
did not think so, for these words and images were heavy
with age, dusty and burdened with a weight of history
that could only be earned after the passage of millennia.
Little more than fleeting glimpses, they nevertheless left
Gregoras in a state of dreadful terror, like a man trapped
in a nightmare of his own making and from which he
knows he cannot ever awaken.

'The truth once learned, cannot be unlearned,' had
been a favourite aphorism of his teachings, but oh, how
he wished it could be...

Each piece was a horror of war and destruction, of
stagnation and doom. As his notes dissolved around
him, they fed new morsels of information into his head
in an unstoppable and inevitable torrent. It was coming
faster now, each unlocked piece of the puzzle adding a
piece to another, larger image, until the entirety of what
had come to Terra in the wake of Magnus's foolhardy
intrusion began to emerge.

It rose from the patterns of light like a black colossus,
a destiny and a nightmare all in one. His mind tried to
grasp the full scale of what he was seeing, but it was too
large, too monumental and too terrifying to ever be contained within one fragile mortal skull.

Gregoras screamed as he saw a dark world of teeming insects, clad in black and grey, toiling endlessly in
darkened hives and subterranean nests of squalor and
misery. This was a world where nothing ever changed,
nothing grew and nothing of worth was created. And yet,
this was a world where such horror was not seen for the

nightmare it was, but as a victory, as an existence to be celebrated and rendered magnificent.

Gregoras could not imagine how the insects could bear to live such terrible lives, never knowing the glory that could be theirs, never understanding that the horror of their daily lives was unendurable. Not only did the insects exist in such stagnation, they actively fought to preserve it. Inexhaustible armies poured from this world to drive back invaders and outsiders, but instead of reforging their destiny anew on the worlds they claimed, they willingly recreated the lightless hell world from which they had come.

He knew this world, just as he knew that these *insects* were not insects at all.

The Pattern filled the chamber, pouring in with geometric accumulation of all that had passed through the whisper stones and the minds of the dead and dying. Gregoras could not bear it all, falling to his knees as the last of his books burned to ashes in the fire of truth that consumed them and poured into his mind.

'Take it back!' he yelled. 'Please, take it back! I don't want this, I never wanted to see this...'

Gregoras fell forward onto his hands and knees as the dream of the red chamber and its fallen angels filled his mind with all its awful truth. He saw everything Sarashina had seen, the clash of blades, the offer and the sacrifice, the honour and the evil. He saw it all in a blink of an eye that went on for an eternity.

And towering over it all was a seated giant atop a monstrous throne of gold, a nightmare engine constructed by lunatics and sadists. The giant's flesh was withered and long dead, a living corpse of metastasised bone and endless agony. Invisible light poured from this giant, and the torment behind his eyes was the purest pain in the world because it was borne willingly and without complaint.

'Oh, no...' whispered Gregoras, as the last fraying thread of his sanity began to unravel. 'Not you, please not *you*...'

The giant turned its gaze upon him, and Evander Gregoras screamed as he finally understood how this nightmare had come to be.

ATHARVA RAN TO the doorway of Antioch's lean-to, searching the darkness for sign of the new arrivals. They weren't hard to find, and were making no effort to conceal their approach. Every third man carried a lit torch, and the flames glittered on the ironwork crows that stared down at the unfolding drama with sculpted indifference.

Atharva counted thirty of them, tall men armoured in contoured plates of beaten iron shaped into a form that was at once familiar and yet subtly different. It took a moment for Atharva to recognise the shapes before him, for their armour was an almost perfect representation of a form of war plate no longer manufactured, a style that had not been worn in battle for hundreds of years and existed now only in revisionist history books and the dusty annexes of the Gallery of Unity. They carried guns that Atharva recognised as a kind he had once touched in that same gallery, weapons that were no less deadly for their age.

Anger touched Atharva, for the appearance of this rabble ran roughshod over the honour of the Legions, whose appearance was openly mocked by such accoutrements of war.

That they were not Legiones Astartes was immediately apparent, but who were they?

'Who in the name of all that's perfect are *they*?' asked Kiron at his shoulder.

'I do not know,' said Atharva, 'but I intend to find out.'

He closed his eyes and let his mind drift beyond the confines of this squalid refuge. He felt the glaring mind presences of the men, recognising the touch of bio-manipulation in their inflated physiques and gnarled genetic code. They were freaks, abominations against humanity crafted by a geneticist with no sense of beauty or the natural workings of a body. The Pavoni bent the base codes of physicality, but even they were bound by the fundamental building blocks of life.

These men had been twisted out of shape and pressed into a mould, the functionality of which their bodies could never hope to maintain. To a man, they were dying, but didn't realise it. Their minds were a crude mesh of aggression, fear and incipient psychosis. On any civilised world, they would have been locked away for the rest of their lives or handed over to the Mechanicum to be wrought into the most basic servitor class.

Yet in the centre of these men was a very different figure, a man whose flesh had likewise been augmented beyond the human norms, but whose body displayed none of the crudity employed in enhancing the others. This man's physique was a work of genius, in the same way that the printing press had been a work of genius in comparison to handwritten manuscripts. And just as the printing press of old had been superseded by more powerful solutions, so too had this man's biology…

Atharva briefly touched his mind, and recoiled at the jagged, razor edges he found in its construction. Like volcanic rock formed from the heat and pressure of the deep earth's forces, it was glassy and scarred, shaped to one purpose and one purpose alone: to conquer a world.

The vitrified scarring on this man's mind was familiar and it took a moment only for Atharva to recall where he had seen such rude psycho-cognitive engineering.

Within the mind of Kai Zulane.

He pulled back as he sensed the rampant hostility of the man's unconscious mental defences, all belligerence and vicious barbs – like an attack dog guarding a threshold. There would be no dominating this man with the Athanaean arts. Atharva opened his eyes, looking at the bulky, crudely-armoured form of the man with a new sense of wonder and awe.

'To destroy you would be to run amok with a flame-lance in a library of priceless tomes.'

'What did you say?' growled Tagore.

'These are no ordinary men,' said Atharva. 'Do not underestimate them.'

Tagore shook his head. 'They will die like ordinary men,' he spat. 'Thirty warriors? I will kill them myself and we will be on our way.'

Atharva placed a restraining hand on Tagore's shoulder and tried not to flinch when the World Eater gave him a ferocious grimace of bared teeth and wild aggression. The implants on the back of his skull hummed with activation, and Atharva saw the danger inherent in the habitual use of such augmetics. Tagore was as much a prisoner of its siren song of violence as Angron had ever been of the slave culture said to have trained him in the arts of slaughter. He wondered if Angron appreciated the irony of enslaving his own men.

'Antioch!' shouted the man with the vitrified mindscape. 'The men in there with you, send them out. Babu Dhakal wants them.'

'Shitting, bastard hell,' hissed Antioch. 'It's Ghota. Throne help me, we're dead.'

Atharva spun to face the cowering chirurgeon. 'Who is he, and who is this Babu Dhakal?'

'Are you serious?' said Antioch, crawling on all fours to get beneath the heaviest table in his shack. 'Babu Dhakal is trouble, like you hadn't brought enough to my door already!'

'And Ghota?'

'The Babu's attack dog,' said Antioch, trying to put as much heavy furniture between himself and the open doorway as possible. 'You don't mess with Ghota if you know what's good for you. People who do end up hung from hooks in pieces.'

Asubha hauled the man from his hiding place and said, 'Who is Dhakal, a local governor? The authority around here?'

Antioch gave a strangled laugh. 'Sure, you could say he's the authority around here. He's a gang lord, one of the last left standing after the blood eagle war. He controls all the territories from the Crow's Court to the Petitioner's Arch and south to the Dhakal Gap. And if you know what's good for you, you'll do as Ghota says.'

'I'm getting tired of waiting, Antioch!' shouted Ghota, his voice a gurgling rasp of cruelty.

Tagore and Subha flanked the doorway, and Severian peered through a gap in the ill-formed brickwork. Atharva moved to where Kai lay in a cursive pose of misery, his body a reeking mess of vomit and expelled matter. Thankfully, he was unconscious, though he shivered with micro-tremors as his body purged itself.

Atharva heard the metallic clatter of weapons being readied to fire and swept Kai into a protective embrace as thirty heavy calibre rifles opened fire.

A sawing blitz of gunfire tore into Antioch's surgery, ripping through the adobe bricks and sheet metal like a las-cutter through flesh. Woodwork splintered, brickwork was pulverised to powder and the air filled with ricochets, flying glass and smoke. The noise was deafening, thunderous and intended to intimidate as much as cause harm.

In a bygone age and against any other targets it might have worked.

Atharva looked up as the barrage ceased, his enhanced sight easily picking out the forms of his fellows. None had been hit by more than a passing sliver of glass or bullet fragment.

Severian grinned and said, 'What's your plan, son of Magnus?'

As much as he loathed resorting to violence, Atharva knew this was no time for subtlety or clever words. Only one plan of action would see them through this encounter.

'Kill them all,' he said.

Tagore grinned. 'First sensible thing you've said all day.'

* * *

THE WORLD EATERS charged from the smoke and dust of gunfire, sprinting with ferocious speed that seemed impossible for such enormous figures. Atharva watched them run with the morbid fascination a man might reserve for watching one alien species destroy another.

Tagore hit first, his fist punching clean through the breastplate of a warrior with twin topknots of black hair and a forked beard. Even as the man fell, Tagore stripped his dead hands of his weapon and turned it on the men standing beside him. The armour Ghota's men wore looked like Thunder Armour, but that resemblance did not stretch to its protective qualities. Thudding recoil and enormous muzzle flare obscured Atharva's view for the briefest second, but in its wake he saw three men cut virtually in two by Tagore's point-blank discharge.

Subha and Asubha charged at his flanks, the energised blades torn from the spears of the dead Custodians flickering with blue light. Subha's charge was the hammerblow of pure force, scattering men like the detonation of a grenade. Though the blade he bore was more akin to a greenskin's cleaver, Asubha wielded it with the precision of a skilled dissector of the dead. Two men went down, headless, a third and fourth with their innards tumbling to the square in looping ropes of wet meat. A fifth lost both his arms and collapsed with a gurgling scream of pain.

Atharva emerged from the bullet-riddled remains of Antioch's surgery with Kai held at his side. He maintained a kine shield around the astropath's body as he watched his brothers of the Crusader Host take Ghota's men apart. Argentus Kiron loosed relentless bursts of plasma from a position of cover in the ruined façade, incinerating heads with every shot and taking cover from the desultory return fire coming his way.

Yet for all the initial damage wreaked by the Outcast Dead, these men were not ordinary mortals who would be cowed by such horrific slaughter. They had been engineered by unknown means to disregard fear or compassion, and fought back with instinctive brutality. Tagore took a round to the side and roared in pain as a shower of bright blood erupted from the wound.

The World Eater shouted, 'In the name of Angron!' and put a fist through the shooter's face, spinning on his heel to unleash a hail of fire into his scattering enemies. Two men were punched from their feet by the impacts. A knot of warriors armed with pistols and long, gutting knives surrounded Asubha stabbing and cutting with manic fury. Atharva saw one blade cut deep into the meat of Asubha's bicep, but the World Eater twisted aside before the blow cut the tendons of his shoulder.

He spun low and cut his attacker in two, darting like a striking snake as he stabbed and thrust with his butcher's blade. Tagore appeared at his side and shot two men in the back before they could turn to face him. The World Eaters sergeant laughed, revelling in the murderous ballet that raged around him, and didn't see the blow that drove him to his knees.

Ghota loomed above Tagore, a heavy hammer of wrought iron spinning around his body as though it weighed nothing at all. Another crashing hammer blow thundered into Tagore's side, sending him spinning through the air as he struggled to rise. Subha threw himself at Ghota, but a backhanded jab of an elbow smashed into his jaw and sent him flying.

'Kiron!' shouted Atharva, edging towards one of the narrow alleyways that led from this battleground. 'Kill that one!'

A bright lance of plasma energy spat from the ruins, but either Ghota had heard Atharva's shout or some preternatural sense warned him of imminent danger, and he swayed aside from the killing blast. The warrior of Fulgrim's Legion vaulted from the ruins and ran towards Ghota, outraged that this upstart had ruined his perfect record of headshots.

Asubha thrust with his crackling blade, but Ghota turned it aside and sent a thunderous left hook into his attacker's jaw. Asubha staggered, his face a mask of shock more than pain. A pistoning jab crashed into Asubha's face, then another, and the warrior reeled as Ghota swung his hammer in a killing arc.

Atharva dropped his kine shield long enough to lift his mind into the lower Enumerations where he could draw on the basic abilities of the Pyrae. With a surge of thought, Atharva hurled a searing bolt of cracking fire towards Ghota. It struck the hulking warrior before he could deliver the deathblow to Asubha, and the cloak at his shoulders erupted with flame.

Ghota roared in pain and tore the blazing cloak from his armour as a fluid shape emerged on the flank of the attackers. The ghostly form of Severian slid from the shadows like a wolf on the hunt. He killed without warning, leaving dead bodies in his wake and moving before his victims were even aware of their danger.

Kiron threw aside his discharged plasma carbine and swept up Subha's fallen blade. The edge no longer crackled with energy, but Kiron did not care. His dirty white hair flowed behind him as he attacked like a swordsman forced to fight with an unbalanced blade.

'You might look like us, but you're just a pathetic copy,' snapped Kiron.

Ghota laughed. 'Is that what you think?'

A duel between a swordsman and a longer-reaching hammer was an unequal contest, but these were no ordinary combatants. As Severian killed with impunity and the World Eaters regrouped in the midst of a furious short-range firefight, Kiron darted and wove between slashing blows of Ghota's hammer. His skill was prodigious, his footwork flawless and his attacks launched with no hint of their target, and Atharva saw him working towards a decapitating strike.

It was a battle of contrasts: precisely controlled skill and perfect discipline against raw violence and hunger for the kill. In the end, there could only be one victor. Kiron ducked beneath a killing arc of the hammerhead and thrust his blade into the narrow gap between Ghota's breastplate and pauldron. The blade stabbed deep into the meat of the man's body, yet he merely grunted as the blade went in. Ghota shoulder barged Kiron, gripping him by the neck and smashing his forehead into the exquisitely handsome features of his opponent.

Kiron's nose and cheeks broke, transforming his beautiful face into a shattered mask of fractured bone and squirting blood. Atharva paused in his escape, stunned at Kiron's wounding. Though gunfire and screams still filled the square, the tempo of the battle seemed to drop as the combatants on both sides watched so perfect a warrior fall.

Ghota's hammer looped around in a bludgeoning curve, and smashed into Kiron's shoulder, destroying muscle and flesh and driving down into his chest in a welter of broken ribs. Atharva heard the crack of bones and felt a sympathetic spasm of pain as Kiron's agony flared in the aether.

Kiron spat a torrent of blood, staring defiantly at his killer.

Ghota's hammer swung around to crush Kiron's skull to splinters.

A heavy fist caught the enormous weapon's haft on its downward arc, a pale, sepulchral hand streaked with blood and empowered with all the strength bred into the warriors of Mortarion's deathly Legion.

Gythua sent a right cross into Ghota's jaw, the blow hitting home like a pile-driver and sending Babu Dhakal's warrior reeling.

'That's my friend you've killed,' he barked.

Atharva knew the Death Guard should not be alive. He should already be dead, a bled-out corpse cooling on Antioch's bench. He shouldn't even have survived the crash, but here he was, unyielding even unto the end. Ghota shook his head and spat blood, taking in the measure of his opponent and giving a crooked-toothed smile.

'You're as good as dead,' said Ghota.

'That's as maybe,' agreed Gythua. 'But come near my friend again and your blood will run with mine on this fine ground.'

'I'll kill you before you can raise a fist,' Ghota promised.

'Then come on, boy,' snapped the Death Guard. 'You're boring me already.'

Gythua's talk was brave, but Atharva knew he could not hope to stand against Ghota. Determination and honour were keeping Gythua on his feet, but they wouldn't be enough against so formidable an opponent.

The sounds of gunfire slackened, and Atharva saw that as Kiron and Ghota had fought, Severian and the World Eaters had finished the battle. Bodies littered the square, some cut open, some headless and some simply torn limb from limb. The odds in this battle had turned on their head, and Atharva saw that understanding in Ghota's blood-red eyes.

The warrior raised his hammer and spat on the ground before walking away from the slaughter. No one raised a weapon against him, though Tagore had one of his victim's guns held across his bloodied chest. Subha and his twin watched Ghota go with a mixture of wary respect and anger, while Severian swept up a fallen rifle and scanned for fresh threats.

With Ghota out of sight, Gythua sank to his knees beside Kiron, his head dropping to his chest as the life ebbed from him. Atharva ran to his side and laid Kai down on the ground in time to catch the Death Guard as his indomitable strength finally gave out. He held the dying warrior and wiped blood from his ghostly pale face.

Beside him, Kiron coughed a frothed mouthful of blood and struggled to speak through the pain of his shattered body. The World Eaters gathered round, bloodied angels of death come to witness the final moments of their fallen brothers. Even Antioch had emerged from the wreckage of his home to see something most mortals would never see through the entire span of their impossibly brief lives: the death of a Space Marine.

'Didn't… think… you'd get a… glorious death… all to… yourself, did you?' hissed Kiron with gurgling, breathy effort.

'Can't say I was… trying… to die at all,' replied Gythua. 'Damn fool of you to go up against that big bastard.'

Kiron nodded. 'He made me miss, and… I never… miss…'

'I won't tell,' said Gythua, and the last of his life bled out.

Kiron nodded and put a hand on Gythua's shoulder before letting out a rattling cough that stilled his breath. Atharva watched the light of his aura fade to grey and bowed his head.

'They are gone,' he said.

'They died well,' observed Tagore, one hand pressed to his side where he had been shot.

Asubha knelt beside the two dead warriors and closed their eyes.

'Their Crimson Path is ended,' said Subha.

Tagore looked over at Atharva and aimed his gun at Kai. 'You still think the astropath is worth this?'

'More than ever,' said Atharva with a nod as Severian emerged from the shadows with a weapon held at his shoulder.

'Good enough,' said Tagore, lifting the weapon as though seeing it for the first time.

Severian turned his gun around in his hands and said, 'You know what these weapons are, who they were made for?'

'Yes,' replied Atharva. 'I do.'

'I heard they were dead,' said Tagore. 'I thought they all died in the last battle of Unity.'

'So history tells us, but apparently Terra holds its own secrets,' said Atharva, staring at the thin wisp of fumes drifting from the hissing patch of ground where Ghota had spat.

'History can wait,' said Severian. 'Our hunters will not, and this will draw them to us like moths to a flame.'

'What about Gythua and Kiron?' asked Subha. 'We can't just leave them here like this.'

Atharva turned to Antioch. 'Do you have any suggestions, chirurgeon?'

'I can't keep them,' he said, shaking his head. 'I'm in enough trouble as it is.'

'No, but as chirurgeon in a place like this, you must be aware of places where dead bodies can be taken.'

Antioch looked up, and whatever caustic reply was forming on his lips remained unspoken as he saw the deadly earnestness in Atharva's eyes.

'Best you can do is to take them to the Temple of Woe,' he said. 'There's an incinerator there if you don't want the bodies picked clean by daybreak.'

'The Temple of Woe?' asked Atharva. 'What is that?'

Antioch shrugged. 'A place where folk that don't want their dead left to rot take their bodies. They say it's run by a priest, if you can believe that. I hear he's some madman who lost his mind and thinks that death is something you can appease with prayers.'

'And how would we find this place?'

'It's a few kilometres east of here, built into the foot of the scarp you can see over the roofs there. You can't miss it, there's dozens of statues carved into its walls. Leave your friends at the feet of the Vacant Angel, and they'll be done right.'

Atharva's psychic senses flared at Antioch's words, and the memory of his recurring vision returned with all the clarity of a lucid dream.

A haunted mausoleum, a stalking wolf and the towering statue of a faceless angel…

NINETEEN

Enemy Emperor
Night is Falling
Execution

KAI FELT WARMTH on his face and a cool breeze caressed his skin with fragrances of glittering oceans, long grasses and exotic spices designed to inflame the senses. He wanted to open his eyes, but some lingering anxiety made him keep them shut for fear that this precious moment of peace might be snatched away from him.

He knew he was dreaming, and the realisation of that did not worry him unduly. The life he had left in the waking world was one of pain and fear, emotions he did not have face in this state of limbo. Kai stretched out his senses, hearing the soft sighing of water on a beach, the rustle of wind through high treetops and the emptiness of space that can only be felt in the greatest wildernesses.

'Are you going to make your move, Kai?' asked a voice that came from right in front of him. He knew the speaker instantly: the golden figure he had pursued through the marble cloisters of Arzashkun. Hesitantly, he opened his eyes, surprised for some reason that he could do so.

He sat on a wooden stool before a polished regicide board on the shores of the lake beyond Arzashkun's walls. The game was underway, and the silver pieces were arranged before Kai, the onyx ones laid out before a tall figure clad in long robes of deepest black. His opponent's face was hooded, but a pair of golden eyes glittered deep in the blackness within. Embroidered words in fine black thread were stitched into every seam and fold of the fuliginous robes, but Kai couldn't read them, and gave up trying when the figure spoke again.

'You have come a long way since last we spoke.'

'Why am I here?' asked Kai.

'To play a game.'

'The game's already begun,' pointed out Kai.

'I know. Few of us are granted the privilege of being present for the beginning of events that shape our lives. One must look at the board one is presented with and make of it what you can. For example, what do you see of my position?'

'I'm not much of an expert on regicide,' admitted Kai, as his opponent pulled back his hood to reveal a face that shimmered in the haze of sunlight that danced through the waving leaves of this oasis. It was a kindly face, a paternal one, yet there was a core of something indefinable, or perhaps undefined, behind that mask.

'But you know the game?'

Kai nodded. 'The Choirmaster made us play it,' he said. 'Something about making us appreciate the value of taking the proper time to make a decision.'

'He is a wise man, Nemo Zhi-Meng.'

'You know him?'

'Of course, but look at the game,' insisted his opponent. 'Tell me what you see.'

Kai scanned the board, seeing that a number of the pieces were hooded, making it impossible to ascertain their loyalty. From what he understood of the game's complexities, it appeared there could only be one outcome.

'I think you're losing,' said Kai.

'So it would appear,' agreed the figure, drawing the hood from one of the pieces, 'but appearances can be deceptive.'

The revealed piece was a Warrior, one of nine remaining to onyx, rendered as an ancient soldier in gleaming battle plate.

'One of yours,' said Kai.

'Then make your move.'

Kai saw the revealed piece had been pushed forward as part of an aggressive opening, but it had been left unsupported by its fellows. Kai moved his Divinitarch from a nearby square and took the piece, placing it on the side of the board.

'Did you mean to sacrifice your Warrior?' asked Kai.

'A good sacrifice is a move that is not necessarily sound, but which leaves your opponent dazed and confused,' said the figure.

'I was told that it is always better to sacrifice your opponent's pieces.'

'In most cases, I would agree, but real sacrifice involves a radical change in the character of a game, which cannot be effected without foresight and a willingness to take great risks.'

And so saying, the figure swept his Fortress down the board and toppled Kai's Divinitarch. The piece in the figure's hand glittered in the sunlight, seeming to shift from black to silver and back to black.

'The sacrifice of a Warrior is most often played for drawing purposes,' said the figure with a sad smile. 'Against the very strongest players it can prove to be quite useful, and one of the advantages of playing so risky a gambit is that the average opponent knows little of how to defend against it.'

'What if you're not playing an average opponent?' asked Kai. 'What if you're playing someone just as clever as you?'

Kai's opponent shook his head and crossed his arms. 'If you allow timidity to guide your play then you will never achieve victory, Kai. All you will find are new ghosts to fear. Too often you allow the fear of that which your opponent has not even considered to keep you from greatness. *That* is the truth of regicide.'

Kai looked down at the board, enjoying this moment of calm in the pain-filled nightmare his life had become. That it was a temporary fiction made it no less real at this point, and Kai had no intention of rushing to embrace the madness of his waking life.

'Do I have to go back?' he asked, moving his Templar forward.

'To the Petitioner's City?'

'Yes.'

'That is up to you, Kai,' said the figure, repositioning his Emperor. 'I cannot tell you which path to choose, though I know the one I would wish you to take.'

'I think the warning I have is for you,' said Kai.

'It is,' agreed the figure. 'But you cannot tell me yet.'

'I want to,' said Kai. 'If you *are* who I think you are, can't you just, I don't know, lift it from my mind?'

'If I could, do you not think I would have done so?'

'I suppose so.'

'I have seen a great many things, Kai, but some secrets are hidden even from me,' said the figure, indicating a handful of hooded pieces that Kai was sure hadn't been there a moment ago. 'I have watched this moment many times and replayed our words a thousand times, but the universe has secrets it refuses to reveal until their appointed hour.'

'Even from you?'

'Even from me,' said the figure with a wry nod.

Kai took a deep breath and rubbed his eyes. The skin around them was irritated and sore.

'The Choirmaster always said regicide was about truth,' said Kai as they took turns to move their pieces across the board.

'He was right,' said the figure, moving his Emperor another square forward. 'No fantasy, however rich, no technique, however masterly, no insight into the psychology of your opponent, however deep, can make regicide a work of art if it does not lead to the truth.'

Despite Kai's averred lack of skill in regicide, the game appeared to be balanced in neither player's favour, though he had more pieces remaining. After the opening salvoes and the mystery of the middle game, it was clear the endgame was now in sight. Both players had lost a great many pieces, but the lords of the board were coming into their own.

'Now we come to it,' said Kai, moving his Empress into a strong position to trap his opponent's Emperor. In the early stages of their game, Kai's Emperor bestrode the board with confident swagger, while his opponent's had remained steadfastly in defence, but now the master of onyx drew nearer the fighting line.

Their pieces jostled for position, and Kai had a growing sense that he had been lured into this attack, but he could see no way his opponent could win without the ultimate sacrifice. At last, he made a confident move, sure he had the onyx Emperor boxed in by his cardinal pieces.

Only when the robed figure moved his Emperor boldly forward did he realise his error.

'Regicide,' said his opponent, and Kai saw with growing admiration and shock how deftly he had been manoeuvred into baring his neck to the executioner's blade.

'I don't believe it,' he said. 'You won with your Emperor. I thought that almost never happens.'

His opponent shrugged. 'During the opening and middle game stage, the Emperor is often a burdensome piece, as it must be defended at all costs, but in the endgame it has to become an important and aggressive player.'

'It was a bloody game,' Kai pointed out. 'You lost a great many of your strongest pieces to bring my Emperor down.'

'Such is often the way with two equally skilled players,' said the figure.

'Do we play again?' asked Kai, reaching for the pieces lost in the game.

The figure reached over and took hold of Kai's wrist. The grip was firm, unyielding, and Kai sensed strength that could crush his bones in an instant.

'No, this is a game that can only be played once.'

'Then why is the board ready to play again?' asked Kai, seeing that all the pieces were restored to their starting positions without him having touched them.

'Because there is another opponent I must face, one who knows every gambit, every subtlety and every end-game. I know this, because I taught him.'

'Can you defeat him?' asked Kai with a mounting sense of unease as a shadow moved on the edges of the oasis.

'I do not know,' admitted the figure. 'I cannot yet see the outcome of our meeting.'

The robed figure looked down at the board, and Kai saw the pieces had moved once more, into a convoluted arrangement that defied interpretation. He looked up and saw his opponent clearly for the first time, seeing the burden of an entire civilisation resting upon his broad shoulders.

'How can I be of service?' asked Kai.

'You can go back, Kai. You can go back to the waking world and bring me the warning Sarashina gave you.'

'I'm afraid to go back,' said Kai. 'I think I might die if I do.'

'I fear that you will,' agreed the figure.

Kai felt a cold knot in the heart of his stomach, and the fear that had consumed him since the *Argo* returned with a sickening lurch. The sky darkened, and Kai heard muttering voices raised in argument from somewhere far distant.

'You're asking me to sacrifice myself for you?'

'No sacrifice is too great for the scalp of the enemy Emperor,' said the figure.

COLD MIST GATHERED around the many benches bearing laboratory equipment, and the hum of generators could be heard beyond the insulated walls of the low-ceilinged chamber. Banks of equipment that would not look out of place in the halls of a Martian geneticist whirred as centrifuges spun clinking vials of raw materials, incubators nursed gestating zygotes and vats of nutrient-rich liquid fostered the growth of complex enzymes and proteins.

That such a well-equipped laboratory existed on Terra was not surprising, but that it was to be found in the heart of the Petitioner's City was nothing short of miraculous. It was akin finding a fully functioning starship buried in the ruins of Earth's prehistory.

Babu Dhakal tended to a silver incubation cylinder in which a chemical soup of elements bubbled with life. The clan lord's armour had dulled with condensation, and the dying flesh of his face was limned with hoarfrost. He no longer felt the cold, as he no longer felt pain or heat or pleasure. One by one, the joys that made existence such a gift were dying.

Just as *he* was dying.

Dhakal's former master had wrought him to be faster, stronger and more powerful than any of the feral barbarian gene-sept warriors that claimed fealty over Humanity's birthrock, a soldier to drag their world back from the anarchy into which it had fallen. Those had been golden days, when the eagle and lightning banner had marched before unstoppable armies of Thunder Warriors.

Battles had lasted weeks on end, with body counts in the millions and duels of titanic warlords that sundered mountains and split continents. Those victories were now dismissed as lurid hyperbole, and historians now refused to believe that such clashes of arms could possibly have been fought. Why their worthless hides were not flogged for this dull-witted blindness was beyond him, but in his heart of hearts he knew that this dreary new age could not sustain such legends without scoffing at the *sturm und drang* of those heady, bloody days.

Dhakal remembered toppling the Azurite Tower with

his bare hands, and wondered what the scuttling little remembrancers that documented this shining bauble of an Imperium would make of the tales he might tell.

The machine before him chimed and Babu Dhakal turned from reveries of his glory days to the task at hand. The silver steel tube vented coolant gasses and a ribbed tube gurgled as nutrient fluids drained away. The upper half of the cylinder hissed open, revealing a gauzy mesh cushion, upon which lay a glistening organ of raw, fresh-grown meat. A web of artificial capillaries fed the organ hyper-oxygenated blood, but patches of necrotic black veined the organ like a diseased lung.

'Not another one' whispered Babu Dhakal, his hands curling into fists. 'I am trying to correct what cannot *be* corrected.'

He closed the incubation cylinder gently, taking deep breaths to calm the rising fury within his chest. He supposed he should be used to such failures, but he was not a man to whom such acceptance came easy. Would he have fought through five battle legions of Grinders had he been such a man? Could he have cast down the Hammer Halo of the Iron Tzar had he been a man to accept failure?

He gripped the edge of the bench in his thick hands, buckling the metal with his furious disappointment. Babu Dhakal wanted to sweep the equipment from the benches and vent his towering fury on the laboratory that had defied him for so long, and only with the greatest effort did he manage to restrain himself. Like everything else in his body, impulse control was eroding and he was a hair's breadth from becoming no better than the barbarian people thought him to be. Yes, he had killed men since the bitter day of Unity, yes he had yoked a city's worth of people beneath his rule, but had he not done that with a greater purpose in mind?

A flashing red light accompanied the rattling of a decompression shutter behind him. Only one other had permission to enter this place of forgotten wonders and miracles, and Babu Dhakal turned as Ghota entered with a downcast expression on his face. Even his eyes, so red with blood, were hooded with failure.

'You return in defeat,' said Babu Dhakal, the word ashen and alien on his tongue.

'Yes, my subedar,' said Ghota, dropping to his knees and lifting his head to expose the cabled veins of his neck. 'My life is yours to end. My blood is yours to spill.'

Babu Dhakal stepped down from the platform upon which he had been working and drew a long dagger with a serrated blade from a thigh scabbard. He rested the killing edge on the pulsing artery in Ghota's neck, and toyed with the idea of driving it home just to feel the warm wetness of the man's blood.

'Back in the day I would have taken your head without a thought.'

'And I would have welcomed it.'

Babu Dhakal sheathed his dagger and said, 'This is a new age, Ghota, and there are few enough of us left alive to continue the old ways,' he said. 'For now, I have need of your heart remaining within your chest.'

Ghota stood and balled his fist upon his chest, a salute that had now fallen out of favour, but which still held meaning for warriors born in a forgotten time.

'Subedar,' said Ghota. 'Command me.'

'The men you took with you?'

'All dead.'

'No matter,' replied Babu Dhakal. 'They were but failed experiments. Tell me of these "Space Marines". What are they like?'

Ghota sneered and squared his shoulders, though he had no right to do so. 'They are not our equal, but they are warriors fit to bear the eagle.'

'And so they should be,' said Babu Dhakal. 'They stand on our shoulders to achieve greatness. Without us, they would not exist.'

'They are but pale shadows of what we were,' said Ghota.

'No, they are the next step in the evolution of the superwarrior, it is we who are pale shadows of what they are. Yes, we are stronger and hardier than them, but our genetic legacy was never meant to last. Old Night may be over, but for us a new night is falling. We were not built to live beyond Unity, did you know that?'

'No, my subedar.'

'Our genes were always flawed but I cannot decide whether that was deliberate or simply ignorance. I hope for the latter, but I suspect the former. This world's master is careless with his creations, and I wonder if his primarchs know that when their task is done they will be cast aside in favour of the mortals in whose name they fight. Like the angels of old, I fear they will not take the idea of such rejection well.'

Ghota said nothing, the reference to the ancient text lost on him.

'How many warriors did you face?' asked Babu Dhakal.

'Seven, but two of them are now dead, my subedar,' said Ghota. 'Only five remain.'

'You killed those two yourself?'

'One of them, the other was dying anyway.'

'Then we must find them, Ghota,' said Babu Dhakal, lifting a metal device from a nearby bench and affixing it to the upper face of his gauntlet. A whirring series of needles, blades and surgical tools snapped from the mountings with a hiss of cryo-cooled air, and Babu Dhakal smiled.

'We are dying every day, but with their genetic material I may yet find a way to reverse the slow decay of our bodies. You understand the significance of this?'

'I do, my subedar,' said Ghota.

Babu Dhakal nodded, and asked, 'Where are these five warriors now?'

Ghota said, 'In the east. I have men watching them. Word will be sent.'

'Good,' said Babu Dhakal. 'We will do this ourselves, my jamadar. You and I. We will rip the bleeding progenoids from their living flesh and we will have that which the Emperor has denied us.'

'Life,' said Ghota, savouring the feel of the word.

MOONLIGHT POOLS IN the open square, bleaching it of colour, but no light from the night sky can dull the vivid redness of the blood splashed around its haphazard mix of cobbles, flagstones and bare earth. Nagasena scans the rooflines for any lingering threat, though he does not expect meet any real resistance here. At least not from their prey. Ironwork crows festoon the eaves and ridges of the buildings, and refuse piles at the edges of the square.

Debris from a daytime market, he thinks.

Tossed in with the rest of the day's refuse are a host of dead bodies, at least twenty-five, maybe more. Each one has been killed without mercy, shot or eviscerated with guns, blades and bare hands.

'This is Space Marine killing,' he says, and Saturnalia nods in agreement.

Hiriko and Athena stare in open-mouthed horror at the damage wrought upon these men, amazed how disastrously a human body could be broken into pieces. They are not used to physical violence, and to see the sheer visceral capabilities of the Legiones Astartes has shocked them to their core.

'It is hard to see is it not?' asks Nagasena, not unkindly.

Adept Hiriko looks up, her face pale and her lips dry.

She nods and says, 'I know what the Space Marines are, but to see just how thoroughly they can dismantle another man's body is…'

'Terrible,' finishes Athena Diyos. 'But is what they were created to do.'

'That and so much more,' says Nagasena.

Hiriko looks at him in puzzlement, but says nothing.

Athena Diyos has led them to this square, following the fading, intangible thread of Kai Zulane's agony, and though it is hard for her to aid his hunters, her loyalty is first and foremost to the Imperium. She trusts Nagasena's vow of honesty, though he is having a harder time in justifying this hunt to himself.

He already knows the Choirmaster's explanation of why Kai Zulane needed to be found was a lie, but that does not offer him any comfort. Especially in light of what Nagasena heard Atharva tell his fellow escapees through the optic feed. Saturnalia and Golovko dismiss the words of traitors, but Nagasena knows that just because a man is labelled a traitor does not make him a liar.

If Kai Zulane *does* know the truth, has Nagasena any right to suppress it?

He rebuilt his life on the basis of truth being the rock upon which all things stood, and he had vowed on the ashes of his old ways never to hide from the truth or allow others to obscure it. Nagasena wonders how that will go at the end of this hunt…

'The bodies are still warm,' notes Saturnalia. 'We are close.'

'Who do you think they were?' asks Athena, grimacing in distaste as Kartono eases past her, making sure he does not touch her. Nagasena's bondsman pulls a dismembered arm from the wet pile of torn meat and wipes blood from a bicep that still twitches with residual electrical activity. A tattoo of crossed lightning bolts has been added to with an artful representation of a bull's head. Nagasena knows that bovine animals were once sacred to the people that lived in this region, but his knowledge of the symbol's significance ends there.

'This is Babu Dhakal's clan marking,' says Kartono.

'Is that supposed to mean something to us?' snaps Hiriko. Her hostility is borne of nothing Kartono has done, but simply of his very nature. He has long grown used to the unreasoning hatred of telepaths, and lets her anger wash over him.

'He is a criminal,' says Kartono. 'The clan master of a gang that runs most of the Petitioner's City. Whores, food, drugs, weapons, you name it, none of it moves without the Babu's say so.'

'So how did these men fall foul of our prey?' wonders Nagasena.

'Who cares?' states Maxim Golovko. 'They're traitors to the Imperium and if they want to kill some crime lord's men then so much the better.'

'Look at these men, Maxim,' Nagasena urges him. 'These are not normal men.'

'They're dead men,' says Golovko, as though that is the end to the matter.

Saturnalia takes Golovko by the arm and holds him fast. The master of the Black Sentinels is a position of great respect, but even he must bow to the power of the Legio Custodes. The Custodian dwarfs Golovko, and his gold armour lends weight to his authority.

'Listen to what Yasu Nagasena has to say,' suggests Saturnalia.

Golovko nods and shrugs off his hand. 'So what's so special about them?' he asks.

'Look at their size,' says Saturnalia.

'They're big, so what?'

'I know it is hard to tell, but I would estimate that most of these men were as tall as the men we are hunting,' says Nagasena, imagining these body parts reassembled into human form. 'And that crossed lightning bolt tattoo was once the symbol of the Thunder Warriors who fought at the side of the Emperor in the earliest wars of Unity.'

'What are you saying?' asks Athena Diyos. 'That these are those same warriors?'

Nagasena shakes his head. 'No, they are long dead, but I believe someone has replicated at least part of the process involved in transforming a mortal man into such a warrior.'

'Impossible,' says Saturnalia. 'Such technology is the domain of the Emperor alone.'

'Clearly not,' replies Nagasena. 'And the question we now face is how these men came to run afoul of our prey? I do not believe it to be simple happanstance. I believe they were seeking them out. And that means that whoever engineered these men is clearly aware of the nature of the men we hunt.'

He looks down at the bodies and adds, 'If not their capabilities.'

'In other words, we are not alone in our quest,' says Saturnalia, reaching the logical conclusion of Nagasena's thought.

Golovko shakes his head and says, 'Then we're wasting time,' before leading the Black Sentinels into the square. They move like the professional soldiers they are, and Nagasena follows them out, knowing immediately where he needs to go as his eyes alight on the smouldering remains of a lean-to structure that has been shredded by heavy calibre gunfire.

'That's bolter damage,' says Saturnalia, levelling his spear and squaring his shoulders.

Nagasena nods, unlimbering his long rifle and unsnapping the safety as he moves towards the ruined structure. He sees a host of battle indicators strewn on the ground, broken blades, torn cloth and brass shell casings that are large enough to have been ejected from a bolter, which makes them far older models than are used today.

Blood splashes and footprints show signs of a furious battle, but the scavengers who picked this place clean have obscured any tracks or clues to their prey's route. He moves to the edge of the ruins, detecting a fragrant smell he recognises as burning qash. For the briefest moment, Nagasena remembers losing himself in a qash haze, sprawled in the silken dragon houses of Nihon with a gun in one hand and an urge to turn it on himself.

He shakes the moment loose and raises his rifle as he sees a thin-boned man seated on a tall stool, the only piece of furniture to have escaped the furious barrage that tore his home apart. He smokes a thin-stemmed pipe amid a storm of broken glass and splintered wood.

Fragrant smoke drifts from the pipe's wide bowl, inviting and redolent with forbidden pleasures.

'You are a chirurgeon,' says Nagasena.

'I am Antioch,' says the man, his manner distracted and his voice slurred. 'I am having a smoke. Would you like to join me?'

'No,' says Nagasena.

'Come on,' laughs Antioch. 'I see the way you're looking at the pipe. You are a lover of the resin, I can always tell.'

'Once maybe,' admits Nagasena.

'Always,' sniggers Antioch as Saturnalia and Golovko pick their way through the rubble.

'They were here, weren't they?' says Nagasena.

'Who?'

Golovko backhands the man from his stool, and he crashes down into the shattered pieces of a toppled cabinet. Glass pricks his skin, but Antioch seems not to care. He spits blood and does not protest when Golovko hauls him to his feet by his soiled nightshirt.

'The traitor Space Marines,' snarls Golovko. 'They were here, we know they were here.'

'Then why did he ask?' replies Antioch.

Golovko hits the man again, and Nagasena says, 'Enough. The man is smoking the *Migou* resin, he will not care or feel it if you beat him.'

Golovko seems unconvinced, but leaves the man alone for now. Saturnalia lifts an overturned table that is sticky with glossy blood. He bends to sniff the table's surface and nods.

'Space Marine blood,' he says.

'They came to you for help,' says Nagasena. 'What did you do for them?'

Antioch shrugs and bends to retrieve his fallen pipe. He gently blows on the bowl, and it glows a warm, inviting orange. He takes a draw and exhales a number of perfect smoke rings.

'Yes,' he says, 'they were here, but what do I know about

their anatomy? I couldn't do anything for the big man.
He was dying before I even touched him.'

'One of them is dead?' says Saturnalia. 'Who?'

Antioch nods dreamily. 'I think they called him
Gythua.'

'Death Guard,' says Golovko with a nod. 'Good.'

'What about Kai Zulane?' asks Saturnalia. 'They had an
astropath with them too.'

'Is that what he was?' replies Antioch. 'Fella had no
eyes, right enough. Never thought he was an astropath. I
thought they all lived up in the City of Sight?'

'Not this one,' says Nagasena. 'He was badly hurt. Does
he still live?'

Antioch smiles and shrugs, as though the matter is
no longer of concern to him. 'I patched him up, sure.
Cleaned up his eyes and packed the wound with sterile
gauze. For all the good it'll do him.'

'What do you mean?'

'I mean that he's dying,' snapped Antioch. 'Too much
trauma, too much pain. I've seen it before in the Army,
some boys just give up when they can't take any more
hurt.'

'But he is still alive?' presses Nagasena.

'Last I saw of him, yes.'

'What happened here?' asks Saturnalia. 'Why did those
men outside come here?'

'The Babu's men? I don't know, but they wanted them
to come out and surrender.'

Nagasena nods, his suspicion that Babu Dhakal's men
knew the Space Marines were here and what they were
now confirmed. In a place like this it would be hard to
keep anything secret, but what could make a man like
that actively seek to engage Space Marines in combat?
Surely such a man would know how deadly these warriors would be? Why risk confrontation unless they had
something he needed enough to risk the lives of so many
men.

'But they didn't surrender,' says Antioch, shuddering at

the memory, even through the bliss of a narcotic haze.
'Never seen anything like it in my life, and hope I never
do again. I watched them take the Babu's men apart like
they were simpletons. Six men against thirty and they
killed them is if it was nothing at all. Only Ghota walked
away alive.'

'Ghota? Is he one of Babu Dhakal's men?'

'He is that,' agrees Antioch. 'Big son of a bitch, almost
as big as the men you're after. And if you don't mind me
saying, I don't think you want to find them. Even though
there's only five of them left alive, I reckon you don't
have enough men to put them down.'

'Five?' says Nagasena.

'Ghota killed the white haired one,' says Antioch, and
Nagasena shares an uneasy look with Saturnalia. The
unspoken question hangs between them like a guilty
secret. What kind of mortal could kill a Space Marine?

'Where are they now?' demands Golovko. 'Where did
they go after you aided the escape of traitors?'

'Ah, now I've been helpful to you, but I don't think
I want to tell you anything else,' says Antioch. 'Doesn't
seem right.'

'We are servants of the Imperium,' says Saturnalia,
looming over the fragile chirurgeon, who looks up at
him like a child defying his father.

'That's as maybe, but at least they were honest,' says
Antioch.

Nagasena steps between Antioch and Golovko before
the man can strike him. He beckons to Adept Hiriko and
says, 'Can you find what you need in his mind?'

Hiriko steps gingerly over the wreckage towards Antioch. The man looks at her warily, but says nothing as she
places her hands either side of his head.

'What's she doing?' asks Antioch.

'Nothing for you to worry about,' Nagasena assures
him.

The chirurgeon is not reassured and looks at her suspiciously, a nervous glint in his eye.

'What is she?' he asks.

'I am a neurolocutor,' says Hiriko by way of explanation. 'Now be still or this will hurt.'

Antioch stiffens in expectation of pain as Hiriko closes her eyes.

What might the mind of a man in a qash stupor be like? Will it even be possible to lift anything of use from him, or will his mind be like a fortress with its gates lying open and every door left unlocked?

Hiriko does not move for almost a minute, then lets out a powerful exhalation as her hands slip from Antioch's head. Her eyes are glassy and Nagasena wonders if the effects of the qash have passed into her mind.

'Oh,' she says, shaking her head.

'Did you get anything?' asks Nagasena.

She nods, still purging the after-effects of delving into Antioch's mind. The man is fearful now, and Nagasena sees that Hiriko has rid him of the qash haze. Forced to face reality without the comforting curtain of the resin to hide behind, the world is a frightening place.

'They are going to a place called the Temple of Woe,' says Hiriko.

'Do you know where that is?' Golovko asks her.

Hiriko looks into Antioch's eyes. 'Yes. It's east of here, I know the way now.'

'Then we don't need this traitor anymore,' growls Golovko.

Before Nagasena can stop him, the Black Sentinel draws his pistol and puts a bullet through Antioch's head.

TWENTY

**Colours and Hues
The End of Everything Good
Kill Team**

WHEN KAI WOKE, it was to a surprising lack of pain and an almost overwhelming sensation of relief. He lifted his head, feeling hard edges of metal digging into his belly. The world around him shone with contours of light and shadow, psychic emanations and dead space. It painted a clear portrait of the buildings, streets and space around him, a representation of the world as clear and vivid as any perceived by those with their birth eyes.

'Stop,' he said, his voice hoarse and parched. 'Stop, please. Put me down.'

The juggernaut upon which he was being carried halted, and rough hands lifted him carefully to the ground. A giant clad in burnished plates of metal stood before him, a warrior of enormous proportions made even larger by the crude plates of sheet steel strapped to his enormous frame and the sharp lines of pistols tucked into his belt. A faint golden haze clung to him, like wisps of cloud caught by the trailing wings of an aircraft.

The image sparked a memory of his dreamspace, but the substance of it drifted just beyond reach, though he was sure that something of vital importance had occurred there. He had a vague recollection of a regicide board and a hooded opponent, but he could not yet grasp its meaning.

'Atharva?' said Kai, as the cold reality of this world intruded.

'Yes,' said the giant. 'You gave me cause for concern. I did not know if you would live.'

'I'm not sure I did,' moaned Kai as he stood on unsteady legs, amazed he could remain upright after so fraught a journey. 'I feel like one of you has punched me in the face.'

'That is not too far from the truth,' admitted Atharva, looking over at the heavily armoured form of Asubha. The Outcast Dead had changed since last Kai last saw them. Armoured in beaten iron breastplates, curved pauldrons and archaic helms, they looked like the barbarian warriors of pre-Unity, the bloodthirsty tribesmen who had ruled Old Earth before the coming of the Emperor. Subha even carried a wooden shield.

Kai had always known his fellow escapees were warriors, but to see them garbed for war was a stark reminder that they were only his protectors because it aligned with their purposes. Should that change, he would be of no more use to them.

'Where did you get the armour and weapons?' he asked, seeing the strange array of pistols and blades they carried, enough to equip three times their number.

'Some very stupid people got in our way,' said Asubha. 'But they are dead now.'

Ghosts of light limned each warrior against the darker, iron blacks, steel greys and umber brickwork of the background. He knew them all by their colours and hues: Tagore, Subha and Asubha in angry reds, purples and killing silver, Atharva in gold, ivory and crimson, and Severian shrouded in stormcloud grey and mist. Kai saw Argentus Kiron and Gythua, propped up against a landslip of rock, the last traces of their auras bleeding into the air like warmth from a cooling corpse.

'We lost Gythua and Kiron,' said Subha with very real pain. 'They had one big bastard who knew how to fight.'

'And we beat him like a whipped cur,' said Tagore.

'But he'll be back,' said Asubha. 'Someone like that won't give up.'

'So next time we kill him properly,' snarled Tagore with bared teeth. Kai saw the aura around his skull flare with a shimmer of cold iron, like the yoke of a hound's master pulling taut. Tagore's muscles bunched and swelled in anticipation of violence, but the World Eater exhaled loudly and turned away before his control slipped away.

'Where are we?' asked Kai, extending his senses.

'Still in the Petitioner's City,' said Atharva. 'But we are almost at its eastern edge.'

Kai nodded slowly. From the background buzz of thoughts and life, he had known they were still in the Petitioner's City. Though the pain in his head was intense, it was manageable and he felt curiously liberated at employing his blindsight instead of expensive augmentations. It had been so long since he had used his psychic abilities to navigate and understand the world around him.

The mountains towered above Kai, so vast it seemed as though there was no end to them. Though the peaks were not alive, they had accumulated a wealth of emotion and experience from those who had clambered over their rocky flanks in the painful epochs since they had been thrust from the bottom of an ancient seabed. A haze of permanence hung over the mountains, split by the searing torrent of psychic energy that speared from the hollow mountain to the farthest reaches of the galaxy. Now that the threat of being sent to its nightmarish depths was gone, Kai found its presence curiously reassuring, like the half-heard voice of an old and trusted friend.

Deeper in the city, the air was a heady mixture of sweat, boiling fats, rotten meat, spices and perfumes, but here it was clean, and the winds coming down from the high ranges were refreshing rather than chilling.

Tagore lifted Gythua's body and slung it over one shoulder, while Asubha lifted Kiron's body with somewhat more respect for his fallen brother. Severian turned and set off towards an opening in the rock that lead towards a sheer scarp of rock climbing almost vertically to a rampart crowned peak.

'Come on,' said Atharva. 'It is just a little farther.'

'What is?' said Kai.

'The Temple of Woe,' said Atharva.

THE TEMPLE OF WOE turned out to be something altogether less sinister that its ominous name had suggested. Built from what looked like a thousand mismatched pieces of variegated marble, it was a formidable structure that rose high above its nearest neighbours. Situated towards the end of a narrowing canyon, its façade was graced with numerous handsome statues depicting weeping angels, mothers holding their stillborn children and skeletal harbingers of death.

Reapers skulked in alcoves, while mourners worked in polished granite clustered around biers of fallen heroes and ouslite pallbearers took the dead to their final rest. Any one of the rival Masonic guilds that had raised the glory of the palace would have dismissed its haphazard beauty with a glance, but it possessed a grandeur and welcoming air the greatest structures of the palace could only dream of.

The road leading towards the temple was festooned with offerings, children's dolls, picts of smiling men and women, wreaths of silken flowers and scraps of paper embossed with poetic eulogies and heartfelt farewells. Hundred of people knelt in supplication, gathered in weeping groups around drum fires placed along the length of the wide road that led towards heavy iron doors that led within. Oil-burning lanterns hanging from the outside of the temple cast flickering shadows that made the statues dance.

'What is this place?' said Subha.

'A place of remembrance and farewell,' said Kai.

He felt a tremendous surge of emotion as his blind-sight took in the full panoply of conflicting auras that swirled around, within and through the building. Enormous sadness washed over him as the weight of grief that filled the street threatened to overwhelm him.

'So much loss,' he said. 'The sadness and pain, it's too much. I don't think I can stand it.'

'Steel yourself, Kai,' said Atharva. 'Grief and guilt are powerful emotions. You know this all too well. You have held yours at bay long enough for this to present no problem.'

'No, there's something else,' he whispered. 'There's something in there that's more powerful that any guilt I've ever known...'

Atharva leaned in close, so that only Kai could hear his next words.

'Say nothing of it,' warned Atharva. 'Our lives will depend on it.'

Without explanation, Atharva followed Severian into the canyon, and Kai felt the hostile gazes of the mourners turn on them. Their anger was matched by their fear, and though every one of them looked like they wanted to hurl some missile or shout an obscenity, none dared move or open their mouth. There was recognition in their anger, but surely that was impossible.

'Whoever those men were you killed, I think they were known here,' he said.

'I think you might be right,' agreed Atharva as the shutter doors to the Temple of Woe opened with a squeal of rusting bearings. A tall man with wild grey hair and a face that spoke of a life lived in the open emerged from the building. His aura was so choked with guilt that Kai drew up in shock to see someone burdened with a heavier share than his own.

Kai became acutely aware of the hundreds of people pressing in around them. They had been afraid of them before, but they drew strength from this man, and their anger was building moment by moment. The Outcast Dead were powerful, but could they kill so many without being overwhelmed? More to the point, could they stop the mob from killing *him*?

'Get out of here,' said the man. 'Didn't you learn anything the last time you came here?'

'We are here for the dead,' said Asubha. 'We were told this was a place to bring fallen warriors.'

'You are not welcome here,' said the man. 'If you're looking for the men you left here, you can tell the Babu they went into the fires, same as all the others.'

Tagore said, 'You will stand aside or you will die,' and Kai felt the pulsing waves of belligerence surrounding the World Eater sergeant. His anger was a wild dog, kept in check by only the slenderest of threads, and the device in his skull frayed that thread with every angry beat of its mechanical heart.

Atharva stepped forward, and placed his hand on Tagore's shoulder. Atharva's golden light bled into the killing red surrounding the World Eater, and the taut aggression of his posture eased a fraction.

'We are not here for killing,' said Atharva, altering his voice so that everyone gathered in the canyon could hear him. Its cadence and tone conveyed a calming effect that diminished the anger radiating from the gathered people. 'And we are not Dhakal's men. We took this armour and these weapons from Ghota's thugs when they attacked us without provocation.'

'Ghota is dead?'

'No,' said Atharva. 'He fled like the coward he is.'

Kai felt the subtle psychic manipulations Atharva was employing, amazed at the power of the Thousand Sons warrior. Like most people, Kai had heard the rumours concerning the Legion of Magnus, but to see him so casually wield such abilities was astounding.

The grey-haired man took a closer look at the Outcast Dead and his eyes widened as he recognised them for what they were.

'The Angels of Death,' said the man. 'You have come at last.'

THE DIMLY-LIT HALLS of the cryptaesthesians were unpleasant at the best of times, and the Choirmaster's senses were vibrating like a badly-struck tuning fork. He disliked coming down here, but Evander Gregoras had ignored his every summons and there was work to be done that required him to forego the study of his precious Pattern.

A trio of Black Sentinels had accompanied him ever since the psychic intrusion of Magnus, though he could not decide whether Golovko had assigned them to protect him or to kill him in the event of another attack. Probably both, he thought.

Black walls of bare stone passed him, feeling like they were pressing in on him with every step he took deeper into the lair of the cryptaesthesians. His head ached from the aftermath of a particularly difficult communion, a garbled message that claimed to be from an astropath attached to the XIX Legion, but had no synesthesia codes verifying its truth. The message spoke of the death of Primarch Corax, and Nemo desperately wanted to believe it was false, a piece of deliberate misinformation designed to demoralise the forces loyal to the Emperor. Though the message had the ring of truth to it, he had chosen not to pass it to the Conduit for fear of the damage it might wreak.

Nor was this the only piece of bad news. Rumours had come from the Eastern Fringe of a cowardly ambush sprung on the XIII Legion around Calth, and two score astropaths had gone mad attempting to make contact with the sanguinary Legions of the Blood Angels. What monstrous fate had befallen the scions of Baal, and why could no word penetrate the Signus Cluster without dreams of madness and slaughter afflicting those who made such attempts?

The astropaths of the City of Sight could not cope

with the demands the palace was placing upon them.
They had reached breaking point, and the Choirmaster
needed the cryptaesthesians of Evander Gregoras to take
their places in the choirs if the entire network was to be
saved. Sifting the psychic debris or hunting for hidden
truths in the background noise of the universe would
have to wait.

At last they came to the correct doorway, and the
Choirmaster rapped his thin knuckles on the shutter, careful to avoid damaging his ring from the Fourth
Dominion. He waited, but no answer was forthcoming,
and he frowned. He could feel the presence of Gregoras's
mind beyond the door, and could hear the sounds of
paper tearing.

'Evander!' he shouted, though he hated to raise his
voice. 'Open the door, I have to speak with you.'

The sounds within the cryptaesthesian's chamber
stopped for a moment then began again, more vigor-
ously than before.

'I need your cryptaesthesians, Evander,' said Nemo. 'I
need them to ease the backlog of communications. We
simply don't have enough telepaths, and with the Black
Ships not coming through, we're burning out. Evander!'

Clearly, Gregoras wasn't about to answer, and the
Choirmaster nodded to the sergeant of the Black Sentinels.

'Open it,' he said, irritated that the master of the City
of Sight could not open every door in his city without
the say so of the Black Sentinels. No door was barred to
them, and the sergeant waved a data-wand in front of
the locking pad. The door slid open, and Nemo stepped
into Gregoras's chambers with a shocked expression as
he saw the disarray within.

The nature of the cryptaesthesians work made them
gloomy and introspective, but given to eccentric behav-
ioural quirks. Gregoras was a cantankerous bastard, but
he was the best there was at sifting the Bleed, and thus
Nemo had tolerated his obsession with the Pattern. He

had seen the work Gregoras had done, but where the cryptaesthesian saw order and meaning, Nemo saw only chaos and happenstance. That work had filled these chambers, every square inch of wall covered with unintelligible script, every shelf bowing under the weight of books, data-retrieval cogitators, statistical compilers, maps, plotters and devices he had devised for the purposes of translating the heartbeat of the universe.

All of it was gone.

Evander sat on a high backed chair in the centre of the room with a book resting on his lap. One hand pressed down on the cover, as though trying to keep its pages from flying open. The other hung at his side, holding a quill that dripped ink to the floor. The Choirmaster took a hesitant step into the chamber, feeling the pressure of an overwhelming psychic presence in the room that had nothing to do with Gregoras or his own powers.

'Evander,' hissed the Choirmaster. 'Your eyes…'

The cryptaesthesian's cheeks were streaked with impossible tears, and the traceries of light that filled his body shone from his eyes in a glittering sheen of organic tissue.

Evander Gregoras was no longer blind.

The cryptaesthesian did not answer, his eyes screwed tightly shut and his face contorted with the effort of holding some terrible fear at bay. His entire body was tense, and the tendons stood out as hard edges against the soft skin of neck. His hands shook on the cover of the book, a black leather-bound *Oneirocritica*.

'Evander, what's happening here?' he asked.

'I saw it all,' said Gregoras, dropping the quill and placing both hands on the cover of the book. 'It needed me to see and it gave me back my eyes! Throne, it gave me back my eyes so I could see it.'

'See what, Evander?' said the Choirmaster. 'You're not making any sense.'

'It's hopeless, Nemo,' said Gregoras, shaking his head as though trying to loose some hideous memory. 'You can't stop it, none of us can. Not you, not me, no one!'

'What are you talking about?' said Nemo.

The Choirmaster took another step forward, crouching in front of Gregoras. A hint of spectral illumination, like starlight reflected on the surface of a river danced beneath his tightly closed eyelids.

'It's all for nothing, Nemo,' said Gregoras, his chest heaving with sobs. 'Everything we did, it's all for nothing. It all stagnates. Nothing really lives, and it's a slow death that lingers for thousands of years. Everything we strove for, everything we were promised... all a lie.'

The knuckles of his fingers were white with the effort of holding the cover of the *Oneirocritica* closed, but he removed one hand long enough to reach inside his robes to remove a small calibre snub-nosed pistol.

The Choirmaster stood erect and moved away from Gregoras as the Black Sentinels raised their rifles and took aim.

'Put the gun down!' barked the sergeant. 'Put the gun down or we will shoot you dead.'

Gregoras laughed, and the pain and soul-sick loss in that sound broke the Choirmaster's heart. What could be so terrible that it could make a man give voice to such a plaintive sound?

'Evander,' said the Choirmaster. 'Whatever has happened here, we can deal with it. We can handle anything. Remember our time on the Black Ships? That boy from Forty-Three Nine? He killed almost everyone on that vessel, but we contained him. We contained him, and we can stop this, whatever it is.'

'Stop it?' said Gregoras. 'Don't you understand? It's already happened.'

'What's happened?'

'The end of everything good,' said Gregoras, putting the pistol in his mouth.

'No!' shouted Nemo, but nothing could stop the cryptaesthesian from pulling the trigger.

His head bucked and a thin wisp of smoke emerged

from his mouth as his jaw fell open. A line of blood ran from his nose and fell to the cover of the *Oneirocritica*. In death, Gregoras's eyes opened, and the Choirmaster saw they were the colour of amber set in rose gold.

The book slid down the dead man's knees and fell to the ground. The Choirmaster took a deep breath as he felt whatever malign presence had occupied the space between worlds begin to dissipate. He stared at the body of his once-friend, trying to imagine what might have driven so rational a man to suicide.

His blindsight was drawn to the fallen book. The droplet of blood on its cover shone with the last vital energies of the dead man, and the Choirmaster felt an immense sadness as the shimmering life-light faded to nothing.

'What did you see, Evander?' he said, knowing there was only one way to find out for sure and wondering if he had the strength to look.

Nemo Zhi-Meng picked up the last *Oneirocritica* of Evander Gregoras and began to read.

KAI FOLLOWED THE Outcast Dead as they entered the Temple of Woe, feeling the weight of grief and guilt that pervaded the air like invisible smoke. Like the outside façade, the interior of the building was also embellished with funereal statuary depicting mourning in all its varied forms: wailing mourners, deathbed vigils, raucous wakes and dignified farewells. Torches hanging from iron sconces filled the temple with a warm glow, and a circular rim of what had once been the cog-toothed wheel of some enormous Mechanicum war-engine now served as a hanging bed for hundreds of tallow candles.

Groups of mourners gathered in sombre groups on wooden benches, the lucky ones whose turn had come to bring their dead inside. People looked up as they entered, some staring in amazement, others too wrapped in their grief to pay them more than a cursory glance. A man and a woman wept beside a body that lay at the foot of a polished black statue of a faceless, kneeling angel.

A faint black haze clung to the sweeps and curves of the angel's wings, and though it had no features carved into its head, Kai sensed something behind that unfinished surface, like a face half-glimpsed in the shadows.

'What is it?' he asked, knowing Atharva was staring at him and would understand his meaning.

'I suspect it is not one thing, but many,' said Atharva. 'The Great Ocean is a reflection of this world, and as the alchemists of old knew: as above, so below. You cannot vent so much grief in one place without attracting the attention of something from beyond the veil.'

'Whatever it is it feels dangerous,' said Kai. 'And... hungry.'

'An apt term,' nodded Atharva. 'And you are right to believe it is dangerous.'

Fear touched Kai, and he said, 'Throne, should we warn these people to get out!'

Atharva laughed and shook his head. 'There is no need, Kai. Its power is not so great that it can escape the prison of stone in which it currently resides.'

'You like my statues?' said the custodian of the Temple of Woe, closing the doors and coming to join them.

'They are magnificent,' said Kai. 'Where did you get them?'

'I did not *get* them anywhere, I carved them myself,' said the man, holding out his hand. 'I am Palladis Novandio and you are welcome here. All of you.'

Kai shook the proffered hand, trying to hide his discomfort as he felt the sharp stab of the man's grief and guilt.

'It is a mausoleum,' said Tagore. 'Why do you gather so much death in one place?'

'They are images of aversion,' said Palladis.

'What does that mean?' asked Subha.

'By gathering so many images of death and grief in one place, you rob them of their sorrow,' said Kai with sudden insight.

'Exactly so,' said Palladis. 'And by honouring death, we keep it at bay.'

'We bring warriors who have walked the Crimson Path,' said Tagore. 'Their mortal remains are not for the scavenger or the vulture to dishonour. We were told you had an incinerator here.'

'We do indeed,' said Palladis, pointing to a square arch at the rear of the structure. Kai felt the finality that existed beyond that door, a barrier that couldn't quite keep the smell of burnt flesh from permeating the air of the temple.

'We have need of it,' said Atharva.

'It is at your disposal,' said Palladis, with a respectful bow.

Kai watched as the Outcast Dead lifted their fallen brothers between them like enormous pallbearers, the World Eaters bearing Gythua, Atharva and Severian hoisting Argentus Kiron to their shoulders.

'The fallen warrior should be honoured in death by his blood-comrades,' said Tagore, 'but these heroes are far from their Legion brothers, and they will never see their homeworlds again.'

'*This* is their homeworld,' said Atharva.

'And we are their comrades now,' added Subha.

'We will honour them,' said Asubha. 'As brothers of battle, we owe fealty to no brotherhood but our own.'

Kai was surprised to hear such words from these warriors. In the brief time he had spent with them, he had not thought them close, but these words spoke of a bond that ran deeper than he would ever know, a bond that could only ever be forged in the bloody cauldron of battle and death.

'Come,' said Palladis Novandio. 'I'll show you.'

Tagore placed a hand on Palladis's chest and shook his head. 'No, you won't,' he said, his teeth bared and a barely restrained hostility razoring the edges of his words. 'The death of a Space Marine is a private affair.'

'I apologise,' said Palladis, recognising the threat. 'I meant no disrespect.'

The Space Marines moved down the central aisle of the

temple, and all sounds of mourning faded as those who bore witness to the solemn parade bowed their heads in silent and unspoken respect. Atharva's power flared like a half-glimpsed flicker of lightning, as the door to the incinerator opened on rust and ash-gummed hinges.

Kai watched them pass from sight, and let out the breath he'd been holding.

It took a moment for him to realise the significance of the moment, but when he realised that he was alone and free, all he felt was a strange sense of emptiness. He no longer knew whether he was a fellow fugitive or a prisoner of the Outcast Dead, but he suspected that hinged upon what he carried within his head.

Kai turned towards the door through which he and the Space Marines had entered the temple. Slivers of torchlight eased through its imperfectly-fitted frame, and that soft glow was the promise of everything he had been denied: the freedom from responsibility, the choice to live or die and, finally, a chance to be no one's slave.

The last realisation was hardest to admit, for Kai had always believed he was master of his own destiny. Here, alone and hunted in a temple dedicated to the dead, he realised how naïve he had been. The worth of the individual was the greatest lie the Imperium had made its people swallow. From soldiers in the army to the scribes of the palace to the workers toiling in the factories, every human life was in service to the Emperor. Whether they realised it or not, the human race had been yoked to the singular goal of the galaxy's conquest.

For the first time in his life, Kai saw the Imperium for what it was, a machine that could operate on such a vast scale only because its fuel of human life was in never-ending supply. He had been part of that machine, but he was a tiny cog that had slipped its gear and was tumbling without purpose through its delicate workings. Kai knew enough of such mechanisms to know that such a random piece could not be allowed to remain within the body of the machine. Either that piece was returned to its designated place, or it was cast out and discarded.

'Death surrounds you, my friend,' said Palladis. 'You were right to come here.'

Kai nodded and said, 'Death surrounds me wherever I go.'

'There is truth in that,' agreed Palladis. 'Do you mean to stay with the Angels of Death?'

'Why do I get the feeling that you're not using that as a nickname?' asked Kai.

'The Legiones Astartes are the physical embodiment of death,' said Palladis. 'You have seen them kill, so you must know that.'

Kai thought back to the bloodshed of their escape from the Custodes gaol, and suppressed a shiver at the ferocious carnage.

'I suppose it's apt,' he agreed. 'The Angels of Death. It has a ring to it.'

'You haven't answered my question,' pointed out Palladis.

Kai thought for a moment, torn between his desire to shape his own future and the insistent voice that urged him to remain with the Outcast Dead.

'I'm not sure,' said Kai, surprising himself. 'I feel that I *want* to leave them, but I'm not sure I *should*. Which is stupid, because I think they mean to take me to… to a place I don't think I'm meant to go.'

'Where do you think are you meant to go?'

'I don't know,' said Kai with a wan smile. 'That's the problem, you see.'

'Then how do you know you are not already there?' said Palladis, before giving his arm a gentle squeeze and making his way towards the man and woman who wept over the body of an old man at the foot of the faceless statue.

Before Kai could ponder the man's last words, the door to the temple opened and a girl with a familiar aura entered. Though his psychic senses told him as much, he knew she had long blond hair beneath her

hood and a blue bandanna wrapped around her forehead. He smiled, finally understanding that there were
no accidents, no coincidences and no pieces of the universal puzzle that were not just links in a causal chain
that stretched back to very beginning of all things.

'Perhaps I *am* where I'm meant to be,' he said softly, as
the girl saw him and her eyes widened in surprise.

'Kai?' said the girl. 'Throne, what are you doing here?'

'Hello, Roxanne,' said Kai.

NAGASENA WATCHES THE approaching vehicles with irritation and a sense of events moving faster than anyone
gathered here can control. Six armoured vehicles, boxy
and reeking of engine oil and hot metal. They have
been forced to wait for these tanks by an order from the
City of Sight. No explanation was forthcoming, and for
nearly ninety minutes they have allowed their quarry to
put ever greater distance between them.

'We should not have waited,' Kartono says to him, but
he does not reply. The answer is self-evident. No, they
should not have waited, but his every instinct is railing
against this hunt. He tells himself that he is foolish to
put faith in omens, that he should have continued without Golovko and Saturnalia.

He knows where his prey has gone, and he could be
there already but for his hunt companions. Yet he did
not set off on his own. He waited. Speed and the relent-
lessness of pursuit are his greatest weapons, and he has
sacrificed them both.

Why?

*Because this hunt does not serve the truth, it is intended
to bury it.*

Saturnalia stands at a crossroads to the east, eager
to be on the hunt, but unwilling to disobey an order
that comes countersigned with the authority of his own
masters. Golovko sits with his men, displaying patience
Nagasena had not suspected he possessed. He is a man
to whom orders are absolute, a man who would kill a

hundred innocents if so ordered. Such men are dangerous, for they can enact any horror in the unshakable belief that it serves a higher purpose.

The lead vehicle grinds to a halt in a squall of rubble and screeching metal. It is painted black and red, with the markings of a fortress gate upon which are crossed a black bladed spear and a lasgun. Golovko and Saturnalia join him as the side hatch opens and a junior lieutenant in a black breastplate and helmet emerges, looking as though he wishes he were anywhere but here.

The lieutenant marches over to Golovko and hands him a sealed, one-time message slate.

A code wand slides from Golovko's gauntlet and the slate flickers into life. Softly glowing text appears on its smooth surface, and the man's face breaks into a grin of feral anticipation.

Nagasena has seen that look before, and he does not like it.

'What does the message say?' he asks, though he fears he knows the answer.

Golovko hands the message slate to Saturnalia, who scans its contents with a nod that confirms what Nagasena is already suspecting. He turns away as Saturnalia offers him the slate.

'We are no longer hunters,' says Nagasena. 'Are we?'

'No,' says Saturnalia. 'We are a kill team.'

TWENTY-ONE

Catharsis
I Might Kill You
The Thunder Lord

ROXANNE THREW HERSELF into Kai's arms with the passion of a long lost lover, wrapping him so tightly that he thought he might break. He returned her embrace, relishing the closeness of another human body and the sight of someone familiar. He and Roxanne had worked together on the *Argo* for many years, though the strict code of conduct enforced upon all Ultramarines vessels had prevented them from becoming truly close.

'You're going to break my ribs,' said Kai, though he didn't want her to let go.

'They'll heal,' said Roxanne, pressing even tighter. 'I never thought I'd see you again.'

'Nor I you,' he said, as she finally released him and took a step back, though she kept a grip on his shoulders.

'You look terrible,' said Roxanne. 'What happened to your eyes? After they separated us on the Lemuryan plate, they wouldn't tell me where you were.'

'Castana's armsmen picked me up and took me to the medicae facilities on Kyprios then left me in the care of an idiot,' said Kai with a sneer. 'But when the Patriarch realised they might be held liable for the loss of the *Argo*, they threw me back to the City of Sight.'

'Bastards,' said Roxanne. 'They took me back to our estates in Galicia and tried to hide me away like I didn't even exist.'

'Why?'

'I was an embarrassment to them,' said Roxanne with a dismissive shrug. 'A Navigator who can't even guide a ship home in the same system as the Astronomican isn't much of a Navigator.'

'That's insane,' he said. 'You can't guide a ship when it's in the middle of a warp storm.'

'I told them that,' she said with an exaggerated gesture, 'but it doesn't look good when a ship is lost. The Navigator's always the first one people want to blame.'

'Or the astropath,' whispered Kai.

He felt her scrutiny, and returned it. The last time Kai had seen Roxanne, she had been a physical and emotional wreck, as haunted by the unending screams of their dead crew as he had been, but her aura showed little sign of that trauma.

Roxanne guided him from the aisle to find a seat in the pews, taking his arm as though he were blind or infirm.

'I *can* see you know,' he said. 'Probably better than you.'

'Typical,' said Roxanne. 'It takes losing your eyes to make you see things clearly.'

He smiled as Roxanne took hold of Kai's skeletally thin hands. He felt the warmth of her friendship, but instead of recoiling, he let it wash over him like a cleansing balm. Ever since he had been evacuated from the wreck of the *Argo*, Kai had been treated like a leper or an invalid, and to be viewed as an equal was just about the most wonderful thing anyone had done for him.

'So what are you doing here?' asked Kai, hoping to steer the conversation away from the *Argo*. 'This doesn't seem like your kind of place.'

'I suppose not, but it turns out it's *just* my kind of place.'

'What do you mean?'

'I'm Castana,' said Roxanne. 'I've never wanted for anything in my life, and that meant I didn't appreciate anything I was ever given. If I broke something or lost something, it would be instantly replaced. Being with the people of the XIII Legion taught me how selfish I'd been. When I returned to our estates I couldn't face going back to the person I was. So I left.'

'And you came here?' said Kai. 'Seems like a bit of an extreme reaction.'

'I know, but, like I said, I'm Castana, we don't do things in half measures. At first I was just going to run off to teach my family that they couldn't treat me like a child. Then, when they realised how much they needed me, they'd come for me and I'd have earned their respect.'

'But they didn't come, did they?'

'No, they didn't,' said Roxanne, but there was no sadness to her at the idea of being abandoned by her family. 'I found a place to stay, but I still had nightmares about the *Argo*, and it was eating me up inside. I knew what happened wasn't my fault, but I couldn't stop thinking about it. One day I heard about a place in the Petitioner's City where anyone could lay their dead to rest and find peace. So I made my way here and volunteered to help in whatever way I could.'

'Did it help? With the nightmares, I mean?'

Roxanne nodded. 'It did. I thought I'd stay a few days, just to clear my head, but the more I helped people, the more I knew I couldn't leave. When you're surrounded by death every day it gives you perspective. I've heard hundreds of stories that would break your heart, but it showed me that what I'd gone through wasn't any worse than what these people live with every day.'

'And what about Palladis Novandio, what's his story?'

He sensed reluctance in Roxanne's aura, and immediately regretted the question.

'He suffered a great loss,' she said. 'He lost people he loved, and he blames himself for their deaths.'

Kai turned to watch Palladis Novandio as he spoke in

a low voice with the people of his temple, now understanding a measure of the man's enveloping grief. He recognised the all-consuming guilt and desire for punishment as the mirror of his own.

'Then we're very similar,' whispered Kai.

'You blame yourself for what happened on the *Argo*, don't you?' said Roxanne.

Kai tried to give a glib answer, to deflect her question, but the words wouldn't come. He could read auras or use his psychic abilities to understand emotions without effort, yet he would not turn that insight upon himself for fear of what he might learn.

'It was my fault,' he said softly. 'I was in a *nuncio* trance when the shields collapsed. I was the way in for the monsters. I was the crack in the defences. It's the only explanation.'

'That's ridiculous,' said Roxanne. 'How can you think like that?'

'Because it's true.'

'No,' said Roxanne firmly. 'It's not. You didn't see what was happening beyond the ship. I saw what hit us, and *any* ship would have been overwhelmed. A squall of warp cyclones blew up out of nowhere and hit a vortex of high-energy currents coming in from the rimward storms. No one saw it coming, not the Nobilite Watcher Guild, not the Gate Sentinels, no one. It was a one in a million, one in a billion, freak confluence. Given what's happening here on Terra and out in the galaxy, I'm surprised there aren't more of them surging to life. It's a mess out there in the warp, and you're lucky you don't see it.'

'You might have seen it, but I heard it,' said Kai. 'I heard them die.'

'Who?'

'All of them. Every man and woman on the ship, I heard them die. All their terrors, all their lost dreams, all their last thoughts. I heard them all, screaming at me. I can still hear them whenever I let my guard down.'

Roxanne gripped his hand fiercely and he felt the power of her stare, though he had no eyes with which to return it. The force of her personality blazed like a solar corona, and only now did Kai realise how strong she was. Roxanne was Castana, and there were few of that clan who lacked for self-assuredness.

'They tried to blame us both for the loss of the *Argo*, so what does that tell you about how little they know about whose fault it was? Someone had to be responsible. Something terrible had happened, and it's human nature to want someone else to pay for it. They told me, day and night, that it was my fault, that I'd done something wrong, that I had to retrain. But I said no, I told them I knew it wasn't my fault. I *knew* there was nothing I or anyone else could have done to save that ship. It was lost no matter what I did. It was lost no matter what *you* or anyone else did.'

Kai listened to her words, feeling each one slip past his armour of certainty like poniards aimed at his heart. He had told himself the same things over and over again, but the mind has no greater accuser than itself. The Castanas told him he caused the death of the *Argo*, and he had believed them because, deep down, he wanted to be punished for surviving.

They needed a scapegoat, and when one of their own wouldn't fall on her sword, he had been the next best thing: a willing victim. Kai felt the black chains of guilt within him slip, a tiny loosening of their implacable hold. Not completely, nothing so simple as the words of a friend could cause them to break their grip so easily, but that they had slackened at all was a revelation.

He smiled and reached up to touch Roxanne's face. She was wary of the gesture, as were all Navigators, for they disliked other people's hands near their third eye. Her cheek was smooth and the brush of her hair against his skin felt luxurious. These moments of human contact were the first Kai had known in months that didn't involve someone wanting to take something from him, and he let it linger, content to take each breath as a free man.

'You're cleverer than you look, do you know that?' said Kai.

'Like I said, this place gives you perspective, but how would you know? You can't even see me with that bandage over your eyes. You never did say what happened to them.'

And Kai told her all that had befallen him since his arrival at the City of Sight, his retraining, the terror of the psychic shockwave that had killed Sarashina and placed something so valuable within his mind that people were willing to kill to retrieve it. He told of their escape from the Custodians' gaol, the crash and their flight through the Petitioner's City, though this last part of his recall was hazed with uncertainty and half-remembered visions where fear and dreams collided. He told Roxanne of the Outcast Dead's plans to bring him to Horus Lupercal, and the mention of the Warmaster's name sent a tremor of fear through her aura.

When Kai finished, he waited for Roxanne to ask about what Sarashina had placed in his mind, but the question never came, and he felt himself fall a little in love with her. She looked over at the door through which the Space Marines had taken their dead.

'You can't let them take you to the Warmaster,' she said.

'You think I owe the Imperium anything, after all they did to me?' said Kai. 'I won't just hand myself over to the Legio Custodes again.'

'I'm not saying you should,' said Roxanne, taking his hands again. 'But even after all that's happened, you're not a traitor to the Imperium, are you? If you let them take you to Horus, that's what you'll be. You know I'm right.'

'I know,' sighed Kai. 'But how can I stop them from taking me? I'm not strong enough to fight them.'

'You could run.'

Kai shook his head. 'I wouldn't last ten minutes out there.'

Roxanne's silence was all the agreement he needed.

'So what are you going to do?' she asked at last.

'I haven't the faintest idea,' said Kai. 'I don't want to be used anymore, that's all I know for sure. I'm tired of being dragged from pillar to post. I want to take control of my own destiny, but I don't know how to do that.'

'Well you'd better figure it out soon,' said Roxanne, as the heavy door at the rear of the temple swung open. 'They're back.'

THE DEAD WERE ashes. Argentus Kiron and Orhu Gythua were no more, their bodies consumed in the fire. Tagore felt numb at their deaths, knowing he should feel a measure of grief at their passing, but unable to think beyond the anticipation of his next kill. Ever since the battle with Babu Dhakal's men, his body had been a taut wire, vibrating at a level that no one could see, but which was ready to snap.

It felt good to have blood on his hands, and the butcher's nails embedded in his skull had rewarded him for his kills with a rush of endorphins. Tagore's hands were clenched tightly, unconsciously balled into fists as he scanned the room for threats, avenues of attack and choke points. The people in here were soft, emotional and useless. They wept tears of what he presumed were sadness, but he could not connect to that emotion any more.

While Severian and Atharva spoke to the grey-haired man who owned this place – he could not bring himself to use the word *temple* – Tagore sent Subha and Asubha to secure their perimeter. His breath was coming in short spikes, and he knew his pupils were dilated to the point of being totally black. Every muscle in his body sang with tension, and it took all Tagore's iron control to keep himself from lashing out at the first person that looked at him.

Not that anyone dared look at a man who was so clearly dangerous. No eye would meet his, and he took a

seat on a creaking bench to calm his raging emotions. He
wanted to fight. He wanted to *kill*. There was no target
for his rage, yet his body craved the release and reward
promised by the pulsing device bolted to the bone of
his skull.

Tagore had spoken of martial honour, but the words
rang hollow, even to him. They were spoken by rote,
and though he wanted to feel cheated at how little they
meant to him, he couldn't even feel that. They were good
words, ones he used to believe in, but as the tally of the
dead mounted, the less anything except the fury of battle came to mean. He knew exactly how many lives he
had taken, and could summon each killing blow from
memory, but he felt no connection to any of them. No
pride in a well-placed lunge, no exultation at the defeat
of a noteworthy foe and no honour in fighting for something in which he believed.

The Emperor had made him into a soldier, but Angron
had wrought him into a weapon.

Tagore remembered the ritual breaking of the chains
aboard the *Conqueror*, that mighty fortress cast out into
the heavens like the war hound of a noble knight. The
Red Angel, Angron himself, had mounted the chain-
wrapped anvil and brought his calloused fist down upon
the mighty knot of iron. With one blow he had severed
the symbolic chains of his slavery, hurling the sundered
links into the thousands of assembled World Eaters.

Tagore had scrapped and brawled with his brothers in
the mad, swirling mêlée to retrieve one of those links.
As a storm-sergeant of the 15th Company, he had been
ferocious enough to wrest a link from a warrior named
Skraal, one of the latest recruits to be implanted with
the butcher's nails. The warrior was young, yet to master
his implants, and Tagore had pummelled him without
mercy until he had released his prize.

He had fashioned that link into the haft of *Ender*, his
war axe, but that weapon was now lost to him. Anger
flared at the thought of the weapon that had saved his

life more times than he could count in the hands of an enemy. Tagore heard the sound of splintering wood, and opened his eyes in expectation of violence, but from the pinpricks of blood welling in his palms, he knew he had crushed the projecting lip of the bench.

Tagore closed his eyes as he spoke the words to the Song of Battle's End.

> *'I raise the fist that struck men down,*
> *And salute the battle won.*
> *My enemy's blood has baptised me.*
> *In death's heart I proved myself,*
> *But now the fire must cool.*
> *The carrion crows feast,*
> *And the tally of the dead begins.*
> *I have seen many fall today.*
> *But even as they die, I know*
> *That our blood too is welcome.*
> *War cares not from whence the blood flows.'*

Tagore let out a shuddering breath as he spoke the last word, feeling the tension running through his body like a charge ease. He unclenched his fists, letting the splintered wood fall to the floor. He felt a presence nearby and inclined his head to see a young boy sitting next to him. Tagore had no idea how old this boy was, he had no memory of being young, and mortal physiology changed so rapidly that it was impossible to gauge the passage of years on their frail flesh.

'What was that you just said?' asked the boy, looking up from a pamphlet he was reading.

Tagore looked around, just to be sure the boy was, in fact, addressing him.

'They are words to cool the fires of battle in a warrior's heart when the killing is done,' he said warily.

'You're a Space Marine, aren't you?'

He nodded, unsure what this boy wanted from him.

'I'm Arik,' said the boy, holding out his hand.

Tagore looked at the hand suspiciously, his eyes darting over the boy's thin frame, unconsciously working out where he could break his bones to most efficiently kill him. His neck was willow thin, it would take no effort at all to break it. His bones were visible at his shoulders and ridges of ribs poked through his thin shirt.

It would take no effort at all to destroy him.

'Tagore, storm-sergeant of the 15th Company,' he said at last. 'I am World Eater.'

Arik nodded and said, 'It's good you're here. If Babu Dhakal's men come back then you'll kill them, won't you?'

Pleased to have a subject to which he could relate, Tagore nodded. 'If *anyone* comes here looking for me, I'll kill him.'

'Are you good at killing people?'

'Very good,' said Tagore. 'There's nobody better than me.'

'Good,' declared Arik. 'I hate him.'

'Babu Dhakal?'

Arik nodded solemnly.

'Why?'

'He had my dad killed,' said the boy, pointing to the kneeling statue at the end of the building. 'Ghota shot him right there.'

Tagore followed the boy's pointing finger, noting the silver ring on his thumb, its quality and worth clearly beyond his means. The statue was of a dark stone, veined with thin lines of grey and deeper black, and though it had no face, Tagore felt sure he could make out where its features were meant to be, as if the sculptor had begun his work, but left it unfinished.

'Ghota killed one of my... friends too,' said Tagore, stumbling over the unfamiliar word. 'I owe him a death, and I always repay a blood debt.'

Arik nodded, the matter dealt with, and returned to reading his pamphlet.

Tagore was in unfamiliar territory, his skills of

conversation limited to battle-cant and commands. He was not adept in dealing with mortals, finding their concerns and reasoning impossible to fathom. Was he supposed to continue speaking to this boy, or were their dealings at an end?

'What are you reading?' he asked after a moment's thought.

'Something my dad used to read,' said Arik, without looking up. 'I don't understand a lot of it, but he really liked it. He used to read it over and over again.'

'Can I see it?' asked Tagore.

The boy nodded and handed over the sheet of paper. It was thin and had been folded too many times, the ink starting to smudge and bleed into the creases. Tagore was used to reading tactical maps or orders of battle, and this language was a mix of dialects and words with which he was unfamiliar, yet the neural pathways of his brain adapted with a rapidity that would have astounded any Terran linguist.

'Men united in the purpose of the Emperor are blessed in his sight and shall live forever in his memory,' read Tagore, his brow furrowed at the strange sentiment. 'I tread the path of righteousness. Though it be paved with broken glass, I will walk it barefoot; though it cross rivers of fire, I will pass over them; though it wanders wide, the light of the Emperor guides my step. There is only the Emperor, and he is our shield and protector.'

Tagore looked up from his reading, feeling the pulse of his implant burrowing deep into his skull as his anger grew at these words of faith and superstition. Arik reached over and pointed to a section further down the pamphlet.

'The strength of the Emperor is humanity, and the strength of humanity is the Emperor,' said Tagore, his fury growing the more he read. 'If one turns from the other we shall all become the Lost and the Damned. And when His servants forget their duty they are no longer human and become something less than beasts. They

have no place in the bosom of humanity or in the heart
of the Emperor. Let them die and be outcast.'

Tagore's heart was racing and his lungs drew air in
short, aggressive breaths. He crumpled the pamphlet in
his fist and let it drop to the ground.

'Get away from me, boy,' he said through bared teeth.

Arik looked up, his eyes widening in fear as he saw the
change in Tagore.

'What did I do?' he said in a trembling voice.

'I said get away from me!'

'Why?'

'Because I think I might kill you,' growled Tagore.

NAGASENA WATCHES THE building from a projection of
rock at the mouth of the canyon, knowing his prey is
close. In the streets behind him, six armoured vehicles
and nearly a hundred soldiers wait in anticipation of his
orders. Though there is only one order to give, Nagasena
hesitates to issue it. Athena Diyos and Adept Hiriko wait
with them, though there is likely no part in this hunt left
for them to play.

Even Nagasena concedes that in the latter stages of
a hunt there is a certain thrill, but he feels none of that
now. Too much uncertainty has entered his life since
he left his mountain home for him to feel anything but
apprehension at the thought of facing Kai Zulane and
the renegades.

Through the scope of his rifle he can see there are no
escape routes from the structure, its statue-covered façade
presenting the only obvious way in or out. Hundreds of
people are gathered before the building, and they have
brought their dead with them. Nagasena understands
the need to cling onto the lost, to honour their memory
and ensure they are not forgotten, but the idea of praying to them or expecting that they will pass onto another
realm of existence is alien to him.

The advanced optics on Nagasena's scope, obtained at
ruinous cost from the Mechanicum of Mars, penetrates

the marble frontage, displaying a coloured thermal scan of the building's interior. Through a fine copper-jacketed wire, that image is displayed on Kartono's slate.

Perhaps sixty people are inside the temple, and the Legiones Astartes are immediately apparent in their heat signatures as well as their size. It is impossible to pick out which of these people might be Kai Zulane. As Antioch had said, there are five of them, and they are gathered around a much smaller individual. Their heat signatures blur. Something behind their overlarge bodies is scattering the readings from his optics, wreathing the entire image in a grainy static that makes Nagasena's eyes itch.

'So much for those expensive bio-filters,' grunts Kartono, slapping a palm against the side of the slate. The image quality does not improve, but they have enough information to mount an assault on the building with a high degree of success.

'We should storm the building,' says Golovko. 'We have over a hundred men now. There's nowhere left for them to run. We can end this within the hour.'

'He's right,' says Saturnalia with obvious reluctance to align himself with the Black Sentinel. 'We have our quarry boxed in.'

'And that makes them doubly dangerous,' says Nagasena. 'There is nothing more dangerous than a warrior who is cornered and has nothing left to lose.'

'Just like the Creatrix of Kallaikoi,' says Kartono.

'Exactly so,' snaps Nagasena, unwilling to relive that particular memory right now. He still bears scars that will never heal from that hunt.

Saturnalia takes the slate from Kartono's hands and holds it up in front of Nagasena, as if he has not yet seen it. He taps the hazed images of the five men they have come to kill.

'There is no reason not to go in,' says the Custodian. 'We have our orders, and they are clear. Everyone here is to die.'

Nagasena has read and reread their orders, searching for a way to interpret them in a manner that will not scar his memories for life and result in the deaths of so many innocents, but Saturnalia is right; their orders are without ambiguity.

'These are Imperial citizens,' he says, though he knows he is wasting his breath trying to convince Saturnalia to alter his course. 'We serve them with our deeds, and to betray them like this is wrong.'

'Wrong? These traitors have been welcomed amongst these people, and they are guilty by association,' says Saturnalia. 'I am a warrior of the Legio Custodes, and my duty is the safety of the Emperor, a duty in which there can be no compromise. Who knows what treachery these men may have already spread among the people of the Petitioner's City? If we allow any they have touched to live, then their betrayal will fester like a rank weed, drawing nourishment from the darkness and growing even greater and more deeply entrenched.'

'You can't know that,' protests Nagasena.

'I don't need to *know* it, I just need to believe it.'

'This is your *Imperial Truth*?' asks Nagasena, almost spitting the words.

'It is just the truth,' says Saturnalia. 'Nothing more, nothing less.'

Nagasena's eyes lock with those of Kartono, but he sees nothing in his bondsman's eyes that give any clue to his emotions. Clade Culexus saw to that. He grips the tightly-wound hilt of *Shoujiki* and knows he should walk away, but that would be as good as signing his own death warrant. For good or ill, he is bound to this hunt until its end.

He nods, and hates that Saturnalia and Golovko share the triumphant grins of conspirators.

'Very well,' he says. 'Let us get this over with.'

Before any attack order can be given, Kartono gives a shocked breath of surprise. He consults the imagery on his slate and looks up in confusion.

'We may have a problem,' he says, pointing down into the canyon. 'New arrivals.'

ATHARVA WATCHED TAGORE rise from the bench and walk stiffly across the nave as he made his way towards their gathering. The warrior's aura blazed with anger, the swirling colours of angry bruises and hot, pumping blood. Just touching that fire enflamed Atharva's own aggression, and he rose into the lower Enumerations to better control himself.

'We may have a way off Terra,' said Asubha as Tagore joined them.

The World Eaters sergeant nodded, his teeth still clenched and his skin drained of colour.

'How?' he asked.

'Tell him,' said Atharva, gesturing to Palladis Novandio.

'At the top of this scarp is the dwelling place of Vadok Singh, one of the Emperor's war masons,' said Palladis with such bitterness and reluctance that it almost made Atharva flinch. 'He oversees all aspects of the construction work to the palace, and he likes the high perch.'

'So?' demanded Tagore, wearing his impatience like a spiked cloak.

'The warmason likes to observe some of his grander constructions from orbit,' clarified Palladis. The man did not want them to leave, and only Atharva's insight had made him divulge this latest morsel of information.

'You understand now?' said Severian.

'He has an orbit-capable craft?' demanded Tagore, his anger morphing into interest.

'He does,' said Palladis.

'We can get off world,' said Subha, punching a fist into his palm.

'Better,' said Asubha. 'If we can get to one of the orbital plates, we can get aboard a warp-capable craft.'

'So we are agreed?' said Atharva, with a sidelong glance at Palladis Novandio. 'We are bound for Isstvan?'

'Isstvan,' agreed Tagore.

'The Legion,' said Asubha and his brother together.

'Isstvan it is,' said Severian. 'I will find us a way to the warmason's villa.'

Atharva nodded as the Luna Wolf slipped away into the darkness at the rear of the temple.

'Where will you go once you are off-world?' asked Palladis Novandio, unable to mask his disappointment. 'You would not consider remaining here? Where else should the Angels of Death be but a temple dedicated to its name?'

Tagore rounded on the man and lifted him from his feet.

'I should kill you now for what you have allowed to take root here,' snarled the World Eater. 'You call a building a temple, and people will find gods within it.'

'What are you talking about, Tagore?' said Atharva.

Tagore held Palladis Novandio at arm's length, as though the man carried some virulent infection. 'He is a promoter of false gods. This is no place of remembrance. It is a fane where the Emperor is held up as some kind of divine being. All this, it is all a lie, and he is its chief prophet. I will kill him and we will be on our way.'

'No!' cried Palladis. 'That's not what we do here, I promise.'

'Liar!' bellowed Tagore, drawing his fist back.

Before Tagore could unleash his killing power, the doors of the temple were flung wide and two enormous figures were silhouetted in the glow of a hundred lamps and flickering torches from outside. Fear billowed in with them on a wave of ash-clogged wind, and Atharva suddenly sensed the predatory minds of hunters beyond the walls of the temple.

He recognised Ghota from the battle outside Antioch's surgery, but the second warrior took his breath away with his sheer scale.

Enormous beyond even Ghota's monstrous size, the warrior was taller than Tagore and broader in the shoulder than Gythua had been. He was clad in a suit of burnished war plate the colour of bronze and midnight. Fashioned in a form worn by a band of warriors long dead, he wore the armour as though born to it. At his side was an outdated model of bolter, and across his back was sheathed a vast-bladed sword.

'I am the Thunder Lord,' said Babu Dhakal. 'And you have something I want.'

TWENTY-TWO

Living History
Temple of Blood
A Worthy Foe

THE WARRIOR BEFORE him should not have been possible. His kind were all dead and gone, slain in the last battle of Unity. It was a measure of their heroic sacrifice that they had all died to win the last and greatest victory for the Emperor. Yet here he was, towering and magnificent, terrible and shocking. The skin of his face was grey and dead, his eyes blood red, and his aura too bright to look upon. His presence had a gravity all of its own, demanding all attention and fear.

'You are Babu Dhakal?' said Atharva, though the question was unnecessary.

'Of course,' said the Thunder Lord.

As though Babu Dhakal and Ghota projected some form of force field before them, every man, woman and child retreated to the back of the temple, huddled in the shadow of the faceless statue. Atharva caught sight of Kai and a blonde-haired woman with a bandanna tied around her temple. He saw what she was immediately, and wanted to smile at the fortune that had sent him an astropath and a Navigator. Truly, the cosmic puzzle of the universe was revealing itself to him little by little.

Tagore bristled at his side, and he felt the spiking anger that threatened to boil over at any minute. Subha and Asubha followed their sergeant's lead, though their battle-rage was nowhere near as volatile as Tagore's. He could not sense Severian's presence, and hoped he had been able to escape the temple already.

'You killed a warrior of the Legiones Astartes,' said Tagore, the words a guttural bark towards Ghota. 'I'll have your heart for that.'

Ghota grinned and bared his teeth. 'I beat you once, I can do it again, little pup.'

Babu Dhakal raised a hand to forestall Tagore's anger.

'I did not come here to fight you, Legiones Astartes,' he said. 'I came to offer you something. Would you be prepared to listen?'

The unexpectedness of the warrior's words took Atharva by surprise. He had not sensed any desire to parley in Babu Dhakal, but then he could barely stand to turn his psychic senses upon him without fear of being overwhelmed.

'What is it you want?' he asked in a voice that didn't betray his unease.

'There are men beyond this building who wish to kill you,' said Babu Dhakal.

'I know this,' said Atharva, and Babu Dhakal laughed, the sound turning into a wet, animal gurgle in his ruined throat.

'You know it because I now allow you to know it,' said the warrior.

'Once I have broken you across my knee, I will kill all of them too,' promised Tagore.

'There are a hundred at least, a Custodian, a clade killer and a man who carries something more deadly than anything any warrior here can face.'

'A weapon?' asked Subha.

'No, the truth.'

'Who are you?' demanded Atharva. 'I know your name to be meaningless. Babu simply means "father" in the

ancient tongue of Bharat. And Dhakal? That is simply a
region of this part of the mountains. So who are you?'

'I have had many names over the years,' said Babu
Dhakal, 'but that is not what you mean, is it? No, you
want my true name, the one I bore in the battles to win
this world?'

'Yes,' said Atharva.

'Very well, since I am here to trade, I will offer you my
name as a gesture of good faith. I no longer remember
my mortal name, but when my flesh was reborn into this
new form, I was named Arik Taranis.'

The name had a weight all of its own, a silencing
quality that stole the anger from the World Eaters and
dumbfounded Atharva with its historic resonance. There
was not one among them who did not know that name,
the battles he had won, the foes he had slain and the
great honours he had earned.

'You are the Lightning Bearer?' asked Tagore.

'A title given to me after the Battle of Mount Ararat
in the Kingdom of Urartu,' said Babu Dhakal. 'I had the
honour of raising the Banner of Lightning at the declara-
tion of Unity.'

Atharva could barely believe his eyes. This warrior was
history wrought into living form: the Victor of Gaduaré,
the Last Rider, the Butcher of Scandia, the Throne-slayer...

These and a hundred other battle-laurels earned by
this warrior tumbled through Atharva's memory, finally
culminating in the end of that great warrior's legendary
life atop a once-flooded mountain.

'History says you are dead,' said Atharva. 'You died of
your wounds once the banner was raised. You and all
your warriors fell in that battle.'

'You look like a clever man,' said Babu Dhakal. 'You
should know better than to take what history says
literally. Such tales as are told of us come from the
mouth of the last man standing, and it would not do
for the Emperor to have to share his victory with others.
Where is the glory when you conquer a world with an

unstoppable army at your back? To begin a legend, you must win that war single-handedly, and there must be no one left alive to contradict your version of events.'

'Are there others like you?' said Subha.

Babu Dhakal shrugged. 'Perhaps others escaped the cull, perhaps not. If they did, they are probably dead by now, victims of their own obsolescence. Our bodies were designed to win a world, not conquer a galaxy like yours.'

Atharva listened to Babu Dhakal's words, amazed at the lack of bitterness he heard. If what the warrior was saying was true, then he and all his kind had been cast aside by the Emperor in favour of the Legiones Astartes gene-template. Yet Babu Dhakal appeared to bear his creator no ill-will for this monstrous betrayal.

'So how is it that you are still alive?' asked Atharva, now beginning to suspect what Babu Dhakal might want from them.

'I am a clever man,' said Babu Dhakal. 'I learned what I could from my creator in the years of war, and I came to know much of his ancient science. Not enough to halt my deterioration, but enough to cling onto life long enough for fortune to smile upon me.'

'Speak plainly,' ordered Tagore. 'What is it you want?'

Babu Dhakal raised his right arm, and Atharva saw a boxy device attached to the armoured plates of his vambrace. It had none of the elegance of the devices employed by the Legion apothecaries, but it was unmistakably a reductor. Alongside the narthecium, it was an essential piece of an apothecary's battle gear.

The narthecium healed the wounded, but the reductor was for the dead.

Its one and only purpose was to extract a fallen Space Marine's gene-seed.

'I want you to help me live,' said Babu Dhakal.

KAI READ THE shock in Atharva's aura, but before the Space Marine could answer, the roof of the temple imploded in a series of detonations that sent timber beams and limestone tiles tumbling to the floor in a rain of flaming debris.

'Watch out!' shouted Kai as a piece of burning rafter slammed down in front of him, crushing an aged man beneath it. He and Roxanne backed away in panic from the tumbling wreckage as black-armoured soldiers dropped into the temple on ziplines in the wake of booming stun grenades.

The throaty grumble of heavy vehicles and the chatter of automatic gunfire sounded from beyond the temple doors. The hard echoes of heavy calibre shells impacting on the canyon walls were punctuated by the screams of terrified people.

'Down!' cried Kai as one of the soldiers loosed a sawing blast of fire from his weapon. Solid rounds tore up benches and chewed the marble walls. Kai pulled Roxanne to the floor and dragged her away from the soldier, but screaming people blocked every avenue of escape through the overturned benches. A man toppled to his knees before Kai, his chest blown out and his head burned by a las-blast.

'What's going on?' cried Roxanne, blinking away the after-effects of the grenade flashes and covering her head as pulverised marble fragments rained down on them.

'Those are Black Sentinels,' said Kai. 'They're here for me.'

He risked casting his mind-sense beyond his immediate surroundings, flinching with every rattle of gunfire and disorientating thunder of grenade detonations. Smoke and expanding banks of smoke rolled through the temple, but such obstacles to sight were no barrier to an astropath's blindsight. He saw soldiers fan into the temple, gunning down anyone they encountered with ruthlessly efficient bursts of fire.

A knot of soldiers moving in perfect concert were coming his way, but no sooner had one shouted a warning than a hulking warrior bearing a broken guardian spear was among them. Tagore hacked three men down in as many blows and gutted another two before the others could even react. Two more died with their skulls caved in, and another fell with his neck broken.

Subha fought at his sergeant's side, killing with artless fury as he strove to imitate Tagore's furious destruction. Kai shifted his gaze, seeing Asubha moving like a ghost through the clouds of thick smoke. Unlike his brother, Asubha was a methodical killer, picking his targets with a clear precision. A Black Sentinel with an auger was killed first, then another with a plasma-coil weapon. There was clear order to Asubha's kills, a methodology that was quite at odds with the seemingly random violence of his brother.

Other figures moved through the confusing flares of psychic light. The red of violence filled the air as surely as grenade smoke, and it became harder to pick out individuals amongst the pulsing anger that allowed combat soldiers to function.

A host of figures blazed amid the crimson fog, individuals whose energy and vitality were undimmed and untouched by this unleashed violence. One he knew to be Atharva, another two as Babu Dhakal and his lieutenant. Blinding flares of psychic energy streamed from Atharva, and dozens of soldiers died in the fire he drew forth from the Immaterium. Babu Dhakal moved swifter than any man Kai had ever seen, slipping through the chaos of the fighting as though simply willing himself from one place to the next. Where men came at him, he killed them effortlessly, but where they ignored him, he returned the favour and let them live.

The barrage of gunfire was unrelenting, and the slaughter of the temple's supplicants was indiscriminate. Kai and Roxanne crawled towards the back of the temple, scrambling over torn up bodies and overturned benches in their desperation to escape. Kai turned to look over his shoulder as a giant in heavy plates of polished armour strode into the temple. Where others were sheathed in crimson or gold, his aura was a pure and lethal silver. Kai felt his entire body flinch as he recognised the baleful, unrelenting purpose of Saturnalia.

Another man came with him, slighter than the Custodian, but no less bright and dangerous. Kai's stomach lurched in sudden pain as he felt the presence of something abhorrent, something that made him think of every shameful deed that had ever troubled his conscience. Kai stopped his crawling and put his head in his hands as his entire body began to shake with unreasoning horror. He perceived nothing that could explain this feeling, but he instinctively curled into a ball as the colour and life bled out of the world.

'Kai!' shouted Roxanne, sounding far away. 'Where are you?'

At the mention of his name, the smaller man with Saturnalia whipped around and unsheathed a sword whose blade was limned with the purest light Kai had ever seen.

'Kai Zulane!' shouted Saturnalia. 'Come forward!'

In response two shapes moved from the red mist, twin smudges of vicious light and fury whose light was the equal of Saturnalia. Where the Custodian was a controlled flame, they burned like the fires that swept over the Merican plains when the summers were long and hot. Subha and Asubha attacked Saturnalia together, their fury and control mingling into the perfect combination to face so disciplined a warrior.

Kai swallowed his sickness back as the swordsman moved deeper into the temple with steps that were swift and assured. He ignored the battle between the World Eaters and Saturnalia. He was here for Kai, and seemed desperate to reach him before anyone else. Kai retched and rolled onto his side. He had to get away, but to where? Black Sentinels filled the temple with gunfire as they fought the Outcast Dead. Kai lost track of his former protectors, now regretting his desire to be free of them.

Kai took a deep breath and pushed himself to a crouch. He followed the amber light of Roxanne's presence. A hand took hold of his shoulder and he tried to shrug it off, but the grip was implacable. Kai was hauled to his feet, and found himself face to face with the warrior bearing the white-lit sword.

He could hear another man next to the swordsman, but he was utterly invisible to Kai's blindsight. The skin-crawling revulsion Kai felt told him there was *something* there, but he sensed not simply an absence of life, but a presence that actively repelled life. Whatever it was, it was a void in the colour of the world, and Kai finally understood the source of his bone-deep horror as his blindsight guttered and slid inexorably into darkness.

'Pariah...' he said.

The swordsman gave him a short bow, the gesture so ridiculous in the face of such slaughter that Kai wanted to laugh.

'I am Yasu Nagasena, and you are coming with me,' he said, the words clipped and precise.

A vast shadow moved in the mist of light and smoke beside Kai. Though his blindsight was virtually extinguished, he instantly recognised the iron taste of shadow's aura.

'No,' said Tagore with a growl that sounded like an avalanche. 'He's not.'

ROXANNE COULDN'T SEE anything. Her eyes streamed and her throat was raw. The caustic banks of smoke obscured anything beyond a metre or so away, but she kept crawling because it was better than staying in the same place. She'd lost Kai, but didn't dare turn back. The noise of rattling bursts of gunshots and the *zip-crack* of lasfire was frightening, but not as terrifying as the softness of bodies she crawled over in her eagerness to escape.

Tears poured down her cheeks, partly from the grenade fumes, but mostly for the dead who now filled the temple. These were her people, and they were being slaughtered. She could hear heavier gunfire coming from outside the temple, and knew that even those who gathered in the canyon beyond were being killed.

A hand reached for her and she cried out as it brushed her arm. She took hold of the hand, but released her grip when she saw the man to whom it belonged was dead. Blood stained his chest and stomach, and his grasping fingers fell away as she crawled onwards. The movement she had felt in his hand had been the result of debris from the roof falling on him.

This was senseless, the wholesale murder of innocents in the search for one man.

She could not understand the mentality of those who would kill their own people in some vague pursuit of a greater good. Didn't they realise that by murdering their own citizens they were killing a part of themselves?

Through a gap in the smoke, Roxanne had a brief glimpse of the furious chaos engulfing the temple. The soldiers Kai had called Black Sentinels still fought the Space Marines for dominance, and were paying a heavy price to win it. Scores were dead already. The warriors of the Legiones Astartes were nothing if not thorough in their butchery.

At the centre of the temple, a warrior with plates of crimson buckled to his body killed the attackers with streaming bolts of blue fire and arcing traceries of lightning. Las-fire bent around him like refracted light, and hard rounds smacked to a halt a metre from his body as though meeting invisible resistance.

The Black Sentinels fighting him burned like pyres or erupted in pillars of boiling blood. There was madness in his eyes, a spiteful need to take decades of frustration out on those who had forced him to hide his true nature. Roxanne had never met a warrior of the Thousand Sons, and seeing the joy this one was taking in unleashing his vengeance, she never wanted to see another.

'Roxanne!' cried a voice over the din. 'Over here! Hurry!'

She ducked as a flurry of lasbolts blew scorched holes in the stone beside her. Squinting through the smoke, she saw Maya and her two children huddled in a makeshift fortress of fallen blocks of stone and roof timbers. Maya beckoned to her, and Roxanne skidded and slipped over the broken flagstones towards her.

'Here, child,' said Maya, dragging her into the relative safety of their ad hoc refuge at the foot of the Vacant Angel.

'Maya,' said Roxanne, hugging the woman tightly.

Arik and her youngest son, a tousle-haired boy whose name she had never learned, lay with their heads buried in their hands, sobbing at the bloodshed unleashed around them.

'What's happening?' said Maya, holding back her tears with visible effort.

'They're going to kill us all,' said Roxanne without thinking. 'No one's leaving here alive.'

'Don't say that, Miss Roxanne,' pleaded Maya. 'My boys, they're all I've got left. It's got to be a mistake! They wouldn't hurt my boys!'

Roxanne couldn't tell if that was a question, and simply shook her head.

'No, they wouldn't,' she said, and Maya gave Roxanne a look of such relief that she hoped she wouldn't be made a liar by these soldiers. Though she was safer than she had been out in the open, Roxanne felt hungry eyes fastened upon her, as though a dangerous beast was poised to leap on her.

She spun around in fear, but saw nothing.

The hot jolt of fear wouldn't leave her and she looked up into the smooth face of the Vacant Angel. The blank head of the statue seemed to regard her curiously, and Roxanne shook her head at the strangeness of the notion. She reached up with outstretched fingers, and it seemed as though the head of the hulking statue leaned in towards her. The sounds of battle grew faint and Roxanne's lips parted in a soft sigh as she saw the suggestion of a pale face swim into focus in the infinite depths of the polished nephrite.

Roxanne rose to her knees, drawn in by the mesmerising allure of that impossible face.

'Are you mad?' hissed Maya, grabbing her robe and dragging her back to the floor. The deafening crescendo of battle swelled, and when Roxanne looked back up to the Vacant Angel, the pale face had vanished.

'Do you want to get that pretty head shot off your shoulders?' demanded Maya.

Roxanne shook her head and pulled herself tight to Maya. She was a big, motherly woman, and Roxanne felt safer just being near her. She saw Arik turning the gleaming silver ring over and over in his fingers.

'They're going to kill us,' said Arik, and though he was only whispering, the words flew to Roxanne's ears with the poignancy of their simple desire. 'Please help us, please help us!'

A shape moved in the swirling fog, and Roxanne grabbed hold of a piece of broken bench with a sharp tip. It wasn't much of a weapon, but it would have to do.

She relaxed as Palladis Novandio emerged from the smoke, his face spattered with blood and his eyes streaming with tears. He staggered like a drunk and Roxanne felt anger overtake her fear at the thought of what was being done here.

'Palladis!' she cried, and he turned towards her in desperate relief. 'Over here!'

'Roxanne...' he wept, stumbling towards here and collapsing just as he reached her. He fell into her arms and she felt his racing heartbeat. He sobbed into her shoulder, and held her tight as the slaughter continued around them.

'I failed,' he said. 'It was never enough... I couldn't keep it away and now everyone else has to suffer.'

Roxanne pulled him behind their flimsy barricade, and he looked up at the Vacant Angel.

'Why?' he demanded of the faceless statue. 'I did everything I could to keep you appeased! Why must you take these people? Why? Take me instead, take me and let them live! I will see you again, my love! My sweet boys, father will see you soon!'

Palladis rose to his feet, screaming at the statue, his words accusing and demanding.

'Take me, you bastard!'

Roxanne wanted to tell him to be quiet, but she knew no words of hers would dam the heartbreaking flow from the depths of his soul.

'Take me!' sobbed Palladis, sinking to his knees. 'Please!'

'GO,' SAYS THE warrior Nagasena knows as Tagore, and Kai Zulane takes to his heels. Kartono is after him in a heartbeat, and Nagasena lets him go. He needs all his concentration for the battle to come. Tagore is a savage, deadly opponent, but Nagasena knows he must fight him. Honour demands it, and if this is the last honour he can salvage from this hunt, then that will be sufficient.

Tagore bears a long, wide-bladed spearhead. Nagasena recognises it as a broken guardian spear, and hopes its edge is no longer energised. Nagasena drops into a fighting crouch and raises his sword above his head, the tip aimed at Tagore's heart.

'You think you can fight me, little man?' says Tagore, a killing light in his eyes.

Nagasena does not reply, his eyes darting over the World Eater's enormous physique in search of some weak spot, any past hurt that might offer him an advantage: a bullet wound in his side, and traces of a yellow black bruise extending beneath the plates of armour he has taken from the dead men at Antioch's.

'I will break that little needle of yours then tear your head off,' promises Tagore, and Nagasena knows he is more than capable of backing up such threats.

Tagore attacks without warning, slashing with his butcher's blade. The blow is ferocious, but not without skill. Nagasena sways aside and lashes out with *Shoujiki*, landing a stinging blow on Tagore's forearm. A return stroke is only just deflected and Nagasena reels from the incredible power behind the Space Marine's strike. He has fought Legiones Astartes warriors before in training cages, though never with real weapons and never with any success. This will be a battle he will be lucky to live through for more than a few seconds.

Tagore reads his hesitancy as fear and grins.

They dance with thrust, slash and riposte, each gauging the other's skill with every blow. For all his rage, Tagore is a fine warrior and a competent swordsman, but what he lacks in skill, he more than makes up for in determination and relentless ferocity. Every attack, from the first to the last, is launched with exactly the same power and desire. Nagasena avoids the most powerful blows, deflects others and launches his own attacks when he can. His bladework is superior to Tagore's, but they have trained in such different forms of combat that it is proving difficult for either warrior to gain the measure of the other.

'You are good, little man,' says Tagore. 'I thought you would be dead by now.'

'You will find I am full of surprises,' says Nagasena.

'I will still kill you,' promises Tagore as Nagasena spins around and launches a dazzling series of low thrusts and high cuts. Tagore parries some, dodges others and allows some to strike him. His armour is dented and torn, but Nagasena has not been aiming for one killing blow. Instead he has been working his attacks subtly towards the cratered bullet hole in Tagore's side.

As the World Eater sways to the right, Nagasena sees his opening and spins low beneath a beheading cut of the guardian spear. He rams his sword forward with all his strength, plunging the blade into the scabbed wound in Tagore's side. The metal hits hard meat and bone, but Nagasena uses his momentum and Tagore's forward movement to drive the point deep into his opponent's body.

Tagore grunts as the tip of Nagasena's sword bursts from his back. His eyes widen in pain and the metal plates driven into his skull crackle with power as it counteracts the agony of Nagasena's blow with pain-suppressants. Nagasena twists his blade to free it from the Space Marine's flesh, but it is wedged deeper than he has strength to overcome. He lingers too long with the effort and a backhanded fist slams into his shoulder.

He loses his grip on *Shoujiki* and falls heavily to the floor.

Nagasena grips his shoulder, knowing at least one bone there is broken. He rolls onto his side as Tagore's foot slams down where he lay, moving as fast as he can to avoid the World Eater's hunger to destroy him. In his haste, he fails to spot a projecting spar of broken roof timber and stumbles as it catches the edge of his foot.

Nagasena manages to avoid falling, but his momentary distraction is the opening Tagore needs. The guardian spear stabs out, catching Nagasena on his wounded shoulder in imitation of the blow he landed on Tagore. The speartip breaks Nagasena's clavicle neatly in two, and severs the tendons connecting his muscles to the bone. It is a precise blow, at odds with the killing fury in Tagore's eyes, and Nagasena again realises he has underestimated the World Eater.

Nagasena is plucked from the ground, hanging suspended like a worm on a hook before his opponent. Tagore grins at him and reaches his free hand towards Nagasena's neck.

'I told you I would kill you,' says Tagore. 'And what I say I will kill, I kill.

Nagasena says nothing. He is in too much pain and there is nothing he can say that will save his life.

Tagore's free hand reaches out and his thick fingers close around Nagasena's neck, easily encircling his throat. All it will take is one squeeze and the bones of his spine will be powder, his windpipe crushed, and the fragile thread of his life will be cut.

But the pressure never comes.

A blinding spear of blue white light flashes past

Nagasena, the heat of it burning the skin beneath his robes. He is momentarily blinded, but hears the wet drool of blood pouring from a broken body and smells the ripe, repulsive stench of seared human flesh. As his sight returns after the flash, he sees that Tagore has been eviscerated by the close range blast of a plasma weapon of some sort.

Tagore drops to his knees, a gaping crater scorched through his body. His face is contorted in agony that not even Legiones Astartes training and genetics can bear. His grip on Nagasena loosens and he slumps to the side, rolling onto his back as his body fights to keep him alive.

It is a fight Nagasena knows he will lose.

Tagore pulls *Shoujiki* from his body with a grimace of pain. The blade is sticky with blood, and he offers it to Nagasena with respect.

'You were… a worthy… foe,' gasps the dying World Eater. 'Fight… well. For a mortal.'

Nagasena accepts the compliment with a deep bow, and takes the proffered sword.

'And you were worthy prey,' he offers in return, though he knows it will be scant comfort.

'I have… walked the… Crimson Path,' says Tagore with a slow nod. He closes his eyes and says, 'My war… is… ended.'

Though it goes against every creed of the swordsman, Nagasena sheaths his sword with the blood of his enemy still upon the blade and turns to see Maxim Golovko with a humming plasma rifle held at his side. The charging coils still hold a faint glow and its barrel drools liquid smoke into the air.

'He was going to kill you,' says Golovko with relish. 'You can thank me later.'

KAI RAN FROM the swordsman, stumbling as the cramping sensation in his gut eased and his blindsight returned the interior of the temple to dim hues of muted colour. His skin ran with sweat at his brush with the pariah, and he dropped to one knee as delayed shock and fear suddenly swamped him.

He had heard of pariahs, in rumours and whispers that travelled the City of Sight, but never truly believed in their existence until now. The abject *emptiness* of that man was terrifying. The gaping, infinite void a human life should fill with memory, life and vital energies was utterly absent in him.

Even the thought of his non-presence was horrifying, and Kai felt the nausea of his soul-absence returning.

'Oh, no…' he whispered, spinning around and hunting the source of his sickness. He could see nothing, but knowing what he was looking for now, he sought out the emptiness of the pariah.

There, a void in the billowing red mist of violence!

Kai turned and ran, but the pariah was faster, Though Kai could perceive the emptiness of the man's presence, he could not evade him. A hand took him by the scruff of the neck and pulled him up short with great strength. The grip was like that of a machine, powerful and unyielding.

'That's far enough,' said a voice that grated like rusty nails along his spine.

Kai wanted to be sick, his entire body trembling in horror at the utter *wrongness* of this man, a man who should not be.

'Who are you?' gasped Kai.

'My name is Kartono,' said his captor. 'And now it's time for you to die.'

TWENTY-THREE

The Crimson Path
Clade Pet
Angel Unleashed

IT HAD BEEN over a hundred years since Asubha and Subha made war together, a century and more since they had fought as brothers on a field so soaked with blood against a foe so terrible. Live or die, the Custodian was a warrior to honour with a glorious death, and Asubha wished his Legion brothers could have witnessed this fight.

Warriors of their skill in a contest of arms with a single opponent should have been no contest at all, but the praetorian was no ordinary foe. He fought with precise grace, his every blow weighted and measured, his movements anticipating theirs on every level. The three of them moved in a graceful ballet of thrust, dodge, counterattack and parry.

Subha fought like Angron in the arena: with fury and unrelenting pressure. He was the perfect foil for Asubha's careful skill. While an enemy was desperately defending against the flurry of Subha's terrible blows, Asubha would be striking with cool precision, hunting for the killing blow that would end any opponent's resistance in a heartbeat.

But this fight was not going the way either of them expected.

The Custodian repelled Subha without apparent effort, his guardian spear moving with such speed that it was surely impossible. Asubha fired his pistol, but the gold-armoured warrior swayed aside as the shot was fired. His spear spun around and hacked the barrel in two before reversing the blow and hammering the barbed haft into Subha's stomach. The colossal impact staggered his twin, and Asubha took the opportunity to slash with the long knife he had taken from one of Babu Dhakal's men.

The blade scraped over the Custodian's shoulder guard and bounced from the cheek plate of his helmet. His foe slammed an elbow into Asubha's face and he reeled at the power behind the strike. Asubha took a step back to reorient himself as Subha circled around to flank the Custodian.

'I always wanted to fight a Custodian,' snarled Subha.

'We wondered who would emerge triumphant,' added Asubha. 'One of us or one of you?'

'There are two of you,' pointed out the Custodian.

'True, but the question still stands. Our debates would always end in stalemate, for there can be no true answer without death hanging on the outcome,' said Asubha.

'You know the answer. I can see it in your eyes. You know you cannot defeat me.'

Asubha laughed and reversed his blade. 'Tell me your name,' he said. 'That we might remember the mighty warrior we slew on Terra.'

The Custodian brought his spear around to the guard position. 'I am Saturnalia Princeps Carthagina Invictus Cronus–'

'Enough!' barked Subha, launching himself at Saturnalia. His twin still bore the blade snapped from the haft of the Custodian they had killed in the Vault. Though a poor mirror of that wielded by Saturnalia, it was still a deadly weapon in the hands of a World Eater. Saturnalia stepped into the attack, going low and driving

his speartip at Subha's gut. His twin spun aside from the
blow, hammering his blade against Saturnalia's shoulder.
A gold plate spun off, but the heavy mail weave beneath
sent the edge skidding away before it could draw blood.

Asubha followed up and aimed a thunderous kick
towards Saturnalia's unprotected side. A burnished hip
plate crumpled under the impact, and drove Saturnalia
to the ground. Asubha thrust with his blade, but the Custodian leaned away from the blow, the tip of the blade
scraping a furrow in his helmet's visor.

Saturnalia's leg swept out in a scything arc, smashing
Asubha from his feet. He rolled as he landed, barely avoiding a guillotine-chop of the Custodian's guardian spear.
Asubha was on his feet a moment later, and saw Subha
slam his fist into the side of Saturnalia's red-plumed
helm. The Custodian went down hard, but before Subha
could press his advantage, he wrenched off his battered
helmet and swung it in a punishing arc that smashed into
Subha's jaw with a crunch of breaking bone.

Subha toppled backwards, and Asubha threw himself at Saturnalia as he discarded his ruined helm. The
two warriors went down in a tangle of powerful limbs,
punching, gouging and jabbing with elbows and fists.
Asubha rammed his forehead into Saturnalia's face and
grinned as he felt the warrior's nose shatter. He dug for
his knife, pistoning the blade towards the Custodian's
jaw. Saturnalia blocked the blow with his forearm, and
the knife blade drove up through his vambrace and
bone. They rolled, and an armoured fist slammed into
the side of Asubha's face.

Asubha was thrown clear by the power behind the
blow. He spat blood and rose to a crouch, ready to
hurl himself at Saturnalia again. All finesse was gone,
his fury had taken over and he and his brother were as
one. Subha was already on his feet, his lower jaw all but
hanging from his skull, but so too was Saturnalia. The
Custodian had retrieved his guardian spear and its tip
was aimed at Subha's heart.

A pumping barrage of shells exploded from the weapon and Subha rocked back as the explosive bolts tore into him. Each one detonated within his flesh, mushrooming from his back in fans of bright blood and splintered bone. Subha crumpled, the life already vanishing from his eyes as he fell onto his front.

'Now you know,' said Saturnalia with a rictus grin of blood.

Asubha felt the red rage take him, and though he had always longed for the butcher's nails, he knew now he did not need them to reach the clarity of undiluted fury. Saturnalia saw the change in him and took a step away. Asubha screamed his brother's name and threw himself back into the fight.

The guardian spear swung out, but Asubha dived beneath its killing arc and swept up Subha's fallen blade. He slashed twice in quick succession as he rolled upright in one smooth motion. Blood sprayed from the twin cuts through the flexible mail weave at the back of Saturnalia's knees, and the Custodian fell into a pool of blood, unable to stand, but still able to fight.

Asubha circled around to face him, his anger filling him with its purity of purpose.

'You will die here today,' hissed Saturnalia through his agony. He held his guardian spear before him, and Asubha took a step forward until the tip was resting on his chest.

'I know that,' agreed Asubha. 'But so will you.'

Asubha drove his bloodied blade down through Saturnalia's skull as the Custodian thrust his spear with the last of his strength. The guardian spear clove Asubha's heart and tore through his lungs, wreaking irreparable damage to his body. Both warriors slumped against one another as though embracing in honour of their fight to the death.

Asubha slid to the side and fell beside the body of his twin.

As he bled out onto the temple floor, he pressed the

broken blade that had ended Saturnalia's life into his brother's dead hand.

'We walk the Crimson Path together, brother,' said Asubha.

ATHARVA SAW A lithe man in a loose bodyglove lift Kai from the ground, and thrust his hand towards him, uttering the fireborn cant of the Pyrae. A horizontal pillar of fire burned its way across the temple, setting alight every single piece of smashed timber and every body in its path. Flames leapt to life, greedily devouring this feast of combustible material, but they guttered and died before they reached the man holding Kai in his grip.

The man turned as Atharva ran towards him with heavy thudding footsteps, and the building of a Pavoni flesh manipulation faded in his mind as he recognised Yasu Nagasena's clade pet. He reached for the blade at his belt, stifling a twist of nausea in his gut at the thought of being so close to such anathema to his powers.

Waving streams of gunfire zig-zagged through the temple, but Atharva pushed them aside with short-lived kine shields as he ran through the flames of his own making. He had seen Tagore fall to Yasu Nagasena, but had no clue as to the fates of Subha and Asubha. With Severian in hiding or fled, he could expect no aid in the fight against this clade warrior.

'Oni-ni-kanabo,' said the man with a wretched grin that made Atharva sick to his stomach. 'Come one step closer and Kai Zulane dies.'

Atharva's lip curled in grimace of distaste. 'You are going to kill him anyway, pariah.'

'How does it feel, warlock?' asked the clade warrior. 'How does it feel to be blind?'

'Liberating,' lied Atharva, taking another step forwards. 'But I can kill you without recourse to my powers.'

'Perhaps,' conceded the pariah, tightening his grip on Kai's neck. 'Though I doubt you can kill me before he dies.'

Though he could see the man clearly with his gen-hanced eyes, Atharva found it difficult to keep his image from blurring. His vision was far superior to that of mortals, but the pariah's umbra made it almost impossible to fix him in his mind's eye. He forced himself into the lower Enumerations, honing his concentration and sharpening his focus. The pariah's blurred form swam into clarity, a black outline against a haze of yellow smoke and orange flames.

Atharva tried to summon even the tiniest morsel of the Great Ocean into his flesh, but the proximity of such an unnatural creature made even that simple task impossible. The pariah was a hole in the world that drained every scrap of energy.

Kai squirmed in the warrior's grasp, his face twisted in pain at the pariah's touch. He let out a cry of such desperation that even Atharva was moved to pity. As vile as it was to be near this man, Atharva could not bear the thought of being touched by him. The clade killer withdrew a long knife with a serrated edge and a blade that ended in two distinct points.

'Whatever you wanted from him is gone,' said the pariah.

Before the pariah could stab Kai, a shape rose up behind him and swung a long spar of jagged timber at his head. The clade warrior sensed the incoming attack at the last moment and twisted out of the path of the blow. He could not avoid it completely, and instead of hammering the side of his skull, it slammed into his shoulder.

Atharva saw the Navigator woman raise the piece of wood to strike again, but the clade warrior was not about to give her a second chance. He ducked under her clumsy swing and slammed an open palm against her chest. The woman flew back, slamming into the faceless statue with a sickening thud of flesh on stone.

Atharva seized the opportunity and lunged forward with his own blade extended. The clade warrior dropped

Kai and bent his entire body back, swaying aside from
Atharva's thrust. His hand chopped down, but Atharva's
flesh and bone were genetically toughened to withstand
pressures greater than any mortal, even a clade-trained
one, could bring to bear.

Atharva backhanded the pariah in the chest, and the
warrior turned the impact into a springing vault. He
landed lightly amid the flames, one leg extended to the
side, the other curled up beneath him.

'So many psykers,' he giggled. 'It's almost too easy.'

Before Atharva could wonder what that meant, a rippling series of metallic plates rose up from the warrior's
neck. As though growing organically at high speed,
curved sections of chromed metal unfolded to encase
the pariah's head in a bulbous helm of gold and silver.
A tubular device extruded the side of the pariah's newly-
formed headgear, and lenses tinted with unfathomable
colours slotted into place over one eye.

Atharva sensed a terrible threat in this strange device,
and put himself between the clade warrior and Kai. He
passed his blade from hand to hand, readying himself
to fight in close combat. Behind him, Kai groaned as the
nausea of the pariah's touch eased.

'I should thank you,' said Atharva. 'It has been too long
since I fought blade to blade. It will make a refreshing
change to kill without my powers.'

The pariah leapt into the air and the strange device
attached to his helmet spat a stream of black light from
the unnatural lenses. Instinctively, Atharva threw up a
kine shield, but the power of the Great Ocean was dead
in him. The bolts struck him in the chest, the plates of
sheet steel strapped to his body offering him no protection against so abominable a weapon.

An inferno of cold fire filled Atharva, a numbing pain
that felt like liquid nitrogen flowing through his veins.
Pulsing waves of dark energy exploded within him, like
the supernova of a dead star. And just as an exploding
sun must collapse into the gravitational hell of a black

hole, so too did Atharva feel his life contracting into a deathly singularity from which there could be no escape.

This was not just death, this was an ending that would deny his life force its release into the Great Ocean where it would exist forever as raw potential. The horror of so bleak a fate gave Atharva the strength to resist it, and he roared as he surged to his feet. The pariah landed next to him, its blade stabbing again and again. Blood oozed from the cuts, and Atharva felt a soul-deep horror at each blow.

His every instinct was to escape this nightmarish being, this abomination that had no right to exist in a world where living things claimed dominion. Unreasoning terror made Atharva want to run and hide, anything to get away from this terrible, abhorrent creature. He fought against the insidious effects of the pariah as another knife thrust opened the meat of his body and a scorching blast of black fire from the clade warrior's helmet enveloped him.

Through the shocking pain, Atharva saw the unfolding battle as though viewed through a slowly shattering window. Black-clad soldiers moved like glacial automatons through the burning temple, the bullets of their weapons stuttering in slow motion as they slaughtered the huddled people taking shelter from the carnage. He saw Tagore lying where he had fallen, his stomach a smoking ruin and a gaping hole cut in his chest.

Across from the dead warrior, Atharva saw Asubha and Subha. The twins lay side by side in death, next to the cloven body of a Legio Custodes warrior. Like Tagore, their chests had also been cut open, and they lay in vast lakes of impossibly bright blood. The temple was lost, and any hope they had of bringing Kai Zulane to the Warmaster was now ashes.

Atharva knew he had only one option left to him, and though it was a monstrously drastic solution, it was the only way he could fight the pariah and prevent what Kai Zulane knew from reaching those who were now his enemies. It was a solution almost as grievous as death, but without making this ultimate sacrifice, he could not fight on. Atharva was a Space Marine, a warrior, and though it was giving up that part of him that made him whole, there was no other choice.

He reached deep inside himself, to the secret place that could look into the Great Ocean and draw on its limitless power. It was a fragile thing, the incalculably precious result of a billion random mutations that had built upon one another over an unimaginably vast span of time. For a frozen instant that lasted an eternity, Atharva wondered whether death would be preferable to being blind for the rest of his life.

'Only those sacrifices that have worth are meaningful,' he said, crushing that secret part of his existence and forever severing his connection to the warp.

He screamed in anguish, as no warrior of the Legiones Astartes had ever screamed or ever would again until the last moments of this war, when men would discover the true depths of suffering the universe could inflict upon them.

Atharva was alone, all his carefully-wrought plans in ashes. With nothing left to lose, and with the last shred of power left to him, he reached up to the faceless angel that loomed above him with a vulture's anticipation. He sensed the gathering anticipation of the neverborn creatures hidden behind its featureless mask, and tore aside the veil that kept them chained within it.

'Kill them all,' he commanded. 'Leave none alive!'

KAI EXPERIENCED ATHARVA'S battle with the pariah through a haze of blurred and overlapping auras. His body was wracked with spasms of pain at its presence, and he fought to hold onto consciousness as its repellent presence turned his stomach inside out. He huddled in the lee of the faceless statue, helpless in the face of the bloodshed that had come to the temple, cradling Roxanne to his chest as a woman he didn't know did the same with two young boys.

He heard Atharva shout at the statue above him and felt a bone-deep chill as a layer of frost crackled into existence on the smooth dark stone. Kai flinched at the sharp cold, and looked up as he felt the sudden presence of something far worse and infinitely more terrible than any pariah could ever be.

The outline of the Vacant Angel shimmered, as though two of them fought to occupy the same space. Like a pair of overlaid transparencies, they jostled and ran together. Kai saw a host of eyes, fanged mouths and claws press outwards from one of the images. As though the universe could no longer cope with two such competing realities, the wavering outlines snapped apart and the temple was split by a shrieking cry of birth more painful and more joyous than any endured by a mortal newborn.

A ghostly form rose from the Vacant Angel, and though Kai's blindsight was not yet restored, he saw its form completely. It resembled a tattered giant in spectral robes with a hood that concealed a depthless void in which galaxies went to die and the empty wasteland that could only exist beyond the event horizon of a black hole. Skeletal arms unfolded, and its voluminous robes billowed in howling winds of aetheric energy. A pair of icy white wings furled into existence from its back, cutting streamers of frozen vapour through the air.

Crackling webs of frost formed on the stone walls of the temple, and glass shattered as the temperature plummeted to below zero in an instant. Kai's breath misted before him and he shivered in terror at the magnificent and terrible creature Atharva had drawn out of the faceless statue.

Its horror touched Kai deeper than any fear he had known, even in his darkest moments aboard the *Argo*. All the grief, all the suffering, all the unendurable pain and woes given voice in this place had shaped its form, a creature of immaterial energy now coalesced into this monstrous, avenging angel.

Death had been wept into its faceless heart and it had

been commanded to unleash that in the most direct way imaginable. The Vacant Angel swept down into the temple with its arms outstretched and a drawn-out shriek of grief exploding from beneath its hood. Kai pressed his hands to his ears as the sound cut into him like a cold knife to the heart.

The Black Sentinels shot at the angel, but nothing so paltry as gunfire could harm such a creature. Bullets passed through its ghostly form and lasblasts simply twitched its form with light as they passed harmlessly through. Men dropped to their knees as it flew at them, driven to madness by even a glimpse of the angel's hooded face.

The angel's gaze was death, and wherever it turned its head, soldiers fell to the ground as their hearts froze in their chests. Its scream was an unending lament for the dead, a solemn, piercing hymnal to the futility of life and the inevitability of death. To hear its scream was to feel the cold touch of the grave, and those Black Sentinels who had not already perished turned their weapons on themselves.

Atharva staggered into the lee of the statue, and though he had loosed this terrible angel, Kai saw his aura was grief-stricken, as though he had lost that which meant most to him in all the world. Even through the haze of the pariah's presence, Kai could see that was exactly what had happened.

Atharva was no longer psychic.

'What did you do?' gasped Kai, his breath misting before him.

'What I had to,' said Atharva, as Kai felt Roxanne stir. Kai turned his horrified gaze from the warrior of the Thousand Sons to the girl cradled in his arms. She lifted her head, but before she could take in the full horror of the daemonic avatar at loose, Kai turned her head away.

'Don't look at it,' he said, and she knew enough to listen.

'What is it?' she asked, keeping her eyes tightly shut.

'It's death,' said Kai, knowing that was only half the truth.

He felt movement beside him, and turned as Palladis Novandio walked out into the chaos of the temple's destruction. The sanctuary he had built from the ashes of his own grief was a charnel house, a tomb for the living and a dreadful mirror of what he had tried to achieve.

'Palladis! What are you doing?' yelled Kai.

'What I must,' he wept as he marched toward the angel laying waste to the living.

'I told you to take me!' screamed Palladis. 'Take me and begone!'

The angel was hovering just below the shattered remains of the temple's roof, its aetheric form bathed in the hellish light of the fires burning beneath it. The darkness beneath its hood flickered, as though the angel recognised something of its creation in the man approaching it.

The creature descended through the air with its arms spread wide, leaving a glittering trail of frozen moisture in its wake. Its keening lament grew sharper, and Kai could only watch in horror as its shimmering, icy wings began to wrap Palladis Novandio in a macabre embrace.

'Palladis, please!' screamed Roxanne as she saw what he was doing. 'Come back!'

The master of the temple turned at the sound of her voice, but made no move to escape the angel's clutches.

'It's alright, Roxanne,' he said, as the wings closed upon him. 'I'll be with them now...'

Like the soldiers before him, Palladis Novandio slumped to the floor of the temple, dead in an instant and his soul now free to join his lost family.

'No!' screamed Roxanne, and the angel looked up, fastening its eyeless stare upon the huddled group of mortals that sheltered below the statue that had imprisoned it for so long. Its mournful cries echoed from the walls like a chorus of all the souls damned to oblivion throughout the ages. Kai heard his death in the sound.

Roxanne took hold of his hands and turned him to face her.

'Kai, this has to end,' she said. 'And it has to end now!'

He shook his head. 'I can't stop this, I don't know how.'

'You do,' she said. 'That's the only thing I know for sure about all of this. Only you can stop this.'

'How?' said Kai, feeling the inexorable approach of the daemonic angel.

'Come with me,' said Roxanne, closing her eyes.

Warmth spread from Roxanne's hands, passing from her flesh and into his. Her breathing deepened, and Kai felt the touch of her strange manifestation of psychic energy. The Navigators were a breed apart from astropaths, and no one beyond the confines of the Navis Nobilite truly understood the full extent of their powers. Kai's breathing deepened, and he felt as though his very essence was being drawn into Roxanne.

He wanted to rebel against this surrender of the self, but Roxanne's soothing voice drew him into her. The sensation was not unlike the early stages of a *nuncio* trance, and though their physical bodies were in mortal danger, Kai let himself be enfolded in Roxanne's strange power. If this was death, then where better to meet it in than in the soul-embrace of a friend?

'Where are we going?' he asked.

'To the *Argo*,' said Roxanne.

KAI OPENED HIS eyes and found himself in the familiar dreamscape of the Rub' al Khali, the endless desert sweeping to the edges of the world in cursive arches of golden sand. He stood by the azure lake, its waters rippling with strange tides and the sun hanging on the far horizon like a semicircle of molten bronze.

The fortress of Arzashkun glittered like a bauble in the middle distance, its towers turned gold in the sunset and its walls shimmering in the heat haze coming off the desert. He knew he should try to reach the safety of the fortress, but felt a curious reluctance to venture in that direction. Instead he turned his gaze towards the shores of the lake.

A regicide board was set up on low table, the pieces arranged apparently at random, for it seemed as though certain pieces were placed on squares they couldn't possibly have reached. Kai remembered playing against someone here, a hooded figure with golden eyes, but the memory refused to divulge any further details.

Roxanne stood beside him, holding his hand as the sun sank slowly to the horizon.

'The sun is setting,' said Kai. 'It's never done that before.'

'This isn't just your dreamspace anymore. It's mine too.'

'I know, but I don't mind.'

'It's beautiful here,' said Roxanne. 'I can see why you come here.'

'It's safe here,' said Kai. 'At least it used to be.'

'Before the *Argo*?'

He nodded, already sensing the lurking presence of the black horror beneath the sand. It felt like an age since he had come here, though he knew it could only have been a day or so. Time was meaningless in a *nuncio* trance, and a dreamer could live an entire lifetime in the course of a single dream.

'It's here, isn't it? The *Argo*.'

'Yes,' said Kai, as the shadow beneath the sand drew ever closer. He could feel the grasping claws of guilt and the tendrils of remorse working their way towards the surface of the sand, but he felt no urge to run for the safety of the fortress.

Roxanne said *he* had to end this, and nothing was ever ended by running away.

This time he would face whatever emerged from the depths of his subconscious.

As though drawn towards them by Kai's willingness to face it, the horror of the *Argo* pushed up from the sand, an oozing black nightmare of screaming death. Kai struggled against its pull, and the fear that Roxanne's presence had kept at bay rose up in a suffocating wave.

'I can't do this,' he said.

'You can,' replied Roxanne, taking his hand. Kai wished he possessed even a fraction of her composure. 'I'm right beside you, and this is my dreamspace too, remember?'

'I remember,' said Kai as the black tide dragged them down like oily quicksand.

'Then let me show you what *I* saw,' said Roxanne.

TWENTY-FOUR

The *Argo*
The Dead Can Forgive
The End of the Game

THE BLACK SAND swallowed Kai, and his panic slammed into him like a resurgent tide. He took a terrified breath, but rather than the oily liquid texture he expected, a breath of achingly cold air filled his lungs. Instead of total darkness, Kai was plunged into a kaleidoscopic hallucination of myriad colours and swirling vortices. He felt sick to the pit of his stomach at the churning maelstrom of phantom images, howling currents and voids of non-space exploding around him.

Yet for all its horror, there was a reluctant beauty to everything, an ethereal quality that thrilled as much as it terrified. It stretched all around him as far as his eyes could see, and it took Kai a moment to recognise that he was seeing this magnificent vista through more than two eyes.

No sooner had the realisation come than he felt the immense, implacable weight of the starship beneath him, its vast bulk stretching behind him like a vast slice of an azure city cut from the metal skin of a planet and set on a course through the stars. He knew this ship, though he had never seen it from such a vantage point.

Whole once again, this immense marvel of technology was the *Argo*.

The entire vessel shuddered like a newborn, and Kai wondered at the forces required to so easily buffet such an incredible weight. A lashing tendril of variegated light swirled down from an unfolding nova of black energy and slammed down towards the ship. A flare of actinic light shimmered on the edge of perception as it struck the vessel's shields, dissipating with what sounded like a roar of terrible frustration.

Another smear of red stormclouds spiralled into existence just off the curving, plough-blade of a bow, and Kai felt the ship's engines strain as it strained to avoid the burgeoning fury. As though sensing the *Argo's* attempts to evade, the stormclouds swelled and threw out grasping spears of hungry light. They too smashed into the shields, and the squalling flare of light seemed more piercing, more strained to Kai.

The entire vessel lurched as yet more tempests blew up around it, slamming it to the side with no more effort than a leaf in the wind. An explosion on the tapering topside flared, and Kai saw a series of towers studded with thin pylons vanish in a searing, short-lived fireball.

A portion of the shields collapsed, a gaping wound in the *Argo's* protection, and he felt the ship's captain turn the vessel away from the most violent monsoons in an effort to protect the open flank.

Whatever beauty Kai felt this region possessed was immediately forgotten. This was a place of terrible, unimaginable danger. No right thinking person would willingly cast themselves here. This realm of existence was anathema to life, and it was not meant that humanity should venture far from its home of placid existence of Terra.

Fresh detonations blossomed along the length of the *Argo*, and more of the vaned towers collapsed as the storms overloaded the pylons' ability to keep them at bay. A forward portion of the starboard flank exploded outwards, venting frozen air like a spray of white blood.

Kai wanted to close his eyes, but he was not cast in this unfolding drama as a participant, merely an observer. He twisted as the ship trembled like a wounded beast, the thunderous detonations wracking its hull eerily silent from his vantage point. The power of the destruction working its way along the vessel was like the hammer-blow footsteps of a Mechanicum battle engine.

The darkness gathered. The red cloud surged towards the *Argo* like a gaping maw and the spiralling arms of the black vortex clawed at the shields with ever greater ferocity. To his untrained eyes, it was as though a gross and malicious sentience guided their fury, for what else could explain the predator's glee he felt from the ugly stains that surrounded the vessel?

He wanted to turn from the horror, to shut himself off from a firmament awash with nightmares, half-glimpsed visions of hungry eyes and mountainous bodies the size of continents shifting in the depths. Yet he had not come here to turn away from this. He had been blind to the reality of the *Argo's* death for too long, and no matter what, he was not turning away from it now.

Roxanne was right. This had to end *now*.

One by one, he watched the shield vanes collapse, and the warp poured in like a polluted sea through a disinte-grating dam. Immaterial energies bathed the vessel, and Kai saw barely visible shapes as they swam into existence within the bounds of those shields that still functioned. Scaled red beasts like skeletal men with long curling horns and clawed arms that flashed like swords. Mon-sters dredged from the deepest nightmares of the crew spun like smoke as they revelled in their newly birthed forms.

The hull was no barrier to them, and they passed through the metres of adamantium to manifest within the crew compartments and companionways of the ship. Formless spawn roamed the hull, their very touch disas-sembling the solid matter of its gun ports, commandways and cargo holds. The vessel groaned and more compartments blew out into space as its collapse continued at a geometric rate. Cathedral-like holds imploded with soundless screams of tearing metal, and Kai wept as he saw thousands of men and women pulled out into the void.

The screams echoed in his skull, but there was nothing he could do to block them out, no fortress of Arzashkun and no Rub' al Khali in which to shut himself away from everything. Here, Kai was forced to face his daemons, and he watched the death of the *Argo* with a heavy heart, knowing it was doomed, but pledged to honour its last moments.

Then, just when it seemed as though the vessel must surely break apart and be claimed by the void, a slender thread of golden light penetrated the darkness. Little more than a sliver against the raging inferno of colour, it was nevertheless a lifeline, and one the *Argo* flailed for in desperation. The ship turned its collapsing prow towards the light, lurching with the last of its strength as a drowning man grasps for an outstretched hand.

Where the golden light shone, no storms could touch, and where it surged strong, they were driven back. A narrow channel of dead space opened up in front of the *Argo*, and Kai's heart soared as the last gasp of the vessel's engines saw it slip into this miraculous channel.

Broken and torn into a raw, ragged shadow of its former self, the *Argo* fell into the fragile gap in the tempests. All around it, blistering squalls of impossible light and sentient cyclones battered at this corridor of serenity, but the light was inviolable and held firm against the warp's every predation. He gasped as his mind was filled with a vision of the greatest mountain on Terra, a hollowed out peak of sadness and service, where the most glorious and most powerful beacon in the galaxy was born.

Kai had never been told how the *Argo* had managed to return to realspace after the monsters attacked. He had

assumed the captain had been lucky enough to find a
warp gate that led back to the Sol system, but he saw
how naïve such a belief had been. The captain and all
the crew were dead, and the only two people left alive
within the dying vessel were Kai and Roxanne. Had Roxanne found this wayward strand of the Astronomican
and pulled them to safety? He knew such an analogy
was crude, but what other way was there to explain it?

Even though this was a memory from another mind,
Kai felt an inordinate sense of relief as the empty corridor of calm space enfolded the *Argo*. The vessel was
plummeting through a web of sticky strands that fought
to cling onto its prize, but the power of the Astronomican was at its strongest here, and the *Argo* was dragged
back into the material universe.

Kai's stomach sank, and he swallowed a mouthful
of bile as his body shifted from one plane of existence
to another. Translating from the warp to realspace was
never easy, but to do it while looking into the heart of
baleful storms was even harder. He fought to hold onto
consciousness, and let out a shuddering series of breaths
as the sickening colours of the warp faded and the distant sprinkling of diamond stars against the darkness of
realspace swam into focus.

Now subject to the principal laws of the universe, the
Argo twisted as gravity tore at it with jealous claws. Portions of the ship buckled inwards, and others tore away
in the violence of translation. How galling it would be to
have survived such violent warp storms only to destroyed
by the very laws held in abeyance beyond the veil of the
Immaterium.

Yet Kai knew they had not been destroyed, they had
lived.

He remembered the salvage crews cutting him from
his astropath's chamber. He remembered screaming and
clawing and biting at them, raving and demented from
his nightmarish solitude. He had heard the crew die,
their every last thought and final moment of agony, and

it had driven him to the brink of madness. To have lived through so horrendous an ordeal was more than most minds could survive, and Kai knew that a man of lesser mental fortitude would have died along with the crew.

For the longest time he had derided himself as weak and foolish, haunted by his own survival and blaming himself for every death to which he had been forced to listen. He knew now that his survival was only thanks to his strength and ability to shut off that part of him that could not hope to deal with such a trauma. Enough people had told him that the death of the *Argo* was not his fault, for good reasons and for bad, but only by seeing it for himself could he truly accept the truth of it.

And with that truth came revelation.

I was there the day Horus slew the Emperor.

The delicious treason of it. The punchline undelivered. Words from another time and another mind. The warrior of the new moon will say it and it will sound like a joke, but it will soon be ashes in his mouth, a bitter memory he wishes he could erase. It is both true and false. Blood spilled through misunderstanding.

Kai sees the Red Chamber.

Crimson light spills over him like oil: thick, slow and choking. It envelops him until it seems there is nothing left of the world but blood.

He is disembodied, or his body has been destroyed. It is impossible to know which.

The Red Chamber is like the interior of a diseased ventricle, pulsing with ruddy light and weirdly angled, as though the fundamental laws of physics no longer apply. Lines and curves intersect and diverge, forming decks and walls and ceilings at impossible angles to one another.

Everywhere drips blood, or is that his imagination?

Red-lit hololiths on one wall show a gently spinning orb of silver and blue, a haze of fire rippling the lower levels of its atmosphere. This world burns with war, and it does not surprise him when he sees the familiar outlines of the Nordafrik continental mass emerge from the storm-lit clouds that gather like gnarled fists over the landscape.

This is Terra, and it is under attack.

Kai has no sensation of form, nothing to give him a clue as to how he can be in this place. Is he a fragment of soul, a sliver of consciousness? A passive observer or a shaper of events yet to come? No matter how he shifts his awareness, there is no sensation of weight or substance.

Flicker. Time shifts.

He sees as he once saw – with his birthsight – and he wishes he did not.

This is a place of carnage, a slaughterhouse where dissected bodies have been hung from the walls, and skulls jangle on hooks like bone totems of primitive savages. Banners of black canvas ripple with no wind to stir them, as though the loathsome devices worked into their fabric quiver with life of their own.

A battle has been fought here. Or will be fought here. It was or will be a battle like no other, and its outcome has yet to be understood by the cosmos at large. This moment, this epochal paradigm shift in the affairs of the galaxy, is his alone to see, but soon it will echo through the aeons like the ringing of the mightiest bell ever tolled.

This is history being written before him, and history demands to be witnessed.

Bodies are strewn around him, titanic warriors in warplate scored with sword and axe wounds, punctured by missile impacts and ripped open by the claws of savage monsters. The ruin of flesh is unimaginable: meat and bone reduced to a gruel of marrow, bodies twisted and gnawed like cast-off butcher scraps. Kai is used to death, and knows full well the horrors man is capable of wreaking on his brothers, but this is something else.

This butchery has all the hallmarks of hatred, and no hate is as bitter as that which was once love. These warriors knew each other, and what was waged in this red chamber was not war, it was murder. It was fratricide of the worst and most unforgivable kind.

His gaze roams the corpses, drawn towards the focal point of the struggle, a stepped dais where a horror like no other awaits him. He wants to look away, to spare himself the awful certitude that will come with seeing what has happened upon the dais. His survival instinct begs him to look away, knowing he will be driven to madness by the sight of it.

Kai knows that to shirk this vision is cowardice. Yet he fears this understanding. He fears it will open a door that cannot ever be closed. Once knowledge moves from potential to actuality, there can be no unlearning, no undoing and no return to the life he once lived.

Flicker. Time shifts again…

Shapes and shadows move around him, vast, cosmic things without shape or form. They are invisible, but he knows they are there. He can sense their horror and disbelief at what has happened here, their galactic rage at an outcome none of them had foreseen. Time skips around him, droplets of blood reversing their course in the air to return to the split arteries from which they fell. Shouts of protest, cries of pain and booming laughter echo and return, echo and return, roosting in the throats of those that wrought them. In an instant, the horror upon the dais is undone and he sees fragments of what has gone before.

Black and red entwined, a golden eye, slitted like a cats. Ivory pinions, a boom of air and a clash of swords. Halo and thorny crown clash, a beating of breasts. Luminous and wondrous rears above hard-edged plate and monstrous ambition. They are clawed and enraged. A stalemate of blows, a battle of wills fought in realms beyond the understanding of mortal senses.

It is martial perfection unmatched. Only one battle in the history of the galaxy will ever eclipse its fury, and it will be fought in the same place in a matter of moments. That one such battle should take place is remarkable. Two is unheard of.

There are no forms he can see, only light and darkness, fleeting impressions of battling titans. These warriors are avatars, numinous and filled with the light of creation at the heart of *the universe. Moulded into ideally-wrought mortal forms and unleashed upon the galaxy, they are brightly burning stars, all the brighter for their achingly short existence.*

Voices take shape, but Kai is relieved beyond imagining that he cannot understand them, for who would dare listen to the words of gods? These incredible beings come together once more, and though their language is unknown to him, meaning seeps into his consciousness.

Gods may be beyond understanding, but they will be heard.

Promises are made. Offers of power and servitude. Seductive bargains offered as promises. Angelic scorn is poured upon them. Hurt tears of rage and rejection. Bloody tears on golden features, a necessary death, the most infinitesimal crack in the most impenetrable armour. A life given willingly, a sacrifice on the altar of the future.

A death for a death. One to provoke the other...

Black and crimson collide one last time. An explosion of red light swamps Kai and time skips back and forth once again. Is this the future or the past? He sees this place as it must once have looked: the sterile, functional interior of a warship's strategium. Breaths of recycled air stir freshly-won honour banners, liveried crewmen attend to their duties with pride, and the limitless potential of the galaxy is a spray of stars in the viewing bay.

In a heartbeat it changes, now a temple to a living god.

A dark-armoured god whose divinity was wrought by his own hands. Once the favoured avatar of a greater god, but now slipped from any notion of servitude, even to those who elevated him beyond the limits set upon his superhuman existence. This is a god who forges his own destiny with brute strength and implacable will, moulding the future to a shape pleasing to him and him alone. He calls no man master, but he will at the end.

Flicker. Forward and back. Flicker, flicker.

The warp makes a mockery of any notion of time as linear.

Kai sees him dead, once a haloed messenger of crimson perfection, now a broken sacrifice who guided the executioner's blade to his own heart. Dead. Unthinkable, and his mind recoils from the horror of this vision. It is vile and spiteful, a parade of horrors conjured for no more reason than to break his spirit.

Yet the warp is capable of so much more, and these are but tasters for a greater horror.

He sees it unfold in unflinching detail, every golden hue of armour, every play of light around features that are ever-changing, but always broken-hearted. He sees hatred, love, guilt, horror, resolve broken and renewed in the same breath, and a depthless well of sadness for a future he sees and knows he has created.

The temporal flow is out of joint, flexing like a broken spine. Though Kai sees this in random flickers of spinning time, he knows this can only be the future.

And it is not distant.

The golden light flinches, and he feels its impossible scrutiny. It is looking back at him. It sees him and knows everything about him in a span of time so small it has no method of being measured. The light sees what he has seen, knows now what he saw upon the raised dais, and he senses a measure of its acceptance of that knowledge.

Words form in his mind, softly spoken and without the need of anything as crude a voice, yet they have the force of the most violent hurricane. He understands these words, and knows now why no mortal should ever hear the voice of a living god.

He sees what happens next in awful clarity, gold and black, master and servant, god and demi-god.

Father and son.

It can end only one way, and the knowledge of what has already happened, but is yet to come is enough to break the sanity of any mortal, no matter how strong their mind might be. Yet Kai has been tempered with guilt and horror, and has a strength beyond that of others.

He has one more task left to perform.

THE VISION VANISHED in burst of golden light and Kai was hurled from the Red Chamber into a place of warmth, aromatic perfumes, scented oils and the sound of a gurgling fountain. He opened his eyes and found himself reclining on a padded couch fashioned from the hide of some exotic beast. His entire body felt as though he floated on an invisible cushion, and all the hurts done to him since his return to Terra were undone.

'Oh, Aniq,' he whispered. 'That we had to see such things...'

He could remember every detail of the Red Chamber, and though it presaged a horror greater than anything he could possibly have imagined, he felt strangely detached from it, as though it was a matter of no consequence to him.

Kai sat up and looked around to see that he lay in one of the principal guest suites of Arzashkun, a chamber so ostentatiously appointed it was almost obscene. Not only was his physical body restored, but a great weight had been lifted from his shoulders, a burden he had not realised was so monstrous until its removal. He took a deep breath and closed his eyes, listening to the fading sound of thousands of voices in his head as they receded into the chambers of memory.

As they pulled away from him, he felt their voices join as one in a wordless sensation of release. The dead could not return, but they could forgive. Kai knew he would never forget these people, and they would never forget him. The thought that they would always be with him made him smile, for they were now part of his story and not a burden to carry.

Kai stood as a warm breeze stirred an invitation at the silken curtain of an opened door that led out onto a balcony. He walked across the marble floor, feeling as though Arzashkun was no longer a place of refuge, but a place of wonder. He had crafted its every tower and chamber from memory, but he had never truly basked in its magnificence. Only now did he appreciate the miraculous skill of its ancient builders, their sense of proportion and joy as they raised its beauty to the skies.

He stepped onto the balcony, but instead of the endless

sands of the Rub' al Khali, he saw a verdant landscape of lush forests, sweeping grasslands and crystal rivers. This was the Empty Quarter before the sands had swallowed it, a bounteous land fought over by kings and emperors since the dawn of civilisation. This was the land where his race had been born, and it shone with the unlimited potential of humanity.

Kai wasn't surprised to see a regicide board set up waiting for him. His opponent from the game by the shore sat before the onyx pieces, and the memory of that conversation returned to him with sudden clarity. Where before his opponent had been indistinct, now he went bare headed, and Kai nodded in respect as he saw a face more commonly seen rendered in marble.

'You look different, Kai,' said the figure, his golden eyes like shimmering coins.

'I am different,' he said, taking a seat before the silver pieces of the board. 'I feel free.'

The man smiled and said, 'Good. That is all I ever wanted for you.'

'You brought the *Argo* from the warp,' said Kai, moving a silver piece forward.

'Are you asking me a question?'

Kai shook his head. 'No. I don't want to know. The truth only spoils things.'

'The truth is a moving target,' said the figure, moving a Templar across the board.

'Did you see?' asked Kai, already knowing the answer.

'I saw what Sarashina hid within you, yes.'

Kai said nothing, and they played in silence, trading pieces back and forth across the board. Mindful of his last encounter over the regicide board, Kai played a cautious game, husbanding his pieces and unwilling to take unnecessary risks.

'Do you not want to play?' asked his opponent.

'I don't know what to say to you,' replied Kai, sitting back in his chair. 'Knowing what you know of the future, you still want to play a game?'

'Of course. At a time like this, it is the best way to stay focused,' said the figure, moving his Emperor forward in an aggressive move designed to tempt Kai to rashness. 'If you want to know a man's true character, play a game with him. In any case, the future is the future, and my feelings towards it will not change it one way or the other.'

'Truly? Even you can't change it?' said Kai, willingly taking the bait.

The figure shrugged, as though they discussed something trivial. 'Some things *need* to happen, Kai. Even the most terrible things you can imagine sometimes need to happen.'

'Why?'

His opponent moved his Divinitarch into a blocking position, and said, 'Because sometimes the only victory possible is to keep your opponent from winning.'

Kai scanned the board, seeing he had no more moves to make.

'Stalemate,' he said.

The figure spread his hands in an empty gesture of apology. 'I know some people think me omnipotent, but there is a catch with being all powerful and all knowing.'

'Which is?'

'You can't be both at the same time,' said the figure with a wry smile.

'So what happens now?'

'I finish the game.'

'This one?' asked Kai, puzzled.

'No,' said the figure. 'Our game is done, and I thank you for it.'

'Will I see you again?'

His opponent laughed. 'Who knows, Kai? If our game has taught me anything, it is that all things are possible.'

'But you're going to die.'

'I know,' said the Emperor.

* * *

KAI OPENED HIS eyes and saw only blackness. He felt cold, and a suffocating claustrophobia enveloped him. He slid his hands from Roxanne's and reached up to rip away the bandages wrapped around his head. He tore at them in a frenzy, pulling away handfuls of textured cloth and wads of sticky gauze as he heard the shrieking moans of the Vacant Angel as it drew closer.

The last of the bandages fell away, and Kai looked into Roxanne's pearlescent eyes. They were the most wondrous shade of gold-flecked amber, and he wondered how he had not noticed that before. The answer came in a heartbeat.

His augmetics, as expensive and precise as they were could not hope to replicate the wonder of human eyes. He saw Roxanne's expression of shock, and reached up to touch his face. Instead of bruised and puffy flesh where Asubha had ripped out his eyes of glass and steel, he touched soft skin and the gentle give of organic tissue.

'Kai,' breathed Roxanne. 'Your eyes…'

He looked up, seeing the interior of the temple with the eyes bequeathed to him by his mother and father, and though they were imperfect organs at best, he revelled in this gift, no matter how short-lived it might be. It mattered not that his first sight in years was of a ruined building that had become a battleground, that he was seeing at all was a miracle.

Bodies lay strewn in disarray, men and women, soldiers and civilians. Amid the destruction, Kai saw Golovko and Yasu Nagasena, their faces twisted in horror at the hideous form of the Vacant Angel as it feasted on the energies of the dead. Kai tore his gaze from the deathly being and watched as his erstwhile protector and captor fought his last battle.

Atharva and the pariah duelled in the shadow of the faceless statue, one a genhanced superhuman engineered to be the greatest warrior of the Imperium, the other a killer of men like him. The pariah moved like an acrobat, his every movement controlled and precise.

Against the bulk of the warrior of the Legiones Astartes, he was a frail and insubstantial figure, but he fought with a confidence born of his unique power to confound and discomfit psykers.

He did not yet know what Kai knew of the Thousand Sons warrior.

Atharva staggered as though in pain, and the pariah leapt in for the killing blow as a long, energised blade snapped from the sleeve of bodyglove.

Atharva righted himself in an instant, and caught him in mid air.

Even though the pariah was helmeted, Kai felt his shock.

'Once I could see, but now I am blind,' said Atharva, with terrible sadness and anger in his voice. Kai knew just how great a sacrifice Atharva had made to fight the clade killer, and he doubted anyone else could truly appreciate what he had given up. The pariah struggled in Atharva's grip, but there could be no escape from such grievous power. The energised blade stabbed down through Atharva's chest, and the warrior grunted in pain as the blade clove his heart.

Atharva hurled the clade warrior away, slamming him into the wall of the temple with a crunching crack of breaking bones. The pariah slumped to the ground, his body a twisted mass of limbs bent at impossible angles for a living being.

Atharva wrenched the blade from his body and stared into the blackened hood of the Vacant Angel.

'Just you and me,' said Atharva as the ghostly form of the angel descended towards him.

Kai knew there was no way Atharva could fight such a terrible apparition, yet he stood firm, putting himself between the Vacant Angel and the mortals at his back. The creature spread its arms, but before it could sweep Atharva into its monstrous embrace, it loosed a piercing shriek of pain. The creature threw back its head and let out a howl of abject agony as portions of its ragged form bled into the air like flares from the surface of a star.

Kai watched as the creature unravelled, its outline wavering and blurring as it was forced back to the realm from whence it had come. He could see no cause for the angel's dissolution until he cast his gaze towards the temple doors and saw a group of lithe figures armoured in gold and silver pushing into the temple.

They wore helms that obscured the lower half of their faces, and each of them was an albino with a white top-knot trailing from the crown of their shaven skulls. White spotted hides were draped across their shoulders, where long bladed swords with wide quillons were sheathed.

They advanced into the temple without words, bearing long spears with crystal blades extended before them. Their supple movements marked them as women, and like hunters driving a dangerous beast back to its lair, they formed a perfect semi-circle around the Vacant Angel.

Its screaming was never ending, but its form was little more than a scrap of dirty, yellowed light as its power was stripped away. Soon, even that was gone, and its keening lament was at an end as the power that sustained it was stripped away.

'The silent sisterhood,' said Roxanne.

Kai had known who these women were, but it was the giant in golden armour who entered the temple behind them that captured all his attention.

'Lord Dorn,' said Atharva.

TWENTY-FIVE

The Only Victory
My Last Hunt
Legacy

To SEE A primarch with his own eyes was a last gift to Kai, and it took all his composure not to throw himself to his knees before the lord and master of the Imperial Fists. With the ending of the Vacant Angel, silence filled the temple as Rogal Dorn marched down the nave. Clad in his war plate of burnished red gold, the primarch dominated the space, a living gravity well to which every eye was drawn.

'Stand down, Atharva of the Thousand Sons,' said Dorn, his voice as hard and unyielding as the stone of the mountains. 'It is over.'

'Nothing is ever over, Rogal Dorn,' said Atharva. 'You of all people should know that.'

The gold-armoured sisters accompanying Dorn flinched at Atharva's use of his given name, but of course said nothing. More people entered the temple, armsmen clad in looped bands of black and bearing an amethyst crest upon their left breast. At their head marched a beautiful woman whose face he had last seen while a prisoner beneath the mountains. There, she had been an illusion, but Kai had no doubt that this Aeliana Septmia Verduchina Castana was the real thing.

Roxanne let out a soft breath at the sight of her family's representative and snapped her head in the direction of a young boy held tight to the matronly women that huddled in the shelter of the statue with them. She knelt beside him and opened his tightly clenched fist to reveal a silver ring set with an amethyst that blinked with a soft purple glow.

The boy's eyes were rimed with tears.

'You said it was a magic ring,' he said.

'And so it is,' said Roxanne with a rueful sigh, taking hold of Kai's hand as they stood together to face Rogal Dorn and his allies. Among them, Kai saw Adept Hiriko and Athena Diyos. Though he knew she must have helped his pursuers, he was glad to have this last chance to see her again.

'Give us the astropath,' ordered Rogal Dorn, and Kai had to stop himself from taking an involuntary step forward.

Atharva shook his head. 'He is not yours to command.'

Dorn laughed, though Kai heard uncertainty in the sound.

'Of course he is,' said Dorn, drawing a vast pistol of chased gold and ebony. 'I am the Emperor's chosen champion. Everything on Terra is mine to command.'

Atharva looked over his shoulder and gave Kai a nod of respect.

'Not everything,' he said as Rogal Dorn's weapon fired with a deafening roar.

Anger touched Kai as he watched Atharva fall, the back of his head a smouldering ruin of blackened meat and skull fragments. The warrior of the Thousand Sons toppled to the temple floor, dead before he hit the ground.

Kai gripped Roxanne's hand tightly, trying not to show how afraid he was. His gaze moved from Lord Dorn to Adept Hiriko and Athena Diyos, and he knew he would not be able to keep them from learning what he knew. He was not strong enough to resist their interrogation, and he dearly wished he could unlearn what he knew.

What he knew would destroy them, its truth too terrible for them to bear, and in that moment Kai knew he could not allow them to take him. Some things were too dark, too impossible and too dreadful to be known. A slow smile crept across his face as he remembered the words of his regicide opponent.

Sometimes the only victory possible is to keep your opponent from winning.

Quite whose victory he was winning Kai wasn't sure, but he knew that the Imperium could not stand against the armies of Horus Lupercal if they dragged the truth out of him. Atharva had failed in his bid to bring him to the Warmaster, and now the fate of millions rested on Kai's shoulders.

This was his moment, his last chance to take control of his destiny and serve the Emperor with the only thing that was his to give.

'Roxanne,' he said evenly. 'I need you to do something for me.'

THE BATTLE IS over, but Nagasena does not yet know who has emerged victorious. The renegade Space Marines are all dead, and the building is secure, but too much has been lost for him to think of this hunt as anything but a failure. He kneels beside the broken body of Kartono, grieving for his fallen companion. His bondsman is a broken thing, his body shattered in every place, and Nagasena does not know how it is possible he is dead.

They had been together for so long, he had never considered the possibility a foe could end him, let along one empowered by the warp. How Atharva could have stood to touch Ulis Kartono, let alone best him like that is a question that will forever go unanswered, and Nagasena is a man who hates to leave matters unresolved.

He wipes a tear from his eye and watches as the House Castana armsmen secure the building, moving with admirable speed and thoroughness to ensure no one is left alive. A striking woman in a dress of amethyst directs

their operations, and when Nagasena sees the elaborate
headpiece that covers her forehead, he knows she must
be Aeliana Castana.

Kai Zulane stands next to the last survivors of this
massacre, a heavyset woman with two young boys held
tight to her, and a pretty girl with a blue bandanna tied
around her forehead. Her features share a clear similarity
to Aeliana Castana, and Nagasena realises he has seen
her face before. She is Roxanne Larysa Joyanni Castana,
the other survivor of the *Argo*, and Nagasena senses a
confluence of events that speak of a universal order at
work.

The warrior women of the Silent Sisterhood have
already withdrawn and Lord Dorn kneels over the bodies of the World Eaters, a look of consternation on his
handsome, patrician features. Maxim Golovko hovers
nearby, basking in the primarch's magnificence like a
devotee.

No one has yet approached Kai Zulane, and Nagasena
understands that they are all afraid of him, even Lord
Dorn. Everyone can see that Zulane's eyes have been
restored, but how such a thing can be possible terrifies
them. But more than that, they fear what he represents.
They fear to learn the truth he knows. They hunger for
it, but he suspects they will come to regret such cursed
knowledge. Truth has been Nagasena's bedrock, but even
he knows there are some truths that cannot be faced
without a heavy price being paid. Kai Zulane's truth is
such a thing, but there can be no turning from it.

Nagasena walks towards the man he has hunted
through the Petitioner's City, and his hand strays to the
hilt of *Shoujiki* as he looks up at the featureless face of
the kneeling statue. Whatever beast Atharva unleashed
from within its stonework is gone, but it retains a grim
aspect. Whatever else happens here today, it will certainly be destroyed.

Kai Zulane speaks animatedly with Roxanne Castana,
and though Nagasena cannot hear what he is saying, he

can read the nature of it without difficulty. Roxanne Castana shakes her head, tears flowing freely down her face, but Zulane is insistent. Nagasena hurries his step, a terrible fear growing in the pit of his stomach.

'Kai!' he shouts, and every eye in the building turns towards him.

The astropath does not respond, as he had known he would not, and Nagasena cries out as Roxanne Castana lifts the bandanna from her forehead.

Kai's eyes widen as he stares into the depths of Roxanne's third eye, and he crumples to the ground with a sigh of what Nagasena can only interpret as relief. Nagasena grabs hold of Roxanne Castana and pulls her towards his body, hoping to break the connection long enough to keep whatever power she possesses from completing its work. Even as he does so, he knows he is too late.

Roxanne turns to him, and Nagasena catches the briefest glimpse of what lies beneath her bandanna. It is milky white and utterly black, a vortex of infinite depths and impenetrable opacity that can see nothing and everything at once. Nagasena feels the alien touch of somewhere far distant, yet all around him, a realm of limitless potential and abject horror that no mortal should ever dare know of for fear of going utterly insane. The thinnest skein divides the domain of Man from the warp, and it chills Nagasena to know how fragile that barrier between worlds really is.

He peers into the nightmare realm of the warp and his spirit is falling, drawn into its unknowable depths. He tries to scream, but he has no voice, and in that fraction of a second, he sees what Kai Zulane saw in Roxanne's eye, but before he can suffer the same fate, a nictitating fold of skin flicks down over the unnatural orb, obscuring it from sight. The terrible connection between Nagasena and Roxanne Castana is broken, and he drops to his knees as she turns her face away and pulls her bandanna back down.

Breath heaves in his chest, and he looks down at Kai Zulane.

The man is clearly dead, yet Nagasena sees a look of such peace on his face that he almost envies him. Kai is serene and the lines of care that aged him beyond his years are softened to the point of making Nagasena think that he is many years younger than his biographical information claimed.

Kai Zulane's eyes are open, and Nagasena sees they are the most intense shade of violet. In ancient cultures, such a hue would have marked a man out for greatness.

'Your journey is at an end, Kai Zulane,' says Nagasena, reaching out to softly close the dead man's eyes. Roxanne Castana kneels beside him, and he covers his face.

'My eye is shut,' she says, and Nagasena looks up.

'Why?' he asks, and does not need to elaborate.

'He was my friend,' says Roxanne through her tears, but before she can say more, the Castana armsmen haul her to her feet.

'Wait,' he says, and such is the authority in his voice that they obey him.

'Was what he knew so terrible?' asks Nagasena.

'I don't know what he knew,' replies Roxanne.

'I believe you, but they will ask hard questions of you, and they will not ask kindly.'

Roxanne shrugs. 'I can't tell them anything. Whatever it was he knew is gone forever.'

'What did he say to you?' pleads Nagasena,

'He said that sometimes the only victory possible to keep your opponent from winning.'

Nagasena knows the words, they are those of an ancient regicide grandmaster, and his heart sinks at the loss of Kai Zulane's truth.

Before any more can be said, Aeliana Castana approaches and Roxanne musters enough courage to meet her disapproval with a haughty, defiant expression of her own.

'You are a disgrace,' says Aeliana Castana. 'Patriarch Verduchina is greatly disappointed. You have brought great shame upon our house.'

Roxanne says nothing, and the Castana armsmen march her away. Nagasena watches her taken from the temple with a mixture of regret and sorrow, knowing that she goes towards an uncertain future. She is Navis Nobilite, and whatever else becomes of her, the Imperium will always have a use for her.

Rogal Dorn approaches with Maxim Golovko in his wake, and Nagasena gives the primarch a deep bow, careful to remove his hand from *Shoujiki's* hilt. Lord Dorn's face is unreadable, a cliff of craggy features that takes in the carnage wrought here with a dispassionate eye.

'Was it all for nothing, Yasu Nagasena?' asks Lord Dorn, staring down at Kai Zulane's body. 'What happened here tonight?'

Nagasena has only one answer for him. 'The truth died here tonight.'

'Perhaps that is for the best,' answers Dorn.

Nagasena shakes his head. 'I cannot believe that. Do we not serve the Imperial Truth? If we do not have truth, then what are we creating? The Imperium must have truth at its heart or else it is not worth building.'

'Be careful what you say, Nagasena,' warns Dorn, and the threat is clear.

'Long ago I took a vow never to speak false, and I will never lie,' says Nagasena. 'Even to you, my lord.'

Dorn places a vast, gauntleted hand on Nagasena's shoulder, and for the briefest moment, he wonders if he too will be sacrificed on the altar of loose ends. But Lord Dorn does not have murder in mind.

'You are an honest man, Yasu Nagasena, and I have need of honest men.'

Nagasena nods and says, 'I am yours to command.'

'Then there is another task I would beg of you.'

'Name it, my lord,' says Nagasena, knowing Lord Dorn honours him by presenting his order as a request.

'General Golovko tells me there is one of the renegades still unaccounted for,' says Dorn.

Nagasena knows immediately who it will be.

'The Luna Wolf,' says Golovko. 'His body isn't here.'

'Just so,' agrees Dorn. 'I would not have one of Horus Lupercal's men at liberty on Terra.'

'I will find him,' says Nagasena. 'But this will be my last hunt.'

The primarch nods and looks down at Kai Zulane.

'What did you know?' wonders Dorn aloud, and Nagasena hears something he would never have expected to hear in the voice of such a singular warrior: uncertainty. 'The first axiom of defence is to understand what you defend against, Yasu, and I fear that this man could have helped me understand…'

'Understand what?' asks Nagasena, when Dorn does not continue.

'I do not know,' says Dorn. 'But this day has diminished us all.'

The primarch marches away, and Yasu Nagasena feels a chill travel the length of his spine that has nothing to do with the katabatic winds sighing through shattered windows and punctured roof of the temple.

What are you afraid of, wonders Nagasena. *What are you really afraid of?*

THE SILVER CYLINDER hummed as it drew near the end of its incubation period. A host of wires and tubes ran from a bank of protein vats, each one encased in temperature-controlled pipework that gurgled as it fed the nutrient-rich broth within. The laboratory was cold, and its lights were dim, as though the work being done here was somehow secretive and its results uncertain.

Shielded and insulated cables connected the silver cylinder to three clear glass jars, each one containing a small, unremarkable looking mass of soft, plum-coloured tissue. A host of fine extraction needles and gene-samplers pierced these strange organs, and they pulsed like childrens' hearts as the information encoded on every zygote and impossibly complex amino-acid chain was decoded.

A bank of monitoring equipment carefully regulated the process, a fantastically delicate operation that could go wrong in a million ways and which had an almost infinite amount of steps that needed to be exactly right before anything approaching success might be achieved.

Eventually, a series of gem-like bulbs on the upper surface of the silver cylinder flickered to life, each one turning green in rapid succession. A soft chime sounded, and coolant gases vented from a grille on the side as the nutrient fluids were drained.

The cylinder slid open with pneumatic hiss, and a mist of chemically-complex vapour drifted from the glistening organ within. It surfaces were glossy red and purple, webbed with myriad networks of super-oxygenated blood. Fresh grown and throbbing with potential, it was as close to perfection as could be imagined.

Only one other laboratory on Terra could have identified this organ, and it was deep beneath the skin of the world, protected as no other place of Terra was protected. No mortal geneticist could have unravelled the complexities of this biological miracle, and only one other individual could have replicated the process of its creation.

'Did it work?' asked Ghota.

'Yes, my son,' said Babu Dhakal with a triumphant exhalation. 'It worked.'

ABOUT THE AUTHOR

Hailing from Scotland, **Graham McNeill** worked for over six years as a Games Developer in Games Workshop's Design Studio before taking the plunge to become a full-time writer. Graham's written more than twenty SF and Fantasy novels and comics, as well as a number of side projects that keep him busy and (mostly) out of trouble. His Horus Heresy novel, *A Thousand Sons*, was a New York Times bestseller and his Time of Legends novel, *Empire*, won the 2010 David Gemmell Legend Award.

Graham lives and works in Nottingham and you can keep up to date with where he'll be and what he's working on by visiting his website.

Join the ranks of the 4th Company at
www.graham-mcneill.com

THE GILDAR RIFT

SARAH CAWKWELL

UK ISBN: 978-1-84970-107-5   US ISBN: 978-1-84970-108-2

AVAILABLE DECEMBER 2011

An extract from the Gildar Rift
by Sarah Cawkwell

THE LINGERING TRACE of blood was everywhere.

It streaked up the walls of the ship's inner corridors. It was smeared on the deck leaving virulent scarlet trails. Brother Temerus, one of Dasan's squad had tried, without success, to link into the *Wolf*'s vox-net. All he had met in response to his hails thus far had been static.

With every step that they took, Ryarus's sense of unease grew. Whatever had happened to the *Wolf of Fenris* had been devastating and worse; whatever it had been that had committed such relentless slaughter may well still be aboard.

During the flight across from the *Dread Argent,* one of Matteus's many observations had been that a complement of more than twenty Space Marines had seemed excessive for a search and rescue operation. Ryarus had quietly agreed with the sentiment. Arrun was being over-careful.

Now, though, he mentally praised the captain's unerring sense of caution.

So far, they had encountered nothing but signs of

battle. No bodies, no injured... nothing. A report from Matteus had detailed a brief diversion into one of the other staging areas which had turned up vast quantities of discarded battle plate. It had been massed into haphazard piles rather than carefully displayed and maintained as was the expected behaviour of an Adeptus Astartes. That was all that either squad had encountered.

The Silver Skulls made their way up from the aft section towards midships. The silence was eerie. No sounds of Chapter serfs or servitors, no distant clash of swords in training cages... there was nothing to be heard except for the heavy, metallic footfalls of Space Marine boots as they moved slowly across the fine steel mesh floors of the dimly lit corridors. The *Wolf of Fenris* creaked around them, the groans of super-stressed metal clearly audible without the usual rumble of the engine.

Tayln, one of Dasan's squad raised his head to listen to the sounds of the vessel. 'She sounds wrong,' he noted. As a promising Techmarine, he had not yet been despatched to Mars for his formal induction into the ways of the Mechanicus. As such, he had undergone his initial training at the hands of the existing Chapter Techmarines. He tipped his head to one side, listening. 'I can hear... something.'